SINFUL HEARTS

A DARK MAFIA ENEMIES TO LOVERS ROMANCE

DARK HEARTS

BOOK THREE

JAGGER COLE

PLAYLIST

Slow Down - Chase Atlantic
Dark in My Imagination
Lost Track of Time - MTNS
Get Out - Frightened Rabbit
vicious - Tate McRae
Hard to Get - Bec Lauder, Two Feet
Angel - Massive Attack
City Of Stars - Gavin James
Diet Mountain Dew - Lana Del Rey
Waiting Game - BANKS
Keep Yourself Warm - Frightened Rabbit
My Moon My Man - Feist
Hypnotic - Zella Day
Shameless - Camila Cabello
bury a friend - Billie Eilish
Francesca - Hozier
Moaning Lisa Smile - Wolf Alice
The Joker - Steve Miller Band
Can You Feel My Heart - Bring Me The Horizon

Someone To Forget - ARMNHMR, Lights
715 - CRΣΣKS - Bon Iver
Love Like Ghosts - Lord Huron

Listen to the playlist on Spotify!

TRIGGER WARNING

This book contains darker themes and graphic depictions of past trauma, as well as mentions of SA. While these scenes were written to create a more vivid, in-depth story, they may be triggering to some readers. Please read with that in mind.

1

ELSA

"WHATEVER YOU DO, don't fuck him."

"Pardon?" I sputter.

Taylor's comment catches me off-guard, spiking my heart rate and bringing a flush to my face. I quickly tuck the last strand of my white-blonde hair into the black leather and lace mask before I turn to face her.

My boss smirks wryly as she finishes adjusting her own mask. Hers is a far simpler gold and matte black piece that just hides the top half of her face—as opposed to mine, more hood than mask, which covers that plus my hair, all the way down to the nape of my neck. Oh, and it has cat ears. I look like some kind of kinky feline Fifty-Shades-themed bank robber.

What is my life right now?

"Dante. Don't fuck him."

Taylor finishes checking herself in the floor-length mirror of the sumptuous blood red and gold private dressing room.

We're both dressed similarly, in what I would consider *scandalously* revealing black cocktail dresses. But Taylor's assured me—or maybe it was more of a warning—that what we're wearing is downright conservative compared to what we'll see once we step out of the private room and dive into the belly of the beast that is Club Venom.

Given that Club Venom is an actual, honest-to-God *sex club*, and she's a member, I'm inclined to believe her.

The difference between us is, Taylor seems to be completely comfortable walking into New York City's most infamous private playground for the dark and deviant. A place where the rich, powerful, and dangerous come to play.

Meanwhile, I feel like I'm standing on the edge of a skyscraper, about to try BASE jumping for the first time. Blindfolded.

My pulse hums in my veins. My mouth feels dry. Sweat slicks the small of my back.

"Elsa."

I flinch, realizing I've been staring wide-eyed at my reflection in the mirror. My gaze flicks over to Taylor to find her smiling.

"Hey, I'm just kidding." Her brows knit. "Probably. It's just that Dante has a certain...*reputation*, as you might be able to guess."

"One that I'm sure has nothing to do with his reputed mafia connections, wealth, good looks, and the fact that he owns this place."

Taylor grins, taking a sip of the champagne that the staff opened for us when we were ushered in here to get ready.

"Ah, now there's the sharp legal mind I hired you for."

I grin back, taking a bigger gulp of my own champagne than perhaps I should. But it calms my jangling nerves, at least a little.

"To be clear, I don't actually think you'd screw a potential client, Elsa. I just want you to be prepared. He's a bit of a charmer..." she frowns. "Okay, he's *a lot* of a charmer. And given that he's..."

"Outrageously good-looking?"

She chuckles, but even though she turns away, I can spot the slight hint of pink in her cheeks creeping down from under the mask.

I like having Taylor as my new boss. Or at least, as one of my *three* new bosses, as of ten months ago when I took the plunge and moved across the pond from London to New York for the *insanely* coveted partner position at Crown and Black.

Taylor Crown is the "Crown" in the wildly prestigious New York City law firm, and the "Black" is actually two brothers —Alistair and Gabriel. They're both great, too. But it's Taylor who's really taken me under her wing.

We're here tonight for our first official sit-down with Dante Sartorre, the majority owner of Club Venom and Crown and Black's newest potential client. It's not lost on me that two women in slinky black cocktail dresses with plunging neck-lines suit Dante's playboy reputation at *bit* better than, say, Gabriel or Alistair—or any other man, for that matter. But that's the game, and I understand completely.

It doesn't make me any less freaked the fuck out to walk out there, though.

3

The nerves, though, aren't *just* because Club Venom is a kink club catering mostly to New York City's dark, dangerous, and powerful. They're not *just* because I fully understand that Taylor choosing me to come with her tonight is a big deal, and I want to impress her.

The nerves are because I'm not merely here for work.

I'm also here on a mission. But I'm the only one who knows that.

Taylor takes a deep breath, glancing over herself once more in the mirror before turning to me.

"Ready?"

"Absolutely."

She frowns a little, her eyes lingering on my Michelle Pfeiffer Catwoman mask.

"You know, they've got other masks you could borrow."

My brow furrows. "Oh. Is this one not—"

"Oh, I mean, it's more than fine. For this place?" She smirks. "Trust me, you look fantastic. No, I meant, are you going to be comfortable in it?"

I mean, it's an S&M black and gold mask with cat ears made from leather and lace covering basically my entire head except my chin, cheeks, and mouth.

"Comfort" isn't exactly its main design function.

Everyone in this club, patrons and staff alike, will be wearing masks. But for the reason I'm here—beyond the business meeting with Dante Sartorre—I need mine to hide who I am completely, with one hundred percent certainty.

Whoever I pick tonight can*not* know who I am. I understand that in a city of ten million people, my chances of being recognized are next to zero. But I want it to be *absolutely* zero. That's the whole point. That's the only way I'll actually be able to go through with this, not to mention how I'll keep my nerves from spilling out all over the floor like raw spaghetti.

Complete and utter anonymity.

"I'm good!" I smile with an eagerness and ease I don't remotely feel. "I kind of like it, actually."

Taylor grins, arching her brow as her gaze rises. "The ears are a cute touch. All right, shall we?"

"Let's."

As Taylor finishes her glass of champagne, I turn and pull my phone out of my bag. I send a quick note to my sister Nora, reminding her that I'll be home late from my business meeting. She sends back a thumbs-up emoji followed by a gif of Juno Temple from *Ted Lasso* smugly smirking with the caption "you've totally got this".

I grin and start to tuck the phone away when it suddenly buzzes again. This time, when I glance at the message, my smile vanishes, and a cold, black dread burrows into my heart.

The text isn't from Nora.

It's from *him*.

FUCKHEAD

I'm not waiting any longer. You will do as I've said. Meet me tonight, or there will be consequences I do not think you are prepared to deal with.

I stare, nauseated, at the text from the man I hate and loathe.

The man who seemingly has followed me all the way to New York.

The man whose disgusting and bone-chilling threats have increased exponentially over the last few weeks, to the point where I've decided to do what I'm going to do tonight, to be rid of him once and for all.

Leo thinks he has power over me. But tonight, I'm going to shatter those chains he thinks he's bound me with.

Because tonight, I'm going to fuck a stranger.

Tonight, at twenty-six years old, I'm finally going to lose my virginity.

At a sex club.

"Just be sure to leave that here," Taylor says. "There's no phones allowed in the club."

"Oh, of course." I quickly close the phone and shove it back in my bag. "I'm guessing that's part of the reason a man like Mr. Sartorre prefers to have business meetings here?"

She smirks. "Ding ding ding. All right, game faces on. Remember, the fact that he's even offered this meeting at all speaks volumes. He *wants* to work with us. We just need to show him exactly how much easier his life will be when he does."

I nod, swallowing back the hammering in my heart. No problem. I just have to help my boss secure a new client with mafia connections who probably represents close to twenty million dollars a year in billable hours, and then for bonus points go find a stranger to unknowingly take my virginity and free me from the chokehold Leo has on me.

No big deal.

Outside the private changing room, two black-masked staff in suits hand us two more flutes of champagne. Then two masked women in flimsy, see-through black gauze cocktail dresses approach, each holding a matte black suitcase. They hold them up and open them, revealing two matching collections of elegant wristbands in varying designs and color combinations.

I glance at Taylor, who just smiles.

"It's the club's kink designations.

My face burns hotly, my eyes widening at the various bands.

"They all signify different...*tastes*," Taylor explains, clearly slightly amused at my own flustered state. "And your preferred role. The red is sadomasochism. So red with black lines across it signifies a Dom. Red with gold lines, a sub."

I swallow thickly, feeling my pulse thud.

"Uh-huh."

"The green is—" Taylor clears her throat, eyeing me. "You know what? Let's just make this easy for both of us. We're here for business, so let's go with the white and gold. It means you're a voyeur only."

"Oh, cool."

I cringe at my own flustered awkwardness. Mercifully, Taylor doesn't push it as she reaches for a white and gold band from the open briefcase in front of her. I pick an identical one from the case in front of me, slipping it onto my wrist with a shiver.

"Elsa?"

I glance at Taylor.

"Relax. I didn't bring you tonight because I thought you had an extensive background in sex clubs or knowledge of the kink lifestyle," she says with a reassuring smile. "I brought you because you're the most promising and brilliant young attorney I know. Okay?"

I exhale, letting a little of the tension out as I force a calmness to my smile that I don't feel.

"Thank you."

She nods, putting a hand on my shoulder as she leans close. "For the record, I'm only a member here because it's where clients like to meet. Don't worry. This isn't my scene, either. We're here for Dante, nothing more. So let's go out there and kill it."

The pep talk definitely helps my nerves. So does knocking back the rest of my champagne in one gulp. Then, wristbands on, we follow our two masked guides further down the hall. The music grows louder. A murmuring din of people talking washes over me. But when it begins to be punctuated by gasping moans of female pleasure, my pulse jumps and my skin tingles.

Then we step out into the main room, and my jaw *drops*.

It's like something out of *Eyes Wide Shut*. Or a Roman orgy.

Holy. Shit.

The room is opulently decorated, full of couches and chairs for the elegant, masked onlookers. More guests talk amongst themselves by two cocktail bars along the sides of the room. But the main focus—and it's impossible *not* to focus on it—is the writhing, thrusting, moaning and grunting mass of bodies tangled in extremely creative ways across the large beds and couches in the center of the room.

A gorgeous, dark-skinned woman, utterly naked but for her wristband and a gold and black mask, gasps in ecstasy as the muscled man bending her over the arm of the couch rams into her. When a second man tangles his fingers in her long braids and guides her mouth to his rock-hard cock, my eyes bulge and my face turns the color of the blood-red hallway we just walked through.

Beside them on the same couch, two blonde women with gravity-defying breasts ride a tattooed, Italian-looking guy who is lying on his back—one of them bouncing up and down on his dick, the other grinding her pussy against his mouth. Another couple fuck on the floor like it's an Olympic event and they're going for gold, and a foursome on an over-sized bed behind them tangles in ways that I wouldn't have thought logistically possible, like an X-rated game of Twister.

I've seen sex before. It's just that I've never, well, *seen* sex before. Not really. Not like this. I mean, no, I might have never gotten around to doing it myself. I've watched plenty of online porn, though.

But watching videos and watching...*this*...right in front of me is like going from a tricycle to a Harley. And very quickly, my anxiety about what the actual fuck I think I'm going to do here tonight skyrockets.

"It's a bit of a shock the first time," Taylor murmurs quietly next to me. She turns to arch a brow, smiling. "Are you okay?"

"Oh, yeah, no, of course," I shrug as casually as I can. "It's just sex. Everyone has it, right?"

Taylor smiles. "Ex*actly*. Ah, here he is. I'd recognize those shoulders anywhere."

I turn from the orgy in front of us, following her gaze to the tall, powerfully built man in his mid-thirties striding across the room toward us. He's wearing an impeccably cut dark suit, clearly custom tailored, and even with the gold and black mask covering the top half of his face, it's obvious he's extremely handsome.

"Ms. Crown," he growls in a low baritone. "Welcome to my humble playground."

Taylor gives him a cool, professional nod and handshake. But when he brings her hand to his lips and kisses the back of it, I can see her cheeks heat.

"And you must be Ms. Guin," he purrs, turning his dark eyes to me. I shiver as I take his hand. Mercifully, he doesn't kiss mine.

"It's a pleasure to meet you, Mr. Sartorre."

He smirks, glancing at Taylor and then back to me. "Please, just Dante. It's a little difficult to be so formal with all *that* going on ten feet away, isn't it?" He nods his chin at the live-action porn movie writhing and moaning behind us. My face heats as something wicked pools in my core.

Dante clears his throat, clasping his hands together as he turns to Taylor. "Slight change of plans. I appreciate you bringing additional talent from your firm tonight. But I'd prefer to hammer out the details of our arrangement between just the two of us."

Taylor arches a brow. "Oh?"

"I can assume that the business I would be bringing to your firm would get me a named partner as my personal attorney?"

"Of course."

"That named partner being you?"

Taylor nods her chin. "Certainly, if that's what you'd like."

"It is. And I'd like to start now. I'm prepared to sign our contract here tonight."

Taylor turns to glance at me, then back to Dante. "Would you give the two of us a moment?"

"Not a problem," he smiles widely.

Taylor smiles as she pulls me aside. "So, plot twist."

"Do you want me to insist on joining?"

She shakes her head. "No, I'm fine. Trust me, I can handle a man like him. I'm just sorry to have dragged you out tonight for nothing. Please, feel free to leave."

When I nod, she turns back to Dante. "Well, lead the way."

He grins an unapologetically wolfish and hungry smile at my boss before turning to me. "Please, Ms. Guin, stay and enjoy yourself. Play, or just watch..." he grins at my white and gold wristband. "Club Venom exists to let your wildest desires come true."

He turns to Taylor, extending an arm that she loops hers through. They start to walk away toward what looks like a private room, when Taylor glances over her shoulder to arch a questioning brow at me.

I mouth "I'm going to go" with a jerk of my thumb, and she nods with a smile before she and Dante disappear through the guarded door.

My pulse thuds.

My skin tingles.

This is going better than expected.

My original plan for the night, which I went over as meticulously as if I were planning to storm of the beaches of Normandy, was…complex. It involved arriving with Taylor, doing the pitch meeting with Dante, and then *leaving* with Taylor. At which point, I'd make up an excuse of wanting to wait for my own ride, stall until Taylor was gone, and then re-enter the club alone. But now that Taylor's busy, well, I guess I've fast forwarded to the alone part.

As a guest, I have full access to the club for the night. Which I very much planned to use in my master plan to find a stranger, lose my virginity, and thereby break Leo's hold on me and shatter his fucked-up interest in me.

I've been his pawn for too long, no matter how well I've avoided him. That ends tonight.

But first…Christ, I need another fucking drink.

Shivering with heat, I pull my gaze from the lurid scene playing out before me and make my way to one of the bars.

"Double vodka and soda, please," I blurt to the bartender. When he brings it, I suck half of it down quickly before I turn to let my eyes slide around the room, heart pounding.

It's no big deal. Or at least, it doesn't have to be. It's just sex, and like I just said oh-so-airily to Taylor, everyone has it.

Except me.

But that changes right now.

I chew on my lip, my gaze sliding across the room and finally landing on a built, older, bearded man. He seems to feel me looking at him, because he turns and arches a dark brow behind his mask. A hungry smile curls the corners of his lips, and I blush.

Maybe?

But then my eyes drop to the band on his wrist: red, with black lines. According to Taylor, that marks him as a sadistic Dom.

I shiver. Yeah, that's going to be a no. I mean, I enjoy watching hardcore stuff online. But who knows *how* hardcore this particular stranger wants to get. And when his gaze narrows darkly and dangerously, and his smile turns downright cruel and hungry, my mind is made up.

No fucking way.

Kinky sounds intriguing. Rough sounds exciting. Getting hogtied, ball-gagged, and flogged while this guy drips candle wax on my vagina sounds like jumping into the deep end when I don't even know how to swim.

I shake my head, shivering again at the way he glares at me before he too looks away for other prey.

My eyes land on a tall man with short, buzzed hair and a clean jaw, with tattoos on his neck. The mix of clean cut and dangerous catches my interest, and I blush when he turns to grin and raise his glass in my direction…

…Until the brunette I didn't realize was on his arm turns to grin at me as well, curling a finger at me.

Well, *that's* more than I'm willing to take on.

Very flattered, but wrong team.

Shaking my head, I sigh and turn back to the bar, realizing I've somehow finished my drink already. I'm in the middle of ordering another when suddenly a laughing voice cuts through everything and instantly sends my stomach plummeting to the floor and my heart rate through the roof.

It's a voice *I know.*

"Well, I should. I come here often enough."

I swallow, my face turning white as I slowly slide my head around. His back is to me. His face is partially covered. But when he brings his hand up to shove his fingers through his long, dark hair, and I see the tattoo on his wrist and back of the hand that I've seen dozens of times—including earlier *today*—I know damn well who it is.

For one frozen moment, I consider running. Or at least slinking away and hoping to God and everything else that is good and holy that I can get out of there and change back into boring, buttoned-up, straight-laced Elsa before he realizes it's *me* in the scandalous black dress and the S&M kitten mask.

There are a million bars in New York City. Tinder is a thing. It's not like it would be remotely difficult for me to get laid the very second I wanted to. But the entire point of doing this at Club Venom tonight was *total* anonymity.

And now here I am a foot away from a man whose family *I work for*, whom I see several times a week, for fuck's sake.

A man who is as arrogant, cocky, and smug as he is outrageously gorgeous.

A man who is a dangerous, murderous criminal. No "allegedly" about it, despite what I say during office hours.

A man with dark hair, tanned skin, piercing ice-blue eyes, and a jawline sharp enough to cut glass. A man with a body built for sin, carved out of marble, a testament to the hours he's poured into working on it in boxing gyms and at the underground fights he's known for.

A man who's *also* known for his endlessly revolving door of women.

Hades Drakos, the dark crown prince of the Drakos Greek mafia family.

I scowl at his back, and a shiver teases up mine.

Of all the fucking gin joints...

Though I'm a partner at Crown and Black, in my spare time I moonlight as the Drakos family's unofficial attorney. Ares, the oldest brother and king of the empire, is professional and courteous in our dealings. Kratos, the third Drakos brother, is also fine in my books, and Calliope, the baby of the family, is a sweetheart with a fantastic sense of humor.

But Hades? Hades is the fucking devil himself.

He's made it his apparent mission in life to be a thorn in my side. A pebble in my shoe. A constant, needling presence, always looming just out of sight, ready to fuck up my day.

He's arrogant. Reckless. Cocky beyond measure. And *painfully* aware of his looks and their effect on the opposite sex. He'd be a harmless, clichéd, trust fund fuckboy brat playing at being a gangster if he wasn't, well, *actually dangerous.*

Viciously ruthless.

Dripping in violence and dark energy.

And the thing is, I could ignore all of those things. After all, it's Ares, not Hades, whom I officially report to. And Hades could be just one more sinfully good-looking if jaw-grindingly annoying and cocky man one could observe from a distance, and then forget about.

Except for the fact that I am wholly incapable of actually *doing* the second part.

I can't forget about him. I can't ignore him. And despite how very, *very* badly I want to be immune to his charms, apparently I am not up to date with my Hades vaccinations.

As much as I want to pretend he doesn't even exist, I simply can't. He's the central character in every single dark fantasy I have once the lights go out at night.

It's bullshit.

It's completely unfair.

A full-body, malignant, systemic takeover with no known cure.

Hades is living proof that what the mind wants and what the body wants are *not* in alignment. Because he makes me want to scream and tear my hair out. But he also makes me want to scream *for him*, while *he* pulls my hair.

"I know who you are, you know."

I flinch, ripped from my stewing, stormy thoughts by a woman's voice. She's on Hades' other side: brunette, model-tall, tits for days, gorgeous, and dressed to fucking *kill* in a little red number that makes what I'm wearing look like a nun's habit.

"Do you, now?"

She giggles, slapping a hand against his chest. I scowl.

"Of *course* I do, Hades," she gushes coquettishly.

I roll my eyes under my mask.

"Ahh, but I don't know you. Perhaps we should change that."

She grins widely. "I don't think my boyfriend would like that very much."

"I don't think you care, though, do you?"

She explodes in a frenzied giggle that makes my jaw grind.

"You're so *bad*," she gushes, slapping his chest again, and this time leaving her hand there.

Oh, just get on your knees and blow him right here, Little Miss Obvious.

I roll my eyes again, turning and slugging down three huge gulps of my second vodka soda.

"You know, you had a thing with my friend once."

"Did I really?" Hades growls, shoving his hair back from his face again.

"M-hmm. Krista Pryce. She said you literally redefined sex for her." The girl giggles obnoxiously again. "She also said you had a magic dick, not to mention huuuge."

My face heats as my lips purse. Jesus Christ, some people have no boundaries.

I make a face, turning away to slug down more vodka. This was a big mistake. I should leave before Hades recognizes me and makes it his mission never to let me forget about that time he saw me dressed like a literal sex kitten at a fucking kink club. Or at the very least, I should leave before this chick starts blurting out more details about Hades than I have any need to know.

Something dark bubbles under the surface of my skin, and I grit my teeth.

Yeah, that's it. I'm leaving.

I swear I'm about to. Really.

Then suddenly, something clicks.

No.

No no no.

I try and shove the thought away, but it's already sunk its claws into me, and they're holding on tight.

Slowly I turn back to let my eyes drag over Hades' broad shoulders and muscled frame beneath his tailored black suit.

I swallow thickly, my pulse thrumming just below the surface.

He might be an arrogant dick and a pain in my ass. Well, no *might* about it, he is. But like it or not, if the rumors and tabloid stories are to be believed, the man standing right in front of me is undeniably something else as well: God's gift to the female orgasm.

This is a very bad idea, Elsa.

Shut up, brain. Maybe it's a genius one.

I came here tonight for a very specific reason. But it doesn't have to suck, right? No pun intended. I don't *have* to get whipped and chained up by the creepy bearded Dom. I don't *have* to mix losing my virginity with experiments in my own sexuality with Mr. and Mrs. "three is a delightful crowd" over there.

If the whole point of the evening was, and is, to get this over with already…why *not* do it with a man like Hades, who obviously *very much* knows what he's doing?

If you're going to learn how to drive, it might as well be in a Lamborghini, right?

What the hell are you thinking, woman?

I ignore the worried voice in my head as I turn to the bartender and order two shots of vodka, chilled. The first goes down easily, and I can feel it doing its job already as I feel myself loosen up.

I'm wearing a mask. My distinct white-blonde hair is covered. And this has got to be the last place on earth Hades would ever expect to find buttoned-up prim and proper Elsa Guin, attorney-at-law.

There's my voice, of course. The London accent could give me away pretty quickly. But I have a solution for even that.

"Jolene" is a twangy-voiced character I made up to amuse Nora with when we first moved to the States—an American southern gal modeled entirely on the incredible Dolly Parton, hence her name, a hat tip to the song. I've gotten frighteningly good it, too.

I take one more breath, still feeling like I'm standing at the edge of a cliff, trying to decide if I'm really going to jump or not.

But I already know I am. I have to.

I won't be anyone's pawn anymore. This is my choice. My power, taken back.

Fuck you, Leo.

In one motion, before I can second guess myself or chicken out, I slug back the second shot of vodka, grab Hades' jacket, and yank him around to face me. His brow furrows, his gorgeous, sinfully dangerous icy-blue eyes stab right into me.

But I don't give them any time to do their damage. Instead, I grab his tie, rise up on the balls of my feet, and yank his mouth down to mine.

And the whole world disappears.

All of it. The music, the people, the anxiety, Leo and his threats, the orgy, even the girl huffing behind him before she stalks off. It all fades away until all I know is the feel of his perfect lips crushed to mine.

The thrill of his hand as it suddenly comes up to grip my jaw possessively. The citrus and whiskey taste of his tongue as it shoves its way past my lips to dance with mine. The hair-trigger effect his other hand sliding over my hip has on the heat pooling between my thighs.

I have no idea how long I kiss him for. A minute? Three hours? Forever? But when he pulls away, something hooks into us. Something that sizzles and ignites as his eyes scorch into me like blue flames.

"That was a nice appetizer," he growls quietly, his grip tightening on me in a way that sends my pulse skipping and my makes my legs quiver.

"What's the main course, darlin'?" I purr in my southern drawl.

I takes everything I have not to gasp, or maybe to pull away and *run*, when I see the dark shadow slide over his eyes, turning the ice blue to the color of a vicious hurricane.

"*You*," he snarls darkly. "Right the fuck now."

2

ELSA

I'd HAVE THOUGHT I'd be at least a little nervous, if not an outright wreck. But when he closes the door to the private room he's taken me to, I don't feel nervous at all.

On the contrary, I feel excited.

Giddy, even.

Hades' jaw grinds as his eyes slide over me lustily, hungrily. I've honestly never had a man look at me with such obvious fire before. But why would anyone hold that back, here at a sex club of all places?

He prowls toward me, making me shiver in anticipation, eager for him to grab me, throw me down, and have his wicked way with me.

But he doesn't do that. He just brushes past me, letting his fingers slide over my hip. I shudder, my breath catching as my eyes close, waiting for the pounce.

Which also doesn't come.

Swallowing, I turn to see him continuing on across the dimly-lit room. The walls are a deep blood red like the hallway downstairs, the floor and ceiling are the same matte black, and the furniture is all done in matching tones of matte black, blood red, and gold.

Two couches sit in front of a crackling fireplace. There's also a fully-stocked bar cart, a door that leads to what looks like a private bathroom, and a bed—a huge, four-poster thing covered in a deep red duvet with the golden Club Venom emblem of the viper emblazoned on it.

"Can I get you a drink?"

Yeah, no. I'm creeping past buzzed right now. If I have anything else, I'm going to be full on drunk, and I don't think I want that.

Not for this.

I want to be loosened up, but I still want to be in control.

"Thanks, sugar, but I don't need one."

Then, in the single boldest move of my entire *life*, I lock my eyes with his, reach up, and slip the straps from my shoulders. The dress slips down my body, pooling on the floor around my black high heels with golden bows on them. I'm not wearing a bra, because in what world do you wear a bra with a dress like this? Which leaves me standing there in front of a man, for the very first time, in only cream lace panties and my heels. And the mask, of course.

Hades' jaw clenches, his eyes roaming over my body. I can feel myself grow warm under his gaze, my nipples puckering to points in the sultry heat of the room.

"So…" I swallow. "Should we do this on the bed, or…?"

He smiles slowly, grinning at me as he takes off his jacket and folds it neatly across the back of the couch. He removes his tie as well, undoing the top few buttons of his shirt as he sits.

I cringe, realizing how clumsily I blurted that out. Okay, maybe I'm more nervous than I think.

"First time here?"

"I..." There's no use in lying. Plus I'm remembering a law professor I had back at Cambridge who used to joke about only breaking one law at a time.

I'm already hiding who I am from a man that *I know and work with*, for the express purpose of him taking my virginity— without knowing it, or me.

Let's not add any more lies to all that.

"Yeah, actually," I blush. "A friend brought me."

"Who's your friend?"

I stiffen. He grins.

"That's a joke. There's no names here."

"And here I was just about to ask you yours, silly me."

His smile turns hungry and dark.

"No you weren't."

I shiver.

"And I think you like that you're about to get fucked by a man whose name you don't know, and who doesn't know yours."

You're about to get fucked.

It's so very Hades—crude, blunt, and yet sinfully arousing.

24

He sinks back into the couch, eyeing me with smoldering blue eyes. I shift on my heels, suddenly wondering if I *do* want that drink to calm my nerves. My arms cross my chest, as if making a pathetic attempt to cover my bare breasts.

Slowly, Hades raises a hand. Heat flushes my cheeks as he curls two fingers, beckoning me over.

"Come."

I take a step toward him, but he shakes his head.

"On your knees."

I shiver, heat pulsing inside of me and mixing with my nerves. For the first time, my eyes drop to the band on his wrist—green, with black lines.

Fuck me. I have *no* idea what that means. Taylor didn't get that far. And suddenly, a little fear sinks into me.

Red meant sadomasochism. White was observing. But green? What the hell does green mean he's into? Hurting me? Or *me* hurting *him?* Tying me up? Something involving urine? No, that would have to be yellow, surely.

I blanch, suddenly realizing I may have just bitten off *way* more than I can chew.

"It means I'm a Dom," he growls quietly, watching where my eyes have landed. "Since it's your first time here."

"Oh."

"It's not red because I'm not specifically interested in hurting or humiliating you, if that's where that fear in your eyes is coming from."

I smile weakly, chewing on my lip.

"I…maybe a little."

"*You*, however, are a puzzle. Your white and gold says you're just here to look. But you grabbed and kissed me, most emphatically."

I blush.

"And you've *definitely* got submissive written all over you. So: yes or no, right now. Are we going to play, little kitten, or am I going to leave?"

It's now or never. Do or die. I could stop this whole insane plan right now.

But I already know I'm not going to.

I shake my head. "I'd like to play," I whisper softly.

"Good girl."

Fuck. Heat throbs between my legs as I squirm under his gaze.

"Now, on your hands and knees."

My pulse thuds in my ears. Almost in a trance, I do as he says, crouching down onto the floor.

"*Now* you may come here."

My face burns. But slowly, I start to move across the floor toward the gorgeous, dangerous man sitting on the couch.

I crawl all the way over to him, ending up between his spread legs. I shiver when Hades' hand reaches down, cupping my jaw and tilting my head up, so that my eyes lock with his.

"Good kitten."

Desire pulls at me, and I suddenly feel my panties grow slick.

Which is exactly when he kisses me again. His lips hungrily slam down to mine, his tongue once again invading my mouth. And I let him, willingly. I moan, shuddering as the eroticism and the craziness of it all hits me like a drug.

I whimper when he nips at my lip before pulling away. His eyes burn hotly as he pats the empty seat on the couch next to him.

"Up here. Crawl."

A nervous sort of energy at the way he's ordering me around and, oddly, calling me "kitten", explodes through my core. But so does desire, hot and hungry, and I crawl up onto the couch.

Kneeling next to him, our eyes lock. Hades suddenly frowns.

"Where are you from?"

Shit.

"Tennessee," I blurt in my Dolly Parton twang.

He smiles curiously. "You look so fucking familiar, kitten."

I swallow, forcing a brave note into my voice that I don't really feel.

"Do you ever get down to Nashville? Maybe we've—"

"Oh, I'm certain I'd have remembered."

Without warning, his hand suddenly raises to my neck, and I shiver as his fingers wrap around my throat. There's no pressure, but it's a small gesture reminding me that at least for tonight, in this room, I'm *his*.

His fingers trail down over my collarbone and drift between my breasts. My breath comes faster and faster, because everywhere he moves is somewhere I've never been touched like this before. His finger traces up the slope of one breast, and he rolls the nipple under this thumb. I shudder, gasping as heat explodes between my legs.

"Turn around."

I'm frozen in place.

"*Turn. Around,*" Hades growls, an edge creeping into his voice.

Finally I do as he says, turning on my knees so that I'm facing away from him, my ass in the air.

Shame, but also desire, pools in my core.

"Show me how wet you are."

Heat explodes in my face.

"*I—*"

"Take your fucking panties off," he growls. "Show me how fucking wet your little pussy is. And do it slowly."

Trembling, my face throbbing, I reach back, still bent over, and slip my fingers into my underwear. I peel it down, feeling the throb in my face only grow hotter and spread further across my body. The lace clings to my arousal for a moment before peeling away, the panties dropping down my thighs to my knees on the couch.

Hades doesn't say anything at first. I feel so fucking exposed, so...*unhidden.* And I'm close to yanking my underwear back up, grabbing my dress, and bolting out the door.

Until suddenly, I feel something I've never felt before. And it feels like pure. Fucking. *Sin.*

I cry out as Hades' tongue drags up my lips, parting them, tasting how unbelievably wet I am. A moan rips from my mouth—hungry and eager—as he growls into me. His strong, powerful hands grip my ass, pulling me harder against his mouth and lewdly spreading me open as his tongue plunges into me, like he's fucking me with it.

He doesn't go slow. He's not doing this to tease me.

He's doing this devour me. To shatter me. To conquer me.

It feels amazing.

His tongue drags up and down my pussy, curling around my clit. His lips wrap around the throbbing, engorged nub, sucking away as my mouth falls open in a silent scream. Pleasure explodes through my whole body as his fingers dig into my skin and his tongue pushes deep into my pussy.

I start to come undone. My vision blurs, my arms shaking, then giving out. My face drops to the couch with my ass shamelessly up in the air as the god of the underworld turns me completely inside out with his wicked, sinful tongue.

His palm suddenly comes down hard on my ass, the spank ripping a sudden cry of pleasure from my slack mouth. He does it again, and again, until my skin is raw with heat.

Until my arousal is dripping down his chin as he devours me whole.

The spanks keep coming, and his tongue is merciless on my clit as I choke my pleasure against the couch, my nails digging into the upholstery. His lips wrap around my throbbing clit just as his palm crashes down against my ass again, and suddenly, I lose all control.

All at once, I'm coming, and I'm coming *hard*.

My eyes roll back in my head as my face caves in. The sob of pleasure rips from my throat, my entire body shaking and trembling. I shamelessly push my hips back against his tongue as I come for what seems like an eternity until I'm collapsing on the couch in a shivering, shuddering pile.

Which is exactly when he pulls my limp, trembling body into his lap. I moan as my legs spread to either side of his hips, realizing that somehow he's naked now too. I stare at him, my mouth hanging open as I truly drink in the sight of Hades Drakos in all his savage, raw, sexual glory.

His tanned skin covered with tattoos. His bulging shoulders and powerfully muscled arms. The flat strength of his chest, and the *unreal* grooves of his chiseled abs and the lines of his hips pointing down to…

Holy. Shit.

I don't realize I'm staring at his enormous, hard, throbbing cock until I hear the low growl in his throat. Then I'm gasping as he takes my hand and pulls it to him. He curls my small fingers around his thickness and drags his gaze up to mine as I sit astride his muscled hips.

"Now be a good little kitten and take my cock. I want you to guide me into that sweet little dripping cunt, and I want you to take every fucking inch of me like a good girl."

Sweet. Jesus.

The way he talks is so outrageously filthy and sexual that it makes my very skin tingle with need. I chew on my lip, shivering, as my chest rises and falls heavily with my breath.

This is it.

I'm really doing this.

I'm shaking slightly as I rise up, using my hand to guide the swollen head of his gorgeous cock against my slick pussy lips. I'm usually somewhat...*cavalier* when it comes to maintenance down there. But knowing I was coming here tonight, to do this, I've shaved myself smooth. And the sensation of the silken head of his cock against my soft, bare lips takes my breath away.

I start to lower myself, eyes rolling back as I feel his head part my folds and sink into me.

And then suddenly, my eyes are staring wide as his strong fingers wrap around my throat.

"I told you to *take* my cock, not tiptoe around it."

I whimper, my eyes locking with his through our masks.

"*Take* my fucking cock, kitten," he growls. "I want to watch you fucking *bouncing* on it."

He's so fucking big, and I'm fairly petite, not to mention, I've *never fucking done this before*. But I'm also so wet that I can literally feel it dripping down his length over my fingers.

So I push down, gasping as I feel him open me up more and more, pushing deeper. There's a sudden sharp pain that makes me wince, but when he growls and rocks his hips up deeper, the discomfort melts into pleasure as his cock ploughs into me.

Hades uses one hand to take both of my wrists, pinning them together at the small of my back. The fingers of the other tighten around my throat.

And then suddenly, without warning, he's yanking me down.

31

Every. Single. Inch of him slides inside me to the hilt. I cry out, the choked sound of my pleasure filling the room as I shudder in ecstasy.

"Good kitten."

And then, he starts to fuck me. Not make love to me. Not tease me. Not move with me. Fuck me.

Hades fucks like he's breaching the walls of a city that dared to defy him, and I'm the evening's conquest.

It's *insane*.

I moan wildly as he bounces me up and down on his thickness, using his grip on my neck and wrists to guide me, as if I'm his personal sex toy. My back arches in pleasure, my mouth hanging open as the pressure and the insanity and the purely sinful heat of his savageness explodes through me.

I'm wetter than I've ever been, bouncing hard and deep on his fat cock. With a snarl he sits up, his mouth fastening around a nipple and biting—fucking *biting*—it. The effect it has on my body is immediate, like electricity crackling through me. I can feel myself tighten around him, the pleasure almost overwhelming as his mouth attacks one nipple and then the next, before moving on to my neck.

My eyes roll back in my head, and I moan wildly, losing all fucking control of myself and any idea of reality as he sucks hard on the soft skin of my neck. He rams into me over and over, biting and sucking and mauling my neck once, twice, three times as the room spins around me.

"I can feel how *greedy* your messy little pussy is, kitten," he rasps into my ear. "So. Fucking. *Desperate* for my big, fat cock. So eager for my fucking cum."

I start to come apart, to lose all control.

"If you want it, you're going to have to earn it, kitten."

He leans back against the couch, dropping his grip on my wrists but keeping it around my neck.

"*Fuck* my cock, kitten. Fuck it good and milk that cum out of my fucking *balls*."

Something changes within me. My customary self, with my usual sense of utter control over everything, is already lying shattered in ruins around us. But the way he speaks to me, and the way he dominates me, and touches me, and *fucks* me is so consuming that something washes over me.

And when it does, I let go. I let go of my shame and my anxieties. I let go of the chains of my past and the confines of my life, so prim and proper up till now.

I let go, and I fucking *ride* him to Kingdom come, bouncing up and down on Ares' god-like cock as the room melts around me. As my back arches, and my nails drag down his chest and abs. As my eyes lock with his through the masks, his fingers squeezing around my throat.

"Come for me, kitten."

When I do, it's like a fucking hurricane smashing into a coastline and destroying it. It's a shift in reality. A force of nature. I scream as I explode, and then suddenly, his mouth is crushing to mine, swallowing my cries and my moans, as if he owns those too.

He owns all of me in this moment—my body, my pleasure, and my release.

I feel his cock swelling even more as he groans into my mouth, followed by the hot flood of his cum spilling into me.

Suddenly, we're rolling over. Suddenly, my back is against the couch with my legs spread wide around his hips.

He's still hard inside of me.

"What—"

"Oh, *kitten*," he growls, lowering his mouth to my neck and biting down hard. "We're just getting started."

I LOSE track of the hours. But after four rounds of the most deviant, insane, body-breaking sex, and more orgasms than I can possibly count, the room is finally quiet. Hades is asleep next to me, his arm wrapped around me possessively, keeping me next to him.

I'm pulsing all over—trembling, as if I've just run a marathon —and I still can't get my heart to stop racing. And I'm sore: *so* fucking sore, everywhere. Between my legs, of course. But also my thighs and breasts from his mouth. My neck and wrists from his grip. My jaw, from when I stretched it so very wide to try and fit his enormous cock into my mouth, still slick from my pussy.

I blush vividly, replaying it all in my mind. Feeling his cum on my skin, tasting him on my tongue. Feeling the soreness from his rough touch all over me, like a deep, sensual ache.

I'm grinning. I'm...*different*.

Lighter. Freer.

It's over. It's done with. Leo's hold over me is gone.

But now, unfortunately, I have to be gone, too.

The Elsa that Hades knows was never here. He won't ever know it was me. Because that was exactly the plan, however derailed it got when I picked *him* instead of a stranger.

But so be it.

It is what it is.

Wincing, I carefully slip out from under his arm. He stirs, but keeps sleeping as I quietly cross the room and quickly pull my panties and dress back on. I carry my heels in my hands as I cross the room back to the bed and lean over him, kissing his cheek softly.

"Thank you," I whisper to my secret sin and my dirty little secret.

Then I'm gone.

3

HADES

Ten hours earlier:

"HERE. You look like you could use this."

With a grunt, I raise my head from the conference table at the sound of my sister's voice. Callie leans against the table, eying me with a mix of amusement and genuine concern. Except that the mix is probably closer to ninety percent amusement and *maybe* ten percent concern, rather than fifty-fifty.

"What?"

She snickers. "This." When she raises the iced coffee and gives it a tempting shake, the fatigue and the pain from last night start to fade just a bit. I usually take it black, but I don't even care that it's got tons of milk and probably way too much sugar in it.

At this point, it could be laced with diesel fuel and fucking arsenic, and I'd probably still slug it back gratefully.

"Please tell me you're not fucking with me."

Callie grins. "Nope. For realsies, take it. You look like shit."

"Well fuck you, too," I mutter through a shallow smirk as I pluck the offered plastic cup from her hand. I suck greedily on the straw and immediately regret it.

"Christ, did you actually get any coffee with your sugar today?"

Callie makes a face. "What? I like it sweet."

"This tastes like diabetes."

"It's gonna taste like nothing but your motherfucker of a hangover when I take it back because you're being an ungrateful dick."

Her hand darts out as if to snatch it back. But I pull away, taking another heavy slug. Tooth-rotting dose of sugar or not, *somewhere* in this candy-sweet mix is some caffeine. Presumably, at least. As I swallow, my nose wrinkles.

"Something's off with this milk."

"Oh, it's oat milk. I'm going dairy-free."

I wrinkle my nose. My sister rolls her eyes again. "Dude, come on. Gift horse. Mouth. No peeking. You ever heard that one?"

"This shit tastes like it *came* from a horse's mouth—*wait*—"

But in my exhausted, beaten-up state, I'm too slow for Callie's sugar-fueled speed as she plucks the cup from my hand again.

"Enjoy the hangover, ass."

I sigh, rolling the ache out of my shoulders and shoving my fingers through my hair. "I'm not hungover."

"Jeez. Could've fooled me." Callie glances at her watch. "How is it that *we're* the early ones?"

She's got a point. Of all my siblings, Callie tends to be my partner in minor clock-related crimes. Like being late for family dinners. Or to meetings called by our oldest brother Ares, the relatively new head of the Drakos family empire.

That's actually why we're here today: a full family meeting in the brand spanking new offices of Thermopylae Acquisitions —so named after the place where the fabled three hundred Spartan warriors held their ground against thousands, because our grandmother Dimitra truly believes we're the descendants of the shirtless guys with the CGI abs from the movie *300* and nobody can convince her otherwise.

This new—and *legitimate*—business venture is the start of a new direction Ares is trying to push our historically criminal family in. I mean, yes, crime is still very much on the table. But with a fully above-board real estate and private equities management firm, we can better *hide* those crimes. Not to mention launder our dirty money much more easily.

"Even a broken clock is right twice a day."

My little sister snickers as she drops into the chair next to me. "Well, I was checking in at The Banshee on my way in. So I was practically right around the corner."

"And how is your new Irish pub?"

She grins widely, the excitement shining in her eyes. "Oh my God, it's looking *so* awesome. You're coming to the soft opening next month, right?"

"Wouldn't miss it for anything."

Recently Callie, my sister-in-law Neve, and *her* sister Eilish went in together on buying an older Irish pub in the West Village. At first, I was skeptical, figuring Callie just wanted a place to party. But as they've gone through the process of remodeling the place into an amazing spot complete with a basement lounge and small stage, hiring staff, and working on branding and marketing, the more I'm convinced Callie might actually be a natural at this.

"Anyway, that's my excuse for being early. You?"

I grunt noncommittally. When she sighs and passes the coffee back to me, I force another mouthful of not-even-close-to-milk and sugar down my throat. Callie gives me a smug look.

"Let me guess, you didn't sleep at your place last night."

I shrug. Callie snickers.

"Shall I bother asking what her name was, or should we stick to something easier for you to remember, like hair color? Or maybe cup size?"

"Ha-ha-haaa," I drawl. "For the record, I was out with Sean."

"Wow. Have you *actually* made your way through every single woman in New York so that you have to bat for the other team now?"

"Oh, we've got all the jokes today, don't we," I mutter. "Sean *Farrell*. And again, I'm not hungover. I'm fucking sore. That motherfucker put my ass through the wringer last night."

Callie bites back a snorting laugh. "There are *so* many taste-less jokes I could make right now."

39

I roll my eyes. "*Boxing*, you fucking weirdo."

She chuckles. "Yeah yeah yeah, I know." She arches a brow. "I'm not surprised you're seriously hurting this morning. Sean is a beast."

Sean Farrell, aka the son of Dominic Farrell, head of one of the vassal families to the Kildare Irish mafia family, has become a good friend of mine. Less than a year ago, if the two of us were fighting, it would have most likely been in the street instead of a ring, and there'd have probably been knives involved, possibly guns, not boxing gloves.

Because back then, the Kildares were our enemies, and we were headed toward an all-out, blood-in-the-streets, nuclear level war with them. Then my older brother Ares married Neve Kildare, joining the families, creating a united front and burying the hostilities.

I'd always known vaguely somewhere in the back of my head that Sean was a top-notch fighter. Then, when we accidentally crossed paths one night at the underground fights I sometimes go to, we hit it off.

I'm pretty good, but Christ. That dude is *phenomenal*. Honest to God, there's a solid chance he could go pro. And from time to time, like last night, I convince him to put me through my paces in a ring. This typically results in me getting my ass served to me. But it's also a great way to learn and get better.

So, no, I didn't sleep at my place in Brooklyn last night, because I was so knocked to shit after ten rounds with that motherfucker that I crashed on the couch of his Lower East Side apartment.

Okay...there *might* have been a couple or twelve shots of whiskey last night too, since Sean insists on embodying every single stereotype of a hard-drinking, tough-fighting Irishman. Yeah, in fact Callie's right: I *am* rocking a small hangover to accompany the full-body ache of getting the absolute shit knocked out of me last night. Fun combination. Not.

Callie sighs loudly and glances at her watch again. "Ares did say ten, right? It's nine fifty-eight. If he's not here in two, I'm—"

As if on cue, the door to the conference room flies open, and the rest of our family crashes in like a wave of chaos, shattering the silence. Ya-ya walks in first, her eyes wide and bright as she clasps her hands together, drinking in the view of Lower Manhattan through the wall of windows. It's our grandmother's first time seeing the Thermopylae Acquisitions offices completely finished, and even though I'm exhausted, sore, and hungover, I grin at the pride and joy on her face.

"Theé mou! Eínai ómorfo!"

My God, it's beautiful.

Kratos, my younger but enormous brother, chuckles a rumbling laugh as he walks in after her.

"Not bad, huh, Ya-ya?"

Behind him, Ares strides in last, like an emperor storming into his war room. I can't help but grin.

Ares was never supposed to be king. And not so long ago, he wasn't, just like he wasn't the oldest Drakos sibling. Back then, it was our older brother, Atlas, who reigned over our family empire, after murdering our father.

Luckily, that reign was comically—or tragically, depending on your point of view—short-lived due to Atlas' idiocy and pride—and it was a dethroning that got him killed in the process. Ares took up the crown after him, moaning and groaning about "not being meant" to be king.

But the truth is, it's a crown he was born to wear.

Atlas was the oldest, but also the cruelest. Years older than all of us, he always felt more like a mean uncle than a brother. And the particular irony of it being *Atlas* who killed our equally unlovable father is that it was Atlas who was always our dad's favorite. The one he poured the most of his cruelty, malice, and pride into.

Ares was smart, though. He took the strength from our brutal upbringing, and left the cruelty and the wickedness on the table. My younger brother Kratos is the strong, silent one. Then there's our *youngest* brother, Deimos, who's currently running the European side of our empire in London and is every inch the God of Terror he's named after. Calliope, or Callie, the baby of the family, well... She's her own force of nature, which is why we get along so well.

And then there's me. The wild card. The unhinged one. The God of the Underworld himself.

It shouldn't be the case, but somehow, even though sometimes we disagree, we all make these personalities work together—both as a family, and as an empire.

Ares pauses near the head of the table, arching a stern brow at Callie and me.

"Thanks for dressing up," he mutters, eyeing Callie's flip-flops, cutoff jean shorts and hoodie, and my black jeans, motorcycle boots and white t-shirt.

"You didn't mention a dress code," Callie fires back.

"I mean, it's a business meeting at our new financial firm, Callie," he sighs. "It's sort of implied."

"Yeah, *Callie*," I grin at her. She flips me off.

"How did you guys not know to dress up?" Kratos grunts, glancing down at his sharp dark blue suit, custom tailored to his large frame.

"*Suck up*," Callie mutters, guzzling her iced coffee.

Ares sighs and shakes his head before taking his seat at the head of the table. Kratos and our grandmother sit across from Callie and I, and Ares leans forward to push a button on the speaker in front of him. After a few rings, the line picks up.

"D, you with us?"

"Loud and clear," Deimos' unmistakably gravely tone rasps through the phone. "Hi, Ya-ya."

"*Geia sou engone*," she chirps back.

"Well, we're all here," I sigh, quickly jutting my arm out to snatch Callie's iced coffee out of her hands. I take another heavy pull, grimacing before I give it back. "Should we start this thing?"

"One sec," Ares glances at his watch. "We're just waiting for—"

The door behind him swings open.

Fuck.

I mean, of *course* she's here. She's our family's legal counsel, and a partner at Crown and Black, the firm we use for most of our legitimate business legal needs. But even still, the second Elsa Guin strides into the room, my brow furrows deeply.

The woman's my fucking nemesis.

Honestly, I don't even know how that started. It's not like we ever clashed over something big and important. It's just...*her*. Everything about her gets under my fucking skin. The fact that she's a fucking ice queen with a stick up her ass the size of the Chrysler Building. Those conservative, drab, gray skirt suits she's always wearing, with her ice-queen white-blonde hair—hair that makes her look like a long-lost Targaryen sister on *Game of Thrones*—scraped back in a severe bun or, on the days she's feeling wild, just a ponytail.

There are some people you meet in life who are just your fucking opposite. And that's Elsa for me. She's the decaf chamomile tea to my shot of whiskey. The electric scooter to my gas-guzzling American muscle car.

The wet fucking blanket to my raging fire.

She's a bloodhound for anything fun, and an *expert* at extinguishing that fun with her schoolteacher-in-charge-of-detention vibe.

But, all of that aside, there's another thing about Elsa that pisses me off beyond anything else. And try as I might, I can't fucking change a thing about it.

She turns me the fuck on.

It's complete and utter bullshit. Something totally fucked with my inner wiring. A critical flaw in my programming. But whatever it is, despite being a thorn in my side and the coldest ice queen in the western world...Elsa's fucking *hot*.

Not in an overt way. I mean the woman is like a robot who's been programmed to find zero humor in anything and speak like a goddamn legal briefing all the time. She wears thick-rimmed glasses, and I honestly doubt she owns a single piece of clothing that isn't office attire in various tones of gray or black.

She isn't hot in the way the women I'm usually attracted to are—leggy model types with vapid thoughts, nothing but slutty clubwear in their closets, and mouths far better suited for sucking my cock than engaging in anything even remotely approaching intelligent conversation.

No, Elsa's hot in that sexy librarian you want to gag with a paperback while you fuck the shit out of her against the shelves of the Classic Lit section kind of way.

...*Not* that I've thought that particular scenario through.

Several times.

I think it's her accent, too. There's something about that posh British tone that makes me want to hear her say *filthy* things with it.

When she walks in, her eyes catch my glare for just half a second. But it's enough for her nose to wrinkle, a small sneer curling her lips before she almost instinctively rolls her eyes and pulls her attention away from me.

Her boss, or at least one of her bosses, Alistair Black, strides in behind her. I don't really know Alistair at all. But I do know that despite being a champion of the law, there's a darkness in him. Call it game recognizing game, or one individual with fucked-up tastes recognizing another. But that blond-haired, blue-eyed charm of his doesn't fool me. Plus, rumor has it that he's a member of the very club I plan on going to tonight. The kind of club deviants like me go to.

Alistair shuts the conference room door before he shakes Ares' hand.

"Hope we didn't keep you?"

My brother shakes his head. "Not at all. We were just starting."

Alistair flashes the room one of his charming million-dollar smiles that seems like it was custom made to win over juries and judges before he unbuttons his jacket and takes a seat at the table.

Elsa, meanwhile, looks around the room like a teacher surveying the detention room she has to monitor. The facade only cracks a little when she gives my sister—who she's been helping with the legal aspects of re-opening The Banshee—a quick flash of a smile before taking her seat.

Ares clears his throat. "Since we're discussing the acquisition today, I've asked Mr. Black and Ms. Guin to sit in on this meeting."

I arch a brow, perking up when he says it. "The acquisition" is something we've been idly talking about for months. But if we're all here to talk about it, with legal representation, I get the feeling it's become more than a hopeful idea.

"As we've all talked about before, Serj Mirzoyan, the head of certain Albanian"...he glances at Elsa and Alistair, clearing his throat..."*enterprises* in New York..."

It's a cute way of avoiding the word "mafia" in front of the lawyers. Even if they're both painfully aware of what our family does and who we are, plausible deniability is always a good thing.

"…wants out. He's done with running things, and he wants to leave with a fat paycheck in his hands. And we're very well-positioned to be the ones who *give him* that fat paycheck, in exchange for full control of all his business assets."

Deimos clears his throat at the other end of the phone line. "Remind me again why he's snubbing his own kids on this? Why wouldn't one of them just take over if he's ready to retire?"

Ares shakes his head. "He's not snubbing them. They'll be compensated well for—"

"Because Melik and Vanya Mirzoyan were raised like trust fund brats, not mafia heirs," I break in. "And Serj is smart enough to understand that a flat payout is a much better inheritance for them than an empire they'll almost assuredly burn to the ground or sell off piecemeal for cocaine and shopping money."

Ares smirks. "That's basically the short version, yeah."

"We're not worried about his motives, though?" I frown. "I mean, Serj has plenty of reasons to try and fuck us over on this."

My older brother nods. "You're referring to the bad blood from years ago?"

"*Yeah*, I'm referring to the fact that our father, may-he-burn-in-Hell, put a bullet through Serj's father. Call me old-fashioned, but I feel like that's not the best foundation for a—"

"Mr. Mirzoyan has been quite open about the…*relationship* between your two families."

47

My jaw grinds as I slide my eyes from Ares to stab my gaze lethally into Elsa.

"I'm sorry, *why* are you here again?"

Callie kicks me under the table. Ares glares at me.

"Because she's been working on this deal since the get-go and has done significant research into the financials Serj provided, *that's why*," he mutters, with a look that says, "knock it the fuck off."

I shrug, leaning back in my chair.

"Yes, there's history between our family and his," Ares nods. "But I'm confident after speaking with Serj that the past is truly in the past. He had about as much love for his father as we all did for ours. And he wants this deal. He's hungry for it."

I frown, folding my arms over my chest. "Okay, so what's the damage going to be?"

"A hundred and fifty mil. That's for the whole thing. Every asset, every business Serj controls."

Kratos whistles. Deimos mutters a curse in Greek over the line that draws a sharp look from our grandmother as she goes to swat the speakerphone.

"It's a lot, I know." Ares steeples his hands on the conference table in front of him, and he glances across to Elsa and Alistair. "Could you please give us a minute?"

The two lawyers nod, standing and closing their legal pads before making an exit.

My brain refuses to acknowledge how good Elsa's ass looks in gray tweed, even if my eyes insist on following it out the door.

When they're gone, Ares grins at us.

"Ya-ya, do you want to take over for this part?"

Our grandmother smiles, drumming her fingertips on the tabletop. She may be small and frail, but the list of people who've rued the day they underestimated Dimitra Drakos is lengthy. The woman is as sharp as a blade, with all the destructive power of a hurricane when she puts her mind to it.

"One hundred and fifty is not a small number," she says in a slow, measured tone. "But, it will get us more than even Serj is aware of."

My brow arches curiously.

"As you know, I sit on a number of boards overseeing rezoning and redevelopment throughout the city."

Despite her age, Dimitra sits on no less than *four* of these boards. First, because she genuinely does want to better New York, and make sure the city keeps affordable housing available, especially for immigrants, given that she's one, too.

But second, because her insider knowledge picked up at the various meetings of these boards helps funnel a *shitload* of construction jobs to Drakos-owned companies.

"One of them is the new West Side Urban Redevelopment Sector," my grandmother goes on. "Which encompasses Nine-Fifty-Two Lincoln Place."

Something clicks in my brain. But Deimos beats me to it.

"That's Serj's parking garage."

Dimitra grins. "It is… At the moment, yes."

I frown. "Why is a parking garage of interest to us as it pertains to this deal? I mean, it's New York, I get that parking is easy passive income. But—"

"It's of interest," Dimitra smiles, "because in nine months the city is going to approve rezoning that whole block for mixed-use housing and retail."

The room goes silent.

Holy *shit*, that's huge. Serj's parking garage—a dismal, brutalist thing from the eighties—takes up almost two thirds of the block.

Ares grins. "Tell them the best part, Ya-ya."

She shrugs, a smug grin on her face. "The rezoning discussion is under a strict gag order. All closed-door meetings, all participants buttoned up with NDAs. Not a soul knows it's happening. Not even Serj Mirzoyan."

The eyebrows of everyone around the table begin to raise as the implications of all this settle in.

"Actually, the *best* part," Ares growls hungrily, "is that given comparable properties in the area, we're looking at a potential two-*billion*-dollar profit from this."

"*Fuck. Me*," Callie breathes.

My own lips curl into a smile. "And Serj really doesn't know?"

Ya-ya shakes her head. "No. None of the property owners will find out about it for another six months, to avoid a price war or any issues with landlords trying to push out existing tenants on the adjacent properties."

Ares' brow furrows. "There's something else, though. Up until two weeks ago, Serj was extremely keen on our deal happening. Since then, he seems to have cooled a little. My guess was that he was courting another offer, and it seems I was right."

He pulls an envelope from of his jacket and slips out a number of black and white photos, which he tosses across the table for all of us to see.

Shit.

"That, obviously, is Serj Mirzoyan meeting with Gavan Tsarenko."

I scowl at the pictures of the older, graying, greasy-haired Serj shaking hands outside of the Russian Tea Room with the young, tall, dark-haired, heavily tattooed, and very handsome head of the Reznikov Bratva's New York City operations.

He's quite possibly one of the most powerful men in the entire city, despite only being something like twenty-four years old.

"Guess we know who Serj's other interested buyer is," Deimos mutters.

Ares nods. "Yeah. And knowing Gavan, there's almost no *way* he doesn't know about that rezoning, or he'd have even less interest in dealing with Serj than we do. The Russians and the Albanians had a turf dispute less than a year ago, and Serj's men capped one of Gavan's top *avtoritets*, whom I gather was also a close friend of his."

"And now he and Serj are doing business…?" I scowl. "Yeah, that wouldn't be happening unless Tsarenko knew for a fact he was screwing Serj over bigtime."

"Exactly," Ares sighs. "So we need to be smart. If we come on too strong, Serj will probably realize we know something he doesn't, which'll spook him. And even if that doesn't happen, we can't win a bidding war against the Russians. They've got *way* deeper pockets than we do."

He frowns as his eyes meet mine.

"You still go to that…" He clears his throat, shooting a quick glance Ya-ya's way before turning back to me. "That *club* of yours, yeah?"

I lift a non-committal shoulder. "At times?"

"Good. Clear your schedule for the night. I want to run something by you later." I nod, and he presses a button on the table in front of him. "Jenna, can you send Ms. Guin and Mr. Black back in, please?"

———

TWENTY MINUTES LATER, we're wrapping up the last bits of legitimate business that Ares needs the lawyers for. Then, everyone's standing and filing out solo or in pairs. It's not until I nod goodbye to Callie that I realize that the only two people left in the room besides me are Elsa and Alistair.

"You're still good for the sit-down tonight with Taylor and Dante Sartorre?"

My ears prick up at the name. Besides being a major player in the New York City underworld, not to mention a majority owner of Club Venom, Dante Sartorre is also a cousin of

Luca Carveli, a west coast big time player with, shall we say, unfortunate connections to our family.

"Connections", as in, our father made a business deal with him years ago in exchange for Callie's hand in marriage when she turns twenty-one. Which is…coming up.

It's something we'll definitely have to deal with at some point. Probably sooner rather than later.

So, yeah, damn right my brows fly up when I hear Elsa and her boss mention Dante's name. I pull out my phone and pretend to be doing something on it with my back to them.

"Absolutely," Elsa replies in that prim, proper, frosty ice-queen with a stick up her ass way of hers.

"Good. Thanks. Taylor's a stone-cold killer lawyer, but it's always good to have back-up. Especially with a guy like Sartorre."

I tap away on my phone, glancing up to give a small nod of my chin to Alistair as he walks past me and out the door.

And then, it's just the two of us.

I swivel my chair around lazily, frowning as Elsa packs her laptop and stacks of legal pads into her giant shoulder-strapped briefcase.

"You have a meeting with Dante Sartorre?"

Her head snaps up, those flinty hazel eyes of hers narrowing suspiciously, like they always do around me, as if she's confident I'm perpetually scheming something.

I mean, it's at least half true.

"Were you eavesdropping?"

"I was sitting eight feet away from you and my ears work." My brow furrows. "Sartorre is a dangerous man, you know."

Elsa shrugs. "Your family is equally dangerous, and I'm just fine."

"Dante is different. You should be careful."

She sighs heavily, like she's waiting for me to drop the punchline of some joke I've set her up for. When it doesn't come, she frowns.

"Is there a reason you care?"

"Just looking out for my favorite ice queen. If you get whacked, how else am I going to cool off a room in the summer?"

Elsa's pink lips curl into a sarcastic sneer. "Hades, it's perpetually *astounding* to me how a man can reach the age of thirty without ever having evolved past children's playground insults."

"I'm twenty-nine."

"I really don't care."

I grin widely. Elsa glares at me over the rim of her glasses.

"Something amusing?"

"Yes. It's *amusing* how immune you think you are to my charms."

She rolls her eyes, shouldering the strap of her bag. "I *am*, in fact, immune to you, Hades. To every dimension of you— both of them, actually. And I'm *so* sorry if no woman has had the heart to tell you this before, but sophomoric humor and trust fund cockiness do not, in fact, make you charming or attractive."

"I think there are *several* woman probably within spitting distance of this very building who would disagree."

Her nose wrinkles in disgust. "Precisely. Hades, let me put it this way," she snaps coldly. "I wouldn't sleep with you if you were the last man on earth and the continuation of the human race depended on it happening."

My brow furrows as I stroke my jaw. "Interesting. Very interesting."

"Oh? *What*, pray tell, is interesting?"

"It just seems like you've put a *lot* of thought into the mechanics of, and situations involving, fucking me."

Her pale face turns crimson in half a second, her eyes widening as her mouth forms a little "O" shape.

"*Fuck off*, Hades."

She storms past me to the door.

"Oh, and Ice Queen?"

She tenses in the open doorway, turning back to glare at me.

I just grin. "Next time you're thinking about me—"

"I *do not* think about—"

"Just know that I could make you come harder than you've ever come in your life with just one finger."

She stares at me, face bright red and fuming as I grin at her.

"Which finger would that be?" She smirks as she brings a hand up. "This one?"

Elsa's middle finger stands stiffly up in the air, a tight grin on her lips, before she whirls and storms out the door.

4

HADES

Present:

I STARTLE as consciousness rips me from the haze I was just swimming in. Groaning, I stretch under the sheet, feeling the sort of ache in my muscles that can only come from a marathon fuck. My lips curl hungrily as I feel my cock thickening heavily against my thigh.

Why stop now?

With a savage grind of my jaw, I roll over to spread her legs and sink myself back into the outrageously pretty, eager, dripping, tight little pussy that's been draining my balls all evening. But I stop short with a start when I realize the bed next to me is empty.

My eyes open blearily as I fully wake up. Scowling, I scan the room. But it's empty. And the door to the ensuite bathroom is open, with the lights off.

Shit.

I sit up, glaring at her side of the bed. My hand lands on the sheets, and I frown.

Still warm. She hasn't been gone long.

For a second, I almost jump from the bed and chase after her. But then I stop myself, rolling my eyes.

I don't chase women. Even a woman who arguably just reset the bar about a mile higher in terms of my own definition of good sex.

I allow a smile to creep over my jaw as I drop back to the pillows, shoving my fingers through my hair.

Fuck, that was good. Really good. Like, "four marathon rounds and I still want more" good.

And I *never* want more from a woman, even if the sex is fantastic. I just don't. I don't chase. I don't call later, or make plans for the next time.

I fuck, I leave.

Veni. Vidi. Vici.

Once we're done…we're *done*. I don't emotionally connect with many people at all outside my immediate family. And I *certainly* don't emotionally connect with women. So it's just sex. And even if it's a good time?

There's always another woman, in another club, with another hopeful smile and twinkle in her eye, like she's going to be the one who fixes me. That *she'll* be the one to keep me wanting more.

But there's no fixing me. I'll never want more. Not from the same woman. A repeat means attachment, and I don't do that either.

I used to think there was something wrong with me because of this inability to be intimate in any real capacity outside the physical mechanics of sex. But as I've gotten older, I've realized that it's not that the ability to feel or experience emotional intimacy is broken inside of me.

It's that it's completely walled off, behind barriers a mile thick and three miles high. Maybe part of it—or probably a lot of it—is what happened to me when I was young. But that's only a piece of it. Somewhere deep down, I know I've always been like this.

For a while, when I first became friendly with Cillian Kildare after my brother married Cillian's niece, I thought maybe I'd found someone else who's the same kind of different as me. Cillian, after all, is a legit, certifiable psychopath. Or at least, he's firmly on the scale somewhere. But it turns out he's not entirely devoid of emotions or unable to have personal relationships. Not just because we're friends—at least as much "friends" as you can be with a man like Cillian. But because he's married to Una now.

They may the darkest, gothiest prom king and queen couple I've ever met. And I'm sure their intimate life involves drinking each other's blood, or pulling the wings off bats or butterflies or some weird shit like that.

But they're in love. Even *Cillian* is in love.

That's never happened to me. And I don't see that changing.

I doubt I'm actually psychotic. I think I'm just...tempestuous. Probably a little fucked up in some fairly profound ways that I have zero interest in examining. Or maybe I'm just a force of chaos, fucking, racing, and raging his way through the world.

Whatever the reason, here I am: approaching thirty without ever having had a meaningful or intimate relationship with a woman that's lasted longer than eight hours.

I glance back to the spot my little kitten recently vacated and replay flashbacks of the evening in my mind, starting with the way she grabbed me and just fucking kissed me.

I've had woman throw themselves at me more times than I could ever count. But never like that. The other times, it's felt almost pathetic—a desperate attempt for me to "pick them". As if they're "special", or in any way different than any of the faceless, disposable women who came before them, or the ones who'll come after.

But the little kitten who kissed me tonight wasn't throwing herself at me. She wasn't begging me to pick her.

She was picking *me*.

And I'm fairly sure that that's never happened to me before.

With a groan, I stretch my sore muscles again and sit up in bed.

Four times.

I grin.

Shit, that was good.

I stand, stretching again before I pad across the room to the bar cart. I pour myself a much-needed whiskey, knock it back, then pour one more and bring it back to the bed with me. I sit on the edge and glance at my watch sitting on the bedside table.

Shit. I'm supposed to be at Leo Stavrin's office—well, *surveilling* his office—twenty minutes ago. And I've already fucked up the first part of the plan involving him tonight.

My mind flashes back to the little kitten kissing me, but then I rewind a little bit further, to the girl I was talking to before Kitten came along.

The girl I actually came to Venom tonight to see. Not because I had the tiniest interest in fucking her, much less *talking* to her. But because Ares asked me to, and family is one thing I will always do *anything* for.

Even seducing Leo Stavrin's utterly brain-dead girlfriend.

It's like this: Leo is Gavan Tsarenko's top captain. Until a few months, he was working lower down the totem pole over in the UK, where Gavan's co-head of the Reznikov Bratva, Konstantin Reznikov, runs things. But when the Russians' war with the Albanians got Gavan's top captain Artyom killed, his position needed to be filled. And it would seem Leo has filled the position well.

That, obviously, puts him close to Gavan. It also probably goes without saying that it makes him intimately familiar with whatever plans Gavan is cooking up when it comes to making a play for Serj's empire.

But there's something else about Leo that few people know: Leo's a cuckold.

I don't mean that as an insult. That's legitimately his thing. Leo's fetish is for his girlfriend Anya—the aforementioned brain-dead brunette with the ridiculously fake tits—to go out and get fucked by random dudes, and then come home and tell him all about it.

There may or may not be a part of that kink that involves, uh, *cleaning her* afterward with his tongue. And, hey, I'm not gonna kink shame anyone, even weaselly little shit-bags like Leo Stavrin, but fucking *ew*.

In any case, that was what Ares wanted to "run past me" after our meeting earlier. Leo's gotten Anya a membership to Venom to help facilitate her random fucks. So the plan was for me to make an appearance myself, find her, seduce her, and get her talking about anything business-related she may have heard from Leo.

That plan went a little sideways when she fucking *recognized me*, of course. Anya might be dumb…and she is…but I doubt even she'd be dumb enough to start talking about her boyfriend's Bratva business with someone who's very obviously a member of a competing family.

And then, of course, Kitten grabbed me and kissed me, and the plan went from merely full of holes to sunk to the bottom of the sea right next to the fucking *Titanic* in about a nanosecond.

Not that I have any regrets. It was honestly a shit plan to begin with, and I get more than a little pissed when Ares wants to weaponize how I am with women for business purposes.

I mean, yes, I have issues. I'm not a fucking whore, though.

I have plans involving Leo too. But mine involve spying on him using the state-of-the-art surveillance equipment I've got stashed in an apartment across the street from the restaurant he uses as an office. Not banging his girl.

And fuck, I should have been there twenty-*five* minutes ago now.

Quickly, I knock back the rest of my drink and get dressed. I glance once back at the bed before I roll my eyes and resist the urge to slap myself.

Then I'm outta there.

———

HALF AN HOUR LATER, I'm pulling the hood of my sweatshirt down low over my face as I slip in the back door of the apartment building. I've rented the studio on the fourth floor through a shell company, just to be safe. I'm not stupid. But you can't be too careful.

As it stands, we're just *potentially* in a business standoff versus the Russians. But I'm hyper aware how it would look getting busted spying on Gavan's top captain in his own place of business when we're not openly in hostilities. Yet.

As much pride as I have in my own family, and as much as I'd love to tell Gavan and his crew to go fuck themselves, that would be epically unwise. We made ourselves much stronger when we partnered our family with the Kildares. But the Reznikov Bratva is a fucking powerhouse. Not to mention allies with about four other equally huge Bratva families.

So the name of the game right now is "make sure you don't get fucking caught".

I can do that.

In the empty rented studio, I leave the lights off as I move to the window. I crack the blinds just enough to be able to see out, looking at the front of Leo's restaurant, The Pearl of the Black Sea: famous—or should I say infamous—for its over-priced caviar, cheap swill vodka poured into bottles with premium labels, and the fact that Leo Stavrin does most of his business out of a third floor, front-facing office.

An office I currently have two cameras with telephoto lenses and a military-grade targeted microphone aimed at.

I slip on the headphones, squinting through one of the cameras as I focus the mic on the office windows across the street.

Shit.

All I'm hearing is garbled static. There's a few hints of men's voices, and even a woman's—Anya, probably. But I can't hear shit. And the shades are drawn, too.

Goddammit.

I pull away from the camera and peer through the blinds themselves. *Fuck.* I glare venomously at the neon sign for the restaurant that hangs just outside Leo's office windows. Somewhere in the back of my mind I remember reading something about the flickering wavelengths of neon throwing off targeted microphones. That might or might not be bullshit, but either way, I can't hear a damn thing.

Fuck.

I try to get anything for a few more minutes before I throw in the towel and admit defeat. This isn't happening. Not tonight, at least.

I'm about to shut everything down and go home, when something catches my eye outside. It's a girl storming out the front door of the restaurant. My brow furrows as I watch her, her back to me as she takes what looks like a shaky breath and shoves her fingers through her long blonde hair.

And then suddenly, the light from the neon sign above her glints off the bracelet on her wrist.

No, not a bracelet.

I go still. My face lowers to the viewfinder of the camera next to me, peering at her now through the telephoto lens.

A *wristband*. A gold and white one.

She's wearing black heels with ornate golden bows on the toes. A backless, sexy—but not *too* sexy—little black cocktail dress.

And even if her face is turned away, I can see the angry red welts—*bite marks*—running up the side of her delicate neck.

Three of them.

Fuck. *Me.*

One similarity would be weird. The combination of all of them piled together is too much to ignore. And the bite marks on her skin that I can still taste, and the gold and white band that is obviously from Club Venom, move it from weird coincidence to fact:

The girl I just spent four hours tangled in bed with in one of the private rooms of Club Venom just walked out of Leo fucking Stavrin's restaurant-slash-office.

I don't for one second believe that's coincidence. She picked *me*, after all.

I'm about to march right down there—the danger of exposure be damned—and grab her to figure out exactly what she was playing at when suddenly, she turns.

And my world goes utterly still.

Her long, white-blonde hair swishes to the side. The neon sign glints in the hazel flintiness of her eyes, and glistens off the soft pink pout of her lips.

Eyes that typically roll at whatever I say. Lips that almost always sneer when they're near me.

And that's when it suddenly hits me like a Mack truck to the face.

The girl standing on the sidewalk outside Leo's place, the girl from the club, *is goddamned Elsa Guin.*

What. The. *Fuck.*

I can feel my throat tightening as my vision tunnels. My jaw grinds painfully as my pulse thuds like a war drum in my ears.

Fuck, I can still taste her on my tongue. I can still feel the velvety sweetness of her cunt squeezing my cock as she erupted beneath me.

But forget trying to wrap my head around the Ice Queen herself fucking anonymous men at Club Venom. I mean, I *will* figure that part out, even if it means ripping it from her piece by fucking piece.

No, right now, I would very much like to know what the actual fuck Elsa Guin is doing walking out of Leo mother-fucking Stavrin's office at one in the morning, after screwing me all evening.

With a snarl rumbling on my lips, I whirl from the window and storm out of studio apartment. I take the stairs two at a time, yanking my hood up as I explode out the side door of the building.

...Just in time to watch Elsa slip into the back seat of an Uber and drive off.

My car is only a block away. If I run, I could make it. I could chase her. I could—

The door to the restaurant opens, and suddenly Leo and four of his goons come pouring out, looking angry as hell.

Shit.

I turn away, yanking the hood down over my face before I slip into the shadows, watching the Uber carrying Elsa slip around a corner and disappear into the night.

This isn't over. Actually, this is the farthest fucking *thing* from over.

Because I've had a taste of the heat that lies buried deep inside the queen of ice.

And now I want the fucking rest.

5

ELSA

THIS NEVER SHOULD HAVE GONE this far.

Wincing, I step out of the Uber I just took from Club Venom. It pulls away from the curb after I shut the door, and I glance up at the garish neon sign blaring "The Pearl of the Black Sea" above me.

He's certainly not expecting me, especially unannounced. But this is where Leo does business. And judging from the number of swarthy, gruff looking men in suits with visible Bratva tattoos milling around the bar and lounge area when I walk in, he's here this evening.

Screw you, Leo. This ends tonight.

I make my way up one of the staircases from the main dining room level to the lounge and bar upstairs, grimacing with every step. I'd always imagined that there might be at least *some* discomfort after doing what I was planning on doing tonight for the first time. But I'd imagined it would only happen once.

I didn't plan on a four-round marathon. Just as I didn't *plan on* Hades Drakos.

I also didn't plan on the instant addiction. The inability to say no or to tap out. The way he teased, manipulated, and played my body like a master. The craving for more, more, *more*.

I also didn't exactly plan on him being hung like a freaking horse.

I grimace again in discomfort as I take the last step up into the lounge area. But even so, a flush creeps up my neck and a warm, sensual feeling pools in my core. Sore or not, that was *good*.

Really, really fucking good. So to speak.

I make my way through the mixed crowd—both regular New Yorkers and the obvious Bratva-connected types—sipping vodka in the upstairs lounge. At the far end, two burly men in suits and wearing earpieces guard the staircase up to the third floor, where Leo holds court in his private office.

The teasing memories of earlier tonight fade as the reality of how I even got to this point presses its foot down on the back of my neck.

Again, this never should have gone this far.

I'd cut Leo out of my life before I was even eighteen. He'd certainly cut Nora and me out of his, which I was more than fine with. And when I decided just under a year ago to move us to New York, it felt like taking an even bigger breath of fresh air. We'd be putting an entire ocean between us and him.

Until he followed us.

Leo has always worked for the Reznikov Bratva—first under Antin Reznikov, when I was small. And then more recently after Antin died, under Konstantin, Antin's son.

In *England*. Or, at times, in Russia.

I've kept tabs on Leo since I was eighteen and took over legal guardianship of my sister. I wanted to know where he was, to make sure that wasn't anywhere near *us*. So I heard about it when he moved to New York right after we did, to start working for Konstantin's co-king of the Reznikov empire, Gavan Tsarenko, the head of the organization's presence in the US.

I told myself it was a coincidence. I told myself New York was a *vast* city, and we could easily never cross paths.

Until Leo very purposefully crossed mine, two months ago, and immediately sank his claws into me again.

Suddenly, Leo *needed* me. Because even worse, he *knew*.

He fucking *knew* I'd never slept with anyone.

I'd never be able to prove it in court. But I know damn well that he got that particularly personal piece of information from a nurse at my OB-GYN's office. A nurse who suddenly had the money, at least according to her ecstatic posts on social media, to quit her job and move with her boyfriend to a lavish beach house in Nha Trang, Vietnam.

A nurse who very obviously sold my personal medical details to Leo. And he's been using that information to torment and threaten me for the last two months.

Because in the fucked-up world of the mafia, and the Bratva, and all of that shit, apparently that's all a woman is: a tradable commodity whose value is determined by whether or not she's a virgin.

It's not like I was ever "holding on to my virtue" or anything like that. Nor am I at all religious, or a prude, or asexual. I mean, I *have* desires. I get sexually turned on. I've just never slept with anyone.

Well, until tonight.

At first, it was that I knew I was too young. Then, I was essentially Nora's mother, and who the hell has time to date or have a social life when you're raising a seven-year-old at the age of eighteen?

After that, there was always just something else to take up my time. University, and then law school. And then absolutely throwing myself into work. My *job* was my boyfriend. And the idea of a one-night stand, or any kind of casual sex just...never appealed to me.

And then there was Hugo.

I was twenty-two and working a hundred hours a week at my first job in London. Hugo was a few years older, and one of the firm's most promising junior partners. He was nice, and charming, and I agreed to go out with him.

Three dates later, I was thoroughly creeped out and had zero interest in seeing him again.

Because Hugo was one of *those* men—the kind of guy, like Leo, who viewed virginity as some sort of commodity. Or worse, as a signal of "goodness"—as opposed to "whorishness", as Hugo so colorfully explained it to me on that third and final date, after I'd finally told him I'd lost interest in him.

But Hugo didn't really hear that, and didn't want to hear the word "no". He got obsessive—not just with me as a human being, but with my "virginal status". It got so bad that I had to move to a new firm entirely. It even escalated to the point where he was stalking our apartment, my new job, and Nora at her fucking *school*.

I finally got a restraining order against him, and it all stopped. But after that, I was officially done with dating. Not when there were men out there who were only going to reduce me to some sort of virginity fetish.

No thanks.

And for a while, it didn't even affect me at all. I've been too insanely busy with work the last few years to have time to date anyway. Vibrators exist. So does internet porn. And I have a *vivid* imagination.

But then two months ago, Leo entered the picture again to once again leverage my lack of sexual experience into a tradable commodity.

But fuck that, and fuck him.

This ends tonight.

The guards at the bottom of the staircase to the third floor glare at me, moving closer together as one shakes his head and holds up a hand.

"No one goes upstairs," he grunts.

I smile a tight smile. "I'm sure Leo will want to know I'm here."

The guy arches a brow, glancing at the other guard before shaking his head.

"Is he expecting you?"

"No."

"Then you should leave."

"You should tell him Elsa is here to see—"

"My my my, aren't we all dressed up?"

I shiver, a mixture of fear and revulsion crawling up my spine as I turn. The thin man with the sunken eyes and the shaved head leering at me has always made me think of a skeleton ever since I first met him two months ago. His name is Pascha, and he's Leo's right-hand man.

He also thoroughly and utterly creeps me the hell out.

Same as the other handful of times we've crossed paths, Pascha looks at me like he's mentally undressing me, which makes my stomach turn. It's even worse tonight, though. Usually, all he's got to work with are drab gray or black pant or skirt suits.

Tonight, I'm dressed like *this*. Which of course, only turns his usual leer into an outright dangerous one.

"You look delicious," he hisses, grinning that bony, creepy grin at me.

"And you look like a sex offender, as always. I'm here to see Leo."

Pascha glares at me. "You would do well to treat me with respect, *malen'kaya suchka*."

"The only little bitch I see here is *you*," I smile sweetly at him.

Pascha's eyes narrow dangerously. "*Careful.*"

"Just tell him I'm here."

"You can tell him yourself." Pascha nods at the two burly guards before grabbing my elbow and yanking me angrily after him as he storms up the stairs. I grit my teeth, still wincing with every step but relishing the triumph I'm going to feel once I tell Leo that his little plan just went up in smoke.

Upstairs, we march down a tacky gilded hallway until we get to a heavy door. The guards step aside as Pascha blows past them and through it, with me in tow.

There are six other men in the room—some drinking at the bar along one wall, a couple of others cleaning handguns on a coffee table between two leather couches. Leo himself looks up from his large, ornate desk when we enter, first with a curious, then amused expression on his face.

"*Ahh*, there she is," he purrs in his thick Russian accent, clearly dulled by vodka by the late hour.

"Hello, Leo."

He scowls. "You could address me as you should, you know."

"Which is how, exactly?"

"As *father*, for a start."

I laugh coldly. "I can promise you, that's not going to happen, *Leo*."

My dad ignores the dig. "Can I assume you've come here tonight to finally follow through with your family responsibilities?"

I can only stare at him. "Family responsibilities?" I hiss. "Where the hell were *your* 'family responsibilities'? Like, *ever*?"

Leo glares back at me. "You were provided for as a child. You had food, clothes, a roof over your head…"

"No thanks to you. My mother did all that."

He rolls his eyes. "How? By sucking dick?"

My temper flares. "*Stop it.*"

"If you don't wish to acknowledge what she was…" he shrugs. "Well, I can't force you."

My mother was many things—amongst them, yes, an exotic dancer.

But she *never* slept with men for money.

"The money for your needs came from me, *moya doch'.*" He sighs, raising a silver-rimmed crystal tumbler and sipping what must be vodka over ice. "But enough. It is in the past. Now, we have the future to look toward, and what it means for you and our family."

I laugh coldly again. "*Our* family? I have my family and you have yours."

He smiles, making a tsking sound with his teeth as he shakes his head. "Blood is blood, *moya doch'*. And you have something this family can use to advance itself."

I resist the urge to throw up as he leans forward across the desk.

"I know you've never been with a man," he growls quietly. "This is good, very good. Because a man like Melik Mirzoyan can appreciate a bride who's never bled for another man."

This time, I do actually have to choke back the vomit rising in my throat.

Because there it is: the reason for all of this. The reason I went out tonight to do what I did, to rid myself of my freaking virginity, so that he couldn't hold it over my head anymore.

My father wants to marry me off like some sort of prize cow to the prince of the Albanian Mafia, Melik Mirzoyan, to secure a deal with Melik's father Serj. Such a deal would allow the Reznikov Bratva to buy out Serj's empire. But apparently Melik is one of those sacks of shit that is only interested in a virgin bride.

Fuck. That.

Slowly, as the silence grows in the room, I start to smile—wider and wider, until Leo's brow furrows.

"This is amusing to you?"

"No, but your choice of phrasing just now is."

It's now or never. I didn't intend to be this dramatic with it, nor did I anticipate there being half a dozen other men in the room, including the ultra-creepy Pascha. But screw it, why not.

"What phrasing?"

A man like Melik Mirzoyan can appreciate a bride who's never bled for another man.

Without saying a word, I bend at the knees and reach down. Leo's face scrunches up in confusion as my hand slips up under the hem of my dress. With a wince, I peel the cream-colored lace panties away from my still-tender parts and pull them down my legs. Then I slip them over my heels, and dangle them from one fingertip, smiling.

Then, before I can lose my nerve, I toss them right onto Leo's desk.

His eyes drop and his face twists when he spots the dark red stain on them.

"What the *fuck*?!" he sputters, standing abruptly and backing away, as if I've just tossed a bomb, or anthrax, on his desk. His eyes drag up to mine, revulsion on his face. "What is this!? Are you on your fucking period or—"

"No, Leo, I'm not."

He frowns. Then blinks.

And slowly, it hits him.

The color rushes into his face, suffusing it with deep a purply-red as his lips curl viciously.

"*No.*"

I just smile. "Oops. So much for the purity pledge for poor widdle Melik and his fragile male ego."

Leo's face contorts with rage, his eyes tightening to slits.

"You. Fucking. *Cunt—*"

"You do *not* get to talk to me like that," I snap. "Actually, you don't get to talk to me at all." I shake my head, keeping my head high as I glare right into his face. "This is *over*. Don't ever come near me again."

Then, with a show of cool confidence I don't feel in the slightest, I turn and stride out of the room, my chin up and shoulders straight.

I keep up the façade until I get outside. Then the air rushes out of my lungs with a wrenching sound as I look up and shove my fingers through my hair.

It's done.

It's over.

The Uber I ordered on my way back down through the restaurant pulls up to the curb. Grinning, I hop in. And then we're off into the night.

NORA'S fast asleep on the couch when I get home. Netflix still thinks she's binging *The Witcher*, so I quietly turn off a shirtless, monster-slaying Henry Cavill, cover my sister with a blanket, make sure the blinds are drawn so the first light won't wake her, and leave her to sleep.

There's almost a twinge of regret when I shower—as if I think that washing his scent, his touch, and his...well, *other things* off me will erase the memory. But I needn't have worried. After I crawl into bed and snuggle under the covers, it's the only thing I can think about.

Part of me feels a little guilty for using him. But not *that* guilty. This is Hades we're talking about, after all. To him, I'm sure I was just one more random girl on one more random night. It's a thought that sits sourly in my brain much more than it should. But I shove the sourness down.

It is what it is. And I have zero regrets.

No one ever has to know.

He can be my own secret sin.

My dirty little secret.

And it's with endless replays of all the ways he made me explode rushing through my head, like a powerful drug, that I slowly sink to sleep.

6

HADES

MY FIRST PLAN after leaving Leo's restaurant involves going directly to Elsa's office, breaking in, and figuring out *exactly* how hard she's fucking my family, since she's clearly working for Leo.

Screwing me was almost certainly part of that.

I *know* she must have heard Anya gushing about "knowing me" at Club Venom. I might have been wearing a mask, but between Anya using my fucking *name,* and my recognizable tattoos—that you can see even when I'm clothed—Elsa absolutely knew who I was.

She didn't just kiss me because she thought I was some random guy.

She kissed me to get *my* attention. To seduce me. Which...worked.

I'm just trying to figure out what the point was in fucking me as it pertains to her working with Leo.

Unfortunately, my plan for burgling her office gets scuttled when I pull up outside the Midtown office building that houses Crown and Black. The bank branch on the ground floor is apparently getting wired up for a new and improved security system, which means there's about twenty cops milling around at every entrance and stairwell.

I mean, the Drakos family has "friends" in the police force. But twenty cops turning a blind eye to me waltzing into a law office at two in the morning? Pushing it.

Five hours later, though, after napping in my car, it's on.

It's Saturday. I'm sure that Crown and Black has their paralegals and interns pulling weekend hours, like every other big NYC firm. But it's still early, and the top three floors that house Crown and Black are empty. Just in case, though, I come in quietly through a maintenance elevator, making sure I avoid the security cameras until I get to Elsa's office.

It's locked, of course. But I've been picking locks since I was ten, and hers isn't exactly Fort Knox.

Once inside, I get to work.

Her desktop computer is my first pick, obviously. But it's password protected, and I don't have the time to try brute-forcing it, nor do I know Elsa well enough to try guessing random passwords.

I just know her well enough to know the sounds she makes when she comes. To know how sweet her pussy tastes. To know she went fucking wild when I pulled her hair, and spanked her ass.

To know she almost came when I fed her my cum off my fingers.

Enough. I grit my teeth, shaking the distracting replays from my head as my dick turns to steel in my pants. Time enough later to jerk off remembering the night I just spent with her.

Right now, I'm here on business.

The locked file cabinet opens just as easily as the door to her office. I comb through it, looking for anything Reznikov or Stavrin-related. Anything to do with Mirzoyan too, for that matter. But all I find is some flimsy shit pertaining to some building permits for Gavan Tsarenko, who I know also employs Taylor Crown herself for his own legal needs.

I scowl as I close the cabinet with nothing to show for my efforts. It's the same disappointing result with the files in her desk drawer, and the only things I find in the closet are four librarian-esque skirt suits in varying shades of gray, gray and gray, and a yoga mat.

Fuck.

I'm making a quick poke around the attached private bathroom, complete with shower facilities, when I hear the office door rattling and then opening.

Shit.

I duck back behind the half-closed bathroom door, peering through the door jamb.

It's fucking *her.* Elsa's panting, her chest rising and falling under the sports bra she's wearing underneath an unzipped hooded running top, together with leggings and jogging shoes.

All black and gray, because *of course.*

She's even got her hair up in its typical severe ponytail. I watch as she turns to frown at the doorknob, because I left it unlocked, and she's probably wondering how she missed locking it the day before.

But she shakes it off, turning to walk over to her desk. I shift to the side to try and get a better view through the cracked door.

…Which fucking *creaks* when I brush against it.

Goddammit.

Instantly, I hear her sharp intake of breath.

"Whoever the *fuck* is in there, I've got a gun!"

Shit.

"And I'm calling the cops!"

"Hang on." I stick my hands out of the bathroom doorway first. "Don't blow my fucking brains out, okay?"

Slowly I poke my head around the corner, where my eyes are instantly met by a furious and spooked Elsa. She's not holding a gun, but she is pointing a can of pepper spray at me.

"That doesn't look like a gun to me, Elsa."

"No?" she spits venomously, still brandishing it.

"No. That's false advertising."

She squints at me. "How about I use it on you anyway, and you can file a complaint about false advertising afterward?"

"Nah, that's okay." My eyes drag from her cold, hazel gaze, to the nozzle of the pepper spray, still aimed at me. "Could you not point that at me?"

"Could you kindly explain what the fuck you're doing in my office?"

Uh, not really.

I also don't want to tell her I know about her double-crossing. Not yet. Not until I've backed her into a corner she'll never get out of.

I step fully out of the bathroom, my hands still raised. "I was just dropping some paperwork off for Thermopylae Acquisitions."

She turns, and for the first time, my eyes land on the three marks on her neck. Something savage growls inside of me—something hungry for more at the sight of my mark on her.

She's obviously slapped concealer over them. But either from her run or because I bit and sucked too hard for them to be hidden away, they're there for all the world to see.

And for me to remember. Which my cock instantly does.

"At seven-fifteen in the morning on a Saturday?" she sneers.

"Yep. Early riser."

"So where are they?"

Well, this is unraveling quickly.

I grin. "Guess I forgot them in the car."

"Right."

Slowly, I lower my hands. Thankfully, Elsa also lowers her pepper spray. She also stiffens and very quickly zips her running top back up over the sports bra—high enough to cover her neck wounds.

"What were you doing in my private lavatory?"

"Taking a piss, what else?"

She wrinkles her nose. "Well, if you're done breaking and entering—"

"I wasn't breaking and entering."

"My office door was locked last night."

"Huh. Damn cleaners."

She rolls her eyes.

"Speaking of which, what are *you* doing here at this hour?"

Elsa frowns. "I *work* here, Hades. Some of us work for a living."

The haughty "over it" tone is the typical one she always uses when she talks to me. But she's overdoing it.

Overcompensating.

I can see it in the flush on her cheeks that's from more than just her run. I can see it in the way she refuses to meet my eyes, as if she knows that if she does so, I'll see right into her, and reveal all of her secrets.

Little does she know that the one secret she's most desperately trying to hide from me isn't a goddamn secret at all.

But I can use that.

I could tell her right here and now. Hell, I could turn on the psycho inside of me, get all dangerous and threatening, and yank the truth about her involvement with the Russian out of her right now.

But I could also wait. I could also slowly box her in and let her build her own cage. If I let her know I know about her double-crossing now, it's all over. I might get something out of her, but what I get is what I get.

If, however, I *don't* let her know I'm onto her, she might just show me even more. If she thinks I have no idea she's working with Leo, and furthermore have no idea it was *her* I was fucking into a whimpering, shaking, subby little *mess* last night, she won't guess that I'm watching her every move.

Learning her every secret.

Waiting for the perfect moment to pounce.

"Little early for the office, isn't it?"

"Little late for you to still be *up*, isn't it?" she shoots back.

I grin. Her usual vitriol is…shaky right now. She's trying too hard to sell it.

It's very amusing to watch.

"Do anything fun last night?"

She groans. "Hades, please leave. I have things to do."

"I'm just making polite conversation."

She rolls her eyes. "My night was fine, thank you."

"Yeah? What'd you do?"

Elsa's eyes snap to mine. "What do you *want*, Hades?"

I chuckle. "Jesus Christ, dial down the suspicions. I'm just trying to be nice."

"Which is exactly why I'm suspicious."

"Want to know what I did last night?"

"Not reall—"

"I met a smoking hot stranger."

Her mouth purses. "How thrilling for you."

"Yeah." I shrug, turning to stroll past her shelves of legal books, running my fingertip over the spines. "Fucked her brains out, too."

Elsa is silent behind me. I smirk, still idly examining her books.

"Three times." Slowly, my brow furrows as I turn to glance at her over my shoulder. "Or was it four?"

Her face turns crimson and her jaw drops open and then snaps shut again, as if we're in the climax of Edgar Allan Poe's *Telltale Heart* and she's terrified that the truth will just tumble out.

"What do you think, Elsa?" I smile broadly. She shivers as I slowly close the distance between us, until I'm standing right in front of her. "Was it three times, or four?"

She swallows uneasily, her face burning hotter and hotter, like it might combust under the pressure.

"I...how the hell should I know?" she mumbles, her hands clenched at her sides.

"That is a *great* question."

The energy between us hums. She swallows again, her lower lip quivering before her teeth firmly latch into it.

"I really think you should leave. I have work to do," she finally blurts.

I just smile, letting my eyes pierce into hers before she yanks her gaze away with a shudder. It's only then that I release her from my gaze.

I turn and make for the door.

"Hades."

Halfway through the door, I turn with a smirk on my lips and a raised brow.

"Don't ever break into my office again."

"Noted. Enjoy your weekend...*kitten*."

She gasps, and I swear she's about to throw up.

Then I leave, with a hungry grin on my face.

7

ELSA

He. Knows.

Three full, long minutes after Hades leaves, I'm still standing in the middle of my office.

Motionless. Stunned. Staring that the door, trying to remember how to breathe.

"Enjoy your weekend...kitten."

A heated shiver creeps up my spine. Flashes of gasped breathes, of fingers and limbs twisting in bedsheets, of nails dragging down his muscled back. Of sweat and pleasure. Of stars flashing in front of my eyes as my body came completely undone at his touch.

I flinch, shuddering and wrenching myself back into the present, blinking as I stare vacantly at the closed door of my office.

I'm losing it.

Hades doesn't "know". Of course he doesn't. If he did, he would have one hundred percent rubbed my face in it, or used it as leverage, or dangled my dirty, sinful secret over my head to gleefully make me dance, and beg him not to tell anyone.

Or he'd have used it to fuck me again.

I tremble, heat throbbing dangerously between my thighs. Then I force myself to take a long, deep breath.

He doesn't know. There's no damn way he does. Obviously, all he said was "enjoy your weekend". And me, being freaked out that he was standing in front of me less than twelve hours after claiming every single inch of my body and redefining my definition of orgasm, simply misheard.

I outright invented that last "kitten", although I have no freaking idea what he could have said that *sounded* like kitten.

I shiver again before I march across the room and lock the door again.

Not that that stopped him before. I know damn well I locked this when I left work yesterday afternoon, and I also know the cleaners don't forget to lock up when they're done.

No. He doesn't know. That wasn't him rubbing it in my face. That was just Hades being, you know, *Hades*. Cocky, obnoxious, arrogant. A bully. A lunatic. A shameless manwhore.

Yeah? Well, you fucked him, sister.

Heat floods my face again as I force myself back to my desk chair.

He doesn't know, and that's the end of that. It has to be, or I'm just going to drown in this thing until I fall apart. I'll just file it away in that lock-box in my head—the place I store and hide anything that trips me up, or pulls me away from my planned trajectory.

Which, obviously, isn't healthy, as all four of the therapists I've seen since I was seventeen have told me, repeatedly. But it is what it is. It's how I deal. How I keep breathing, both for me, and for Nora. I take all the things that drag me down or lie across the path in front of me, and shove them deep into the very back of a closet I can then forget about.

One day, of course, the closet will have to be cleaned out.

But not today.

That's how I've managed to get where I am. And, not to toot my own horn *too* hard, but you don't get to be where I am, at the age of just twenty-six, without some seriously unhealthy mental health habits. But, therapy will still exist later, once I've hit my stride and can finally take a breath. Once I've created an iron-clad life for Nora and myself I can fix the parts of myself that got broken along the way.

Until then, though, this train doesn't stop. For anything.

Certainly not for Hades fucking Drakos. Or his mind games.

Or his God-like dick and tongue.

I flush deeply, shaking those thoughts from my head for the last time. Then I do what I always do to bury or hide away things I don't want to deal with: I open my laptop.

And I work.

For Nora. For me. For the future. Because I will *not* be our mother, chained to a life that grinds her under its heel and to a man who controls her, hurts her, and takes away everything that makes her herself.

I've been running from that potential future since I was fourteen. And nothing, not even the God of Hell himself, is going to stop me now.

———

"STOP."

I gasp, almost spilling my coffee. I spin toward the voice behind me.

"Jesus, you scared the hell out of me."

Fumi—my colleague who has the office next to mine, and who's also my *only* real friend in New York—makes a face as she leans against the door frame. It's not uncommon for her to launch directly into the middle of a conversation, whether you're in a scheduled meeting or in neighboring bathroom stalls.

But normally it doesn't give me a heart attack like a jump scare moment in a horror movie.

I blame the cocky and gorgeous menace that broke into my office two days ago.

"Sorry," Fumi winces, tucking a strand of jet-black hair behind her ear. "I just had something really important to ask you."

I nod as sink into my office chair and gingerly take a sip of my steaming hot coffee.

"Of course. Come in."

She steps into my office and drops into one of the two chairs across the desk from me, nodding slowly as she taps her fingertips together meditatively.

My brows knit. "Is this about the Chesterman case? I talked to their family counsel on Friday afternoon. He seemed to think they'd be amenable to a—"

"Nice try, but I'm not asking about work."

I swallow, arching a brow as a grin spreads across Fumi's face.

"Okay..."

Her grin widens. "How was your weekend?"

I lift an easy shoulder. "Fine, mostly. I just stayed in and caught up on work. Made sure Nora didn't get into any trouble. Dinner in. You know, the usual."

"Uh-huh, uh-huh," she nods slowly, her dark eyes locked on mine.

I clear my throat. "So, how was your—"

"I'm just wondering which part of catching up on work, managing your teenage sister, and cooking dinner gave you your hickeys."

My face explodes with heat as my hand flies to my neck—only to remember quickly that I'm wearing a silk scarf around it. I simmer, trying to look as nonchalant as possible.

"What hickeys?"

Fumi rolls her eyes. "Really? You're a professional lawyer and you're actually *this bad* at lying?"

I purse my lips, trying to will the heat from my face.

"I'm not *lying*—"

"Objection. You've never been into neck scarves."

"Maybe I want to give them a go."

"How very Parisian of you."

When my face burns even hotter, she just grins wider.

"C'mon! We don't work for a fucking convent, Elsa. You're allowed to go out and get your freak on. But…" She shakes her head, sighing heavily.

"But…what?"

"But you have to fucking *tell me all the details afterward*, so I can live vicariously through your sexcapades!"

I can feel the redness engulfing my face. But I still force a snorted laugh and a roll of my eyes.

"It's nothing like that, trust me."

She groans. "Elsa! We have to present a united front on this! Sisters helping sisters! I *crave* gory details. Now go! And don't you dare tell me you've forgotten the pact."

I grin widely. "The pact" is something that came out of a *very* long night of drinking after work one day, not long after I joined Crown and Black. Both of us were commiserating about being married to our jobs, and how we didn't understand how anyone working the hours we worked could possibly find the time to date, even casually.

It was comforting enough to hear that I wasn't the only one who felt that way. But coming from someone like her, it made me feel even more seen. Because with her Japanese father and Korean-Italian mother, Fumi is freaking *gorgeous*. Like, outrageously, knocking it out of the park, winning-the-genetic-lottery beautiful.

So if even *she* wasn't even finding dates, it really was the job. Not my neurotic nature. Or at least, not entirely that.

Our drunken pact was a two-parter: one, if we were both still completely and utterly married to Crown and Black by the age of thirty, we'd marry each other. Not because of any latent gay tendencies. But solely to make sure neither of us died alone only to be eaten by the cat, or something tragic like that.

The other part of the pact was that one of us would tell the other if and when she somehow, by some miracle, managed to go on a date or, better yet, get laid.

Fumi, as close a friend as she is, does *not* know that I am—or *was*—a twenty-six-year-old virgin, though. Because who the hell wants to have that conversation?

I laugh and wave a dismissive hand. "It's seriously not what you think. I saw some TikTok or something with this girl wearing one, and thought I'd try rocking the scarf look. That's it."

"Oh, okay," Fumi nods. "Well, if that's all—"

She's up before I can even register it, lunging around my desk and yanking the scarf off before I can stop her.

"Hey—!"

"I *knew it!*" she crows triumphantly.

My face burns hotly as I yank the scarf back into place.

"Details, woman! Now!"

I groan. "It was really nothing. I went to this dumb club—"

"Ugh, I hate clubs."

I know this. And same. But Fumi means *dance* clubs, not the kinky and dangerous sex club variety.

"Exactly. And as a perfect example of why we do, this guy was all over me."

She scowls. "Like, didn't take no for an answer ? Because I'll fucking stab him." She shrugs. "Legally speaking."

I grin. "No, no, it was fine."

She arches a quizzical brow. "Are there more hickeys...*elsewhere?*"

I flush hotly.

Yes. Yes, there are. On my tits, my nipples, my hips, probably down my back, on my inner thighs, at my bikini line. Vicious ones, at that.

"*No*, jeez. It was just this dumb thing."

"Did you..."

"No!" I blurt, shaking my head. "We never left the club."

Sustained on a technicality. Proceed.

"And will there be a repeat performance? Like, should I be stocking up on fashionable neck scarves for future Christmas and birthday presents?"

I roll my eyes. "I was just having some drinks and blowing off some steam. That was it. We didn't even trade names."

She groans appreciatively. "God, that sounds hot. Lie to me. Tell me you banged him in the bathroom, or at least got fingered under the bar. Give me *something* for the wank-bank, for fuck's sakes."

I blush deeply, shaking my head as I roll my eyes. "You need professional help."

"No, I need *dick—*"

"Ms. Guin."

I jolt at the sound of my boss' voice in my doorway. Fumi turns the color of skim milk, going absolutely stock-still as Gabriel Black's deep, rough baritone rumbles into my office.

"A moment?"

"Of course, Mr. Black."

Taylor and I are on a first-name basis, at her insistence. Alistair is the same way, so long as we're not with clients.

Gabriel is unequivocally, unimpeachably, "Mr. Black", and God help anyone who tries to call him anything else. Though to be honest, with his black hair, black eyes, and swarthy jaw that somehow always makes me think of an eighteenth-century pirate king or something equally menacing, "Mr. Black" does fit him rather well.

Fumi grimaces at me before typing something at lighting speed on her phone. Mine buzzes on the desk in front of me, a text from her reading "he did not hear me say that, right?" popping up on the screen. I glance at her and give her the most subtle head shake side-to-side.

Even if I'm at least fifty percent sure he *did* just hear her say she needed dick.

Fumi stands, clearing her throat and taking a breath before she turns to smile brightly and professionally at our boss.

"Good morning, Mr. Black."

"Ms. Yamaguchi," he growls. She darts past him and out the door.

When we're alone, Gabriel closes my office door and then leans against it.

"How's the Chesterman case going?"

It's funny. Up till last week, even given how cool I am with Taylor and Alistair, Gabriel Black has always thrown me off a little. I mean he throws *everyone* off to varying degrees, ranging from "a little" to "pee-your-pants", which is kind of his evil superpower. It's also what makes him a viciously ruthless and successful lawyer.

But now, in the three days since I last saw him, I've come face to face with a more ferocious darkness.

A more lethal villain.

A more consuming force of nature.

And I'm realizing that it's a little tough to be intimidated by anyone, even Gabriel Black, after you've fucked the God of Hell.

Four times.

"Great, actually," I beam. "I spoke to the family's personal counsel last week, and I think they'll be amenable to a settlement. Nobody on their side wants to see the inside of a courtroom."

He nods slowly. "Good. Keep me up to date, but feel free to proceed as you see fit."

"Of course, Mr. Black. Thank you."

I smile. He doesn't. He just stands there, his dark brow furrowed.

"Is there something else I could help you with?"

"There is." He clears his throat. "Ms. Crown and I just got out of a meeting with Gavan Tsarenko."

I nod. Gabriel's eyes narrow slightly.

"He'd like to speak to you."

A shiver runs down my spine. I have no illusions that this has to do with anything other than my father, Gavan's top captain.

"Oh? When did he want to set up a meet—"

"Right now."

My pulse grows weak.

"Will that be a problem?"

"Not at all."

He nods, getting ready to go. "Good. Oh, and you're still fine for tonight?"

I resist the urge to grimace. Tonight, I'm meeting a potential new Crown and Black client for a pitch dinner. On the one hand, I'm honored that the name partners have the faith in me to do this solo.

On the other hand, Howard Kenmore, the potential client, specifically *requested* me. Howard is fifty-three, disgustingly wealthy, and has a very public history of dating petite blondes less than half his age, the last two of which wore thick-rimmed glasses.

Obviously, this begs the somewhat troubling question of whether I'm going out tonight to pitch Howard on Crown and Black, or to audition to be his next girlfriend.

But of course, I'm not mentioning my concerns to Gabriel. Instead, I just nod and smile. "Of course."

"Excellent. Oh, and don't overthink the Gavan thing. He's about to dump a lot more work on us—much more than Taylor can reasonably be expected to handle herself. I think he just wants to meet a few of our top people who'll be taking on some of that work. It's all above-board. Don't let the rumors spook you."

"Absolutely, Mr. Black."

He nods and raps his knuckles against the door behind him. Then he's gone.

8

ELSA

I EXHALE as Gabriel closes the door, trying to compartmentalize the various things flying around my brain: the dinner with Howard later, the impending meeting with the co-King of one of the most dangerous and powerful Bratva families in the world...oh, and the lingering memories of screwing Hades.

Which is exactly when the door swings open with barely a knock, and Gavan himself billows in like a black cloud.

At twenty-four, Gavan Tsarenko is even younger than I am. Tall and built, the man looks every inch the Bratva king that he is: black hair, steely gunmetal gray eyes, heavily tattooed. Even in his impeccable, tailored suits, the lines of ink creep out of his cuffs and snake across the backs of his hands, as well as up his neck to his jaw.

I stand and keep a neutral, professional smile pasted on my face as he enters. But inside, I can feel my blood chilling just a little bit. He's not known to be ill-tempered or prone to random acts of violence or anything. In fact, by reputation, he's as cold and calculating as a machine. But it doesn't stop me from biting back a shiver as his dark energy flows into the room like black ink spilling across paper.

And then all the effort I'm putting into maintaining a calm appearance vanishes when Leo walks in behind him, followed by the consummately-creepy Pascha.

My father just glares at me, half a snarl on his lips. Pascha shuts my office door and very deliberately leans against it while mentally undressing me.

Puke.

"Ms. Guin," Gavan purrs quietly. "I don't believe we've ever officially been introduced."

He crosses the room with the air of a man who owns every single one he enters. He shakes my hand firmly across the desk, then clears his throat. "May I sit?"

"Of course, please."

Gavan undoes his jacket button and settles his muscled frame into one of the two chairs facing my desk. When I remain standing, he arches a brow.

"Will you be joining me?"

I lean against the credenza behind my desk. "I'm fine here."

His lips curl at the corners. Angry? Amused? I can't quite say.

"Let's skip the part where we pretend we don't understand all the convoluted histories and relationships in this room," he begins. "It's a waste of time and we're both busy people. As I understand it, your father—"

"I don't consider him my father," I murmur icily.

Leo and Pascha glare daggers at me. Gavan just inclines his head gracefully. "Yes. Well, *Leo*, then, wished to aid my organization in an important business acquisition, by offering your hand in marriage to Serj Mirzoyan's son, Melik. Do I have that correct so far?"

I nod stiffly.

"However, I gather there have been certain...*actions* taken on your part recently that have rendered this deal no longer acceptable, as Melik exclusively wanted an..." he clears his throat. "*Inexperienced* bride. Is that also correct?"

"Apparently so."

"And is this true? I mean that you—"

"I'm not going to discuss my body, my personal choices, or my sex life with you or your men, Mr. Tsarenko."

Gavan shakes his head. "You misunderstand. That isn't why I'm here, Ms. Guin."

"Then why *are* you here?" I mutter in a tone that I fully realize is approaching dangerous considering the man I'm using it on. "Because I know it's not about 'meeting the other lawyers in our firm who will be handling your legal needs', as you told my boss."

He smirks. "Perceptive."

"Thank you."

Gavan clears his throat. "I don't honestly give a shit who you choose to sleep with, Ms. Guin. And while I can appreciate my captain's *zealousness*," he turns to arch a brow at a glowering Leo, "in trying to secure this deal for me through whatever means he saw fit, no one's forcing anyone to marry anyone else."

I turn to sneer at Leo. He looks like he's got a lot to say. But he just glances at Gavan before leaning against the wall with his arms folded over his chest and remains silent, glaring at me.

"Now, as I understand it, the Drakos family is *also* interested in doing business with Serj Mirzoyan?"

I raise one brow, dipping my chin and keeping pointedly silent. Gavan grins.

"Right, of course. Attorney client privilege and all that. Even so…" He leans back in the chair, drumming his fingers on the arm rest as his gray eyes stab into mine. "Some deals, like Mr. Mirzoyan's, are too important to leave up to whichever way the wind might blow at a negotiating table."

"Then I suggest you retain great counsel and bring a large check to that negotiating table, Mr. Tsarenko. I'm afraid I can't divulge any information about other clients I may or may not be representing."

"Watch your fucking tone, *daughter*," Leo spits venomously.

Gavan holds up a hand, his eyes still locked on mine.

"Brass tacks, Ms. Guin. What would it take for you to divulge information on these hypothetical clients of yours?"

I blink, stunned at his brazenness.

"I'm sorry, Mr. Tsarenko—"

"Gavan is fine."

"*Mr. Tsarenko*," I say again. "Are you implying that you'd like to bribe me into breaking my attorney client privilege in order to give you sensitive information about a business rival of yours?"

"Oh, I'm not implying anything, Ms. Guin," he smiles. "I'm flat out asking you."

I bristle, shaking my head. "I'm afraid that's not going to happen. And I'm not comfortable with the tenor of this conversation."

Gavan says nothing. His eyes don't leave mine.

I swallow. "I think it would be best if you left now."

His brow arches, and the corners of his lips curl slightly.

"You're sure? Because once an offer of a gift in return for information goes away, it generally doesn't come back."

"Mr. Tsarenko, I am flat out telling you I will not be taking money in exchange for breaking my professional code of ethics, not to mention the law."

Gavan takes a deep breath. He doesn't make a single move to stand. His fingers drum the arm rest over and over, jacking my anxiety through the roof until it feels like I'm going to explode.

"*Mr. Tsarenko—*"

He sighs. "I suppose we'll have to go with the threat, instead."

I go cold as something frosty glints in his steely eyes.

"Excuse me?"

"If you don't want to accept the carrot, Ms. Guin," he says in his deep, growly tone, "then we'll have no choice but to use the stick."

A shiver ripples down my spine. "Mr. Tsarenko, all due respect. But for professional and legal reasons, given that I am not your attorney, I'm afraid I have to ask you to leave—"

"Oh, for fuck's sake!" Leo finally snaps, surging from the wall and slamming his knuckles on the front edge of my desk and leaning menacingly across it. "Do what he's fucking telling you to do, or so fucking help me God, there'll be *another* Guin sister—one who presumably hasn't whored herself out yet—offered to Melik to secure this deal."

I go *livid*.

"You come anywhere fucking *near her*—!"

"Leo."

There's nothing sharp or loud in Gavan's voice. And yet it holds a power that money can't buy, and instantly chills the room. He turns to glare at my father.

"That won't be happening."

"Gavan, I can sell Serj and Melik on—"

"You are *not* offering up a fifteen-fucking-year-old-girl as marriage bait," Gavan snarls, his voice suddenly shockingly vicious and cold. "And frankly the fact that I even have to say that out loud to you is concerning. The sister is off the goddamn table, in any capacity. Is that clear?"

Leo scowls.

"Is that fucking *clear*, Leo."

My father shoots me a venomous look before he turns to Gavan. "Yeah, boss. Clear."

Gavan lets his gaze rest on Leo for another few seconds before he pulls his eyes back to me. I'm wondering if I'm supposed to thank him or not, when he answers the unasked question.

"Don't."

I frown. "Don't—?"

"Thank me. Your sister might be off the playing field, but I still expect to get what I want, Ms. Guin."

"Look, Mr. Tsarenko—"

"You've gone to great lengths to hide your connection to your father, Elsa. Taking your mother's maiden name, distancing yourself and your sister from him. Working your way through school by yourself."

I glare at him. He just shrugs.

"And I can respect that. But I can—and *will*—have zero problem with exposing all of those secrets you so *very* much want to keep hidden, if it will get me what I want."

It takes me a few seconds to realize the gravity of what he's just said. And when it does hit me, I go white and stiff.

"I—"

"You're one of this firm's fastest-rising stars, if not *the* fastest. A non-equity partner at twenty-six, and already on the path to equity partnership? That's very impressive."

Dread pools in my stomach.

"I wonder," Gavan sighs, absently turning to look out the windows past me, drumming his fingers on the armrest of his chair, "I wonder how they'd feel if they knew who your father was?"

My legs shake and threaten to buckle. My face pales. Leo and Pascha both smirk. Gavan's face remains eerily neutral.

Slowly, I take a breath, trying to calm my racing pulse before I speak.

"Is that a threat, Mr. Tsarenko?"

He doesn't answer. He simply smiles, stands, and walks back toward the door. When he reaches it, he turns, pushing his fingers through his dark hair as his gunmetal eyes land on me.

"I *will* get what I want, Ms. Guin. Take that how you will."

He nods, turns, and strides out the door. Leo sneers at me, and without a word, follows his boss out. Pascha lingers one more second, his eyes sliding over me one last time as he licks his lips thoughtfully. Then he slithers out too.

What the *fuck*. It's nine-thirty a.m., and I'm officially being blackmailed by the Bratva to spy on the Greek Mafia.

How's *your* morning going?

9

HADES

"So... What do you think?"

I moan as I chew slowly, letting the steak dissolve in my mouth. When I don't say anything—I can't, because this shit is way too good to interrupt with words—and only shake my head, Sean grins.

"It's fuckin' amazing, right?"

I give it another few seconds, letting the flavor spread over my tongue a little longer before I finally swallow. I glance at Sean, nodding.

"That's fucking good, man."

His grin widens as he clinks his glass of whiskey to mine. "What can I say, man? That's my girl."

We're at Shank, a brand-new steakhouse with a modern vibe in the Meatpacking District, down the street from the Whitney Museum. Sean's an investor in the place, and his girlfriend Maya is the chef de cuisine of the joint, which was recently short-listed for a James Beard award.

Restaurants are notoriously iffy investments, since something like eighty-five percent of them close within the first year, usually way in debt. But I think Sean picked a winner here—both with the spot, and with the girl.

The food is fucking *insane*. The cocktail list is cool and trendy without being hipster and obnoxious. And they've got a killer wine list, curated by one of New York's top sommeliers. Plus, the ambiance is great—low lights, German brass fixtures, exposed brick and dark hardwood everywhere. Sean and I are posted up at the bar, but there's also a wine lounge on the second floor, the main dining room behind us, and even a few glass-walled private dining rooms along the back wall. The glass on those can be turned opaque with the touch of a button. Which is supremely cool.

"Sean, this place is going to kill it. Congrats, man."

He grins as I raise my glass to his.

"Nah, man. It's all Maya. She's a fucking force."

"Remind me why you haven't been smart enough to wife her yet?"

He makes a face as he takes a sip. "I dunno, man. I mean I love her and shit, but it's a big step, you know? And we're not even thirty yet. Who knows what the future holds?"

I roll my eyes. "Dude, as your friend, I'm going to level with you."

"Yeah? Please do."

"Sean, you're a six-foot-four ginger giant with generally shitty people skills and table manners, a moderate drinking problem, and a below average dick."

He snorts a laugh. "You are *such* an asshole."

"I'm just saying, man...the 'future'? For you? Maya is *way* out of your league and I don't know how she agreed to go out with you in the first place. Don't be a fucking moron. Put a ring on that yesterday."

He grins.

"How's the steak, boys?"

Sean sputters into his whiskey as we both turn to see the chef herself standing behind us, her hair slick against her temples under the white chef's hat, a flush on her face from the chaos and heat of the kitchen.

"Maya," I shake my head, waving my fork at the plate in front of me. "This is fucking....*dayum*."

"Hades is about to make a mess of his underwear over your steak. And I'm not sure how I'm supposed to feel about that," Sean grins at his girlfriend, leaning in to kiss her cheek.

She laughs. "Well, try not to make a scene, Hades. But if you and the steak need to get a room, the Standard is right down the street. No questions asked."

"Don't threaten me with a good time, Maya."

She chuckles as she gives me a quick hug, then pulls back. "All right, well, try not to jizz on any of the guests. I need to get back in there."

"Love you," Sean growls, pulling her close.

She blushes. "Stop it, I'm a sweaty mess."

"Yeah?" he grins, nuzzling her neck. "Good."

She kisses him once more before she dashes back into the kitchen.

"Seriously. Like *yesterday*, you dumb Irish fuck," I mutter under my breath. "I'll shove you into traffic myself if you don't marry her."

He laughs, draining his glass before motioning to the bartender for another.

"Yeah yeah yeah. I know. Look, anyway, I wanted to ask your opinion on something else, too."

"Shoot."

"You know Bob Warren?"

I stare at him. "Bob Warren as in the boxing promotor Bob Warren?"

"Yeah."

"Yeah I've heard of him. Have you heard of this guy Michael Jordan who used to play some basketball?"

Sean snickers. "Well, he wants to work with me. What do you think—"

"I think if you have to ask me another dumb-ass question like 'should I marry the best woman I've ever and will ever meet' or 'should I work with the most famous boxing promotor in the world who will make my career', I'm going to have you fucking committed. Jesus fucking Christ, dipshit. You call him right the fuck—"

I don't finish my thought. I can't.

Because behind Sean, Elsa Guin just walked into Shank.

Elsa, who is looking *stunning* in a dark gray—of course, but here it works—sleeveless dinner gown, her hair swept up.

Elsa, who is clearly here *with someone*.

Something vicious and monstrous snarls and claws inside of me. A red mist I don't quite understand, that I haven't met before, creeps around the corners of my vision as my eyes land on the two of them: Elsa, and the fucking guy she's out to dinner with.

The guy I want to, for whatever insane reason, break in fucking half with my bare hands right now.

He looks old enough to be her fucking *dad*, for fuck's sake. And he's got "schmarmy moneyed douchebag" written all over him. I could overlook the cocksucker grin he flashes at the whole place as if everyone should stand and applaud him for simply existing. I could ignore the overly-bronzed tan from whatever island he just came back from, and the comical combover to hide his baldness.

But I cannot—*cannot*, for reasons that mystify me in this moment—overlook the way he puts his hand on the small of Elsa's back as they follow the maître d' across the dining room.

Suddenly, I want to kill him. I want to rip that fucking hand away from her, remove it and the arm its attached to from his body, and beat him to death with it while she watches.

Or, even more disturbingly, maybe while she rides my cock.

What the fuck is wrong with me?

Sean is saying something to me. I have no idea what. I can't look away from watching Elsa and this fucking dude walk across the restaurant and into one of the private, glass-walled dining rooms behind me, where they sit across from each other with smiles on their faces.

I'm filled with rage.

And it's all very, very confusing.

Why the fuck should I or do I care who Elsa goes out to dinner with? Because I fucked her? I've fucked more women than I can remember. And I've never once given a single shit about them the second it's over.

I don't do followups. I don't call. I don't have second encounters.

Veni. Vidi. Vici.

I come, I…well, *come*, and I leave. And I give zero fucks afterward.

So why can't I pull my eyes and my gaze away from the two of them?

"Yo, Hades. Hello? Hades. Ground control to Major Tom."

I blink, finally managing to tear my gaze from where Elsa is smiling and chatting away happily with the walking dildo. When I turn back to him, Sean is giving me a confused look.

"Who's the girl?"

"No one," I mutter, entirely too fast.

He smirks. "Really."

"Yeah, really."

He frowns, peering past me. "Well, someone should tell her she can't blow her date in the restaurant."

I snap my head around so fast I see blurs.

Goddammit.

Sean chuckles as I whip my gaze back to him. Elsa and fuck-face are just sitting at the table like regular people, having a conversation.

"See, this is why I always beat your ass in the ring, brother," Sean laughs. "You're way too easy to fuck with emotionally."

"You beat me in the ring because you're a giant ginger monster with a tiny cock."

"Bro, I swear to God—"

"Hold that thought."

I stand. And before I know what I'm doing, I'm marching across the dining room, as if I'm going to war.

"Hades!" Sean calls after me. But I ignore him.

I ignore everything.

Everything except for the fact that some fucking guy thinks he can just take Elsa out to dinner. Talk to her. Look at her. Fucking *touch* her.

And even if I don't quite understand it myself, I do know one thing.

He's dead fucking wrong. And he's about to learn that the hard way.

10

HADES

It takes Elsa a second to comprehend what's happening as I storm into the private room carrying one of the chairs from out in the main dining room, plop it down at the table between them, and slide into it.

But when she does, her flinty hazel eyes narrow to slits.

"*What are you—*"

"You guys been here before? Great place."

Fuck-face frowns at me. "I'm sorry, this is a private—"

"Kennedy Rockefeller DuPont the fourth," I chirp, shoving my hand in his face.

"Howard Kenmore," he mutters, shaking it out of habit, looking more than a little bewildered.

"So, what are we drinking tonight?" I smile brightly at the two of them. Howard McFuck-Face looks confused. Elsa, meanwhile, looks like she wants something heavy to fall through the ceiling onto me and only me.

"Uh, this is a 1969—"

Howard frowns when I pluck his glass from the table and drain it in one gulp.

"Mmm. Tasty. Very….wine-flavored."

His brow furrows. "I'm sorry, exactly who the hell are—"

"Kennedy Rockefeller—"

"This is Hades Drakos, Mr. Kenmore," Elsa interrupts tersely, looking pale. "And Mr. Kenmore," she hisses, glaring at me, "is a very important gentleman who's considering Crown and Black for his legal needs."

"Huh. No shit."

Howard frowns. Elsa groans, pinching the bridge of her nose as she turns back to him.

"I am *so* sorry, Mr. Kenmore. Hades' family also works with Crown and Black."

His brow creases. "*Drakos...*" he muses, trying to connect the dots.

"Yes, well, sadly, Hades sufferers from..." she clears her throat politely. "Well, the family does what they can, of course, but when he doesn't take his meds..."

Howard nods. "Ahh, I see." He turns to me. "Son, is there perhaps a car I could call to take you—"

"Get the fuck out."

Elsa's eyes just about pop out of her head. Howard frowns.

"Excuse—"

"I said get. The. Fuck. Out. You. Old. Fuck. Before I drag your ass out by that ridiculous combover."

His face goes livid. "Young man, do you have any goddamn idea who I am?"

"Not really, to be honest, and I don't care," I growl, making him pale as I leer into his face like a maniac. "But maybe I could tell you about *my* family."

He frowns. "Drakos, as in—?"

When his face turns a shade of white, I can see he's finally connected the dots.

"Whatever you're thinking, you're right," I mutter. "Now, I'm here tonight to tell you that unfortunately, there isn't space for you on Crown and Black's client roster. They're all full. No room at the inn. So, again, *fuck off.*"

Elsa looks like she's going to throw up. Howard has that look I've seen on a hundred other people—a mix of wanting to hit me, but fully understanding how horribly it would end for them if they did.

So, because he's a big pussy, he turns his wrath on Elsa.

"This is completely unacceptable, Ms. Guin."

"Mr. Kenmore, I sincerely apologize for—"

"I believe I *will* be leaving after all," he hisses. "And then calling Gabriel and Alistair Black, along with Taylor Crown, and telling them in one fell swoop exactly how badly *you* fucked up this potential deal."

My temper turns black as he leers across the table at Elsa.

"I will be taking my business elsewhere, Ms. Guin. Perhaps when I call your bosses, I'll suggest that as fuckable as their pretty little blonde pretend lawyer is, perhaps next time, they should send a professional—"

He gasps sharply, his words dying in his throat as his face turns pale, as if someone's holding a steak knife to his balls.

Which is probably because someone *is*.

Me.

"I'm going to stop you right there, fuck-face," I growl icily, leveling my vicious gaze at him. "Before you say something you—or at the very least, your balls—will regret. Now: are you listening?"

He makes a pathetic mewling noise as I press the tip a little harder against his shriveled nuts through his trousers.

"I didn't hear you."

He nods eagerly. "Yes!" he bleats. "I'm listening!"

"Wonderful. Here's what's going to happen, Mr. Ken Doll."

"Kenmore."

"Interrupt me again. *Please.*"

He turns the color of oatmeal, his lower lip quivering.

"Here's what you're going to do, fuck-face. You're going to get up, try not to piss all over the restaurant's floor, and go pay the bill. And you're going to tip like the rich fuck that you are. After *that*, you're going to call whoever you have to call at Crown and Black and tell them that unfortunately, you're happy with your current legal representation, *but* you were so blown away by Ms. Guin's acumen and profession- alism that you're going to be hiring Crown and Black as accessory legal counsel. You're going to promise them five million a year in billable hours—"

"You extorting little—"

Howard bleats again, turning a greenish white color as I ease the tip of my blade a little closer against his manhood.

"Make that six. It's now *six* million a year in billable hours. And you're going to be *damn sure* that you give all the credit to Ms. Guin for that. Now, have I made myself abundantly clear?"

He nods vigorously, trembling.

"I'm sure I don't have to mention that should you fuck this up, or screw her over in any way, I *will* be removing your balls from your body while you sleep. And furthermore, since you've pissed me off, if and when it comes to it, I'll be using something more like a fork instead of a knife."

He looks like he's going to throw up. But he manages to nod as he whimpers pathetically.

"Now get up. And *get the fuck out.*"

The second I pull the knife away from his nuts, Howard is *gone*. I watch in amusement as he bolts across the restaurant, dumping a few hundred-dollar bills at the host station before all but falling out the front door into the street.

"He's a spry little motherfucker for a guy his age—"

"What the *fuck* is wrong with you!?"

I swallow back the groan. It's that fucking posh, polished accent of hers. Specifically, that posh, polished accent when it says completely unpolished things. Like the word "fuck", which apparently makes me instantly hard whenever she says it.

I pour another splash of the wine into my glass and bring it to my lips as Elsa stares at me like I'm a maniac.

"*Hades*," she hisses.

"Yes?"

Her eyes bulge. "What the hell are you doing here?"

I fix her with a look. "Really?"

"Really *what*?"

"Do you really want to play the 'why are you here' game?"

"I have no idea what you're talking—"

"Okay, if you insist. I'll go first. Why were you at Leo Stavrin's restaurant on Friday night?"

Her face pales. She swallows, her lips pressing together. Her hand tightens on the stem of her wine glass so hard that I'm legitimately worried it's going to snap.

But slowly, like the goddamn pro that she is, she swallows it all back. Her mouth twists into a grimace, and her eyes turn accusatory.

"Were you following me?"

"Answer the question."

"I don't have to answer a thing, you arrogant dickhead," she mutters. "What I do on my own time is none of your business."

"Well, I'm making it my business."

She glares at me. "Hades, I do have other clients, you know."

"Whom you see at one in the morning?"

Her eyes flare. "Stalker much?"

"Leo Stavrin is not a client of Crown and Black."

"Why do I feel I don't have to mention that his boss, Gavan Tsarenko, *is?*"

"Gavan wasn't at The Pearl of the Black Sea the other—"

"Oh my God, you're a complete lunatic." She shoves her chair back, standing abruptly as her eyes bore into me. "Hades, stop following me. Leave me alone and stay the fuck away from my career. *Please.* I do have other clients besides you and your family. Now if you'll excuse me, I'm leaving."

She makes it almost all the way to the glass door out to the main dining room.

Almost.

"Do those other clients know that you enjoy putting on a cat mask, going to kink clubs, and getting fucked like a bad girl?"

You can hear the record scratch on her life as she comes to a frozen stop. Her entire body tenses and then convulses, and for a second, I'm worried that she's about to vomit. Her back to me, I watch her shudder, her hands clenching and shaking at her sides.

"*Do* they?"

Elsa takes a shaky breath, shivering.

"I have no idea what you're—"

"You have a small mole just south of your left breast, on your ribcage."

She flinches. Hesitantly, she half turns her face toward me, not meeting my eyes.

"No, I don't—"

"And a birthmark in the shape of two overlapping dots, like a Venn diagram, on your inner thigh."

Whatever color is left in her face drains through the floor.

"That…no…" she mumbles. "That isn't true—"

"Yeah? Well, it sure as fuck is true that you took my cum four fucking times the other night. Twice while deep in your dripping wet pussy, once across your back and ass, and once more down your throat like the greedy little cumslut that, apparently, you are. Tell me that isn't true, *kitten*," I hiss. "Just try. I was *there*."

She starts to shake. I watch her throat rise and fall heavily as she tries to swallow the lump caught there. And when she turns to stare at me with wide, horrified eyes and a face completely devoid of color, I almost feel bad.

Almost.

But my tolerance for people who use me is pretty fucking low.

"Keep denying it, please."

She opens her mouth, but nothing comes out before it slowly closes again, dread dripping down her face.

"Wh-what do you want?"

Her voice is so small and frail. The usual haughty, bored, disdainful tone she typically uses when speaking to me is *gone*.

On one hand, it's almost disheartening. Because for all the way we needle each other, I actually *like* her usual all-business, take-no-shit attitude. Honestly, it's a turn on.

That said, on the *other* hand, seeing her shrink a little bit, and watching her...dare I say...*submit* to me is...

Well...*also* a turn on.

A huge one.

"What do I *want*..." I muse, swirling the wine in my glass. "Hmm...I wonder now."

When she turns to eye me with a cold, terrified look, I grin wickedly and waggle my eyebrows up and down. Instantly, heat floods her face.

"Don't even think about it," she hisses quietly.

I feign shock. "Don't even think about *what*? Jesus, Elsa, where did *your* brain go with that?"

"That you're going to blackmail me," she mumbles. "It's not going to work."

"Oh, I think it would definitely work. But also, who do you think I am?"

"A criminal psychopath?"

"I mean, don't hold back or anything," I growl.

She swallows, chewing on her bottom lip.

"Hades..." Elsa hugs herself, looking pale. "I...my career...If you tell them about Venom..."

My brow knits. "Wait, exactly how repressed *are* you that you're worried about your bosses knowing that you had consensual sex?" I smile thinly. "I really don't think they give a shit—"

"What do you want? I mean for you to not tell them about seeing me at Leo Stavrin's place."

There's that small, broken tone again. Part of me wants to laugh. I mean, shit, she's a rockstar lawyer. She probably breaks this tone out all the time in court to get little old ladies out of vehicular manslaughter charges because they can't see over the steering wheel anymore. I bet judges and juries eat it right the fuck out of her hand.

But I'm generally pretty damn good at reading people. It's one of my superpowers. And when I look into Elsa's eyes, I don't see bullshit and practiced lines and a rehearsed tone right now.

I see fear. Real, actual fear.

And instead of my brain going to dark places involving making her submit to me—say, for instance, on her knees whimpering "yes daddy, please daddy" with my cock in her mouth—I find myself inexplicably switching tracks.

Suddenly, I don't want to use this against her. Rather, I want to save her from whatever is scaring the hell out of her so much right now. And she's right. It's obviously not the part about having been to Club Venom, and everything that happened there. It's not even *me*, though I'm pretty sure Elsa would like nobody in the world to know she slept with me.

No, it's Leo. Or possibly Gavan. That's what's scaring the hell out of her. And when I see that fear on her face, I find myself wanting to protect her from it.

I want to stand between her and whatever's just shaken the strength right out of her.

And that's a new one for me.

"Hades—"

Her phone rings from within her bag. She shoves a hand in to silence it, swallowing as her eyes raise to mine.

"I just—"

Her phone rings again. This time, she pulls it out of her bag and peers at the screen, frowning.

"I—hang on, this is my building super." Her eyes raise to mine, as if seeking permission. I just nod, and she answers the phone.

"Hi, George? What's up—"

Her face goes white. Her hand flies to her mouth as it falls open, her eyes wide and horrified.

"*Oh my God*! Hang on! George, can you—no, keep them out if they don't have a warrant! I'm getting in a cab right now!"

Forget how pale and terrified she looked before. Now, she looks like she's going to explode.

"Elsa—"

"I have to go."

She spins and makes a run for it—crashing out of the private room and fleeing across the dining room. I don't really realize how quickly I've followed her until I catch up with her right outside the front doors of the restaurant.

Elsa's madly trying to flag down a cab when I grab her arm.

"What's going on?"

"It's fine!" she blurts, her eyes wild as she keeps waving a hand in the air. "I—I have to get home. Now."

"What—"

"It's my *sister*, okay!?" she screams. "I have to get home to my—"

"Come on."

She gasps as I grab her by the arm and the hip, hustling her down the street.

"Get off me!!" she yelps, twisting under my grip. "I need to get a cab—"

"No, you don't."

We come to a stop right in front of my dark green '67 Camaro Z28, and I yank open the passenger side door for her.

"Get in."

She blinks, looking shocked and numb as she turns to me.

"What?"

"I'm driving you. Get in."

"I—Hades, I need a cab."

"I'm way faster than a cab, trust me. Now get in the damn car."

11

ELSA

"I DIDN'T KNOW you had a sister."

Not many people do. I keep my personal life personal. Especially after I got passed over for a highly competitive job at a firm in London when they learned I had a ten-year-old living with me. Not one person in that interview room believed that she was a younger sister, and that there just weren't any parents around anymore. I could see the same look in their eyes that I used to get when I'd take an even younger Nora to the playground.

When the age difference between you and your sister is as large as it is between Nora and me, people don't see a teenager with her baby sister.

They see a *very* young mother with a cataclysmic mistake.

They see someone they can silently judge while smiling benignly.

That particular firm, after fawning over me for three months, suddenly told me that they didn't think I was "the right fit" for their "culture".

"Most of our junior partners work hard and *then* start families of their own," one of them told me.

I walked out before I could tell them all to go fuck themselves. That *they* could try raising a child alone when they were still a teenager themselves after their mother dies.

But there's no judgement in Hades' tone. And when I turn to look at him as the lift rises, all I see is a genuine look of interest in his sharp, ice-blue eyes before he turns to face the doors again.

It takes me a full two seconds to realize I'm still looking at him before I manage to rip my gaze away.

Goddammit, why is he so fucking attractive?

Again, it would be *so* easy to write Hades off as some sort of trust fund brat who's only playing at being a gangster. He was born with more wealth that I can even imagine. The Drakos family home on Central Park South is a neoclassical mansion from the British countryside—as in it was *literally* a mansion in England that Hades' great-grandfather had moved, brick by brick, and rebuilt on the roof of a forty-story building overlooking Central Park.

Hades has never wanted for anything. He's never had to pull all-nighters for days on end in order put food on the table while raising a kid sister *and* going to university. He received an allowance from his trust fund while he fucked and partied his way through Harvard.

And yet, as easy as it would be to think of him as this soft, moneyed, pampered brat...even I know that's not really true at all. And let's face it, words like "soft" and "pampered" are the last ones I would use to describe Hades.

He's not good looking in the way a rich trust fund brat usually is. His is a dangerous, lethal beauty. And it's not just the viciously piercing blue eyes, the dark brows and tanned skin, the tattoos and muscles, or the razor-sharp jaw and cheekbones that give him this overall deadly attractiveness.

It's the fact that he *is* deadly. He *is* savage and vicious. He *is* lethal.

He's a killer.

Hades isn't pretending to be a tough guy. He's pretending to be normal. And the times I truly realize that are the times when my sinful attraction toward him despite my fear of him burns the fiercest.

"Her name is Nora," I finally say. "She's fifteen."

Hades nods. "And she's living with you right now?"

"She's always lived with me." The lift comes to a stop, and the doors slide open. Hades starts to exit with me, but I stop, turning back to him with a furrowed brow. "Look, I'm fine, you can go. Thanks for driving me," I mumble.

He nods, his eyes lancing into me in a way that sends a ripple of heat down my spine.

"See ya," I blurt.

I turn and start walking down the hallway.

See ya?

Seriously?

I groan, but when I walk around the corner and see the two police officers standing outside my apartment door, my cringey interaction with Hades and his sinful hotness melts away.

The two cops are here because a neighbor called to complain about the loud music and the smell of pot smoke coming from my apartment.

"Good evening, officers," I venture with a professional smile. I extend my hand to shake theirs. "Elsa Guin. I'm the owner of the unit."

They both nod politely and shake my hand before one of them—an officer Gonzales, as it says on his badge—sighs.

"Look, we hate to bother you like this, miss, and we'd love to just drop it now that you've arrived. But unfortunately, since we could smell the marijuana from out here in the hall ourselves, and being that the other oocupant is a minor, we need to file the paperwork."

I grit my teeth.

Goddammit, Nora.

"Now, you can refuse us entry, of course. But we would like to speak to the two young men in there as well."

I stiffen. "I'm sorry, the *what?*"

The two cops glance at each other unhappily.

"There, uh, appear to be two other individuals in there with her. At least that's what it sounded like when we first knocked."

"Uh, okay, yeah…" Anxiety is flooding my system as I brush my hand over my tightly pulled back hair.

Officer Gonzales gives me a sympathetic look, his lips twisted. "I'm sorry, miss. We're not trying to bust your balls. But while New York might be a recreational legal state—"

"Yes, I'm aware. The legal age is twenty-one," I mutter, finishing for him. "And you smelled what you smelled."

He shrugs. "Unfortunately, yeah, we did. We're going to have to file—"

His eyes suddenly snap past me, and his whole demeanor changes. He stiffens, as if a supervisor has just walked in.

"Mr. Drakos, sir."

What?

I whirl, frowning when I see a grinning Hades striding over, his hand extended.

"Jose, how are things, man?"

Officer Gonzales beams, nodding eagerly.

"No complaints over here, Mr. Drakos."

Hades grins that smooth, charming grin of his that he uses when he's trying to get his way.

"And, Chuck, hi, how's your boy?"

"Real good, Mr. Drakos," the other cop grins. "Just made the varsity team."

Hades whistles and points. "Basketball, right?"

If officer Chuck grins any wider, I'm going to beg Hades to just give the man an autograph before he pisses himself.

"Yes sir, Mr. Drakos sir."

"That's awesome, Chuck. Give him my best."

Hades clears his throat, sighing as he claps his hands together.

"Look, fellas, I think this is all just one big misunderstanding. Don't you?" He rolls his shoulders before his hand slides into his jacket pocket. It comes out a second later holding a wad of cash.

The color drains from my face.

He's not seriously insane enough to try to bribe—

"What do we think, guys?" Hades shrugs casually, grinning that lopsided, charming grin of his as he brazenly extends the hand holding the money between two fingers. "You guys are, what, just ending your shift, right? How about dinner on me?"

I'm hyperventilating. Black spots dot my vision as I count the seconds before these two cops drop Hades like a bag of bricks and haul him down to the precinct for the *very* serious crime of attempting to bribe a police officer.

I mean there's cocky, and then there's sheer lunacy.

Except all that happens is Officer Gonzales turning to Chuck, and the two of them just shrugging.

"Yeah, I could eat. How about you, Chuck?"

"Starvin'."

Hades smiles and my jaw drops as he hands the stack of hundreds to Officer Gonzales and then firmly shakes his hand.

"Enjoy, guys."

"Great to see you, Mr. Drakos."

The two cops barely even look at me as they legit tip their hats to Hades and then saunter off around the corner. When I hear the elevator door close, I turn to the psychopath standing next to me, aghast.

"Did you just fucking bribe *the police*?!"

He lifts a casual shoulder, shoving his fingers through his hair.

"What bribe? I gifted them dinner in appreciation of the amazing services they do for our great city."

I scoff. "That's called bribery, and it's a felony."

"You don't have many friends, do you?"

"I have plenty of *friends*. I just don't have crooked cops at my beck and call."

"Well, if you *want* your sister to be processed for possession and use, I can call them back."

I glare at him before I shove past him to angrily stick my key in the door.

"You're welcome, by the way," he grunts behind me.

Ignoring him, I push the door open. Instantly, I'm assaulted by the lingering scent of pot and way, way too loud music. I storm down the hallway into the main living room, and suddenly stop dead in my tracks as two boys all but levitate off the couch with white faces.

"Who the *fuck* are you?!" I bellow at them.

One of them ventures an uneasy smile. "Uh, we go to school with Nora—"

"Where is she?"

"Uh—"

Their eyes suddenly shift past me and somehow get even wider.

"*Oh fuck.* Mr. Drak—"

It happens so fast, I can't even take it in. Hades storms past me like a force of nature, grabbing the two guys by the collars and yanking them off their feet so hard they both fall to their knees.

"*Where. Is. She?*" he snarls viciously.

"In her room!" one of them blurts, looking like he's about to cry, or maybe pee himself. Or both. "She's in her room! We were just hanging out, Mr. Drakos! I swear! Just a little smoke and some music! That's all we—"

Without even blinking, Hades suddenly turns and literally drags them out through the glass sliding door to the balcony off the living room.

"Hades…?"

I start to follow him, but then my face goes white as he yanks both boys up and shoves them hard against the balcony railing, to the point that they're bent backward over it with their feet scrabbling to keep on the ground.

"Hades!" I scream. "Are you fucking crazy!?"

But he ignores me, his eyes two dangerous, lethal slits as he stares at the two teenagers who clearly know him somehow.

"You're both eighteen," he rasps darkly as they choke back sobs and whip their heads around to gape at the ground thirty stories beneath them. "And Nora is *fifteen*, you little fucks," Hades snarls. "From now on, you leave her the fuck alone. You don't come near her. You don't come over to her fucking house. And you *do not* give her drugs. Is that fucking clear?!"

The two guys nod so hard and with so much fear and panic in their eyes, I almost feel sorry for them.

"Yes, sir, Mr. Drakos!" one of them bleats pathetically. "We won't! We swear!" The other boy swallows, the question obviously hanging on his lips.

"*Speak*," Hades hisses.

"Uh, my dad—"

"Are you smart enough to understand what I'm telling you?" Hades spits back.

They both nod wildly.

"Then I don't think either of your fathers needs to hear about this. If you ever come near Nora again, though, believe me, that *will* change. Are we crystal fucking clear, you little shits?"

Cue the painfully hard head nods again, and the choked apologies.

"Good."

I'm still staring at the whole scene like it's some sort of insane fever dream. Hades hoists them back over the balcony to safety and keeps a hold of their collars as he drags them back through my apartment before he shoves them out the door and slams it shut.

When he turns back to me, he smirks.

"Are you *insane*?!" I blurt. "What the hell was that?!"

He shrugs. "They're eighteen, and they should know better. Also, both their fathers work for my family."

"Oh, same as those two cops?"

"Are you typically this much of an asshole when people do you fucking favors?"

I'm about to tell him to pack up his crazy and get out when I hear Nora's voice.

"Hello?"

With a final glare at him, I pull my attention from Hades and march back to the living room. I grab the remote for the stereo and click it, instantly silencing the loud, awful rock music blaring through the speakers.

"Nora?" I growl through clenched teeth.

She's silent.

"Nora, get out here."

There's a heavy sigh and a squeak from her bedroom door as it swings open. A second later, my sister shuffles out of the hallway that leads to both of our rooms in leggings and a hoodie, her dark hair down and framing her face and her hazel eyes, which are currently clearly unimpressed with me.

"What?"

I arch a brow. "Really? You're going to open with attitude? That's seriously how you're going to play this?"

She rolls her eyes. "El, you're over-reacting."

I stare at her. "Over-reacting? Nora, *the police* were called to our apartment, and you were smoking weed! Are you fucking serious right now?!"

"It's legal now, in case you missed the memo!" she barks back at me. "You're the lawyer, aren't you?"

"Not if you're fifteen years old it's not! And those boys are *way* too old for you!"

"I'm not a fucking kid, Elsa!"

"Legally speaking, yes you are. And they are, legally speaking, *adults.*"

"Did they hurt you?"

The dark, edged note in Hades' voice startles even me. Nora just about jumps out of her skin before her eyes whip past me to where he has just emerged into the living room.

"Uh, who the hell are you?"

"Answer him," I murmur quietly, dread pooling in my stomach.

Nora rolls her eyes again. "*No.* They didn't hurt me. Jesus."

"Were they in your room?"

Her face turns crimson as she shoots daggers at Hades.

"Oh my God, *seriously?!*"

"Nora." My brow furrows as I move toward her. "Given their ages and yours—"

"Holy fuck, you're serious." She stares at me. "What do you think I am? Yeah, Elsa, I *blew them* both for pot." She rolls her eyes. "That's a *joke*, by the way. Just making sure you got it."

"Nora, what were you thinking?"

"Honestly? I was thinking I just wanted to smoke some weed and listen to some cool music! What, like you never let loose and partied when you were my age?"

"*No!*" I snap. "I didn't!"

"Well, you should have!"

"I couldn't! I was too busy raising *you!*"

The room goes silent, and I cringe.

Fuck.

"Nora, I'm sorry. I didn't mean—"

"Whatever."

She starts to turn to go back to her room.

"Where's the weed?" Hades asks.

She stiffens, turning back to glare at him. "Again, who *are* you, and what are you doing in our house?"

"This is Hades," I mutter. "He's…a client."

Nora smirks, arching a brow. "Dude, your name is seriously *Hades?*"

"Last time I checked."

"Like, the god of the underworld?"

"My father was a little obsessed with Greek mythology. Don't change the subject. Hand over the pot."

She sighs. "I don't even have it. They came over with some, but all they wanted to do was talk football and play shitty music. So I hung out in my room and played my own stuff." She sighs, glaring at me. "I didn't even smoke any. Happy?"

"I mean, yes, I suppose?"

"Can I go back to my room now?"

"We're going to talk more about this later, but yeah."

"Can't wait."

Nora turns and snags a stack of magazines off the coffee table before she starts to head down the hall.

"Yeah, I'll take that pot now."

She stiffens, turning to shoot a wary look at Hades.

"What?"

"The bag of weed you just scooped up with those magazines. I mean, props for trying. That was a nice move. But I feel like you're not really the target demographic for *Legal Digest* magazine."

I blink, just now realizing what magazines Nora picked up. She glares at Hades, her lips zipped before she marches over and dumps the stack back onto the table, plucking out the little Ziploc bag of weed shoved between two issues.

"*Narc,*" she mutters, handing it to Hades before she whirls and stomps down the hall. I flinch when her door slams shut, then exhale slowly.

"Thank you," I mutter under my breath, not looking at him.

Trying not to think about the fact that less than an hour ago, this man looked me in the eye and told me *he knows.*

Game over. Secret well and truly spilled.

Hades knows what happened at Club Venom. I can tell myself that he doesn't as much as I like, but all that's going to do is make me look ridiculous.

I slept with the god of war.

And he damn well knows it.

"I need a drink," I blurt, striding into the kitchen and grabbing a bottle of vodka out of the freezer. "Do you want one?"

I'm scrupulously avoiding direct eye contact with him, as I have been ever since the restaurant. But I catch the slight shrug of his broad shoulder out of the corner of my eye.

"Sure."

What am I doing? Why do I *want* to keep him here?

But somehow here I am: pouring two vodkas over ice, handing him one, and walking outside to the balcony with Hades right behind me. I stare out at the glittering lights of Chelsea and the west side of Manhattan as I take a slow slug of my drink, my pulse still thudding from the heated exchange with my sister.

And from what just spilled out that we're not talking about, apparently.

"I don't get it."

I frown, glancing back at him. "Get what?"

"You've got this killer career, a great apartment—"

"Oh, please, I'm sure your penthouse or wherever you live is much nicer."

He lifts a shoulder. "*And* you're raising a fifteen-year-old."

"Barely," I mutter.

"I think it's more than barely."

I swallow. "So, what don't you get?"

When he doesn't answer, I turn around. Immediately, my jaw drops as I see him rolling a joint on my patio table with the pot he just confiscated from Nora.

"Excuse me, what the fuck are you doing?"

Hades licks the edge of the paper, seals it up, and then sticks the joint between his lips. He flicks the Yankees branded lighter that was in the baggie, torches the end, and inhales deeply.

"*Hades—*"

"Toke?"

"Um, *no*? Get rid of that right now!"

He grins, exhaling out of the corner of his mouth with the joint hanging from his lips. It has the extremely unfair effect of making him look outrageously hot, like a smoldering young Marlon Brando.

"You do know it's legal in New York now, right? Also its fucking *weed*, not heroin." He inhales again, his brow furrowing as he plucks the joint from his lips with a sour look. "Ugh, shitty weed, though."

"Great. Can you get rid of it now?"

"Depends. Can you tell me why the fuck you were at Club Venom?"

I'm so unprepared for the question that I actually flinch at his words. My face heats, my throat tightening as I swallow nervously and try to stop myself from shaking.

"Why were *you* at Cub Venom?" I throw back in an obvious attempt at deflection.

"The drink specials and nachos, obviously," he drawls sarcastically, stamping out the joint under his heel. "Why do you *think* I was there?"

My lips curl into a sneer. "So, I was just a warm, available hole for you?"

"Don't," he growls, the playful, teasing smile gone from his lips in a heartbeat as his icy blue eyes turn to slits. *"You're* the one that kissed *me,* remember? *You're* the one that threw herself at *me."*

"I don't remember you protesting too hard."

"Has the lawyer in the room ever heard of sexual assault by deception?"

I stare at him. "Are you fucking serious?"

"You knew exactly who I was."

"That's not *deception,* Hades," I blurt. "And I don't seem to remember you asking me *my* name."

"Yeah, funny how that doesn't happen at *anonymous sex clubs,*" he snarls. "You know, the kind where you wear fucking *masks*?!"

I swallow, my hand tightening around the rocks glass in my hand. Hades gets up from the patio table, making my core clench as he looms over me with those piercing blue eyes stabbing into my very soul.

"I want to know *why."*

"Why *what,* Hades? *You* can go fuck a stranger no problem at a place like Venom because you're a man? But I'm the bad guy when I do it, because I have a fucking vagina?"

"Trying to bring up gender stereotypes is a nice lawyer play, *kitten*," he grunts, making me shiver when he uses that name. "But I'm not a jury of soccer moms, so you can save it. What I want to know is, why *me?*"

I swallow, flushing as heat pools in my core.

"I had no idea who you—"

"You're a pretty shitty liar for an attorney."

I roll my eyes. "*Fine*! I heard you talking and recognized your tattoos. So *yes*, Hades. I knew who you were, okay!? And now you know who *I* am, or was, or whatever. We're even—"

"Not quite."

It happens so fast I don't even have time to gasp. His big hand comes up and wraps around my throat just as his mouth drops to mine. And suddenly, Hades is kissing me with all the aggressive force of a conquering army.

His lips bruise against mine. His tongue demands entrance, pushing into my mouth and tasting my own. I shudder, and when the whimper hums in my throat, I swear I can feel him smiling triumphantly through the kiss.

Half of me wants to shove him away and slap his goddamn face.

The other half wants him to dominate me and bring me to my knees again, like he did at the club.

And the longer I kiss him, and the warmer my body gets as it sinfully and traitorously melts against his rock-hard chest, the more that other half of me is winning the battle.

"Did you go grocery shopping? I'm starving."

The sound of Nora's voice is like having ice water dumped over my head. With a startled gasp, I yank my lips away from Hades and shove him back. I stumble from him, panting, my eyes wide as my hand comes up to touch my puffy, swollen lips.

"Elsa."

Turning from the Greek god in front of me, I turn to see Nora padding into the living room and glancing curiously at me through the open glass door to the balcony.

"I'm going to do delivery. Burritos work for you?"

I just nod, still numb.

Still tingling everywhere.

Still trying to keep myself away from the swirling dark vortex of a man standing less than two feet from me, who just kissed the absolute fuck out of me.

"Uh, yeah, thanks."

She nods her chin past me. "Is the narc staying for burritos too?"

"I could do some serious damage to a barbacoa—"

"He is not," I say thinly.

Nora shrugs and walks into the kitchen fiddling with her phone as I turn back to Hades.

To those eyes.

To those lips.

To that fierce look in his face that says he's ready to devour me.

"I want you to leave. And *now* we're even—"

I almost choke on the last word as Hades surges to me, forcing me backward until my back hits the glass wall next to the doorway into the living room. I whimper despite myself as he melts against me, pinning me to the glass as his lips brush the sensitive skin on my neck where my bruises—*his* bruises—have just started to fade.

"Hades—"

I gasp sharply when his lips fasten over one of the fading marks, and his teeth sink into my skin. Hard. So hard, in fact, that something heated flickers and licks its way down my spine to pool between my thighs.

"We're not even close to even yet, *kitten*."

Then he's gone. And I'm still slumped against the glass, trying to remember how to speak or walk, when I hear the door to my apartment close behind him.

12

HADES

"So. Who is she?"

I'm barely inside the lobby of the building my family's home sits atop when I hear Castle's voice behind me.

Like Sean Farrell, Castle is another unexpected friend courtesy the Drakos-Kildare partnership that came about when Ares married Neve. The one-time Army Ranger, who was once bodyguard to Neve and her sister Eilish, is now Cillian's de facto number two. After Ares and Neve tied the knot, Castle and I still bumped heads on more than one occasion. But in the last few months, we've been getting along tolerably well.

I think realizing I wasn't sniffing after Eilish Kildare helped settle whatever problems there were between us. Castle's fiercely protective of the two women, who are like kid sisters to him.

Not that Eilish isn't smoking hot, but she's not my type. What can I say: innocent and sweet is a turnoff for me.

Castle and I connect through boxing as well, same as Sean. But we've also gotten friendlier simply by working together than I think either of us would have expected. It's nice.

When my brother married Neve, the whole point was to create a truce: Drakos and Kildare setting all previous hostilities aside to present a united front against any and all enemies. In terms of business, the original idea was that each family would maintain their own empire independent of each other. That's still mostly the case, although some of our...less than legitimate business interests have started overlapping.

Like, for instance—and I'm speaking *completely* hypothetically, of course—if a Columbian gang who'd been trying to muscle in one of our poker games in Harlem needed to be reminded who's fucking game it was, and we needed to burn a warehouse they used for their drug imports down to the ground.

All hypothetical, of course...

As it turns out, Castle knows his way *remarkably* well around a gas can and structure supports. After I discovered that, and furthermore after we realized we were evenly-matched sparring partners, things have been pretty cool between us.

"What? Who?"

"Whoever you've been cheating on me with, dick. You stood me up at the gym twice last week."

I snort, shaking my head as we both step into the elevator. I use my thumbprint to unlock access to the top floor where the Drakos estate is perched, and the elevator starts to rise.

"Shit, sorry, man. I've been slammed with work."

"All good, I'm just fucking with you. Congrats on the launch of Thermopylae Acquisitions by the way. How's it feel, going legit?"

All I can offer in response is a non-committal grunt. Castle chuckles.

The doors glide open with a soft chime, and the two of us step out into the lavish front entrance of the Drakos estate. Even though he's been here about ten thousand times by now, Castle still whistles under his breath, his eyes dragging up to the high vaulted, gilded ceiling, taking in the elegant and supremely English wainscoting on the walls, and out the glass front doors to the grounds.

Yeah, we're on top of a building overlooking Central Park South, and there are private *grounds*.

Grandpappy Drakos didn't fuck around with this place.

"Try not to drool on the parquet floors, okay? Ya-ya will be pissed."

Castle grins, shaking his head and running his fingers through his short blonde hair. "Sorry. Gets me every time, this place. It's fucking insane, man, you know that?"

"Dimitra literally maintains a separate landline number exclusively for all the real estate agents and brokers who call offering to cut off their own hands to get the listing if we ever decide to sell. You gotta listen to the messages sometime, it's embarrassing. This one guy left a message once literally offering to blow me, Ares, and Kratos. And the dude is straight and married."

"He also might have a fairly loose definition of 'straight.'"

I chuckle as the two of us walk down one of the gilded hallways and out one of the side doors leading to the grounds. It's Sunday, which means family dinner night. This has always been Ya-ya's "thing", and ever since the merger of the families, she's started including the Kildares as well. It's exactly what it sounds like: both families sit down together to eat, drink, and laugh, with the only rule being no business at the table whatsoever.

Tonight, since the weather is nice, my grandmother's decided we're eating al fresco. And once again, I try not to roll my eyes too much at Castle's low, impressed whistle when we follow the white gravel path around the corner to the arbor that covers the outdoor dining area.

White, creeping floral vines, twinkling garden lights, and polished wood tables and chairs underneath a pergola draped with gauzy white curtains. Hashtag: natural life. Hashtag: family. Hashtag: live laugh love. It's like dining in a fucking Pinterest board.

That said, I fucking *love* eating out here.

Yeah, you can still hear the hum of the city down below. But you also feel removed from it. And if you completely lose yourself in the meal, and the conversation, and family—or at least in a couple of strong drinks—you can pretend you're in Greece somewhere, eating under the same skies the Spartans looked up at.

The staff is still setting the dining area up. Ya-ya stops supervising and breaks away to come over and give me a big hug and a kiss on the cheek when she spots us. Then she turns and reaches up on tiptoe to pat Castle on the cheek, calling him her "Apollo"—a nickname she recently gave him, given his height and blonde hair and...yeah...his good looks.

It's seriously Greek mythology all the way down the line with this fucking family, I swear.

Castle pats my shoulder and heads over to where Cillian and Una are chilling with drinks in all their dark gothy glory. I'm about to grab myself one when Kratos appears, handing me a beer.

"Mind reader," I smirk, knocking my bottle to his and then taking a sip. When my brother keeps eyeing me as he slowly works on his own beer, I arch my brow.

"Something on your mind?"

"You could say that."

"Well, don't keep me hanging. Spit it out."

"What the fuck were you doing at Elsa Guin's apartment the other night?"

I choke on my beer, caught off guard.

"What? I wasn't."

Kratos gives me an "oh-please" look.

"You were. Donnie Petrakis' kid Theo told his dad you scared the piss out of him over there."

Shit. I'd completely forgotten about threatening Theo Petrakis and Nick Eliades with telling their dads about the weed.

I frown, arching a brow at Kratos.

"Wait. Did the kid seriously rat on *himself*?"

My brother smirks. "Apparently so."

"What a fucking moron. Donnie seriously better straighten the kid out if he ever wants him to lead." I shake my head, drinking my beer. "I mean who fucking squeals on *themselves*—"

"So?"

I glance back at him. "So...what?"

"*So*, do you want to tell me why you were over there at ten o'clock at night?"

I shoot him a skeptical look. "Why do you think? Ares wants to head hunt her away from Crown and Black to work exclusively for us on a full-time basis."

"Yeah?" he grunts. "Well I'm pretty sure that you *fucking her* isn't part of his game plan to win her over."

I feign righteous indignation.

"Just what exactly do you think I am?"

"Kind of a whore, if we're being honest," Callie interjects as she joins us with a smirk on her face and a cocktail in her hand.

"Well, fuck you, too," I mutter as Kratos chuckles along with her. "Let's break out *your* sordid personal life, Callie."

She shrugs, taking a sip of her drink. "Me? I have no sordid personal life. But don't worry, Hades, yours is sordid enough for all of us!" She smacks me affectionately on the arm.

"Yeah, keep talking shit and I'll rat you out to Ares about that drink." I nod at the glass in my twenty-year-old sister's hand.

"You wouldn't dare."

"You sure? Keep calling me a whore and you'll find out."

151

She scowls. "The man is the head of a literal criminal empire, and I get dinged for a having a fucking drink at a private family dinner? It's such bullshit."

"Gotta draw the line somewhere," I say with a grin. "It's what separates us from the animals. Right?" I glance at Kratos, who shakes his head with mock sadness.

"It's us or the monkeys, Callie."

She rolls her eyes. "Me having a pomegranate martini is not going to make society devolve into troops of monkeys." As if to prove her point, she takes a sip of the purplish cocktail in her hand before letting her eyes wander back to me.

"Hey, by the way, how was Elsa the other night?"

Ex-fucking-cuse me?

"I heard you were hanging out at her place."

Oh, that *night.*

"I saw Eva Petrakis at lunch a few days ago. Apparently you almost made her little brother Theo piss himself."

I shrug. "I was just dropping off some paperwork. Theo was trying to get Elsa's little sister high. She's only fifteen."

Kratos arches a brow. "Elsa has a little sister?"

"I know, right? News to me too."

Callie rolls her eyes. "Oh my god, how did you guys not know that?"

"How did *you*?"

"Umm, because we hang out? She's actually really cool."

I simmer. "She's actually *not*, by any definition, cool."

"Why, because she wouldn't blow you within four minutes of meeting you at some gross club, like the typical woman you go for?"

You'd be surprised...

"I mean, he *was* at her house at ten o'clock at night," Kratos grins.

"True." Callie shoots me a warning look. "Seriously, don't perv on Elsa. She's a friend."

I gasp loudly. "Oh shit, Callie! Here comes Ares."

"Yeah, better hide the evidence," Kratos mutters.

Callie's eyes widen frantically, and in one gulp she downs the rest of her drink, trying not to choke as she turns to set the empty glass on a side table.

Kratos immediately starts to crack up. Our sister frowns in confusion before she turns to glance over her shoulder.

...To where Ares is *not* coming over.

"Okay seriously, *fuck you* both."

TWENTY MINUTES LATER—AFTER Ares *does* finally arrive, with Neve on his arm and Eilish in tow—we hear the familiar sound of Dimitra hitting the small brass dinner bell on the sideboard, signifying that dinner is served.

We all take our seats. We laugh, we eat, we drink. And life is fucking good. Or at least, as good as it gets for me, I guess.

Because even though I bury it underneath my crude jokes, my cavalier attitude to the world in general—and to women specifically—and my myriad faceless, meaningless, emotionless one-night stands, I'm still very aware that I'm different.

A little broken, maybe. A little fucked up.

Wired wrong. Or at least, differently from most people.

And as much as I love my family and love these dinners, when I look around the table, it's just a giant reminder of how different I am.

I see Ares, sitting next to Neve and grinning as she pops an olive into his mouth. I watch him turn and cradle her chin in his hand, kissing her deeply before pulling away with another grin.

They used to be mortal enemies, and are now two of the most disgustingly in-love people I've ever laid eyes on.

Then there's Cillian and Una—Cillian in his customary all-black Johnny Cash look, and Una in a scooped-back black cocktail dress, showing off that badass tattoo across her entire back. The literal psychopath and his arguably equally psycho bride. I mean their Hollywood meet-cute involved Una putting a fucking knife into Cillian.

Yeah, even *those* two fuckin' weirdos found love.

Kratos is single, but only because he chooses to be. Because he's—as one of the several therapists I've had over the years liked to say—"happy with himself". Whereas I waffle between hating myself and hating the rest of the world.

Callie's also alone, but then again, she's young. Plus there's the whole mess with her arranged engagement to Luca Carveli to be sorted out. Eilish is unattached, at least as far as I know. But she's like Elsa in that she's married to her books, given that she's just started at Columbia School of Business.

Castle's the same way: utterly wedded to his job, and completely fine with that.

I could—and *do*, often—tell myself that I'm single by choice. Because I'm a wild man, and an agent of chaos, and love the thrill of the hunt and losing myself in a different stranger every time I go out.

But that's bullshit.

I'm alone because I'm a self-destructive time-bomb.

And that's never going to change.

————

AFTER DINNER, I'm sitting with Callie in a couple of lawn chairs, gazing out at Manhattan over the edge of the roof, when Ares strolls over.

"Where's your better half, bro?"

He rolls his eyes. "Neve and I are actually two separate people. We're not joined at the hip."

I glance side-long at Callie. She glances at me. The both of us crack up. Ares sighs.

"Hilarious. Anything interesting happening at Leo's place these days?"

My jaw tightens. I mean, yes and no. I've gone back to spy on his restaurant from the studio apartment across the street a few times since the night I saw Elsa walk out. But I haven't picked up anything more of interest regarding the Albanians. Maybe because they are—or at least Gavan is—smart enough not to talk about major, hundred-million-dollar business acquisitions in rooms full of windows facing other rooms full of windows.

I also haven't seen Elsa back there.

That's a major sticking point. I've done some more digging since that morning when I broke into her office. Actually, I've been back to her office twice since then—both times at night, so I could take my time. I even slipped into her apartment just yesterday, while she was at work and Nora was at school, to paw through her home office.

Nothing. There is nothing *anywhere* that connects her to Leo or Gavan. And the more I think about it, the more I doubt she's working for or with either of them.

Which begs the question: what the actual fuck was she doing at The Pearl that night after Club Venom?

"Nothing." I shake my head. "If they're talking about the Mirzoyan deal, they're not doing it at the restaurant."

Ares nods. "Okay. Anything at all, though?"

"Nope."

I haven't mentioned seeing Elsa outside Leo's restaurant that night to anyone. Not even anyone in my family, including Ares.

I'm not quite sure why.

"All right then, on a separate note, you wanna tell me why you were at Elsa's apartment at ten o'clock the other night?"

"Oh for fuck's sake…"

Callie snickers as I roll my eyes and groan.

"Well?"

"He was perving on her."

I raise my middle finger to Callie.

"I was dropping off some paperwork."

"What paperwork?"

I sigh. "Just *paperwork*. Why the fuck is everyone so up my ass about this?"

"Because you've historically mixed with her about as well as oil does with water, that's why. What's going on?"

Aside from the fact that I fucked her four times the other night, and then kissed her again a few days ago? Not much.

But even that's a lie. I *want* to be able to say there's nothing between Elsa and me. That she's an honest-to-fuck ice-queen, a prude—well, most of the time—and a serious pain in my fucking ass.

Except I've gotten a peek behind that ice-queen I. And I don't just mean because of our marathon, masked fuck-a-thon at Club Venom—okay, maybe that's a huge part of it. But more than that, ever since that night, when I've crossed her path, I see a different Elsa than I used to see. And again, I don't just mean because now when I look at her, I imagine her naked, moaning, and writhing on my cock.

I used to view Elsa as my nemesis. The Toby Flenderson to my Michael Scott, if life were an episode of *The Office*. A fun-hating, all-business, uptight, frosty little *bitch*.

Now, I kinda get it.

Elsa's a fucking partner at the most prestigious law firm in New York at the age of twenty-freaking-six. That's insane when you think about it. I'm unable to fathom the work and the hours it must have taken to get there.

And on top of that, as if *that* wasn't a Herculean achievement enough, she's got her teenaged sister living with her.

"And she's living with you right now?"

"She's always lived with me."

What the hell is "always" supposed to mean? Like, Elsa never left home while going to school in England? Or that she did, and Nora came with her? It occurs to me that I don't know a damn thing about Elsa or her family.

But bottom line, for whatever reason, I *get* the head-down, all-business strictness and the general frostiness now. I'm not sure it's so much that Elsa's an ice-queen bitch, but rather the way she walls off the world, to give herself space to even take a breath.

"Nothing, Jesus," I say with some irritation, running my fingers through my hair and pushing it back from my face. "Relax, man."

He eyes me with a look that says he's not necessarily buying my shit, but that he's ready to leave it on the shelf for the moment. Then he clears his throat.

"Do you, ah, still talk to Vanya Mirzoyan at all?"

Mother. Fucker. I was wondering when he'd bring that shit up. So I play dumb.

"About the acquisition of her dad's Albanian Mafia empire? No, sorry."

Ares frowns. "You know what I mean. Since you two dated in college."

My jaw clenches. "We did not *date*."

"I was trying to be polite. Fine, I'm asking you if you still keep in contact with Vanya since fucking her in college."

"First of all, one drunken, way-too-toothy, not-to-completion blowjob does *not* mean we dated."

Callie makes a barfing sound.

Second of all, I couldn't say no...

"*Nor* does it mean that I was regularly screwing her. For fuck's sake, why does this entire family have the absolute lowest opinion of me when it comes to women?"

"Hades, I'm not trying to bust your balls. I just want to know if there's a connection there that we could leverage to put a little pressure on the deal. I've shied away from using the fact that you and Vanya went to Harvard together because it seemed like a cheap play that Serj would *see* as cheap. But now that we've got Gavan Tsarenko and his infinitely deep pockets in the mix, my gloves are coming off. Do you or do you not still have any contact with Vanya Mirzoyan?"

"No," I snap. "She hates me and the feeling is decidedly mutual."

Ares sucks on his teeth, turning away with a glare. "Well, suck it up, buttercup, and swallow your fucking ego. I need you to see if you can get her to like you again."

"Not happening."

"How about shoot for 'not hating you', and we'll call it a start." He sighs, turning back to me. "Look, I know this is a beyond shitty ask, man. And I apologize. I'm not trying to imply anything about your social life, trust me. I'm just grasping at any fucking straw I can find to keep the Russians off our asses and nail down this deal."

I nod slowly. "All right, fuck. Fine. Yeah, I'll send a 'sorry you bit my dick and I never called you again' card."

Ares smirks. "Thank you."

"I mean, as long you're sure it's not going to be a problem with your lawyer girlfriend, Hades?" Callie giggles.

"Weren't you going to get another pomegranate martini, *Callie*?"

She glares at me. Ares frowns at her.

"Callie, c'mon. We talked about this. Not while you're still twenty."

She rolls her eyes. "Well, as much fun as it is to get scolded by your own brother, Eilish and I have to take off. Bye, dorks. Don't have too much fun with Little Miss Jaws, Hades."

I grin at her as she walks away. When she's gone, Ares sighs and sinks into the chair she just vacated. I shoot him a look.

"Dude, you gotta chill on the whole dad routine with Callie. She's an adult—a competent, well-rounded, intelligent one at that. Like, she's not out there pounding shots and getting behind the wheel of a car. It's a responsible drink at dinner with her family. Pick your battles, man."

He nods, rubbing his chin. "I know, I know. You're right. I just still think of her as this little kid we have to protect from the world."

"Well, we could start with cancelling that fucking deal with Luca Carveli. She's almost twenty-one, bro, and you know that fucking pig has it marked on his goddamn calendar in red ink."

Ares scowls. "I'm working on it. The problem is the deal Dad cut with him was huge, and there's interest baked into that contract. Frankly, breaking it would mean paying Luca more money than we've got." He sighs, turning to glance at and give me a reassuring nod. "But don't worry. That shit is not going to happen. You've got my word on that."

I nod, pulling my gaze back to the glittering lights of the city.

"One battle at a time, Hades," Ares mutters. "Get in touch with Vanya, and for fuck's sake, please tell me you're not actually screwing Elsa."

I roll my eyes. "I am not screwing Elsa. Relax."

I mean, it's not a *total* lie. I am not currently, at this exact moment, literally fucking Elsa and sinking my teeth into her neck as her pussy clenches and comes all over my dick.

But the past happened. And as for the future?

I grit my teeth as something dark, vicious, and *hungry* stirs deep inside of me and begins to swell my cock.

Well, we'll just have to find out.

13

ELSA

THIS IS EMBARRASSING. I mean *I'm* embarrassed enough for myself as it is. But if someone else were to walk in here and see the homage to Hades Drakos covering my twin desktop computer screens, it would be fall-through-the-floor mortifying.

It's research. Not an homage.

Research. Yeah, that's what it is. Reconnaissance on the man who was supposed to be my dirty little sinful secret, who now seems to be bulldozering his way into every facet of my life.

And my thoughts.

Not to mention my goddamn dreams—vividly and nightly, ever since he kissed me on the balcony the other night like a king staking his claim to his rightful territory. And the worst part is, even though I know I should be incensed that he just "decided" to kiss me like that—brutally, savagely, and completely unapologetically...

I'm not. In fact, the more times I replay it, the more turned on I get. The faster my pulse beats. The more erotically detailed my nightly, dreaming fantasies of him become.

I shiver as I return my focus to the screens in front of me. On them, there's a whole litany of articles and online gossip about Hades pulled up. There was a piece in the *Financial Times* recently on the launch of Thermopylae Acquisitions—with zero mention of the *other* business interests of the Drakos family. Which I'm betting means they're either friends with the guy who wrote the piece, or they made him the proverbial offer he couldn't refuse.

My eyes skim over it. A little ways past the part where it gushes about the "strategic financial wisdom" of Ares Drakos, I find the bit about Hades. The author, one Mark Duccet, goes on to paint Hades in an extraordinarily favorable light as the resilient middle brother, learning to flex his wings beyond his older brother's shadow.

I roll my eyes at phrases like "confident and grounded", or "the poised voice of reason and the steady hand at the helm that helps guide King Ares' ship."

Give me a fucking break.

I minimize the article before I vomit. Then, I'm suddenly blushing as images of Hades fill the screen—other windows I've had open behind the *Financial Times* article.

Images of Hades in an impeccably tailored suit, at a police-man's fundraiser. Or jogging across the pitch of the football —sorry, *soccer*—club the Drakos family once owned, and presumably laundered money through, back in England.

And then, there are other pictures: candid, paparazzi shots of Hades, shirtless, lounging on the bow of a yacht somewhere.

Hades poolside at a luxury resort—also shirtless. Hades crossing the finish line of the London Marathon.

Shirtless, again, because why the fuck not.

There are more. Pictures of Hades outside the premiere of some dumb B-list movie, arm-in-arm with the vapid-looking starlet-of-the-month whom he was apparently "seeing" at the time.

I scowl, closing *that* particular window immediately.

I sigh, leaning back in my chair as my eyes scan the no less than *ten* pictures of Hades up on my screens.

Yeah, research. Sure.

Keep telling yourself that, stalker.

It's not that I'm losing myself and getting all tangled up in the man that I slept with and keep fantasizing about now.

It's *not*.

That said, I'm in the middle of googling "Hades Drakos beach swimsuit" when there's a knock at my door, and it swings open before I can even respond. Lunging forward while just about having a heart attack, I slam my screens off before raising my eyes past them to the doorway.

Instantly, my face hollows, my skin turns clammy, and my stomach knots with dread at the sneering, leering man standing in my office doorway.

"Knock knock," Pascha grins lecherously as he saunters in.

"I'm in the middle of—"

He shuts the door behind him with a resounding click before he turns back to me, a creepy smile on his pock-marked face.

"As I said, I'm in the middle of something," I hiss evenly. "Leave."

Pascha ignores me, turning to stroll casually across my office, meandering his way past shelves of legal texts toward the little couch area I've got set up in the corner.

"Your father would like an update."

I stand, walking around to the front of my desk and leaning against it with my arms folded.

"You can tell Leo I'm working on it," I mutter.

"Yes, well, I'm not in the habit of lying to my boss."

"It's not a lie. I'm working on it."

He swivels to leer at me, his eyes brazenly and nauseatingly sliding over my body in that way he does, making me cringe.

"Yes. Well. Work harder."

He turns back, strolling casually over to the couches and bending over the one faced away from us. He chuckles to himself and starts to poke around at something, I can't see what.

"Excuse me, what the fuck are you—"

Horribly, it dawns on me that it's the gym bag I dropped there on my way in today—just as Pascha stands upright and turns toward me.

Grinning lecherously.

Holding one of my fucking *gym socks* in his hand.

"Put that down, you fucking cree—"

He lifts it to his face and sniffs deeply, making my skin crawl as the bile rises in my throat.

"Mmm...delicious."

"Put that *down!*"

I bolt toward him, yanking the sock from his hand, grabbing my gym bag, and then storming back across the room to throw them both under my desk. When I whirl back to him I gasp. He's standing right behind me.

Looming over me. Sneering at me. Undressing me with his eyes.

"Get out of my office," I hiss quietly.

Pascha's grin just widens.

"Don't play innocent and bashful with me, little girl," he chuckles darkly. "We both know you're neither of those things when it comes to men now."

My stomach heaves. I *hate* that this man knows about, and probably *thinks about*, my sex life.

Fucking *ick*.

"Get. Out," I spit at him.

His smile threatens to split his face. "I'm curious..."

"I don't give a shit—"

"Which position were you in when you first got fucked like a ten-dollar whore by a stranger?"

Nausea and anger explode through my system.

"Why do you want to know, Pascha?" I sneer at him. "Jealous?"

I regret saying it the second it leaves my lips. Because the way his jaw clenches tells me I'm righter than I ever wanted to be about that.

And it terrifies me.

He terrifies me. And the fact that I'm alone with him right now sends my anxiety skyrocketing.

"*Or...*" he leers. "Perhaps it never happened? Perhaps you *lied* about whoring yourself out to another man in order to get out of the arrangement your father made with you?"

"Oh, believe me," I snap. "That was no lie."

"I'm not so sure. Why don't we check?"

Pascha grabs me and shoves me back hard against the side of my desk. Terror and fear explode through me as his hand jams down between us and shoves under the hem of my skirt.

"Get the *fuck* off of me!!"

I hit him, hard—once, twice...

And then I go still and cold as the naked edge of his knife presses to my throat. Panic and terror claw their way through me as I stand there, horrified, pinned to the desk with his hand resting on my thigh and his weapon against my jugular.

"You would do very well indeed to be nicer to me, bitch," Pascha snarls into my ear.

I swallow with difficulty, the sound of my pulse roaring in my ears as I force myself to glare right into his face.

"You can't touch me."

"*Watch me.*"

"My father—"

"I am like a *son* to your father," Pascha snaps. "You, on the other hand, are nothing more than a whore."

His hand grabs my thigh, reaching higher as bile and vomit churn together in my stomach.

"I can do whatever the *fuck* I want—"

The door to my office swings open. Instantly, Pascha's hand yanks back out from under my skirt as he jumps back from me. Still frozen, all I can do is swivel my eyes to the door, just in time to see Leo walk through, distracted by the phone to his ear.

I shudder as Pascha moves closer to me again, his sour breath on my neck.

"Not a fucking *word*," he hisses quietly. "Or you will regret it. And we both know he trusts me over you anyway."

I hate how right Pascha is. He really is like Leo's son, from everything I've seen. If I told Leo what Pascha just did to me, he'd probably tell him to go ahead and do it some more.

My pulse is still racing and my skin is still crawling from being touched by that fucking creep when the door opens again.

Doesn't *anybody* fucking knock anymore?

This time, it's Nora who walks in. My face drains of color.

"What are you doing here?!" I blurt.

My sister's brows fly up as she tears her eyes from her phone. "We...have a lunch date?"

I wince.

"Right, sorry. Of course."

Suddenly, Leo's done with his call and slipping his phone into his jacket pocket. He turns to smile icily at me.

"Aha. Just the lawyer I was looking for."

My heart is racing, fear surging through my veins. Only now, it's not because I'm scared of what Pascha or Leo might do to me.

It's because Nora just unwittingly walked into the middle of all this.

I force a smile to my lips as I turn my attention to her.

"Nora, can I get a minute with"...I clear my throat, turning to level my gaze at my father..."Mr. Stavrin?"

Nora's brow furrows. But then she grins. "Oh, you mean Leo?"

My face turns even whiter.

Leo chuckles. "We rode up in the elevator together. I was telling Nora here what a great lawyer her big sister is!"

I go numb as he lays a hand on her shoulder, smiling fixedly at me.

"And she was telling me all about school. And her *dancing*, actually!"

"Nora..." I choke, hardly able to form words as I stare, terrified, at where Leo's hand is resting on her shoulder.

"You know, Nora," Leo sighs, "my wife was a dancer, too. She passed, sadly."

I want to throw up. Or scream. Or stab him in the face with whatever even remotely sharp object I can get my hands on. Or all three of those things together.

Instead, I can only watch in horror as Nora's face fills with sympathy as she eats up his bullshit.

"Oh, Leo, I'm so sorry—"

"Nora." I bark her name way more harshly than I intended to. But it does snap her attention to me. "Sorry, but I do need a quick minute alone with Mr. Stavrin."

Her brow knits, but she nods. Generally speaking, for all her teenage angst and occasional sass, she's pretty great about respecting my work.

"Yeah, no problem. I'll be outside—"

"Why don't you stay here with my business associate?" Leo grins. "Your sister and I can talk business out on the balcony."

Before I can say a thing, he surges toward me, wraps a hand tightly around my forearm, and starts to pull me after him toward the sliding door that leads out to the balcony off my office.

"Nora—"

"She'll be just fine with Pascha," Leo chuckles with an affable laugh as he slides open the balcony door. He tugs me through it and then slams it shut, leaving us alone.

I yank my arm violently out of his grip, snarling. "You stay the *fuck* away from her!"

Leo laughs, grinning. "Oh, but there's *so* much to tell her, Elsa."

"What, like that she's your goddamn daughter?"

His smile drops. "She's not my daughter."

I could cheerfully murder him. It's the same shit he used to say to my mother when I was eleven and Nora had just been born. That since my mother hadn't been "putting out enough" for him, Nora was obviously some other man's child.

The accusation was absurd. My mother was stuck on Leo. Sick with him, like a disease, despite all of his cruelty, violence, and womanizing.

But the one silver lining to Leo's suspicions and accusations about Nora's parentage was that it was the straw that broke his back. My sister wasn't even one yet when Leo finally up and left for good.

It's the nicest thing he ever did for us.

"I'm not doing this with you again, asshole," I hiss at him.

"She *isn't*, Elsa," Leo snaps back. "I'm sorry if the truth hurts, but she—"

"Oh my God, you just don't ever stop—"

"Your mother was a whore!"

"*Shut. Up.*"

"I mean that literally!"

"She was a *dancer*."

"Who sucked cock for money."

I know I could run a paternity test on Nora. In fact, I've almost done so, perhaps two dozen times. But I never go through with it. Sometimes, I wonder if it's the fear of him being right, and what it would do to Nora's and my relationship if it turned out that way.

But that's ridiculous. Because even if Leo was right, or even if my mother straight up *found her* on the streets, Nora would still be, and would always be, my sister.

I turn, flinching when I see her talking to Pascha back inside my office, unaware that she's talking to a predator.

"What the hell do you want, Leo?" I snap coldly.

"I want to know where things are sitting with you getting us what we want."

"I'm working on it."

"Work harder."

I glare at him. "I'm their attorney, not their confidante, Leo. And I'm not personally involved in whatever you think they're involved with concerning Serj Mirzoyan."

"Don't bullshit me."

"I'm *not*," I hiss. "At the last meeting I was at with them, they asked me and the other attorney present to leave the room when it was about to come up . I am *not* involved. I know none of the details."

"Then change that."

I roll my eyes in exasperation. "That isn't how it works. I'm a *lawyer*, Leo," I snap. "Not a mafia henchman."

"Get close to them," he growls. "Learn about their plans. I don't know, *fuck* one of them if you have to. I hear that's your thing now."

I stare at him, wide-eyed.

"You *will* do this, Elsa. It's not a negotiation."

"Get the hell out of my office—"

"You'll get me what I fucking want, or we'll move on to Nora and see what she can offer."

Leo smiles coldly at me.

"Being that she's...*unsullied*, unlike you."

Sick surges in my stomach and threatens to rise up my throat.

"You won't go fucking *near* her."

"Won't I?"

He turns his head. Shuddering, I follow his gaze inside the office. Instantly, I go cold. Inside, Pascha is showing Nora something on his phone. They laugh together at whatever they're watching, and then he lays the phone down on my desk.

In horror, I watch Nora bend over, her elbows on the desk to get a better look as she laughs at the video. Pasha, meanwhile, stays standing. He slowly turns, letting his creepy gaze stab into mine through the glass between us. Then he turns back, his eyes dropping lasciviously to Nora's ass.

I make for the door, a roar in my throat. But I'm stopped and the sound is abruptly cut off as Leo grabs me by the throat and shoves me back against the balcony railing.

"Get the fuck off—!"

"*Shut up.*"

I jolt, stiffening as he pulls back his jacket to flash the butt of the gun in the holster under his arm.

"Shut up, and just watch."

"*Please…*"

Inside, Pascha grins at me, chuckling as Nora laughs at whatever she's watching on his phone. He turns his gaze thoughtfully to her ass again, still grinning as he runs his hand sickeningly close to her—not touching, but only two inches away. He turns back to me again, his smile lecherous and hungry before he throws me a kissy face that makes me want to throw up.

"*She's off-limits,*" I choke. "Gavan said—"

"Gavan is young and trying to find balance," Leo hisses. "But his priority is always and will always be the business. He cares about the results, not my methods. Trust me on that."

He nods inside to Pascha, who grins at me as he makes a big show of slowly licking his lips and glancing back at my sister.

"*Get him the fuck away from her.*"

"Then get me what I want, you little cunt," Leo snarls.

He releases my arm. Instantly, I bolt inside, storm over to the desk, and yank Pascha's phone away from Nora.

"Hey, I was watching that—"

"Mr. Stavrin and his friend need to leave."

I say it pointedly, glaring death at Leo as he steps back inside, and then leveling pure hatred at Pascha. He plucks his phone from my outstretched hand, smirking at me in that creepy way of his before he heads to the door.

When Leo does the same, I follow him, ready to slam and lock the door behind him. But he stops suddenly in the doorway, turning to lower his mouth to my ear.

"I have no problems doing the worst you can imagine to the offspring of the woman you called mother and whatever five-dollar-fuck brought that brat into the world. Get me what I want, Elsa. Or you'll regret it. And I can promise you, Nora certainly will too."

14

HADES

"FUCKING HELL, man. You were a beast out there tonight."

I grin through the blood in my mouth, spitting some of it out onto the grimy floor between my feet. I look up from the locker room bench to see Sean shaking his head.

"Bring that intensity to one of our sparring matches, and you might actually beat me."

"Now I *know* you're jerking me off."

He chuckles and snaps a towel at me. "Well, you might not lose as badly, at least."

The dingy locker room we're in is so gross it's actually legitimately condemned. The whole building is—an old Boys and Girls Club of America gymnasium that was shut down in the late eighties for fire code violations and lead paint or some shit.

Normally, it would be unheard-of for real estate like this to sit around unsold or undeveloped for so long in New York. But we're *way* out in Brooklyn—past the hipster hangouts and ironic bars, past the Marcy Projects, past, well, everything.

This is no-man's land. Which actually makes it pretty ideal for the underground boxing matches and occasional EDM raves the two Israeli dudes who own this place use it for.

"How's Lamar?"

"Ech, he'll be fine. But you reset him to default passwords with that last hit. Holy *fuck*, Hades."

I grimace. I know these underground fights are supposed to be outlets for anger. It's where you're *meant* to go to blow off steam, and everyone involved understands that.

But I doubt Lamar—whom I've fought before—expected me to come at him like a grizzly bear on cocaine tonight. Like, I'm sitting here with just a couple of bruises, and they're still peeling him off the floor of the ring.

"He's really okay?"

Sean chuckles. "Relax. He's gonna be fine. But for real, man. Where the fuck did that come from tonight? Who were you fighting out there?"

Elsa, that's who. I was fighting *Elsa* out there.

I mean, not literally or figuratively. I wasn't hitting Lamar picturing her face or anything psycho like that. But I *was* swinging to smash away the chemical addiction to her I seem to have developed.

Break the chain that keeps me circling her like a snarling dog, unable to run away. But I have to break it. I *have* to pull myself back from whatever insane, irrational attraction I have toward the snarky, frosty little lawyer.

There's no way anything good would come from any of that. Not a chance. The best-case scenario that could come of me pursuing...whatever this is with Elsa Guin...is that she would become just one more woman out there with an ax to grind with me after I invariably piss her off or ghost her.

Worst-case scenario, she could drop my family from her legal schedule. Not just refuse to become our full-time counsel, like Ares keeps gunning for. I mean drop us as in quit whatever she's working on with us through Crown and Black. And that's a *lot*.

Attorney-client privilege is one thing. But as much as I've grumbled about her, there's something about Elsa that just *works* when it comes to handling my family's legal—or at times not-so-legal—needs.

I know Elsa makes a big show of distancing herself from the darker and more sinister work she's done for us—like overseeing the removal of that dead body from Ares and Neve's wedding, for instance, and locking down the band and the guests on the official story. But I can tell she secretly kind of *loves* it. There's a thrill she desperately tries to hide in her eyes that I know I've spotted while she's working things like that for us, and it makes her just click with the Drakos family.

That's a rare thing to find. And I don't think it would be easily found again in other legal counsel. Which means fucking around with her, and inevitably pissing her off, is a gigantically terrible idea.

If I could just convince the rest of me that can't stop thinking about the taste of her lips, the whimper of her submission, the silken feel of her cunt swallowing my cock, and the sensual way her body begged me for more...

Well, that would be fucking swell.

After I shower and get dressed, Sean and I head over to the other locker room to check on Lamar. He gives me a wary look from where he's slumped on a bench. But he does grin and shake my hand when I squat down to tell him what a good fight it was.

"Bro, you were a fuckin' *animal* out there."

"Sorry about that."

"All good, brother. All good."

When we're done there, Sean takes off to go meet Maya after her shift at the restaurant. I sit on the fender of my Z28, sipping a beer under the dingy glow of flickering streetlight.

"Does it work?"

I frown, startled by the voice from the shadows. When I turn and peer into them, a slender, pale young guy with dark, beady eye, a shaved head, and a pock-marked face slips out of the darkness. The acid-wash jeans and tight jean jacket paint him pretty clearly to me as European.

I eye him warily, not moving from the car.

"Does what work? The Camaro?"

He grins a toothy, yellowed smile.

"No. Fighting in the gutter. Does it make you feel less like the privileged little princeling you are?"

Nope, not European.

Russian.

And slowly, I realize I know him: Pascha Andreev, one of Leo Stavrin's goons. I've seen him around The Pearl here and there, and skulking around with Leo the couple of times I've tailed him.

He obviously knows who I am. But I don't know a thing about him, aside from the fact that he looks like a complete, utter creep. And that fixed smile of his and the unblinking way he's just staring at me aren't exactly doing much to change that impression.

"Nope," I shrug, answering his question with a dry smile. "But what can I say? I just like hitting people."

I keep my body language casual. But I do tense a little on the inside when he slips a hand into the pocket of his jacket. The hand comes back out, but only with a pack of Russian cigarettes, not a weapon. I watch coolly as he slips one between his lips and lights it before holding the pack out to me.

"You want?"

"I'm good."

He nods, inhaling. "You Americans don't smoke anymore, do you?"

"Nah. Apparently they're bad for your health."

He nods, his eyes locking with mine. "So is continuing to spend time with Elsa Guin."

I go still, my hands involuntarily curling into fists as my jaw clenches.

"Excuse me?"

A smug grin spreads across his face.

"The Englishwoman," he grunts. "Stay away from her."

Slowly, I slide off the fender of the Camaro, my gaze lasering through the flickering light from the streetlamp between us.

"Might be a little tough, given that she's the family lawyer."

Pascha smiles eerily. "Socially, I mean."

I slowly cross the distance between us. "You know what? I've got something else you can add to that list of things that are bad for your health." I come to a stop right in front of him, glaring darkly at him. "*Giving me orders.*"

He doesn't respond. He just drags on his smoke, his eyes never leaving mine.

Yeah, fuck this.

I turn and begin to walk away. Then he opens his goddamn mouth again.

"She's a whore, you know."

And I see fucking *red*. Pure, malignant, vengeful *red*. I know strategically I should cage my emotions right now. But one, fuck that. And two, there's no way I can contain the snarl of fury that explodes from my mouth.

"*Excuse me?*" I hiss venomously.

Pascha's grin widens. "She fucks random men."

My vision glitches from the effort it's taking not to snap right now and break his face.

Hitting Pascha could, in fact probably would, launch a not-so-great chain reaction. We're not in open hostilities with the Bratva, but we're also not exactly bound by any sort of peace treaties with them, either.

But honestly, the fact that I'm even *at* this point, that it even bothers me this much, is much more worrisome than the fact that I'm ready to throw down with one of Gavan Tsarenko's underlings.

Because I am *not* this man. I don't get all territorial with women. Not because I'm a pussy or because I'm not willing to fight for what I want, or what's mine. But because I've simply *never given a shit*.

Well, apparently, that's changed. Because right now, I very much give *a lot of* shits about what the fuck this little creep is saying about Elsa.

"I'm going to give you some free diplomatic advice," I snarl quietly. "Walk away. Right—"

"Yes, she fucks random men, little prince," Pascha leers at me, clearly enjoying himself. "She fucked one to lose her maidenhood just the other night, like a complete slut."

Everything goes still. I tense, blinking, as I try and process what he just said.

What. The. FUCK.

My lips curl dangerously. "What did you just say?"

He laughs. "I said Elsa Guin let some man take her one valuable, tradable asset at a club of sin just the other night."

Holy.

Fucking.

Shit.

She jumped me that night and had me bring her back to one of the rooms to fuck her...to take her goddamn *virginity*?

"What *club of sin*," I snarl.

Pascha all but giggles in his glee to tell me. "Club Venom. A place for whores like her to fuck strange men with masks on, as if to hide their shamefulness."

I can't tell if I wanted him to say something different—to name some other club where Elsa might have recently gone to screw some other guy and lose her virginity. Or if hearing that would have sent me into a murderous rage.

Either way, there it is, right on the table.

Club Venom.

The other night.

A stranger taking her virginity.

And that fucking stranger was *me*.

"Who knows?" Pascha chuckles, tossing his cigarette away. "Maybe it wasn't even only one man. Maybe she fucked a whole room full of dick—"

"You will shut your fucking mouth and you will go tell your boss to keep his nose out of my family's business. Whom we do business with, or who we use for legal services, are none of his concern. Consider this a warn—"

"It's a shame, isn't it?" Pascha drones on. "What a sweet, fuckable mouth she has, no? And that tight little ass? I'm actually a little angry. The number of times I've emptied my balls imagining being the first man to pound through that sweet little cunt—"

He chokes as my fist smashes into his nose, shattering it and sending blood streaming down his face. He squeals like a stuck pig as he collapses to the ground, holding his ruined face. I crouch down next to him, my lips curled dangerously.

"Next time I tell you to shut your mouth," I snarl. "I'd suggest you *do it*. And tell Leo to go fuck himself."

I stand, spit on him, and leave him where he is on the filthy ground before I storm back to my car and roar away.

DESPITE SMASHING PASCHA'S NOSE, and driving around the city like a maniac for the last two hours, by the time I finally get back home I'm still on fire.

I'm still ready to crack the world in half.

I pour a heavy splash of whiskey into a glass and flop onto the couch with my laptop. Glaring death at the screen, I immediately start bringing up everything I have on Elsa.

It's honestly not much.

I really don't think there's any connection between her and Leo, or Gavan. Unless it's all under-the-table shit, but I sincerely doubt that. Even the times she's helped our family with less than squeaky-clean things—like the body at Ares and Neve's wedding—she's insisted on billing us the hours using squeaky-clean methods. Even if it meant invoices with things like "privacy and marriage consultations", in the case of that wedding.

No, she's not working for the Russians. Though, that does beg the question of what the fuck Leo's little bitch-boy was doing telling me to stay away from Elsa. Like, why do they care?

I slug back half of my drink, my jaw grinding as I go through the dossier I've compiled on her. There really isn't much. Government-funded schooling in the UK's version of a poor, crumbling public school, and then a merit-based scholarship to Cambridge, where she got her BA in law in two years instead of the usual three. Top of her class, because obviously.

She clawed her way up through three of the most prestigious firms in the UK, rising all the way to senior associate at her last job before the offer of partner status at Crown and Black brought her to New York. Her trial record is nearly perfect, too, with a staggering ninety-two percent win rate.

Pounding back more of my drink, I bring up some of Elsa's social media pages.

She's twenty-six. *Twenty-fucking-six*.

As much as the idea of her being with any other man makes me want to crush the crystal tumbler in my hand to dust, there's no goddamn *way* I was the first guy she slept with. I understand I've had a less than healthy sex life that started entirely too young. But *nobody*—especially anyone as fucking hot as Elsa—stays a virgin until they're twenty-six. Not a chance.

But the more I scroll through and stalk her admittedly sparse social media presence, the less sure I become of that conviction.

Sure, there's pictures of her all dolled up at galas and work functions, some where she's even standing next to and smiling with men. But none of them look even remotely like romantic or sexual partners. They're very obviously coworkers and colleagues.

I keep digging, finding more recent pictures of her here in New York—some taken at a function standing next to Gabriel and Alistair Black. A few with some other legal-looking dipshit.

But that's it. There's not a single man in any picture with her who looks like an obvious boyfriend.

Swallowing, I sit back, letting it all sink in.

It *can't* be true.

Unless it is.

I mean, she works a million hours a week. Her workload is insane. And on top of that, she's basically been raising a kid. Maybe she's truly never had time for a boyfriend. But you don't need to be in an established relationship to get fucked now and again. I mean I've literally never had a girlfriend, and I've been with more women than I can remember.

A vicious scowl suddenly tightens across my face at the thought of Elsa out there having casual sex with random men.

Or any sex at all, with any man who isn't *me*.

Just like earlier, in the parking lot with Pascha, the violence I feel rising up inside me even thinking about her with another man shocks me.

What if he's right?

What if the other night with me, despite all the improbabilities, really was her first time? I know most guys would feel smug about that—all triumphant and puffed up.

Not me.

I've never wanted to be anyone's first. Because *fuck that*. It's not because I'm worried about virgins "getting clingy", which seems to be a serious concern for every male character in every teen comedy ever.

I've never wanted to deal with virgins because your first time means something.

Or at least, it should. And I've never wanted that responsibility.

Sex is an escape for me, nothing more. A way to tune out the world and the darkness inside of me. I don't lose myself in women.

I use them to stop feeling anything at all.

But the other reason I'm not fist-pumping or patting myself on the goddamn back for the very real potential that I was Elsa's first is that she *used* me, from the sounds of it.

And I fucking *really* hate when a woman uses me and sex to get something she wants.

Gritting my teeth, I close the laptop, plunging the room into darkness. I can feel my fury surging inside, my anger at Elsa and her bullshit boiling up into a frenzy.

Except it doesn't boil over. I *want* it to. But every time I try to push it there, I get sidetracked by replays of that night.

Her mouth. Her skin. Her eagerness.

That hungry look in her eyes as she dragged her nails down my back and begged for more.

Something dark inside of me snarls and licks its lips.

I was her first.

I've never wanted to be someone's first. Except suddenly, the idea of being *Elsa's* first fills me with…

Hunger.

Desire.

Possessiveness.

And a fucking insatiable need for *more*.

15

ELSA

My eyes ache. Blinking and wincing, I pull back from the computer screens, rolling my shoulders, realizing I've been mere inches away from them as I pore over the legal briefing Taylor forwarded me earlier today.

Hours ago. Hours that have flown by in a haze of legal jargon. I dimly remember Fumi being the guardian angel and amazing friend that she is, dropping off lunch for me earlier. Then checking in on me again at the end of the workday.

But even that was…

I glance at my watch and groan.

Five freaking hours ago.

I did check in with Nora earlier, and sent her a delivery from her favorite sushi spot for her dinner. I glance down at my phone and grin at the text message from her still sitting on the screen:

NORA

> Best. Sister. Ever. I'm saving you some - NOT
> ALL - of this jaguar roll. Love ya

My smile widens. We bicker at times. I mean she's fifteen: of course we bicker. But at the end of the day, she's my sister. A flicker of anxiety sparks inside me as my mind flashes back to two days ago, when Leo and his little creep Pascha were in here.

Threatening me. Worse, threatening *her*. The thought of Pascha coming anywhere near my little sister makes me simultaneously want to vomit and stab him.

And I am not, by nature, a violent person.

I take a breath, shaking those thoughts from my head as I lean back in my office chair. My door is closed, but I'm sure I'm the last one still here. Even Alistair the workaholic is usually gone by nine.

I quickly reread the last paragraph of the briefing I've just spent eleven hours going through.

Finished.

I'm about to open a new document to type out the notes I've taken on the briefing for Taylor, because even if she doesn't even need this until next week, I'm a psycho like that. But just then, my phone dings with a message.

TAYLOR CROWN

> You'd better not still be at the office with that
> Klein briefing.

I grin as I pick up the phone and tap out a quick reply.

ME

Guilty as charged. I just finished, though, and was about to get my notes to you.

TAYLOR CROWN

OMG, no. NO. Fuck everything about that. I can't believe you read the whole damn thing today. Get out of there right now! That's an order!

ME

You're the boss. Okay, I'm packing it in.

Honestly, thank God for her rational thinking, because writing my notes out tonight would have been pure insanity.

So I close down my work computer. But I don't immediately get up. Even though there's a sister and sushi waiting for me at home. Instead, blushing even though there's *no one* here, I pull up Instagram on my phone.

He's, shamefully, at the top of my recent searches.

Most of Hades' feed is filled with pictures of his car, or boxing gloves, or old books, which the skeptic in me assumes is curated to look artsy and interesting, probably to woo and impress women.

As if he needs any fucking help in that department.

You seemed to have screwed him no problem without seeing his artsy, book post-y self.

I simmer, biting my lip as I scroll through his posts. Past the pictures of his dark, British-racing-green Camaro, and the boxing stuff, and the books, and a couple of promo posts about the Irish pub I've been helping Callie, Neve, and Eilish get ready to open, there are...*other* pictures. Pictures I would normally use, at least to myself, as ammunition to make fun of his vanity and his whole "hot, rich, and dangerous to know" vibe.

At least I would if I could stop drooling over them.

Pictures like the one of him shirtless, half in shadow and dripping in sweat, as if he's just come back from a run or the gym.

God, it's getting embarrassing. I need to stop looking at this picture.

But I can't.

Obviously, it's his abs that pull the eye first. Half in shadow, and the way the light hits them, they look insane, almost as if he's photoshopped them. Except I know he hasn't.

Because I know that's what they look like in real life.

I know what they feel like grinding against my ass, or pinning me to the wall.

I flush deeply.

I know what the sweat on those chiseled abs and sinfully grooved hip lines angling down into his gym shorts *tastes like*.

I know what a lot of him tastes like…

It's not just the shadowed abs, hip grooves, and chest that I like about this picture. It's his face. It's also half shadowed in the shot, with one side almost completely dark.

Except for his eye.

The one on the lit side is sexy enough, with that cool, ice-blue stare. But it's his eye on the shadowed side of his face that I think is what I like most about this picture.

It's the intensity of it. The way that even if the rest of that side of his face is in shadow, the eye seems to spark. It's intense, and powerful, and makes me shiver.

But somehow, it also reveals a vulnerability in him. There's something haunting in that shadowed eye that grips me and won't let go.

The—no joke—*two thousand* comments on this particular post are almost exclusively from women, of course. Every single one a fawning, nauseating, emoji-filled gush about his looks, and his abs, and how *sexxxy* he is.

My lips tighten even skimming them.

But not one of them, at least not that I've seen, mentions the shadowed eye.

And I kind of like that. It's as if that look I see every time I perv this picture is for me and me alone. My dirty little secret.

Just like the rest of him.

I obviously know about Hades' reputation. I know ours was probably one of a string of a million nights just like it for him, all with different women ready and willing to do anything and everything with him.

That makes me furious. Like, stabby furious, even if I have no right to feel that way. Because I *did* trick him into sleeping with me. And I did it knowing exactly who and what he was. Is.

I mean, that was kind of the point.

But still, even if thinking about all those other girls being with him makes me want to scream, I can block them out.

And I do that by letting my mind go blank and simply reliving that one night.

Every touch. Every kiss. Every whimpered moan from my lips and growled command from his. And once I'm drowning in the heat of those memories, everything else fades away until I can imagine that it's just him, and me.

No one else. No other girls.

Just me.

Me and my secret sin.

The loud knock on my office door sends my heart into my throat.

…And my thumb fucking *double-tapping* the picture of Hades I've been drooling over.

Mother. *FUCK.*

My face goes white as I stare at the solid red heart icon. Crap, I don't even *follow* Hades. As far as I know, he doesn't even know I'm on Instagram at all, let alone creeping his pictures.

And I just "liked" one of the hottest pics on his feed, which was posted like fifteen months ago.

Holy *cringe.*

I could unlike it, but he'll still get the notification. Groaning, I close the app and drop the phone on my desk before my eyes drag up to the door.

"Yeah? I'm still working in—"

The door opens, and I turn to stone.

I was ashen enough for "liking" Hades' abs. When Pascha walks into my office at ten-fifteen at night, I go white with fear.

He smiles cruelly as he steps in, closing the door behind him.

"You're working late."

I swallow, feeling my pulse begin to thud heavily in my ears as my throat closes a little.

"What do you want?" I croak.

Pascha's lips curl up at the corners, as if he's caught the scent of my fear, and he's getting off on it. Which might actually be the case.

I shudder and quickly stand as he moves toward my desk.

"I said, what do you *want?*"

My nails dig into my palms, trying to keep myself from shaking.

Or running.

"Look, it's only been a few days. If you want me to find something on the Drakos family, you're going to need to have a little more patience—"

"That's not why I'm here."

He keeps strolling toward me—slowly, unhurried. The fear begins to knot and twist in my stomach, turning my blood to ice.

"I beg your pardon?"

Pascha comes to a stop by my desk, leaning against it casually with that thin, creepy smirk on his face.

"I know what you did, you know."

My brows knit. My jaw clenches tightly, as if to stave off the fear.

"I have no idea what you're—"

"It was no random man who fucked you, was it?"

My insides turn so cold they could actually freeze and crack. I try to swallow, but it's futile. I try to breathe, to utter a single word, but nothing comes.

Pascha's lethal smile curls demonically at the corners.

"It was Hades Drakos, wasn't it…you little whore."

Beneath the ice, something heated and furious snaps.

"Whom I sleep with is the furthest thing from your business you can possibly imagine," I hiss quietly.

"Ahh…" he grins, slowly raising a finger and shaking it, along with his head from side to side. "But not in this case. Because he's the enemy. The very enemy your father wants you to be spying on. And instead you went out and *fucked* him." Pascha's eyes turn dangerous. "This does not paint you in a very good light, now does it?"

The room goes quiet. My pulse thuds heavily, my blood thick in my veins as I try and hold back the sheer terror. Because Pascha is like a shark right now, circling me, sniffing for blood in the water. If I show fear, that's like opening a vein. And he won't waste a second in tearing me in half.

"I think you should leave."

He smiles coldly. "No. I don't think we're even a little bit close to done here."

I swallow. "Okay...so what's your plan, Pascha?" I hiss through clenched teeth. "Go tattle on me to Leo? He himself suggested I screw one of them to get close to the family. Do you really think he'd care?"

His lips curl. "There's getting close, and getting *too* close. One could consider what you did spying. *Or*, that you're working with the Drakos snakes against your father's and Gavan Tsarenko's interests. And that would *not* be wise..."

I bite back a gasp as he takes a step toward me.

"...or healthy."

My face pales, my nails digging *hard* into my palms.

"I won't tell, though."

He says it with a sudden smile, and I stiffen.

"I won't, really."

He moves close. I don't want to, because I do *not* want to show him how scared I am right now, but I take a step back almost on instinct.

Pascha grins.

The shark has caught the scent.

"I'm *sure* we can come to an...agreement."

My skin crawls at the lascivious way his eyes slowly drift up and down my whole body when he says it.

"*Leave*," I choke.

Pascha shrugs, his eyes still locked on mine.

"Are you sure? If I leave right now, it's not going to end well for you."

His voice rasps out like broken glass.

"Ask me what I want for my silence."

My teeth grind, hatred and abject fear twisting in my stomach like two blades as his words hang in the air.

"*Fine,*" I hiss. "What the fuck do you—"

"Show me your tits."

I go numb. Bile rises in my throat, and the room spins.

"*No.*"

His eyes bore into me as he tilts his head to the side.

"No? Then things are about to get ugly for you." He grins. "And for your sister."

No...

"Maybe *she* will be happy to show me what's been growing under that training bra—"

"*Fuck. YOU,*" I snarl, venom dripping from my lips.

"Gladly. Now fucking *show* me, or I *will* be at Nora's door next, and I won't be asking her for the same thing quite so nicely."

"Here!"

It's the pure, unimaginable horror of him harming Nora. The very idea of this monster touching her, or even thinking about her like that, smashes down every last barrier and shred of resistance I have left.

"Fine! Here!"

Shaking, tears in my eyes, I unbutton my blouse and yank it open.

"Happy?!" I sneer. "You fucking creep!"

Pascha's brows lift. "A little. But not completely. The bra, too."

I look away, tears starting to trickle down my cheeks.

"*Please…*"

"Oh yes. I'll enjoy this *so* much more if you use that word."

I could try to protest or fight him on this. But it's already over, and he knows it. Threatening Nora was the final stroke.

I'd do anything to keep him from hurting her.

Anything.

I go into a numb, fugue state, like I'm shutting down or checking out of reality. I look away from Pascha as I unclasp the front of my bra, feeling the cool air against my skin.

Feel the malignant touch of his gaze drift across my body, slowly turning me to stone.

"Get on your knees."

I choke, actually dry heaving as the horror of what's happening fully crashes down on me. My eyes drag back to him, pleading.

"*No—*"

I sob when I see the blade flick open in his hand, his beady eyes filled with predatory hunger.

"Get. On. Your. Knees."

"*Don't do this…*"

I choke, sobbing as Pascha shoves me to my knees, frenzied mania in his eyes as he frantically works his belt open.

"Make it good, my little whore," he snarls. "No teeth, or I'll cut your throat and fuck that in—"

The door to my office slams open so hard it almost breaks off the hinges. I can't see properly through the tears blurring my vision. All I see is a dark shape *fly* across the room, roaring, and slam into Pascha like a truck.

It's only then, as I watch them both go crashing over my desk chair, that I realize it's Hades.

There's no long, drawn-out fight. They don't trade blows. Hades just kneels astride Pascha's heaving chest—arms bulging, teeth bared, and eyes demonic—as his hands wrap tight around Pascha's throat.

And squeeze.

And squeeze.

And *squeeze*, ignoring the flapping, flailing motions of the Russian's arms. Ignoring the knife as Pascha makes one weak, futile attempt to stab him. Ignoring even the way I'm staring at this grisly scene unfolding right in front of me, as if I'm in a nightmare from which I can't wake up.

Suddenly, it's all over.

Pascha's arms drop and go limp. His body stops jerking and writhing. His chest stops rising and falling, and his head lolls to the side, eyes wide and staring at nothing.

Lips blue and lifeless.

I blink, and slowly, my eyes lift. They find Hades', blazing right back into me with a look of pure, lethal power.

Pure snarling rage.

Pure *possessiveness.*

I can't look away.

I don't ever want to look away.

16

HADES

SHE'S SO white that for a moment, I worry that the piece of shit cut her. That the paleness in her face and the blue of the veins across her neck are because she's bleeding out from a wound I can't see.

But that's not it, thank God.

It's just that she's more terrified than I'm guessing she's ever been in her life.

It's "just" that.

I have no words for that.

She's immobile, barely even flinching as I close her blouse and pull her to her feet. Her eyes have a lost, faraway look in them as she stares past me at Pascha's body.

Wordlessly, I drag her into the bathroom and away from the grisly scene spread across her rug. That seems to help, because suddenly, she's focusing again—blinking, looking confused, unsure how she got from there to here as I sit her down on the closed toilet seat.

Then her eyes lock onto mine.

"Hades…"

"Stay here."

Her hand grabs my wrist in a death grip as I turn to walk out of the bathroom.

"I'll be right back," I growl quietly, lowering to look her in the eye. "I'm not going anywhere."

Elsa has a bar cart in her office, like any self-respecting high-powered lawyer who never sleeps and runs on pure ambition and drive. Ignoring the searing pain in my shoulder from where the fucker sliced me, I pour a *very* heavy splash into a tumbler and then bring it back to the bathroom.

"Drink."

She blinks, shaking her head as she looks up at me.

"I—I don't want a—"

"It wasn't a request."

She nods, trembling as her hands wrap around the glass and bring it to her lips.

"The whole thing," I growl quietly. "And then I need you to stay right here."

She nods again.

Back in the office, I work quickly, rolling up the rug with Pascha's body in it, and doing a cursory sweep for any blood. This will never be a crime scene, so it's not like I need to go out and buy bleach and a black light. Once I'm confident there's no obvious blood or any other signs of what just happened here, I pull out my phone.

Kratos answers on the second ring.

"Hey, what's up—"

"The ninety-ninth street development that Ezio Adamos' crew is working on. They're pouring the foundation tomorrow, yeah?"

The line is silent.

"Kratos, I need you to answer the fucking—"

"Do I even want to know who?"

"Probably not."

He sighs heavily, slowly. "Yeah, first thing tomorrow at eight. I'm guessing you want me to tell the foreman not to look too hard in the pit before pouring?"

"Bingo."

"*Shit*. Okay, yeah, consider it done."

"Thanks."

"Hades…you good, man?"

I glance first at the gash on my shoulder soaking my T-shirt with blood, then at the body rolled up in Elsa's rug.

"I'm fine. Thanks, brother."

Back in the bathroom, Elsa's glass is almost empty, and Elsa herself is looking a lot better, with more color to her cheeks. She frowns, stiffening when she sees the blood on my shoulder.

"Is that from…?"

I shake my head. "That's all me."

Her frown deepens as she suddenly stands. "Let me see it."

"Sit. You're in shock."

"And you're bleeding, a *lot*," she throws back. "Let me see it."

I lean against the sink, watching Elsa as she stands next to me and delicately pulls back the sliced-open T-shirt sleeve. She winces and makes a face as her eyes drag up to mine.

"Hades, you need stitches."

"Yeah, well, I don't really have time for stitches right now."

"I can take care of it."

I'm sorry, what?

My brow arches as I eye her incredulously. "Excuse me?"

Her lips purse. "I can do it, trust me."

"*You* can sew up a knife wound."

Elsa nods, turning and opening one of the vanity drawers. She pulls out one of those little sewing kits for putting buttons back on dress shirts. My jaw tightens, and she glances at me.

"You don't believe me?"

"It's more that, one you're not a doctor, and two you just drank a triple shot of whiskey. But yeah, aside from that, no issues here. All golden."

She smiles.

Good. If she's smiling, it means the shock is wearing off.

"Sit," she nods at the toilet seat. After I do, she clears her throat, her cheeks flushing. "Can you, uh…"

I peel my t-shirt off, smirking at the way she looks away from me.

"The patient's ready, doc."

She nods, swallowing nervously. It doesn't exactly inspire confidence. But I wasn't trying to be tough before: I genuinely *don't* have time to go get stitches right now—definitely not at a hospital, not even from the doctor that I know Cillian uses for circumstance like this.

Elsa washes her hands, threads the needle, and then dips it in the dregs of her whiskey to sterilize it. She leans down to my shoulder, takes a deep breath, and then gets to work.

I grimace, but watch as she deftly pushes the needle through the clean edges of the knife cut. She works slowly, but she *does* clearly know what she's doing. Which is...a little curious.

"How do you know how to do this?"

"My mother."

"She was a nurse?"

Her eyes darken as she inhales deeply.

"My father used to..." Elsa grimaces. "He hit her a lot. Sometimes badly, and often *with* something. She never wanted to go to the police or the hospital, because he was a dangerous man. That, and he always threatened to make sure she'd lose me if he ever got put away."

Rage boils inside of me.

"I'm sorry."

She shrugs. "It was a whole other lifetime ago." She swallows, pushing the needle through once again. "So is the whole 'show no pain' routine like a macho thing you do?"

I smirk. "I'm just used to it. I box a lot."

Elsa nods.

"That, and my oldest brother used to beat the ever-living fuck out of me when we were young."

She frowns, glancing sharply up at me. "Atlas?"

"Yeah. I think you met him once, when you were still in England?"

She nods.

"He was an asshole, and I'm glad he's gone, even if he was my brother."

I have no idea how or why any of that pops out. I don't tell anyone about how Atlas used to pummel me. And I've never put how I feel about his death into actual, out-loud words, even to my siblings.

Elsa finishes the last two stitches wordlessly. Then, with a nod, she uses a pair of nail clippers to cut the remaining thread away with a satisfied nod.

"There. All done."

"Just like sewing a button back on."

She smiles briefly, but it quickly fades as worry crosses her face and she turns to stare at the door to her office.

"So… Now what?" she says in a small voice that makes me want to stand between her and the world.

I sigh. "Now, we move a rug."

THERE'S a zero percent chance that we can walk out the front doors of this building and onto Madison Avenue with a fucking body rolled up in a rug without getting arrested. Further complicating matters is the fact that most of the office has cameras set up—trust me, I know. I've broken into this place four times before.

In the end, I manage to jump from Elsa's balcony to the one attached to the office next to hers, and then to the one next to *that*. From there, I can reach the window-washers' platform, where I snag a spare coil of rope, and then jump back to Elsa's.

I use the rope to hoist the rolled-up rug from her balcony up to the roof of the building. From there, we take the maintenance elevator down to the garage beneath the building and deposit Pascha in his carpet casket into the trunk of my waiting car.

Yes, we.

Elsa's silent as we drive uptown to the project on ninety-ninth street that the Adamos family—one of the Drakos family's several vassal families—is overseeing. The one that is slated to have its foundation poured tomorrow, which will now and forever be this piece of shit's final resting place.

"Stay here," I murmur when I stop the car just inside the construction gates.

I half expect her to fight me on that, because why break with tradition. But Elsa does indeed stay put as I close the gates, pop my trunk, and then drag Pascha's dead ass to the edge of the foundation pit. In he goes, carpet and all, followed by a generous scoop of dirt from one of the earth-movers nearby.

It's done.

When I get back to the car, I shut the door, but don't turn the engine on quite yet. Instead, we both just sit there in the dark, staring out into the city night.

Slowly, I turn to her. She's still looking straight ahead. The glow of the dashboard illuminates her soft face and tight jaw.

She looks so vulnerable. So desperately in need of protection.

"That night, at Venom…"

I don't *have* to bring this up right now. But I can't *not* bring it up anymore, either.

Elsa swallows, chewing on her lower lip as she turns to face me with guarded eyes.

"Why did you jump me like that?"

She blushes deeply.

"I didn't *jump*—"

"Potayto, potahto. Why'd you kiss me? Why'd you pick me?"

She swallows again uncomfortably. "I needed an outlet. You know, to blow off steam."

"But why *me*," I growl quietly.

She shivers, still chewing on her bottom lip as she looks away. "I… I don't know."

"I think you do."

"I guess because your reputation told me you'd at least know what you were doing."

I smirk. "I feel like I should be insulted."

"But you're not."

She grins a little as she hazards a glance back at me.

"So, do you do that a lot?"

The smile drops from her lips.

"Do what?"

"Go to Club Venom, or any club for that matter, and fuck some random guy to blow off steam?"

Elsa's face heats as her throat bobs up and down. "I...do what I need to—"

"I know I was your first, Elsa."

The car goes silent, and she goes stock still, apart from the pulsing vein in her delicate neck and at her temple.

She doesn't have to say a word for me to know I'm fucking right. Her sharp inhalation and the way her eyes bulge a little give her away.

So it's true.

I was the man to take her virginity and sink a hard cock into her for the very first time.

And, again, I can't tell if that pisses me right the fuck off, or fills me with a savage, primal sense of *entitlement*.

Possessiveness.

Covetousness.

"Hades, please," she laughs nervously. "I'm twenty-six years—"

"Stop."

Her mouth snaps shut. Her eyes dart to mine, widening when she sees the raw hunger in mine, tinged with anger.

"I don't like being used, Elsa."

She laughs coldly. "Oh yes, I'm sure you positively *hated* being 'used' like that."

"You knew who the fuck I was, and *what* I was, and you let me fall right into that bed with you, without telling me you were a virgin."

She bristles. "Would it have changed a single fucking thing if I had?!"

"Yes!"

"*Bullshit!* We both got what we wanted—"

"Not quite."

It just happens. I don't think, it's not planned, and I have no idea where to go from here. All I know is, one second she's talking and I can't stop staring into her eyes, and the next second I'm grabbing her face in my hands possessively and kissing her like she belongs to me.

Because she *damn well does.*

Elsa moans into my lips, whimpering before she suddenly pulls back with a gasp. Her hand comes up, her fingertips running softly over her puffy lips as her eyes lock on mine.

"What are you doing?" she breathes, whimpering once more when I cup her jaw again.

"Taking what's mine."

Her eyed widen and her cheeks heat.

"I—Hades, I'm not yours—"

"Yeah, you keep telling yourself that."

My mouth crushes to hers again.

Fiercely. Violently. Unapologetically.

And this time, I won't be stopping anytime soon.

17

ELSA

WE'RE TUMBLING into the back seat of his car before I can even comprehend it. It doesn't do a thing to stop the voracious way I'm kissing him, just as hard and as recklessly as he's kissing me.

I moan as I fall back, my legs wrapping around his hips as his tongue invades my mouth. He pulls away from me just enough to yank off his t-shirt, his muscled torso chiseled and lean in the shadowy darkness of the car.

He hisses as I reach up, kissing and then sucking on his firm chest, dragging my teeth across his skin. As if I want to gnaw a hole in him and crawl all the way in. I bite him again, and Hades snarls, grabbing a fistful of my hair and yanking me back to slam his mouth to mine.

He all but rips my blouse open, sending at least two of the buttons scattering onto the floor. My bra is next, and suddenly I'm arching my back and hissing in pleasure as his lips wrap around one of my nipples. I cry out as his teeth bite down, sending an electric shock of pleasure ripping through my core before he pulls back to level his fierce gaze at me.

The way he looms over me in the darkness, like some sexy, predatory animal, has my skin tingling and my core throbbing with need. Like he's this conquering, savage Viking, ready to stake his claim after razing a village.

But that is only part of it. He isn't *just* the man who took my virginity in that club. He's not *just* the gorgeous, dangerous man who's managed to slide his way into my brain and invade my every thought and desire.

He's the man who literally just killed for me, and now, he's taking what he's owed.

And, as fucked up as it is, everything about that is *outrageously*, sinfully hot to me.

Hades kisses me fiercely again before his mouth drags to my neck. I moan when he bites hard—so hard he might have drawn blood. All it does is make me rip and yank harder at his clothes with an urgency that sends me reeling.

I shove his jeans down, shuddering and moaning as I slip my hands into his boxers and wrap my fingers around his hard, thick cock. Hades snarls, pushing my thighs wide apart as he shoves his jeans and boxers down.

My mouth sears to his as he yanks the crotch of my panties to the side, and in one thrust, he savagely buries every inch of his huge cock deep inside me.

I cry out, whimpering and moaning into his mouth as he fists the back of my hair. He snarls, his hips rolling as he pounds in and out of me, shoving me right to the edge of my release in seconds. I cling to him, my nails clawing down his back and his biceps as they ripple beneath his tanned, tattooed skin.

"*I* was your fucking *first*," he rasps against my lips. "*I* was the man to tear into this pretty little pussy for the first time. To feel you squeeze so fucking tight around my cock. To feel you come undone around me."

I moan deeply, nodding and drowning in the savage possessiveness of him—the way he consumes me entirely.

"*I* was the first man to fuck you, kitten. And I'll be *the only man to fuck you.*"

Maybe it's the way he's fucking me like he's trying to kill me. But even more than that I think it's those words snarling from his lips that shove me over the precipice. I cry out, shattering and exploding as the orgasm rips through my body.

Hades doesn't even slow down. He keeps pounding into me, fucking me right through my climax even as I scream for more. Then he pulls out, fisting his cock until suddenly, his hot, white cum is spraying across my skin in thick ropes across my stomach, my breasts, and my pussy.

His gaze locks with mine as he leans down to kiss me deeply. Then he's pulling away, and his finger drags up through the sticky cum on my chest, scooping it up before he brings it up to my lips.

"Open wide, kitten."

I whimper as I suck his finger into my mouth and lick it clean. I do it again when he brings his finger back with more, and then a third time. My pulse thrums at the primal lust in his eyes and at the sight of his clenched jaw and coiled muscles as he suddenly moves over me, straddling my chest.

His hand tightens in my hair, our eyes locked as he guides his swollen, still hard, glistening cock to my mouth.

I take him in, shuddering with heat and whimpering at the low growl that rumbles from his chest.

"Good girl."

He pushes deeper, thrusting his thick cock deeper into my throat, his eyes never leaving mine, that lethal ice-blue stare stabbing right into me. His abs clench, his hips pump, and he shallowly fucks my mouth until he's hard as iron.

I gasp, sucking in air as a mix of spit and precum and my own pussy juice drips down my chin. He kisses me hard again, invading my mouth with his tongue before he suddenly pulls away.

I whimper when he flips me over like a rag-doll.

Like his own personal fuck toy, ready for more.

Both of us panting, he shoves my skirt up, brutally yanks my panties down to my knees, and straddles my hips with his knees, flattening me onto my face in the back seat of the car. His swollen cock sinks between my thighs and opens my lips, easing inside.

"Tell me what you want, kitten," he growls darkly.

"I—I want you...to..."

"To what."

"Fuck me."

"Good girl."

He rams in ruthlessly, crushing the air from my lungs as I cry out in pleasure. I choke into the leather of the car seat, moaning and writhing under him as Hades fucks me like a wild animal. His hips and muscled abs smack my ass with each thrust, and I gasp when he grabs my hair and tugs on it hard as he pounds into me. His hand slips under me, pinching my nipples and mauling my tits as I writhe and beg for more.

And more.

And more and more and *more*. I never want him to stop fucking me, ever. I never want him to stop consuming me, or drowning me in his vicious, weaponized sin.

When I come, the world explodes around me.

It's not an orgasm. It's an awakening.

A rebirth.

Like I'm breathing air for the first time.

His body presses to mine, one arm around me cupping my breasts and the other squeezing my throat as he rams his huge, gorgeous cock into me all the way through my orgasm. Suddenly, he bites down hard on my neck, and his cock swells and surges inside me. His cum spills deep, taking whatever breath I have left away, until we're both sinking down into the abyss, weightless.

And I never want to come back up.

IT'S two hours later when we pull up outside of my building.

I'm a *mess*.

Bruises and bite marks cover my body, from my jaw down to my thighs. My hair looks like I just went through a hurricane. Or like I just got fucked silly.

My clothes are ripped to shreds. My makeup is a mess or smudged off entirely, and I can feel his dried cum on my breasts, my stomach, between my thighs, possibly still on my chin and throat.

What the *fuck*.

And yet through it all, the one pervasive thought I have is: *more*.

A *lot* more.

I turn toward him, blushing when I realize he's already staring at me with that cocky smirk and those lethal blue eyes.

Tempting me into sin. Making me want to tell him to drive us somewhere so he can ravage me all over again until I can't walk for a week.

Which is exactly when my phone buzzes with a text.

Nora: r u almost home? It's...late?

And just like that, the bubble I've been existing in for the last few hours, wrapped up in him and only him, pops. And reality hits me like a slap in the face.

What the fuck am I thinking?

I have a life. I have a career, and responsibilities. I have *Nora*, for God's sake. Exactly what do I think I'm doing playing gangster girlfriend to Hades fucking *Drakos*?

"Elsa—"

"We can't do this again."

It tumbles out of me before my over-analytical mind can chew it up and reformat it as a compelling legal argument.

Hades raises a brow, his cocky grin morphing into a hard look.

"Do what, exactly?"

"*This*. This…whatever this thing is between us."

"Oh, do you not *want* to do this? Because if so, that was a fucking stunning performance just now. Oscar-worthy, even."

I simmer, my face heating. "That's not what I mean. I don't not *want* to…"

"We're two consenting adults, Elsa. I don't see what the problem is."

"It's more complicated than that."

"Why."

"Because…it just is."

"But why does it have to be 'complicated'?" He frowns. "I enjoy fucking you and watching you bounce up and down on my cock, begging for more like a good girl."

My face suffuses with heat.

"And you in turn seem to enjoy *being* that good girl bouncing up and down on my cock and begging for more. There's really nothing complicated about that."

"So, that's what this is? Purely sex, nothing more?"

His jaw clenches.

"If that's all it was, would you be okay with that?"

Say no. Say no to all of this and just walk away. Walk away before the insanity and the gravitational pull from orbiting this close to Hades Drakos sucks you in.

"*Maybe?*" I whisper quietly.

His jaw grinds, and then slowly, that cocky smirk returns.

"So, we have an agreement. No feelings. No attachments."

As if he's even capable of either of those.

"Just fucking."

I blush, chewing on my lip.

"Just fucking," I breathe.

"Deal," he growls.

I swallow as I reach over, taking his hand and shaking it like we're closing some house purchase or something, ignoring the shiver of heat that slides up my spine at his touch.

"Deal."

I want to kiss him. But then I wonder if that crosses the line we've *just* drawn from "just fucking" to "feelings", even though there's been a whole lot of kissing involved in our "just fucking" thus far.

So in the end, I don't. We just lock eyes, me shivering and shuddering as the soreness and the aching need in my body throbs incessantly.

"So…" My throat bobs up and down. "See you soon."

He nods.

Upstairs, I manage to sneak inside and get to my room so I can shower the sins of my night away. I slip into a tank top and shorts, then think better of it and change into longer pajamas that cover the marks of my aggressive and savage sexual encounter with the god of the underworld.

Now I can face Nora.

Sort of.

We end up chatting for a bit and then watching the newest *Ted Lasso* episode before we both head to bed.

Damn. Should have kissed him.

It's the last thought I have before I sink into sleep.

18

ELSA

"I HEARD A JUICY RUMOR ABOUT YOU."

I stiffen at the sound of Fumi's voice behind me in the doorway to the staff lounge.

A juicy rumor?

Dread knots in my stomach, and my face pales. Because when it comes to "juicy rumors" and me, the only place my mind goes is *Hades*.

She knows. How does she know?

Slowly, I turn from the espresso machine to face her.

"*Oh?*" I croak, heat flooding into my face.

Fumi grins widely, arching a brow.

"Yeah, that you banged out the entire Klein briefing in one day. But now I'm really curious as to what sordid little secret you just *thought* I was talking about."

I squirm as my face throbs.

"Nothing. You just caught me off guard, is all."

Fumi rolls her eyes. "Elsa, you're a great lawyer. But I am a *ruthless* prosecutor because I can't be lied to. I mean I literally cannot be. I see right through that shit."

Mercifully, that's the precise moment the espresso machine finishes with a ding. Laughing as lightly as I can manage, I turn and then take my time picking up the little ceramic cup and blowing on it.

"Believe me, Fumi, I wouldn't dare try."

"Well, you *would*, because you just did. But now you know. Bullet-proof, baby. So spill."

I swallow back the heat from my face, turning to her as I sip the espresso.

"There's really nothing to spill."

It's been two days since the insane night in Hades' back seat. The night where I fell into sin *again*, because I'm clearly completely unable to control myself around him. Which is a problem because one, he's *Hades*. But more to the point two, given that his family employs me, he's technically my client.

And that's a *big* problem. Not just morally and ethically, but also *legally*. If one is following the very strictest letter of the law, a sexual relationship between a lawyer and their own client is considered sexual abuse.

Technically, this could cost me my license.

And yet somehow, this isn't throwing me into a tailspin. I'm not in panic mode, worrying about this thing looming over me, ready to wreck my life or blow it to smithereens.

I'm mainly wondering when it can happen again.

God, what is wrong with me.

Because not worrying about the implications of whatever this thing is between Hades and I isn't the only thing going on with me right now. The other one also has to do with that same night.

Pascha.

I've seen dead bodies before—on morgue tables, at crime scenes, when I had to identify our mom, heck, even at Ares and Neve's wedding.

But I've never seen someone *become* a dead body. I've never seen someone murdered right before my eyes.

Never, that is, until two days ago, when Hades strangled Pascha out of existence not three feet from me, in my office.

This should have me falling to pieces. I should be a fucking *wreck* of anxiety, panic, and moral quandaries.

And I'm not.

I thought for sure that yesterday, when I had to walk into that same office and act like I *hadn't* seen Hades choke the life out of a man there the night before that I'd have a nervous breakdown. But I didn't.

And this morning, I'm not even sure I could tell you exactly where on the floor it happened. I even picked out a new rug online.

I don't know...does that make me some kind of psycho, devoid of empathy? I mean, *should* I have even a little empathy for someone losing their life, if that person was a monster? This morning in the bathroom mirror, I decided I didn't.

And I'm fine with that.

"No?" Fumi needles. "So you just decided to randomly bring neck scarves back into your rotation again? For absolutely no reason?"

Don't blush. Don't blush. Don't blush—

I blush.

It's not for no reason. It's because I've got fresh battle wounds courtesy of the god of the underworld all across my neck. And my breasts. And my ass, and hips, and thighs.

Apparently, fucking Hades Drakos is a full contact sport. Or maybe a gladiatorial match to the death.

Fumi grins. "You're totally fucking someone."

"I am *not.*"

"Girl, you know you're an adult, right? You're allowed to have whatever sex you want and not hide it away like a dirty little secret. It's kind of the one perk of having to age, pay taxes, and go to work every day."

I shake my head as I look away.

"Okay, okay. *Yes*, I've been…seeing someone."

Fumi squeals. "*Yes*. YES. Get it, lady. Dude, I didn't know how to say this without sounding like a total jackass, but you *needed* to get laid. Like, doctor's prescription time."

I roll my eyes, blushing.

"You're not going to tell me anything about him or who he is, are you?"

"Nope."

She starts to laugh, but then suddenly stiffens. "Oh shit, it's not one of the brothers, is it?"

"Brothers?"

She leans close, grinning conspiratorially as she lowers her voice. "Alistair or Gabriel?"

I make a face. "God, *no*."

"You're sure about that."

"Fairly certain, yeah."

She grins. "I was going to say, speaking of lurid rumors, the shit I've heard about those two..." she waggles her brows. "*Yikes*."

"Yeah, well, *no*. I am not sleeping with any of our bosses."

"Someone else from the office?"

"No."

"Matthew McConaughey? Because that's not cool. You know I have dibs."

I laugh, shaking my head. "*No*."

"Timothée Chalamet."

My nose wrinkles. "Ew—no."

"*What*? He's gorgeous."

"Agree to completely disagree. I think he looks like a chimney sweep straight out of Dickens."

She rolls her eyes.

"Oh, I know! The hot bartender at the place across the street that Taylor like to go for lunch."

"Negative."

"Mick Jagger."

I giggle. *"Nyet."*

"A Saudi prince."

"Nein."

"Henry Cavill."

"Non."

"Hades Drakos."

I almost have a heart attack. I cough, eyes bulging out of my head as my jaw hits the floor. Mercifully, Fumi is looking past me at something, and doesn't catch the shame and sin written all over my face.

"What?"

"Hades Drakos."

I swallow, taking a shaky breath just as her eyes slide back to mine.

"Why on Earth would you—"

"Because he's *here*, and currently marching toward us looking at you like he's about to rip your clothes off and ravish you against the office fridge whether I leave the room or not."

Goddammit.

I hate when she messes with me.

"Ha bloody ha. Right. Let me just turn around and say hello to my nightmare client—"

"You got a nightmare client? Bummer."

The floor drops away when I hear his voice—for real, in person—right behind me in the doorway to the break lounge.

Fumi clears her throat. "I, uh, wasn't kidding."

Fuck.

I don't turn around to face him. I can't. Because if I do, I'm not sure I'd be able to say no even if he *did* start to rip my clothes off and ravish me against the fridge right here and now.

"Good afternoon, Mr. Drakos," Fumi says brightly.

"Afternoon, Ms. Yamaguchi. I need to speak to my attorney."

"Of course." Her eyes slide back to mine, *very* full of questions. Her brow cocks just enough to say "I'm going to drag this out of you later" before she clears her throat. "I'll catch up with you later, Elsa?"

"M-hmm," I nod, my throat bobbing.

When she's gone, instantly, it's like the whole room's gotten warmer. I still have my back to him as I walk over to the sink and dump out my undrunk espresso.

"What do you want?" I murmur.

I shiver as I hear his footsteps bringing him closer.

"I need to see you in your office."

"I'm busy."

"That's a real shame."

I jolt, gasping as Hades boldly grabs a fistful of my hair. He tugs just hard enough to pull my head back and pull me against him as his lips brush my tingling neck.

"Because in sixty seconds, I'm bending you over the nearest flat surface and fucking you until you see *God*. If you'd like me to do that here in the break room, I'm game. How about you?"

Heat explodes across my face and down my chest to pool between my thighs. My pulse thuds wildly, my legs shaking as they squeeze together with an achy need.

For him.

I could tell him to fuck off. But I'm wet, and on fire, and I want him. *Badly*.

Also, he's crazy enough to make good on that threat, and we both know it.

"We..." I swallow, shivering as I feel his hand grab my hip possessively. "We said we wouldn't do this again."

"You're a lawyer," he growls. "Don't people lie all the time?"

Tell me about it. I've been lying to myself nonstop for the last two days about him. How I'll never do it again. How it has to end. How this is a beyond terrible idea and there's no way I'll sleep with Hades ever again.

Vicious, ruthless lies, the lot of them.

Because I'm fairly certain I'm going to sleep with Hades again.

Like...right now.

"Tick tock, kitten," he rasps into my ear, making me bite my lip so hard I almost taste blood to stop the whimper. "Your office, or right here in the break room, so the whole firm can watch you getting fucked like the greedy little cum slut you are."

I shiver, panting and gripping the counter in front of me with white knuckles as something sinful and hot erupts inside of me.

"I…"

"Three. Two—"

"My office," I choke out.

I pull away, still unwilling to look him in the eye lest I cave and jump him right here. I walk on unsteady legs, trying to keep my head held high and my expression business-like as I thread my way through the cubicles across the main floor.

Hoping to everything that is good and holy that it just looks like I'm headed to my office with a client to talk legal matters.

Not to get thoroughly and utterly *fucked* by said client.

"Right through here," I mumble through the adrenaline and lust roaring through my veins, gesturing toward my office door as if Hades hadn't ever been here before.

I stop outside it, still not meeting his eye as I gesture with my hand. Raw black energy and a throbbing magnetism radiate from his body as he slides past me into the office. I step in after him, turning to close the door behind us.

"Hades—"

I gasp as he suddenly pins me hard to the door, my face against it as his mouth devours my neck. Whimpering, I shudder, clawing at the door as his teeth rake across my tender skin, his lips fastening onto my neck and sucking as his hands slide around to my front.

The buttons of my blouse open violently, and I whimper when his big hands slide inside. He opens the front clasp of my bra, spilling my breasts into his hands. Strong fingers pinch and twist my nipples as I clamp my own hand over my mouth to muffle my unstoppable cries of pleasure.

Suddenly, he's dropping down to his knees behind me. My eyes widen as he shoves my skirt up, as if there's *not* a huge, fully-staffed legal firm all working and milling around just on the other side of my office door.

I cry out when he bites—literally *bites*—my ass. His fingers grab the waistband of my thong, yanking it down my hips and thighs to tangle at my knees. His powerful hands grip my ass, lewdly spreading me open as I feel his hot breath against the back of my thighs.

"You'll want to keep that hand over that mouth, kitten."

"I—"

My face caves and my eyes roll back in my head when his mouth dives between my thighs to cover my pussy. His tongue drags slowly through my lips, making me squeal into my hand as my toes curl in my high heels.

Hades growls deeply, his thick, powerful fingers digging into my ass as he drags his tongue up and down my pussy. I cry out when he pushes it inside, delving deep, as if he's devouring me from the inside out. My head swims with pleasure, one hand clawing at the door I'm panting against, the other clamped painfully between my teeth.

His tongue moves lower to swirl around my aching, needy clit. He wraps his lips around the throbbing nub, sucking on it, making my legs shake. My eyes squeeze shut, my brow creasing as I moan into the hand caught in my mouth.

The wet heat between my legs grows and throbs. The way his tongue drags across my throbbing clit as I drip all over his chin has me seeing double as my vision blurs.

Slowly, his tongue moves lower, and then back. Then further back. His hands tighten, spreading me wider open as I feel his tongue suddenly start to drag up toward...

"*Hades...*" I choke, caught between the heady, sinful pleasure the tip of his tongue is dragging out of me as it teases closer and closer to my asshole, and the shame that this is...dirty.

Too dirty.

Too shameful.

This... This shouldn't feel so good.

"Hades—"

I reach back, my fingers sliding into his hair to push him away, even if it feels so fucking good I want to scream.

"Wait—"

I whimper as he grabs my wrist and pins my hand to the small of my back.

"Don't interrupt me while I'm trying to eat, kitten," he snarls against my skin.

"That...I mean...you can't—"

"I can't, or you don't *want* me to?"

I swallow, shivering.

"*Answer me*, kitten."

Mother*fuck*. It's like that word—that little pet name—is now hardwired into my brain like a trigger. I'm pretty sure I could be at a freaking funeral, or in the dentist's chair getting a root canal, and if he said it, I'd *still* get instantly wet.

"I…" My eyes squeeze shut, heat pulsing through my face. "You…*can't.*"

Hades growls deeply. "I'm going to interpret that as 'you want me to, you're just too ashamed to ask for it'."

My teeth sink into my bottom lip, a whimper bubbling up my throat as I feel his tongue drag up the inside of my thigh.

"*Hades…*"

"*Answer me.*"

My eyes squeeze shut tightly.

"*I want you to…*" My voice is a whisper.

"What a good kitten."

I moan as he yanks my pinned hand down to my ass. He reaches up and pulls the other hand away from my face, bringing that down as well.

"Now *spread them* for me, kitten."

Holy fuck.

I'm practically shaking as I slide my hands over my ass, grabbing my cheeks.

"*Spread.*"

I do. Heat explodes in my face as I feel his eyes brazenly dragging over me in this incredibly intimate and exposed position. But I'm not ashamed. I'm not knotted in anxiousness, wanting it to be over.

I'm eager for it to *begin.*

I moan when his thumb brushes my clit. His mouth lowers, and suddenly, as his tongue drags lightly over my most private place, I see fucking *stars*.

"Oh my God..."

The sensation is *insane*. It's like discovering nerve endings and pleasure points I never knew I had. His tongue swirls over my hole, teasing and prodding and licking, sending my head reeling as the filthy pleasure explodes through my core.

It's the combination of the act itself and the sensation being both sinfully dirty and outrageously intimate at the same time. It's his thumb rolling my clit and two of his fingers curling deep into my pussy. His deep, savage, hungry growls as he tongue-fucks my ass and intermittently spanks me at the same time.

It's taking everything I have to keep from screaming in pleasure so loud that someone on the other side of the door calls the police.

His wet, sinful tongue pushes deeper. His thumb adds more pressure on my throbbing clit. And my world is just beginning to crack and shatter at the edges when suddenly, Hades pushes a third finger into my dripping wet pussy. And it's game over.

I bite down on my lip so hard that the taste of copper floods my tongue. I cry out through clenched teeth and bleeding lips, spasming and shaking and writhing—pushing shamefully back against his tongue and his fingers as my body explodes.

19

ELSA

THE ORGASM CURLS my toes and arches my back, tearing through me like a hurricane until I'm not sure I can even stay standing.

Which is exactly when he pulls away, spins me around, and pins me hard against the door. I moan, still shuddering from the explosive release he just wrenched out of me as his mouth descends to my neck to leave fresh battle scars.

He grabs me, easily lifting me up against his body, his hands gripping my ass and my legs wrapped tight around his hips. Turning, he marches me across the office, and with one sweep of his arm, he clears my desk of just about everything except the computer monitors.

I shudder, whimpering as he plants me on the edge of it, spreads my legs wide, and unzips his pants. Moaning, I'm ripping at his shirt and dragging my tongue down the throbbing vein in his neck as I feel him pull out his cock. I glance down, my breath catching and my eyes flaring at the sheer gorgeous size of him.

Hades' jaw clenches as he wraps a hand around his cock and pushes the fat head against my clit, making me whimper eagerly.

"Exactly how many times have you thought about my cock stretching you wide open and filling you to the fucking brim since the other night?"

I moan, locking eyes with him.

"Se-several times."

"Be. Fucking. *Specific*, counselor," he snarls, rubbing the swollen head over my throbbing clit and sending fresh fireworks exploding through my system.

"There's no way I could keep track."

He groans. "And how many times have you played with this pretty little pussy, thinking of me fucking it until you come all over my balls?"

I whimper, my face flooding with heat.

"I…"

"Tell me."

"Four times," I blurt, heat flooding my face and chest.

"Good girl."

I gasp, clawing at him as he sinks the thick head of his cock into me. My eyes roll back as he pushes another hard inch inside, only to draw back.

"I *like* that I'm the only man who's ever felt this sweet little cunt snug around his cock, kitten," he growls.

God, is that outrageously sexy.

"I *like* that this pussy belongs to *me* and me onl—"

"That's a bold statement," I breathe. "Who says—"

I almost scream, my eyes rolling back as he buries every inch of his cock inside me with one swift, powerful thrust of his hips.

"*Me*," Hades snarls savagely. "*I* say so. I'm the one who taught this little pussy how to fuck. How to come with my cock buried deep inside it. How to get wet and achy and needy when I'm *not* inside it. So yes, kitten," he rasps. "It's fucking *mine*."

He punctuates his words by rolling his hips back and then driving hard into me again.

"*All. Fucking. MINE.*"

I moan as he suddenly shoves me back across the desk, grabs my thighs, and shoves my legs up high and wide. His hips pound against me, his cock ramming deep and hard as I start to drown in pleasure.

Which is exactly when he stops, and slowly pulls out of me.

"What…"

The wet, slippery, swollen head of his cock slides down, and I tremble as I feel it tease against the tight ring of my ass.

I don't tell him to stop.

Even though I know he's crazy enough to do it.

Because I'm crazy enough to *want him* to do it.

"I was the first to claim that pouty, smart mouth of yours," he growls. "And the first to take this pretty little pink cunt."

I shiver as his thumb rolls over my clit and his cock throbs against my asshole.

"I believe there's one other hole I need to claim."

Holy. Fuck.

I can't tell which is more insane: the idea that Hades is about to fuck me in the ass for the first time, at my job, *on my desk*, with an office full of people twelve feet away. Or the fact that I'm seconds away from *begging him to*.

He groans as he strokes his slippery cock against my tight hole, dragging his piercing eyes up to lock with mine.

"*Open up for me, kitten—*"

There's a firm knock on my door.

I jolt, almost falling off the edge of my desk before I manage to catch myself. Hades snarls, whirling to glare daggers at the door.

"Uh...hang on!" I blurt. "I'm with a client!"

"Ms. Guin?"

Fuck. Me. It's Erin, Taylor's personal assistant.

"*Yes?*" I choke.

"Ms. Crown wanted to know if you could come to her office to go over the notes on the Klein briefing?"

Goddammit.

"Uh, when?"

"Right now?"

Shit.

Hades turns, smirking as he teases the head of his still very hard cock over my ass. I bite down hard on my lip, shivering as my eyes start from their sockets.

"*Stop*," I whisper.

"*Why.*"

"*Because I have to go see my boss!*" I hiss.

"Tell her you're busy taking every inch of my fat cock up your virgin ass."

My eyes bulge at the outrageous vulgarity.

…That should *not* be as hot as it is.

"Ms. Guin?"

"*Yes*, Erin!" I blurt. "I'm coming!"

"Wow, already?"

I shoot Hades a look before I begrudgingly push him away.

"*I have to go.*"

"The fuck you do."

"Hades…" I chew on my lip, eyeing him. "Please."

His brows furrow. "This isn't over, kitten."

Heat floods my face. "I'll be there in two minutes, Erin!"

I'm still shaking as I slide off my desk, ignoring the disaster zone of papers and files he's just swept to the floor. I fix my blouse and my skirt as best I can, then go to the mirror over the sink in the bathroom.

Good God, I look like I've just been fucked sideways. In a tornado.

I pull my hair out of the bun—it's already mostly out anyway —shaking it loose in the mirror.

"You should wear it down more often."

I start, blushing as I look past my reflection to where Hades is buttoning his shirt up behind me.

"I've always worn it up for work."

He arches a brow, and I blush.

"And…basically…all the time."

"Wear it down. It's sexy like that."

My core tingles.

"Yes, because that's exactly what I want to convey walking into a deposition or a courtroom, Hades. 'Sexy'. Very professional."

"Sexy doesn't have to mean unprofessional. I don't mean you should walk into your next case in sheer lingerie and thigh-highs." He stops, his lips curling wickedly. "Although I can think of other occasions where that exact outfit would work."

I flush deeply.

"Seriously. Sexy can convey power, too. You don't have to be buttoned up like a nun with your hair scraped back so tight it affects your vision to come off as professional or powerful. Your reputation will do that all on its own."

I frown. "My reputation?"

"That you're a beast of a lawyer."

Heat tingles through my cheeks as I bite back a grin.

"Oh."

He inclines his head, taking me in. "Just my opinion. You should wear your hair down more often. It doesn't make you look any less professional or ass-kicking."

I chew on my lip. "Well...maybe I will."

"Good."

I'm still throbbing all over as we walk to the door together. Then I stop him.

"Uh...you go first. I'll leave in a few minutes."

He smirks. "How clandestine."

I roll my eyes. "I just—"

I jolt as he suddenly surges into me, grabs a handful of my hair in his fist, and kisses me.

Brutally.

"I *will* be finishing what we started, kitten," he growls into my ear.

Then he turns, strides for the door, and swings it open.

"Oh, and Elsa?"

I'm still burning up as I meet his eyes.

"If you were looking for these..."

Dear lord.

He's dangling my *thong* from his finger, right there in the fucking doorway to the rest of the firm, with only the fact that his shoulders are so broad stopping everyone from seeing it.

"*Give me—*"

"You know where to find me."

He slips them into his pants pocket as I stare at him.

Then he's gone.

What. The. FUCK am I tangling myself up in?

It takes me another three minutes to calm myself, catch my breath, and put some concealer on the fresh bite and suck marks on my neck. Then I walk upstairs to Taylor's office, doing everything I can to ignore the aching need still throbbing between my thighs.

That, and the fact that I'm not wearing underwear.

"I'm so sorry to keep you waiting."

Taylor looks up as I step in. She smiles.

"No problem at all. Have a seat, and we'll—" She stops suddenly, looking at me curiously.

I go cold. Did I miss a spot?

"What—"

"Oh, nothing!" she beams. "I was just going to say, *love* the hair-down look on you. You should rock that more often!"

Two hours later I'm back in my office, sitting in my chair, surrounded by the chaos Hades left in his wake. Files and documents are strewn across the floor, together with two legal pads, a desktop clock, and a handful of pens.

I haven't made the first move to clean them up since I got back from my meeting with Taylor ten minutes ago.

Because all I'm doing is staring at the edge of my desk, and remembering the feel of him.

The taste of his mouth.

The power of him, twisting and tying me into knots.

And that's exactly when the door suddenly bangs open. I look up quickly, paling as Leo comes storming inside with a dark cloud looming in his eyes. He slams the door shut behind him, his eyes narrowing at me lethally.

"*Yes?*" I hiss.

His eye twitches as his lips curl.

"Where the fuck is Pascha?"

With Hades, I'm utterly incapable of hiding the truth, or any of my emotions. Mercifully, when it comes to pretty much anyone *but* him, my experience in a courtroom serves me well.

I gaze blankly at Leo. "I have no idea."

"Well, then maybe we involve Gavan in this, then."

"Yes, maybe we do," I mutter quietly. "And I can tell him how your creep of a lackey tried to touch me, or how you threatened a fifteen-year-old girl. Think that would help?"

Leo's lips curve down. "So, my little girl has claws after all."

"Get out of my office, Leo."

He snarls at me. "This isn't going away. My man is missing."

"Have you tried the zoo? Maybe they finally locked him up where he belongs."

Leo bristles. "If I don't find him, I'm coming back. And when I do, I'll be *much* less agreeable about it."

"Get. Out."

He shakes his head, smiling darkly at me.

"Careful, little girl," he mutters as he turns and opens the door. "You're walking a dangerous tightrope here. I'm not sure you understand just how close you are to falling."

Then he's gone.

He's wrong about that last part. I'm not unaware of how close I am to falling.

I know full well that I *already have*.

The god of the underworld has just made me his real-life Persephone.

It's just that I'm pretty sure I'm not supposed to be this excited to be dragged down into sin and temptation.

I'm also pretty sure I only want *more*.

20

HADES

When I pull up outside the Jamaican grocery store where I'm having my meeting with Jayden, I actually have to stay in the car measuring my breaths for another ten minutes.

You can't exactly waltz into the closing of a lucrative business deal sporting a raging hard-on.

Also, blue balls are a real thing, and between my swollen balls and my rock-hard cock, the discomfort in my slacks still has me gritting my teeth a full hour after leaving Elsa's office.

At the same time, though…*fuck*, that was good.

Too good.

Way too good.

She's too good, too much, and the way my body craves hers, like a drug I can't find anywhere else is almost scary.

It's a very new concept for me.

It's been a month since that night at Club Venom.

I haven't been with a *single other woman* since.

But that creates a "which came first", chicken/egg situation. Am I disturbingly obsessed with and utterly hooked on Elsa because I haven't let myself drown in my usual ocean of hedonistic, meaningless sex that typically leaves me feeling empty inside? Or have I chosen to forgo my usual self-medication with strangers I don't give a shit about, and who don't give a shit about me as anything more than a fun story to tell later, because I'm obsessed with Elsa?

I scowl, glaring through the windshield into the middle distance as I replay what just went down in her office. It's not even anything I planned, either. I walked in there today, at Ares' request, to *actually* talk to her in her capacity of our family's attorney—to have her give one last look at the contract sitting on the passenger seat next to me.

I told myself it was fine. That despite what's been going on—and *on*—between us, we're adults. And we're capable of discussing normal, grownup things without it devolving into carnal chaos fueled by pure, unbridled lust.

Or not.

Because the second I laid eyes on her when I walked into the Crown and Black offices, that shit went right out the window. One. Fucking. Look at that tight blonde bun, and her even tighter ass in that gray skirt, and I knew I had to devour her whole.

I don't do repeats. Ever. And yet somehow, unbelievably, I've been with her *seven times*—four times at Club Venom, twice in my car, and once in her office an hour ago.

Groaning, I glance at my watch, and then down to the bulging erection tenting my slacks.

Fuck. I have to stop thinking about any of this shit, or I'm going to miss my meeting with Jayden and I won't close this deal.

I inhale, switching my mind to that and away from the vivid thoughts of watching Elsa's pink, pretty pussy swallow my cock whole.

Jayden Robinson is the uncle of Lamar, the one I tore into at boxing the other night, and the head of a relatively low-key Jamaican crime syndicate in Queens. And the deal with him is one we've been hammering out for two months. It's also kind of a precursor, a trial run if you like, for the Albanian acquisition. Even though we're technically buying part of a criminal operation from Jayden, like us, he's got things hidden behind legit fronts. And it's those legit fronts that we'll be purchasing through Thermopylae Acquisitions, to the tune of three million dollars.

It's not Albanian acquisition money, nor is it redeveloping the parking garage at nine-fifty-two Lincoln Place money. But hey, three mil is still three mil. And it's a solid deal for both parties. Jayden gets to walk away from a property he doesn't really have the manpower to run, or even the interest in keeping anymore. And we get another waterfront storage facility to run things out of.

I glance down again.

Finally. My dick has decided to sit down and be quiet. Thank you.

Seizing my opportunity, I grab the contract, jump out of the car, and walk around to the back entrance of the store. The smell of oxtail, rundun, and curried goat makes my stomach rumble as I knock on the back door.

A huge dude with dreads and a face like a mountain opens it a crack with a icy look. But when he sees who I am, he nods, flashing a warm, welcoming grin.

"Hades, how you doin'?"

"Can't complain, Danny."

He smirks, opening the door wide to let me in. "Heard you tuned up Lavar pretty good the other night."

I wince. "How's he doing?"

"Talking in tongues, brother."

I frown. Danny cracks another grin.

"I'm just fucking with you, man. He's fine. Probably looking for a rematch. But hey, come on in. You're here for Mr. Robinson, yeah?"

"Yeah," I wave the contract in my hand. "He's expecting me."

Jayden's big bodyguard chuckles. "It's all business all day long in here today, I guess."

"Oh?"

Danny shrugs, leading me through the back of the market, past huge open barrels of spices and curry leaves, and then up the stairs to Jayden's office.

"Yeah, brother. The big guy's got his boss-man hat on today, I'm telling you. Didn't even come out for lunch.. We had the Italians in here this morning, a couple of mean-lookin' Russians an hour ago, now you—"

"Did you say Russians?"

Jayden's family and mine go pretty far back. Our grandfathers did business together here in New York, back in the day. But even so, there were precautions in place when we first sat down to make this deal. Namely, precautions to keep it *quiet*.

This was a good deal for both of us, and neither party wanted or needed anyone else coming in and trying to fuck things up with a bidding war. Or doing anything else that would put too much scrutiny on the deal, the warehouse, or either of our shell companies involved in the process.

On Jayden's side, he was nervous about the Haitians seeing the deal as sign of weakness, or of him getting ready to step down as head of the organization.

On our end? Well, *Russians*. Namely, the Reznikov Bratva. We didn't want them to even hear a whisper about this deal, because Gavan is a smart motherfucker. And he'd see this for exactly what it is: a test run for something bigger.

Like Serj Mirzoyan's empire.

So, yeah. Damned straight I tense the fuck up when Danny mentions Russians.

He shrugs. "I don't know, man. I'm just security. But yeah, they were Russian." He frowns. "I think. Maybe Ukrainian? Or Polish?"

I relax a little. As much as I like Danny, it's like he says: he isn't exactly part of the inner circle. Who knows who the hell Jayden was talking to earlier. It could've been Lithuanian grain importers, for all I know.

At the door to the office, Danny knocks a staccato rhythm that I'm sure is code. A little window slides open all the same, with dark eyes glaring out before the face nods. The window shuts, the door unlocks, and then it swings open.

"Good luck in there, brother," Danny pats me on the back. "Oh, hey, you didn't bring any of that baklava again, did you?"

"Shit. Slipped my mind. Next time, for sure."

He grins as I turn and stride into the office and close the door behind me. I nod at a couple of familiar faces around the room before I walk over to shake Jayden's hand. At sixty-five, he's put on some pounds around his middle, and his long dreads are gray. But he's still a formidable guy.

Luckily, the Greeks and the Jamaicans have always gotten along pretty damn well in this city.

"Big day, Jay," I grin, plopping into a chair and dropping the contract on the desk between us. "You ready to make this official and take my money?"

The room is completely quiet. And I'm suddenly aware that I'm the only fucker smiling in here. Jayden frowns, clearing his throat.

"First of all," he smiles awkwardly at me, "I want to thank you for the interest in the property, Hades. I know our families go way back, and I appreciate the way you worked out a deal that was good for both of us."

Was good? I don't like how this is starting. At all.

"You want to tell me what's going on, Jay?"

His brow furrows. "You, ahh, want a drink, Hades?"

"I want to know what's up, actually," I growl.

He sighs. "Look, there's no easy way to say this, but I wanted to tell you face to face, like men."

Fuck..

"You getting cold feet, Jay?"

"Shit, Hades, I didn't mean for this to happen. I said no at first. But he just kept putting money on the table, brother. And at a certain point, it becomes impossible to keep saying no."

My jaw grinds.

"*Who* kept putting money on the table," I growl.

Jayden sighs. "I'm sorry, Hades. I know this is going to look like a snub, and I didn't mean for it to be. It's just business—"

"*WHO.*"

He drags his fingers through his gray beard.

"Gavan Tsarenko."

Son. Of. A. Bitch.

"He came in less than an hour ago, Hades. I never invited him, and I truly don't even know how he knew it was for sale. But he did, and the more I told him it wasn't for sale, the more he was telling me everything can be for sale at the right price, and throwing more money on the table."

Jayden looks legitimately sorry, and a little scared as he shrugs and raises his arms in appeal. "I mean what was I supposed to do, brother? All respect to you and your family, Hades, it's the fuckin' Russian *Bratva.*"

I look away, my jaw grinding.

"How much."

Jayden sucks his teeth. "Seven."

Fucking. Hell.

"He dropped *seven mil*?!"

Jay nods.

"That's fucking insane."

"You're telling me."

"Also…" Desmond, Jayden's nephew and the next in line for the throne, gets up from one of the couches across the office. "Gavan rolled up with thirty big fuckin' Russian dudes, who literally surrounded the place." He shrugs. "I don't think he was planning to start anything, but Gavan definitely meant to send a message."

"Which I got loud and clear, you hear what I'm saying?" Jayden mutters.

"Yeah," I growl. "I hear you."

Except I don't think the message was for him.

It was for *me* and my family. Tsarenko comes by with thirty men, and then pays one hundred and thirty-three fucking percent over the current price?

Yeah, *no*. That wasn't a bidding war. That was a shot across my family's fucking bow.

"Hades, I'm sorry, brother. I didn't—"

"It's fine."

I stand, cracking my neck before I reach over and shake Jay's hand.

"Hades, we go way back—"

"Which is why I'm only pissed, and not *furious*," I growl.

"We can make this right. I've got other—"

"Don't worry about it."

When Jay swallows nervously, I force a smile and pat his hand.

"Seriously, Jay, we're good. Shit happens, you know? Like you said—it's just business."

I'm guessing this was the other part of Gavan's little surprise attack: to get us pissed off at the Jamaicans for selling to him instead of us.

To divide us.

And that's actually even *more* concerning than him buying a fucking warehouse he doesn't need just to "send a message".

A *lot* more concerning.

Which is why making sure Jay knows we're cool is really, really important.

"Seriously, we're good," I smile at him. "Listen, my sister's opening this new bar in the West Village, and they're doing this family and friends soft opening in a few weeks. Why don't you and Desmond swing by?"

The concern around his eyes melts a little. "Yeah?"

"For sure. I'll put you both on the guest list."

"Stock up on the Red Stripe," Desmond chuckles. "It's all Uncle drinks."

I grin through the darkness swirling inside of me. "I'll see what I can do."

———

"*FUCK*."

Ares turns to stab his gaze through the big windows of the Thermopylae Acquisitions conference room. I got our mother's piercing icy-blue eyes. Ares got our father's dark, brooding ones.

"You're sure it wasn't Jayden's idea?"

I shake my head. "Positive. Never mind the history between our families, we've always been a bit bigger and more powerful than him anyway—and that was before we joined forces with the Kildares. No, he's got too much respect for our history, and too much appreciation for the power dynamic to fuck that up."

"Even for four fucking million over our price?"

I nod. "Even that. Jay's not an actor, man. And he looked scared as shit when I walked in there. This was a shot across our bow, but it rattled Jay's windows too."

Ares shakes his head. "This deal was locked the fuck down. I mean the only people who knew were us, Neve's family, and Jay's crew. Maybe one of his guys let it slip? Or, fuck, I mean I know Cillian and Castle just brought on some new blood. Maybe—"

"Ares." I drum my fingers on the conference table, glancing up at him when he turns back to me. "I think part of the reason Gavan did this was to make us suspicious of our allies. Same as how I'm betting he was hoping it would drive a wedge between us and the Jamaicans."

His eyes narrow. "He's trying to divide us."

I nod.

"And sow discontent."

"Yep."

His jaw clenches. "In war or politics, those are both moves you make on your enemies before you *invade...*"

I nod slowly. "They sure are."

"We need to find out how the Russians knew about this deal, Hades. And we need to find out yesterday."

21

ELSA

You'd think by now, I'd have become immune to Hades'...*filthiness*. His ability to rattle me by saying things that should make me livid and disgusted, instead of warm and wet.

Immune, or at least slightly numb. Desensitized. But apparently, I'm not. Case in point: the way I've been staring at my phone screen for the last five solid minutes, re-reading over and over the last text he sent me.

HADES

does your ass miss my tongue?

I've literally re-read it close to a hundred times. And it has *not* lost its edge yet.

I still tingle every time I read it. Still feel my pulse quicken, still squeeze my thighs together at my desk.

Still squirmy, achy, and needy. I mean, what the fuck, self?

I've been like this since yesterday, when he...*yeah.*

Pinned me to my office door, yanked my panties down, and tongued my clit. Then my ass, until I came like a wrecking ball. And as much as I still want to feel—I don't know, embarrassed?—for something so insanely dirty feeling so good, I can't.

All I feel when I think about it is the need for more, like an addiction.

And that's Hades in a nutshell: something dirty that feels so good.

My phone buzzes on the desk in front of me.

HADES

Is this you ignoring me, or are you too busy playing with your pussy while thinking about me to answer your texts

My face throbs with heat. I mean, the *audacity* of the man.

ME

You're the one texting me, Hades.

I bite my lip, grinning as my thumbs tap over the screen.

ME

Like a stood-up prom date, I might add.

HADES

did you even go to prom? or were you too busy organizing your receipts and ironing your underwear

ME

You're the one currently in possession of a pair of my underwear, you tell me: do they look and feel ironed?

HADES

> No, but they smell like your pussy, and it's making me hungry

I mean, sweet *JESUS*. This is what I'm dealing with. How do you even respond to that? And why the *hell* does it turn me on so much when he talks to me like this?

I simmer, squirming in my chair as heat pools between my thighs.

ME

> We don't have prom in the UK. At least, we didn't when I was in school. We had school formals.

HADES

> that sounds like prom but with pinkies out and a guy called Jeeves taking your coat and riding boots at the door

ME

> lol. We were poor, and so was the school I went to. My formal was biscuits and fruit punch served off a folding table in the gymnasium with a bad DJ. And then an afterparty at a sketchy motel where everyone could screw.

I chew on my lip as I make an addition to my last text.

ME

> I mean, obviously not EVERYONE. I'm pretty sure I was too busy telling everyone not to get drunk to do any of that, lol.

HADES

> You mean too busy to screw guys

I roll my eyes. I can almost *feel* his possessive glare through the phone.

> **ME**
>
> Oh, no, I did a ton of that. Dick all night. The whole rugby team, actually. Choo-choo!

There's no response for a full minute. I grin.

> **ME**
>
> You KNOW I'm joking. What are you doing, sulking?

> **HADES**
>
> I do know you're joking but don't

I roll my eyes again.

> **ME**
>
> And why is that?

> **HADES**
>
> because I don't even want you joking about being with other men

Oh. My. God. Possessive much?

> **ME**
>
> Why?

> **HADES**
>
> because you're mine

Heat explodes in my core. My pulse begins to beat even faster, and I start to shiver. Goddammit, there's something insanely sexy about this ridiculously over-the-top caveman routine, even though there's no way I would have ever found this even a mild turn-on in anyone else.

But...that's Hades.

Something new. And wild. And insane.

> **HADES**
>
> and I wasn't sulking, I was looking up your
> class list from your school

> **ME**
>
> I'm sorry, what? Why?

> **HADES**
>
> So that I could check through all the guys
> who might have been at that post-formal
> afterparty, or any party, who might have
> touched you

My pulse pounds in my ears. My breath becomes shaky.

> **ME**
>
> Why is that?

> **HADES**
>
> So that I could find them and fucking
> kill them

There's no "lol" at the end of that statement. No funny gif. No cute emoji.

It's not a joke. He's legitimately that insane, and dangerous, and more than capable of doing that. And apparently, I'm *far* more than capable of getting wetter than rain when he says shit like that.

> **ME**
>
> You'd seriously kill someone for touching
> me?

> **HADES**
>
> yes

> **ME**
>
> That's ALL?? Just for touching me?

HADES

Does there need to be any other reason

I stare at the screen, eyes bugging out of my face, my mouth hanging open.

And my panties a fucking *mess*.

Maybe there really is something off with Hades. Maybe he's even more of a psycho—like, legitimately so—than I've ever guessed. But if he is, then there's a strong chance, given how much this whole act is turning me on, that I am, too.

HADES

and you're deflecting. we were talking about your ass missing me

I blush fiercely.

ME

No, YOU were talking about that.

HADES

yet again, deflection instead of an honest answer.

ME

Too bad.

HADES

answer me or I'll come over there and ask it myself and this time I'll leave the fucking door open

Fuck. My entire body clenches and squirms. My skin feels electric under my clothes. What the hell has this man done to me?

ME

Fine. No, it does not.

HADES

I said an HONEST answer

I flush deeply.

HADES

you're too busy being this buttoned up good
girl to admit you came like a fucking geyser
with my tongue in your ass, aren't you

ME

Who even talks like this?

HADES

me, obviously

in any case I'm glad she misses me

ME

Who?

Fuck. I walked right into that one.

HADES

your ass. don't worry, I'm not done with her.
next time, it won't just be my tongue opening
her up

I stare at the screen with wide, scandalized, but oh-so-*eager* eyes.

Holy. *Shit.*

ME

Meaning?

HADES

you know what I mean, kitten

ME

I might need clarification.

Three dots appear and then disappear. And then suddenly, a picture just pops right up on my screen that sucks the air from my lungs and sends my jaw crashing to the fucking floor.

His cock.

Hades' *fully*-erect, VERY large, very thick, very bulging-with-a-vein-running-down-the-length-of-it *cock*.

...and the icing on the cake is my stolen thong wrapped around the base of it.

Sweet. Tap-dancing. Christ.

You're supposed to be angry at unsolicited dick pics. And normally, I damn well would be.

...Unless, apparently, that unsolicited dick pic comes from Hades Drakos. Because when his *gorgeous* cock fills my screen, all I want to do is freaking lick it. All over.

I am absolutely, one hundred percent, going insane.

HADES

how's the clarity on that

I shiver.

ME

When did you take that?

HADES

just now

ME

Are you at home?

HADES

I'm sitting in traffic, why

Oh my God, he's an animal. He just took a picture of his massive dick with my panties wrapped around it in midtown traffic. Like, who does that?

And also...

My eyes slide over the image, heat spreading through every single nook and cranny of my body. My nipples feeling electrified against my bra. My clit aching to be touched under my slick panties.

Hades has a freaking *beautiful* dick. Like, that thing is the Brad Pitt or Benicio del Toro of dicks. It's ridiculous.

It's also *huge*. Like the sort of huge where I'm actually confused how it fit inside my vagina. And *that's* built for delivering babies, for fuck's sake.

ME

I feel that I need to set some expectations.

HADES

concerning

ME

Concerning my ass.

HADES

please elaborate

ME

As it pertains to your penis.

I cringe. I really did just say "penis", didn't I?

264

HADES

talk dirty to me, baby. tell me more about my penile member and your vaginal cavity

I giggle, loudly.

HADES

or any other bodily cavities we were discussing. And these expectations you wish to set

I blush.

ME

There's no way your cock is going in there.

HADES

that's factually incorrect

I grin.

ME

I'm being serious. It isn't physically possible.

HADES

what makes you so sure

I scroll up to the picture in the middle of our conversation, screenshot it, and then text him the screenshot.

ME

Uuuuhh…because your dick is the size of a baseball bat??!

HADES

you don't have to win me over with flattery, baby. I'm what they call a sure thing

I roll my eyes, grinning impishly.

ME

> Take that however you will. Bottom line...no pun intended...my arse wants nothing to do with your dick.

HADES

> I'm looking forward to the moment when you admit how wrong you were

ME

> Dream on. I have to go. I have actual work to do.

HADES

> not before you show me you don't

ME

> Show you what?

HADES

> how soaking wet you are thinking about my fat cock sinking into your ass

Heat explodes across my face.

I've never done that. I mean, *obviously* I've never sent someone a picture like that.

But apparently, this man is able to unlock each and every first of mine he wants. Because before I know what I'm doing, before I can stop myself, I'm lowering my phone under the desk and slowly spreading my legs.

Click.

I wince. The first shot is...not sexy. Blurred, badly lit, and basically of my thigh. Yeah, no thanks. I try a few more, but it's the same result. Finally, realizing it's the lack of light under the desk, and after finding out the hard way that flash photography of your crotch is about the least sexy thing ever, I get up and move to the small sitting area by my windows.

I try a few more angles in there, before I finally just say screw it and drop my panties. Blushing, I lie back on the sofa, legs spread and my skirt bunched up as I bring the camera lens to my privates.

"Smile..." I murmur, blushing as I—oh my God—snap a couple of pictures of my pussy.

The first few are meh. But then...there it is. The money shot, where you can actually see the glistening heat of my arousal and the pink flush on my lips.

I don't second guess it. Don't overthink it. I just hit send, and then immediately turn my phone face down as my face heats.

What the fuck did I just do?

I swallow. It's fine. It's not like my face is in it. And as insane as he is, I feel that Hades is the last person who'd ever share something like that, given his lunatic possessive streak.

ME

I hope that suffices. I'm going to work now.

HADES

keep the panties off when you do

ME

Lol, no way.

HADES

it wasn't a request. do not put them back on

I bite my lip, grinning.

ME

And how would you even know if I did or not?

HADES

> by walking into your office or maybe waiting until you're in one of your bosses' offices, bending you over, lifting your skirt, and checking. THAT'S how

Aaaaand again, he's crazy enough to fucking do it, too.

ME

> Psycho. Fine, they're off. I'm working now. Bye.

I open my photo app and delete all the pictures I just took of my pussy, because *yikes*, I do not need those popping up in a meeting or something.

Then, I pluck my panties off the couch. I'm about to slip them back on, because honestly, why not? But then, heat surging into my face, I walk back over to my desk and slip them deep into my bag instead.

When I sit, I feel a shiver of desire tingle up from between my legs all the way up to my cheeks.

My phone dings once more.

HADES

> do it

ME

> ??

HADES

> you won't be able to get any work done until you do

ME

> What are you talking about?

HADES

> you making yourself come

It's like he's got a remote control to my libido. To my brain. And to my pussy. Because instantly, it throbs with a need so desperate it actually makes my head spin.

ME

Sounds like projection to me. Did our conversation get you so hot and bothered that you had to jerk off?

HADES

you tell me

I'm about to ask what that even means when another picture comes through.

A picture so outrageously lurid, so ridiculously dirty, that I almost drop my phone.

And yet a picture so fucking hot, my thighs squeeze together involuntarily as my core coils and writhes with need.

A picture of Hades' swollen cock, my panties still wrapped around the thick base, with sticky, glistening white cum dripping down every magnificent inch of him and pooling in my thong.

It's quite possibly the sexiest thing I've ever laid eyes on.

HADES

have fun, kitten

I've barely closed the bathroom door behind me before I'm leaning against the sink with one hand under my skirt and the other muffling my strangled cries.

22

ELSA

A FEW HOURS LATER, there's a knock at my office door.

"Come in."

When I look up and see Neve, Eilish, and Callie walk in, I grin.

"Hey!"

Neve makes a face, nodding at the legal briefings spread out across my desk. "Shit, sorry, are you in the middle of something?"

"You've just described ninety-nine percent of my waking life and maybe thirty percent of my sleeping life. But it's nothing that can't wait. What's up?"

Eilish holds up a file folder. "Final liquor licensing and fire code stuff. They just need your once-over and a signature, and then they can forever be locked in the safe at The Banshee."

I smile at the three of them. "You guys getting excited for this?"

Callie beams. "Uh, *hell yes*. You're coming to the soft opening, yeah?"

"Of course!"

I find myself almost unable to look Callie in the eye, since I spent close to an hour of my day earlier *vividly* sexting her brother. Which, given her and my friendship, I feel kind of weird about now.

I take the file folder and leaf through it. "I can get these back to you guys later tonight, if you like?"

Neve shakes her head of red hair. "It totally does not have to be tonight."

"Honestly, it's no big deal. Want me to drop it at one of your places?"

"You're kinda near the West Village, right?"

I nod. "West seventeenth and ninth. Right by Chelsea Market."

She shrugs. "Would you just be able to drop it off at the Banshee itself? You know the safe combo, right?"

I grin. "I do, and yeah, that's no problem."

Eilish makes a face. "You sure? We're not looking to make more work for you."

"Seriously, you're really not. I wouldn't offer if it was a problem."

"Thank you," she sighs. "It would be a huge help, if you really don't mind. I've got a late class tonight, Neve's got some function dealio with Ares, and Callie…" she turns to eye Hades' sister, who makes a face.

"I've got a video chat," Callie mutters darkly. "With my *fiancé.*"

I wince. "Sorry, lady."

Being that her fiancé is a fifty-year-old, grotesque and notoriously vile Italian Mafia don from Los Angeles…*ouch.*

"Well, I'm happy to drop it off and stick it in the office safe."

"Thanks, Elsa," Eilish grins. "Oh! Before I forget, we changed the keypad lock on the back door. It's seven-nine-nine-two-zero-five now."

"Got it." I make a mental note.

"Oh, and also?" Neve holds up a finger. "This is off the topic of the Banshee, but do you have the easement filings for the fourteenth street development? Ares asked if I could grab those from you if I swung by here."

"Yeah, not a problem." I cross back to my desk and open my email. "There's a bunch of different documents, hang on. I'm going to email you…*these* ones…" I frown and then glance at her. "Actually, I know the last two are saved as PDFs on my phone. Feel free to grab it and email them to yourself."

"Yeah?"

"Yeah, it's right there." I smile, nodding my chin at my phone sitting on the corner of the desk. "Password is eleven-nine-teen-twenty-three."

"Awesome, thanks."

"It's probably in my recent photos. Hang on, I'm sending you the first five docs—"

"Ooookay, WOW. Yeah."

Neve almost drops my phone as she quickly places it face down on my desk and all but leaps back from it.

"Sorry!! I…yeah, *sorry.*"

My brows knit. "What—"

Oh holy fucking mother of Christ.

I deleted all the X-rated selfies of my own privates earlier.

…But I did *not* delete the screenshot from my conversation with Hades, including the picture of his dick, that I sent back to him.

I have a fairly good idea what Neve just saw in my photos.

I turn the color of ripe strawberries as it hits me. I actually gag, like I'm going to actually throw up right here on my office floor, but manage to stop myself.

Callie grins as she makes a beeline for the phone. "Whoa. Okay, whatever this is, I have *got* to see—"

Neve, mercifully, gets to it first, slamming her hand down over it before Callie can snatch it up and be forever scarred.

"Not for our eyes, Cals."

"Oh c'mon!" Callie protests." This sounds juicy as *fuck!*"

Eilish grins at me. "Is Ms. Elsa Guin *sexting* with someone?"

"*No*," I blurt. "I…"

I'm drowning. Hyperventilating. Possibly having a minor panic attack.

"Guys, it's none of our business, okay?" Neve shoots the other two a look. "So, can we just leave it?"

Eilish shrugs. "Sure. Sorry. Didn't mean to pry."

I swallow. "No problem."

"Ugh, buzzkill," Callie sighs. "But I need to get going anyway."

"Same, actually," Eilish nods. "Gotta get to class." She turns to Callie. "You heading uptown? Castle's downstairs. We can give you a ride."

"Perfect, thanks."

Neve clears her throat. "I actually have to go over some other contract stuff with Elsa." She turns to eye me warily. "If you've got a sec?"

I nod stiffly. "M-hmm."

"Great. See you both later."

I manage a weak wave at Callie and Eilish. When they're gone, I drag my eyes to Neve, mortified.

"I am *so* sorry—"

She shakes her head. "It's your phone. *I'm* sorry I pried."

"Still. I'm sorry you saw…*that.*"

She snickers, chewing on her lip as she eyes me.

"So…you and Hades?"

"*What?!*" I sputter.

She sucks her teeth. "I saw the pic. I could tell."

I stare at her, my face on fire. "You can *tell* based off of…." I swallow. "*That?*" I croak.

"I mean, I'm married to his brother. Family resemblance, who knew."

I keep staring at her, stunned. A second later she breaks, cracking up and grinning at me.

"I'm *completely* joking. I saw his contact name at the top of the screenshot."

The air whooshes out of my lungs as I catch myself on the edge of my desk.

"Relax. I mean, I saw a quarter second of a dick and then I looked away. Believe me, I've retained *nothing*."

I simmer, chewing on my lip. "Well, aside from the knowledge that I'm...*yeah*. With Hades."

"Aside from that...yeah." She grins at me. "I did *not* have that on my Bingo card, not gonna lie."

"Is saying 'it's complicated' too cliche a phrase in this case?"

"I literally cannot imagine a more appropriate situation for its use."

I smile. Neve does too, before her brow furrows.

"Is it..." she frowns, like she's hunting for the right word.

"It's not serious," I blurt.

She chuckles. "That's not what was I going to ask, and that's none of my business anyway. No, I was trying to find a tactful way of asking if he was pressuring you into doing anything or being too...well, *Hades*."

I shake my head. "He's not."

"I just mean—and please don't take offense to this, but you're not really..."

"His type?"

She winces, making a face. "No! Well, yeah, but that sounds like a put down when I'm trying to play you up and shit on his usual terrible taste in women. And I might be totally wrong about this, and if I am, please tell me, but you've never struck me as much of a dating type. That's all."

"Because I'm married to my job?"

"Ding ding ding."

I blush, smiling. "You're right. But it's…"

"Complicated."

"Very."

"I'd ask if you're having fun, but I'm going to assume from that goofy-ass grin on your face that that's a yes."

And there I go, grinning even wider.

"Does anyone else know?"

"*No.*"

"Cool. It's staying that way, at least on my end."

"You're not going to tell Ares?"

"That I saw a picture of his brother's boner? Uh, no, Elsa. I like living on a planet that hasn't been blown apart by a nuclear firestorm."

I snort a laugh.

"No, for real, I'm not. This is between you and Hades." She peers at me. "He *is* treating you well, though, right?"

I nod. "I'm in total control."

Well, that's only maybe ten percent true, but who's keeping score.

"Good. But for real, can we agree to literally never tell Ares that I caught even a millisecond glimpse of his brother's genitals? Actually, please can I ask you never to tell Hades, either?" She frowns. "Look, could we just collectively agree to forget any of this ever happened, and tell no one about it, *ever*?"

"Neve, we one hundred percent have a deal."

We both laugh as we shake on it. Then we hug. She turns to leave.

"Hey, Neve?"

She stops at the door, turning to look back at me. "Yeah?"

"That's, uh…" I clear my throat uneasily. "That's the *only* picture you saw… Right?"

She wags her brows, zipping a finger across her lips.

I exhale slowly.

"Just, you know, let me know who your bikini waxer is sometime."

Oh my fucking GOD.

Neve snorts another laugh, grinning at me as she opens my office door.

"Love ya, Elsa."

HOURS LATER, though not nearly as late as I've had to stay sometimes, I'm finally leaving. I grab my gym bag off the couch in my office, lock up, and grab an Uber home.

When I get there, I frown when I see the food delivery I sent to Nora a couple of hours ago still sitting on the kitchen counter. One, because I seriously need to start finding the time to make my sister actual home-cooked meals instead of feeding her nothing but takeout. But two, I sent it hours ago, and it's still unopened.

"Nora?"

She's not in the living room when I poke my head in there. I check her room next, knocking lightly on the closed door.

"Hey! I'm home. How was your day? Also, you must be starving! The Italian I sent—" I frown. "Nora?"

I creak the door open. She's not there.

Pulling my phone out, I send her a quick text. I'm not super hardcore about a curfew, or about where she can or can't go. She's fifteen, she's a smart kid, and it's New York. As long as she lets me know where she's going to be, and that everything is okay, she's got a lot of freedom.

ME

Hey, just checking in. You good?

Her reply comes almost immediately:

NORA

Yeah, sorry, forgot to text earlier. A lot going on. I'm at Gemma's house. Fill u in later?

ME

Yeah, of course. And no problem. Uber or taxi if it's after ten, ok?

She sends me a thumbs up emoji, and that's that.

She was obviously home earlier after school when I had the food delivered, since it's sitting on our kitchen counter. But I guess something came up with her friends. I hate making light of her teen drama, because I was that age once too. But sometimes, it's hard not to roll my eyes at the latest earth-shattering catastrophe that usually revolves around literally nothing.

In the kitchen, I realize I'm starving. So I open up the takeout bag and pop some of the cavatelli with spicy sausage and broccolini in the microwave. I'm halfway through devouring it, along with a big glass of pinot noir, when the unit phone buzzes with a call from the front desk down in the lobby.

"Hey, Gerry."

"Evenin', Ms. Guin. Gotta package here for you."

My brows knit. "Work files?"

"Nnno, I don't think so. Big black box with a ribbon, and the courier said he was paid not to say who it came from."

Okay…that's weird.

Just then, my phone buzzes with a text:

TAYLOR CROWN

> Hey, hope I'm not interrupting your evening. Just wanted to say thanks again for the superwoman act with the Klein briefing. The notes and the recommendations on proceeding are top notch. I can't stress enough how psyched the brothers and I are to have you with us, Elsa. Don't even reply to this. Just enjoy your night. And again, our sincere thanks.

I grin. Whatever the package is, I think this explains where it came from.

"Ms. Guin?"

"Yeah, sorry. I'm here."

"Want me to bring it up?"

"Nah, I could do with stretching my legs. I'll be right down. Thanks."

Ten minutes later, I'm back upstairs sitting in my living room, staring at the matte black box tied with a black satin ribbon and bow sitting on my coffee table. There's no note or anything, but I grin at the sweet gesture from Taylor.

ME

> Hey Taylor, thank you so much, and my absolute pleasure. I'm so happy at Crown and Black. It's everything I've ever looked for in a firm for the long-term. Thank you, really. Your feedback means a lot to me.

Taylor's a stickler for her bedtime routine and sleep health, so she's already got her "do not disturb" auto reply set for texts. But still, she'll see it in the morning and know I got the package.

I re-read her text again, my smile growing wider. I love working for her, and Alistair and Gabriel. It's a wonderful chance at a fresh start, away from Leo, and the less fun memories of childhood, and from Hugo the stalker creep. So it really is incredibly validating to hear that they're glad I'm here, too.

I take a big slug of my pinot noir and then pull open the ribbon tied around the box. I take off the lid, smiling curiously at the matte black crepe paper inside, before I pull it aside—

…And go very, very, still.

I am *fairly* confident this is not a gift from Taylor. And if it is, I have, well, *several* questions. Because it's not a bottle of wine, or a fruit basket, or a laser-etched Lucite plaque, or something else your boss would send you for a job well done.

Inside the box, I'm staring at the most erotic and provocative, skimpiest lingerie I've ever laid eyes on, bar none.

My mouth falls open, my cheeks burning as I stare at the contents. The demi-bra is transparent black lace, with just enough fabric to basically—sort of—cup the undersides of your breasts without really covering much of anything.

I start to pull the matching panties out—in the same delicate, black, see-through lace as the bra—before I stop, my eyes going wide.

There's skimpy, and then there's, well, *this*. It's like a thong, but…not really. The front is about two inches wide, leading down to the gusset, which I realize as I hold them up actually splits apart.

My face blooms bright red as it clicks.

Crotchless panties. They're freaking crotchless panties.

The back is even flimsier. After the lace in the front splits into two, to not at *all* cover your vagina, it comes up the back over the ass in two strips, one over each cheek, to where they connect with the delicate waistband again.

That's it.

The box also contains lacy black thigh-highs with a matching black lace garter belt.

So, no—this is pretty obviously *not* from Taylor. And it doesn't take much of a genius to figure out who *did* send it.

Hades, clearly.

Then I realize there's something else in the box. *Two* something elses, actually, both in smallish black satin boxes. I pick up the first, without the faintest idea what it could be as I open it.

I immediately turn bright red.

It's a vibrator. A little, shiny, gold vibrator. The kind that's in a sort of "U" shape, where you slide one end up and *inside*, and the other end hugs the front against your clit.

I mean, so I've heard...

I shiver, chewing on my lip as I stare at the outrageously sexy lingerie and the golden—or at least gold *plated*—vibrator, courtesy of Hades bloody Drakos.

Which seriously begs the question: what the *fuck* is in the other box? Handcuffs? A freaking *ball gag?*

I simmer with forbidden heat as I lift open the lid of the second box.

Immediately, something hot pulses and sizzles in the pit of my stomach as stare at the little bulbous toy sitting inside the box, also gold.

It's a butt plug.

The man got me a fucking golden *butt plug.*

My hand trembles as I reach for it. My breath comes heavier as my fingertips brush over the polished surface and pick it up.

It's heavy. And...*thick.*

Just like him.

A throb of molten lust pulses through my body.

Swallowing, I place the plug back in the box, which I set down on the coffee table. I breathe deeply as I let my eyes drink it all in.

I've never owned anything like this. Never *worn* anything even close to this. And certainly never been *given* anything like this, by anyone.

My eyes dart to my phone.

Stop. I shouldn't even engage.

Oh, who am I kidding.

ME

What the hell is all of this?

HADES

are you just now working up the guts to text me? My courier dropped that off half an hour ago and I know you're way too impatient to have waited this long to open it

Shit. It's...disturbing, how inside my head he is.

ME

It has nothing to do with courage. I was just deciding whether or not to throw it away.

HADES

we both know you're not going to do that

ME

And if I do?

HADES

another box just like it would arrive fairly
quickly

I shiver with excitement.

ME

What is all of this?

HADES

you might only recently have gotten fucked
for the first time but don't pretend you don't
know exactly what all of that is

I roll my eyes.

ME

I know what it IS. I mean what is all of this as
it pertains to me. Or to you?

HADES

it's what you'll be wearing the next time I
see you

I snort.

ME

You wish.

HADES

I don't wish. I demand. and you obey

He's seriously un-fucking-believable. Real humans do not talk like this. And yet, here I am, grinning and blushing like a schoolgirl with a crush, playing his game.

Very, very willingly.

But just as I'm typing out a cheeky reply, the door to the apartment suddenly slams open.

Fuck.

Choking on my wine, I shove the extremely adult contents of the package back into the box. Then I jump up and bolt down the hall to my bedroom to shove it all in my closet.

Outside my room, I hear Nora slamming the door to her own room shut.

Shit.

Time to put on my big sister hat.

I step out of my room and knock on her door.

"Nora?"

"Come in."

Fear and worry stab into me at the soft, utterly broken tone of my sister's voice. I quickly push the door open.

"Nora?"

Oh, fuck.

"Oh, shit, Nora, honey, what's wrong?!"

I sit on the bed next to her and wrap her in my arms as she cries her heart out.

"Hey, it's okay! Shh, it's okay. I'm here. I'm here."

I stroke her hair as she clings to my arm, sobbing.

"Do you want to talk about it? Did something happen with someone at school?"

She shakes her head, then twists, lifting her eyes, blurry with tears, to mine. "Some kids from school got jumped tonight."

My brow furrows. "Jumped as in mugged?"

"As in they got the shit beat out of them."

Holy shit.

"It's why I ran over to Gemma's house. At first we all thought they'd been in a fight. But it's a lot worse than that."

"Oh my God, Nora." My face falls as I hug her tightly. "What happened? Who got hurt?"

She doesn't say anything.

"Hey," I smile, lifting her face to mine. "You can tell me anything. You know that."

"Promise you won't get mad?"

"One thousand percent."

"Theo Petrakis and Nick Eliades."

The two boys who were over here smoking pot that day Hades drove me home.

"Two other guys, too, Evan Chan and Kyle McMasters. But Nick and Theo got the worst of it."

I wince. "How bad?"

Nora shudders, choking back a sob. "They're both in the hospital. Nick has a broken arm, broken leg, and a fractured eye socket."

Jesus fucking Christ.

He may be one of the little shits who tried to get my fifteen-year-old sister high, and that damn well better have been the extent of his plans for that evening. But still, he's just a kid.

"God, that's horrible," I murmur, hugging her closer.

Nora's face pales. "Theo got it even worse. I guess they knocked him out, then doused him with vodka and lit him on fire."

Holy shit.

"Oh my God, Nora, I'm so sorry." I squeeze her tightly. "Did they catch the guys who did it?"

She shakes her head miserably. "No." She suddenly shivers violently. "They're still out there. Elsa, what if they're targeting kids from St. Mark's Academy?"

I shake my head quickly, pulling her tighter to me. "*No*, Nora. No. Nobody is targeting anyone. It's horrible and senseless, but I'm sure it was just a random act of violence. I mean they're all wealthy enough kids, from families with money. Maybe these guys who jumped them saw four teenagers with fancy watches and figured they were easy targets?"

"But why hurt them so badly? Elsa, Theo is in *really* bad shape. And Nick's going to lose his spot on the Cornell hockey team next year." She shudders and tears up again. "Why the fuck did they have to hurt them like that?!"

I shake my head, rocking her. "I don't know, Nora," I murmur quietly. "But I'm *sure* it was just senseless, random violence."

She doesn't need to know that both Theo's and Nick's fathers work for the Drakos family. She also doesn't need to dwell on the idea that being doused with *vodka* and lit on fucking fire is a pretty cut and dried Bratva message.

She also *really* doesn't need to know that suddenly I'm worried that something very, very bad is looming on the horizon.

23

HADES

TECHNICALLY SPEAKING, I *have* an office at Thermopylae Acquisitions. I've just never once actually *used* it. To me, this whole city is my office. Sometimes my office is my home. Other times, a bar or a café. Still others, the nature of the work I do for my family doesn't really entail an "office" at all.

I mean smashing someone's nose in or lighting their car on fire doesn't really come with a casual Friday dress code or mandatory holiday party.

Today, since I *am* actually doing work-work, as opposed to hurting people or trashing their personal property, I'm at the family home on Central Park South. We lived here when we were kids, back before Mom died and our father moved us all to London—a city he always preferred to New York.

Since we've returned, the full-time occupancy has dropped. Ares and Neve are in their glass and steel loft over on the west side. I've got my place in Brooklyn, though I do keep a room at the main house. And Deimos is in London, obviously. Which leaves Callie, Kratos, and of course Ya-ya, who never left at all.

It's a *comically* large house for just three people. But it works for them. And I do love catching up on my work here, especially when I can set up shop outside, like today. Even if that work entails answering emails, which is arguably my least favorite thing in the world to do.

Who the fuck still even sends emails? I barely ever check mine. We all have smartphones. Why are we not just texting? Email is all just digital junk mail these days anyway.

But, as *I* am doing my least favorite activity, I'm also taking breaks roughly every two minutes to check my phone.

Like a complete. Fucking. Jackass.

Because, obviously, I'm compulsively looking for anything from Elsa.

Because, *also* obviously, I have somehow turned into one of those incredibly lame, simpering guys who checks his phone every ninety-eight seconds to see if the girl he likes has texted him.

It's all incredibly pathetic and uncool.

But it's been a quiet few day on the Elsa front, since the night I sent her the lingerie and the toys. I'm actually regretting sending those, because it seems to have shut her right the fuck up.

She went completely offline that night without really ending our text conversation, which is unusual for her. She gave me some bullshit excuse the next day about her sister needing her or something. But even after that, it's been a few days without much of anything besides the odd message here and there.

I can tell myself all I like that she's busy, and married to her job, and all that shit. Or that Crown and Black has a giant gala event for their high-roller clients tomorrow night, that's probably eating up a bunch of her time.

But still…

I glance at the phone for the umpteenth time.

Still nothing.

You fucking pathetic pussy.

"Well, now I get why you're never actually at the office."

I turn, nodding at Ares as he walks across the garden to where I'm sitting at the outdoor dining table. He drops into a chair across from me and drums his fingers on the top of the table.

"What can I say, Ares, I'm just livin' that vagabond life. Midtown, Brooklyn, Little Odessa, K-town. The world is my oyster. Who knows where I'll end up next?"

He smirks, shaking his head before his brow furrows.

"I need to ask you something."

"Shoot."

"You're not going to like it."

"Ruh-row, Shaggy."

He gives me his signature big brother Ares "stop fucking around" look. I shut my mouth.

"What's going on with you and Elsa?"

Shit.

I clear my throat. "Elaborate?"

"C'mon, man. Don't make me wade through the bullshit. I know you're seeing her."

"I'm not *seeing* her—"

"Hades..."

I scowl at his scolding tone. "And what if I am, anyway? It's none of your concern or business."

"Actually, it *literally* is. Because you know we've been trying to get her to come work for the family full-time. And because you're *you*, Hades..."

My lips curl.

"...and this is one woman I *cannot* have running off or losing her shit because you fuck her over or make promises you're never going to keep."

"Oh, *fuck off*, Ares."

"I'm *not* trying to be an asshole here, brother," he growls. "I'm really, really not. But even now, as our person at Crown and Black, she's an important part of our business, and you're—"

"*Fuck. You.*" I hiss. "You *know* why I'm the way I am."

Ares looks away, his jaw tight and his face grim.

"*I know*, man," he finally says quietly, turning back. He reaches across the table, gripping my shoulder firmly as he nods. "Look, I'm sorry. I'm not trying to imply that you're this—"

"Man-whore who's obviously just only ever thinking with his dick and who will obviously do anything, maybe ruin everything, just to get laid?"

"I didn't say that."

"You kind of did."

He sighs. "So, you're seeing her. Yeah?"

I look away. "It's complicated."

"Well, let me simplify it, then, since it's obvious neither of you have thought this through."

"Ares, so help me God, if you try and 'dad' me right now, I'll fucking snap."

"I'm not trying to *dad* anyone," he barks. "I'm trying to help you."

"Really? Is that what this is?"

He rolls his eyes. "Man, have you even thought about how badly this could blow up in her face? She's worked her ass off her entire life to get this position."

"And?"

"And she's in a professional relationship with our family. Are you even aware that you sleeping with her creates a *massive* ethics violation?"

"Yeah, but it's like jaywalking. No one enforces—"

"She could be *disbarred*, Hades. Or at the very least, if Taylor, Gabriel, or Alistair finds out, they could fire her. They'd almost *have to* fire her to cover their own asses legally."

I'm silent.

Fuck.

Admittedly, I didn't actually know that.

But it doesn't change a thing.

Not when she's under my fucking skin and haunting my every waking moment like a fucking addiction.

"Hades—"

"You know what, man?" I stand. "The office has been a real grind today. So I'm taking a lunch."

He exhales, shoving his fingers through his hair. "Look, I'm sorry. I'm just—"

"Do us both a favor and stay the absolute fuck out of my personal life. Case closed. Okay?"

He sucks on his teeth. But then he nods.

"Anything else we need to *chat* about?"

"Yeah, actually." He sighs. "But you're going to like it even less."

"Jesus Christ, now what?"

"Serj Mirzoyan's reached out with a personal ask. He floated the idea of you taking Vanya as your date to the Crown and Black gala tomorrow night."

I snort, rolling my eyes and looking away.

Then I realize he's serious.

"Wait, you're *not* fucking with me?"

"Nope. Look, I know you're not a fan of hers. But..."

I sigh. "But it's a request from Serj, and if he says jump and we ask how high, that puts us in a good position to close this deal before Gavan can muscle in on it."

Ares sighs. "Well…yeah."

I grit my teeth.

"*Fine*. I'm really leaving now—"

"He'd also like for you to come over today to meet with her, get re-acquainted…" He grimaces. "And formally ask his permission to take her to the Crown and Black thing."

"It's a fucking *gala*, not a wedding chapel."

He sighs again. "I know. And I don't enjoy asking you to do this. But…" he shrugs. "All Serj is asking for is for you to wine and dine his daughter a bit and play nice with him. I think it might help us. A lot, actually."

I grimace. "Fuck it. Fine."

Ares nods. "Thank you. Really. I appreciate it."

"Don't worry about it," I mutter before I turn back to him. "And you *did* enjoy asking me to do this, didn't you, asshole?"

He grins. "Maybe a little."

"Maybe go fuck yourself a little."

24

HADES

"Ahh, Mr. Drakos."

Serj Mirzoyan hauls himself to his feet from the couch in the office of his lavish Bronx mansion, grinning at me.

"Come, come. Please, sit."

The gruff-looking man in the suit who led me here from the front door nods at his boss, and closes the door to the office on his way out.

Serj is a big, bruiser type—the kind of guy who built his empire out of brutality and by chopping hands off his enemies. And it shows. He's got the cauliflower ears of a street fighter, the scarred face of a man who's gone to war a couple of times, and the wealth and power of a man who's not only won those wars but crushed his enemies.

All that said, he's extremely charming. At least, right now he is. I've only met him maybe once before, just in passing, so I have no idea. But I have the feeling I'm getting a little bit of a red carpet rolled out for me.

He strides over and takes my hand, giving it an almost ridiculously firm shake as he grins.

"A drink, yes?"

"That would be great, thank you, Mr. Mirzoyan."

"Please. My friends call me Serj."

"Are we friends, then?"

He glances over his shoulder at me from the bar cart. "I would very much like that, Mr. Drakos."

"Then it's just Hades, *Serj.*"

He chuckles, bringing me a glass of something clear, and I hide my smile. I can smell the anise from three feet away.

Yeah... If he's pouring traditional Greek ouzo for me, he's rolling out the red carpet. And I'm suddenly wondering if maybe Gavan's gotten bored of this ongoing battle over Serj's empire and has backed off. It would certainly explain Serj cuddling up to me.

He clinks his glass to mine.

"*Gëzuar.*"

"*Stin yit mas.*"

We drink, and he nods. "To a wonderful future, and to burying whatever bad blood there was between our families. It lies in the past, yes?"

Maybe Serj really is over the fact that my father killed his, something like thirty years ago. Maybe he's not. Either way, money talks.

And a hundred and fifty million fucking *yells.*

"I know things have dragged on perhaps a little longer than you would have liked with your family's purchase of my business. But I need to do what is best for my children and their future. This, I hope you can understand."

"You want to get the most money possible, of course." I grin. "Yes, I can completely understand that. Money doesn't buy happiness, but it sure covers up a lot of bullshit."

Serj chuckles, clinking his glass to mine. "Exactly. I was just telling my good friend—"

The door to the study bangs open loudly. When I turn, I cock a brow as I lay eyes on Melik, Serj's douchebag of a son.

"What the fuck is he doing here, Papa?"

I resist the urge to roll my eyes. I mean, yes, as I understand it, Serj's decision to sell his empire rather than pass it down to his kids hasn't gone over so well with either of them. But this isn't just Melik being pissed about that. He's *always* this much of a prick.

I know Melik and Vanya from Harvard—Melik was in my grade, and Vanya was two years younger. Their father is an immigrant with *lots* of money, so of course, he sent them to the flashiest, most prestigious school he could.

Vanya actually managed to graduate. Melik got kicked out for literally never going to class. And assaulting a professor. And driving his G-wagon into the side of an administration building while he was drunk. And selling coke. And...well, just basically being a trust fund douchebag pretending to be gangster.

He's somehow both a coward and a hothead, and Serj is wise to sell his empire rather than leave it to him. If he thinks his empire would last two weeks under Melik's guidance, he's being generous.

I mean the dude put out a rap album three years ago under the name "Pussy Slayer", without a shred of irony or satire involved. That tells you everything you need to know about Melik Mirzoyan right fucking there.

"*Hesht!*" Serj snaps at his son, glaring at him. "He is our guest, Melik."

"He's a fucking invader, is what he is." He pulls his contemptuous gaze to me. "You have no business in my home, *Drakos.*"

I smile politely. "How's the rap industry these days, Melik?"

He scowls. "The game is rigged. Thanks to the Jews."

Right. *Right.* There's also the fun little fact that Melik is a *raging* neo-Nazi fuckwad. So that's a nice cherry on top of the whole steaming pile of shit that he already is.

"We've talked about this, Melik," Serj chides his son. "The Drakos family has made a generous offer—"

"To pillage what is rightfully mine!" he spits. "Barbarians at the fucking gates—"

"*Melik!*"

Even I flinch at the booming sound of Serj dropping his "civilized rich guy with the big house" act and revealing the street-brawler hiding underneath.

"You will leave us," he snarls at his son. "*Now.*"

Melik glares at me, muttering something in Albanian before he whirls on his heel and storms out of the room.

Serj sighs heavily. "You have my sincere apologies, Hades."

"It's not a problem." I shrug. "I sometimes have that effect on people."

"He's upset about the direction I've chosen to go. Please, forgive him."

"Of course, Serj."

Fuck off, Melik.

"And he's angry about a girl. There was a marriage proposal recently concerning the daughter of a would-be ally that..." Serj's brow furrows." Well, is no longer favorable to a traditional man like my son."

"I'm sure there are plenty of other fish in the sea for a man like Melik."

The older Mirzoyan pointedly clears his throat. "Yes, well. Anyway, I wanted you to come here today, because I wanted to ask a favor of you."

He wants me to bring Vanya to this fucking gala tomorrow. I already know this. *He* already knows I know this. But Serj is so old school that we're going to do this whole "allow me the honor of taking your daughter to the dance" bullshit routine. Whatever.

"Anything I can do, Serj."

He nods. "The Crown and Black gala tomorrow evening. I do some business with Gabriel Black, and as such, I've received an invitation. Unfortunately, I have a work engagement. But it would break my daughter's heart not to go. She so loves these things."

I smile benignly, grinding my teeth on the inside.

"Would you do me the honor of taking her as your date? She'd be over the moon to walk in there on your arm, my friend."

In every other situation but this one, I would say no.

I somehow got through four years of Harvard almost perpetually drunk or fucked up on coke, which I don't touch anymore. There's *a lot* of those four years I don't remember as anything more than a haze.

But I remember Vanya.

Back then, the image I had of Vanya Mirzoyan was that of a fairly vapid, hard-partying trust fund mob-princess type. I sort of remember her trying to get with me a few times, and me saying no every time.

But I absolutely remember the time she cornered me, when I was too drunk to say no, even if every cell in my body was screaming it.

I don't get drunk out of my mind and have sex, because I fucking despise it. It brings back all of those dark memories from when I was younger.

I was beyond wasted the night Vanya shoved me into a dark bedroom at a party and tried to blow me. I was so drunk and so petrified by the flashbacks that I sort of lay back and just let it happen until I simply couldn't take it anymore. I finally bolted from the room, and we've never spoken since.

So, no, escorting her to a fucking gala isn't exactly high on my wish list.

But the other reason, for reasons I'm not sure I'm even ready to think about, is that Elsa will be there too. She'll be there, and she'll watch me walk in with some other woman.

And I have a feeling that's not going to go over very well.

I might be possessive as fuck, probably to a psycho degree. Frankly, I'm surprised hasn't scared her off yet. But she's got that streak too. I've seen it in her eyes when the subject of me with other women, or my past, has come up.

But I'm stuck. I can't actually say no to Serj. Because this "favor" is clearly part of our deal. And there's *way* too much money on the table for me to let my own shit get in the way of my family's success.

"I'd be honored to take her, Serj."

He beams widely, clapping me heartily on the shoulder.

"*Excellent*, my friend. Excellent. She's here right now, actually. Would you like to talk details about tomorrow? Maybe you could coordinate your tie to her dress or something. I don't know how these things work."

"Well, I'm sure she and I can speak on the phone—"

Nope. Serj marches right past me, flings open the door, and bellows.

"VANYA!"

He turns to smile at me. I hear the sound of heels clicking on marble floors as she approaches, and suddenly, Serj's daughter walks in, dark hair billowing around her like a villain's cloak. She gives me a polished, practiced smile.

"Hades. *So* good to see you again."

"Likewise," I mutter.

Serj beams. "Well, I'll let you two discuss. Hades, my thanks again."

I nod as he steps out and closes the door. Then, we're alone.

Vanya sighs, her shoulders relaxing a hair as she wanders over to the bar cart and pours herself a vodka.

"So, it looks like you're my date for tomorrow," she says dryly.

"Great," I growl.

She sighs, cocking her hip as she eyes me. "Look, I know you don't like me very much, Hades."

I snort. "I wonder why."

She shrugs. "I…actually *have* wondered that. I thought we got along okay back at school, you know? I've always assumed it's because I wouldn't fuck you."

I stare at her in disbelief, my jaw tight.

"Are you joking?"

"Nnn…o?"

I laugh coldly. "You have no idea why I might not be your biggest fan."

"I genuinely don't. But I also don't care that much, Hades, so it's okay. We can go to this dumb gala thing tomorrow because my father is insisting that I go—and I'm guessing he's holding your deal over your head to make *you* go as well. So, we can go, get drunk, not talk to each other, and call it a night. Sound good?"

The gall of this woman is unbelievable.

"You seriously don't remember what happened at that frat party at the Sigma house. Your freshman year, my junior one."

"Hades, that was like nine years ago. I really don't, sorry."

Anger begins to make my blood boil.

"It was a Halloween party. Your freshman year."

She looks at me like I've got two heads. "Hades—"

"You were wearing a Cleopatra costume, with a gold mask," I hiss. "I was drunk, Vanya. *Very* drunk. And you used that to—"

"Hades, I wasn't in the *country* on Halloween my freshman year of Harvard. My father paid for me and some girlfriends to fly to Ibiza."

My face darkens. "That's bullshit."

"It's…not?" She frowns. "Why would I lie about that? And what exactly do you think happened between us, anyway?"

"You really want to go there, Vanya?"

"I've already told you: I don't really care. But you seem to. Look, it's not like I actively *dislike* you, Hades," she shrugs. "We've just never run in the same circle. We didn't back then when I was a party girl…the only party girl at school who wouldn't screw you because I had some self-respect…and we don't now, either, trust me. So if you want to 'go there', please, by all means—"

"You found me so fucking drunk I could barely see straight, shoved me into a room, and tried to suck my dick even though I was telling you to fucking stop," I snap. "And don't give me that fucking 'a guy can't say no' bullshit," I hiss. "Because I fucking *did*."

Her brow worries, and her face pales a little.

"That happened to you?" she says quietly.

I glare at her.

"Hades," Vanya says gently, walking toward me. "I'm so sorry."

"I don't want your fucking apologies—"

"I was in *Ibiza*, Hades. I'm really, truly sorry that someone did that to you. It's awful." Her face darkens as she looks away. "I woke up to a guy trying to put his hand down my pants in the basement of a party once, my senior year." Her eyes raise to mine. "I mean, if you ever want to talk about it—"

My blood is roaring in my ears. "It was *you*. I know it was you, Vanya. You wore a Cleopatra—"

"Wait, Halloween my freshman year?" She frowns, trying to remember. "Cleopatra?"

Then she purses her lips.

"Whitney fucking Gerrard," she says quietly.

"Excuse me?"

"Whitney Gerrard. She was in my dorm freshman year. Dark hair, and her mother is Albanian, so we have a similar complexion." She blinks, shaking her head. "She wore a Cleopatra costume that Halloween. Definitely. And she told everyone you two were dating for like a month after. I remember distinctly, because she had these Polaroids of the two of you hugging at that party tacked up on her dorm door. You both looked pretty wasted."

The room blurs.

Fuck.

I'm vaguely aware of Vanya approaching. And of me flinching a little when she puts her hand on my arm, then relaxing.

"You wanna sit?"

I nod, letting her guide me to the couch.

"Here."

She hands me a glass of whiskey. I mumble a thanks and knock it back in one gulp.

"I'm so sorry, Hades. Oh my God, *fuck* Whitney. What an utter piece of shit."

I nod.

"Is that why you've never liked me?"

I glance over at her sitting next to me.

"Mostly." I smile wryly. "That, and I kind of always thought of you as this trust fund mob-princess brat."

She grins. "I mean, *I am* a trust fund mob-princess brat."

I chuckle.

"But I've accepted that. Melik is all bent out of shape about this deal. But, please…" she rolls her eyes. "I mean, he can't unclog a toilet without calling for help. There's no *chance* he could lead our father's empire. He's just power hungry. That's why he's pissed."

I frown. "I was under the impression both of you were upset about the sale."

She snorts. "*Me?* No. No, Hades, I just want the cash, not power, not an empire. I just want to spend the rest of my life on a beach somewhere, where women who look like Gal

Gadot dressed as Wonder Woman reapply my sunblock and keep my wine glass topped up."

She grins as heat creeps into her face.

"That was my awkward way of telling you I've realized I'm gay, by the way. Something my father refuses to acknowledge, hence you being my date for tomorrow."

"Yeah, getting rubdowns from Wonder Woman is kind of a giveaway."

She laughs, still a little embarrassed. I smile curiously.

"I didn't actually know that about you."

"No, you wouldn't. I'm fairly private about it."

"So why tell me?"

She shrugs. "Because you told me something I'm guessing you don't tell many people. It seemed fair."

Today is one hundred percent not going as I expected it would. And I'm very okay with that.

"I don't suppose I can sweeten the pot at all to get you to help me push this deal through?"

"You don't have to sweeten anything. I'm already pushing for it. And my dad—"

She breaks. And suddenly, she starts to cry.

Shit.

"Hey, I've got you."

I wrap a platonic arm around Vanya's shoulders, giving her support as she sniffs back the tears and dabs at her face.

"I'm so sorry, I don't know where that came from. I... I'm sorry."

"Don't be." I frown. "Are you okay?"

"I..." she looks down. "*No*, actually." She chokes out another sob as she raises red, puffy eyes to mine. "He's got cancer, Hades. My dad, I mean. He just found out recently that it's terminal."

I wince. "Jesus. I'm so fucking sorry, Vanya."

"Thanks," she sniffs. "I'm still trying to wrap my head around it. But...that's mainly why he's doing all this. He doesn't have a lot of time, Hades. I don't want the empire, and Melik would be a disaster if he got it. So that's why Dad's burying the past between our families and making this deal."

Christ. I kind of feel a little guilty now, knowing how much one of the properties we're about to purchase from Serj is actually going to be worth someday. But it is what it is. Vanya and her brother will get a massive payout. And he'll be dead anyway.

Vanya's face twists as she looks up at me. "I shouldn't have said that. Please—"

"I'm not going to use your dad being sick as a negotiating tactic, Vanya," I growl quietly.

Her lips twist. "The Russians would."

"Well, I won't. And neither will my brother."

"Thank you."

"Of course."

But thank you for confirming that Gavan is also after your father's empire.

25

ELSA

"You're not bringing anyone tonight?"

I'm in the research library at work—a gorgeous, glass-walled room with floor-to-ceiling bookshelves full of legal texts. I've been pouring over case studies until my eyes blur, but I push the work in front of me aside when Fumi enters.

"What?"

"To the gala. You're not bringing anyone?"

"Says who?"

She smirks, holding up the tablet in her hand. "Says the RSVP list."

"Oh." I shrug. "Nah. I was going to bring Nora, but she made plans with her friends instead and ditched me."

"Brutal."

I snicker. "I'll live. Are you bringing anyone?"

Fumi makes a very dry, very *Simpsons*-inspired *"ha-ha"* sound.

"I thought you were giving apps a try?"

"Oh, I was, for about thirty seconds. But as it turns out, men are awful. Breaking news, I know."

I make a face. "That bad?"

"The number of wieners I've been shown without asking to see them is a legitimately terrifying commentary on the state of the world. Like, who does that? Hi, what do you do for work? What do you like to eat? Anyway, here's a photo of my not-very-impressive worm of a dick. Can we fuck now?"

I snort out a laugh as she shakes her head in despair.

"Elsa, it's brutal out there, I'm telling you. I mean, I could kind of wrap my head around it if you had a *nice*-looking dick, right? I mean if you've got a supermodel cock? I mean, sure, probably still ask first. But if it's that nice? Yeah, maybe I'm down to take a peek, you know?"

I'm cracking up. First, because Fumi is fucking hilarious. And second, because laughing covers the sudden redness suffusing my face, since I'm now thinking very hard about the dick pictures Hades sent me the other day.

"But holy shit. Please spare me those badly-lit, blurry shots of your micro-dicks. And why the fuck is there *always* a toilet in the background? I mean if I'm taking pictures of my pussy, that shit is going to be glamour city, not taken in some fucking toilet. Like, have a little respect for your privates, right?"

I almost fall out of my chair laughing.

"Looks like your boyfriend is coming tonight…"

That knocks the laughter right out of me. I stiffen and stare at her.

"Excuse me?"

Fumi grins and sings his name at me. "Hades Drakos."

I sputter, quickly shaking my head. "He's *not* my boyfriend."

"Well, he's clearly *something*."

"Absolutely not. For fuck's sake, he's a *client*, Fumi."

"Yeah, I've got clients too, girl. Even a few that are almost as criminally hot as Hades. But *I'm* not the one getting dragged off to my office by any of them to get fucked silly for an hour in the middle of the workday."

My eyes widen and my face burns brighter than the sun.

"I—Fumi—" I swallow. "I did *not!* We had a meeting—"

"You do understand that I'm not a fucking idiot, right? Like, you know that?"

My lips press together tightly, my cheeks still tingling.

"Yeah," I mumble. "I know that."

"Cool. Just wanted to clear that up."

I give her a wry smile as I finally force myself to look her in the eye. Fumi arches her brows, sighing.

"So…not your boyfriend."

"No."

"But…"

"But. Nothing. He's my client, Fumi. That would be completely unethical."

"Uh-huh," she sighs dryly. "Sure."

"And I could get into heaps of trouble for it."

"Gotcha. Which is why you definitely are *not*"—she uses her fingers to make air quotes—"*hooking up* with Hades Drakos."

"Fumiii—"

"*Elsaaa.*"

I roll my eyes. She laughs, then sighs. "I'm not going to say a word, relax. Plus, trust me. There are *way* more egregious breaches of counsel-client *entanglements* going on in this place than you and Hades."

My jaw drops. "*Who?*"

She drags a finger across her lips. "Ah-ah-ah. Steel trap. I say nothing."

I grin.

"So: Hades."

I sigh. "Complicated. The actual dictionary definition of complicated."

"Well, he's certainly easy on the eyes."

I blush, and Fumi laughs.

"I'm just saying, if someone *had* to send me a dick pic, solicited or otherwise, and that person was Hades Drakos, I'm not sure I'd complain that much."

"You can say that again."

Shit. I did not just say that out loud.

Except I just did. Fuck.

Fumi giggles, waggling her brows at me. "Oh, it's like *that*, is it?"

I groan, burying my face in my hands. "I plead the fifth."

"Bullshit. How big are we talking here?"

"Oh my *God*, really?"

"Uh, yes?" She holds her hands out and moves them closer and further apart, like she's measuring. "This? Or this?"

"I am *not* talking about this with you."

"Which almost *always* means it's either tragically tiny or porn-star huge. And given the glazed look in your eyes after he left the other day, I'm gonna go with door number two on that one."

My face burns hotly as I shake my head at her. "You're a lunatic."

She laughs, dropping her eyes back to her tablet. Then her brow furrows.

"What?"

She purses her lips, still staring at the screen. "He's really not your boyfriend, right?"

"No. Definitely not."

"Okay, good. I don't have to murder him, then."

"And why would you have to do that?"

"Because he's got a plus one on his RSVP for tonight."

Something black and vengeful suddenly rises up inside of me, snarling. Something that rips through me with sharp claws and leaves me wanting to scream, or break something, or both.

"Oh?" I say thinly.

Fumi arches her brows. "Yeah. A Vanya Mirzoyan?"

"Oh. Cool."

I look away.

"No. Fuck that."

"Fumi, we're not a couple or anything—"

"Well, still. That's fucking bullshit. You need to make him sweat that he didn't bring you."

"What? No. I don't care."

"Sure, you don't."

I glare at her. But she does this ridiculous pout-face glare right back at me that always cracks me up, and I laugh.

"You're getting ready at my place tonight before the gala. We need to make sure you're all dressed up."

"I dress up!"

"Elsa, I love you. But your idea of dressing up makes it look like you've got a hot date with a deposition. We need you dressed up like you've got a hot date with *big porn star dick*."

I groan, blushing.

"We need you looking like Princess Diana in the revenge dress after Charles stuck his dick in Camilla."

"Fumi—"

"No negotiating, it's happening. Trust me… You're going to look *hot*."

———

She's not wrong.

Eight hours later, after I grudgingly submit to Fumi's "glow up" makeover, I walk into the gala feeling like a freaking movie star.

I even stop in the foyer of the Plaza Hotel, where the event is being held, to glance at myself in one of the floor-length, golden-edged mirrors. Heat tingles through my cheeks as I grin.

I mean *damn*, self.

There's a hint—maybe much, much more than a hint—of truth to what Fumi said earlier. I don't really ever dress up. At least, not like this. Not glamorously. But tonight, I'm wearing this stunning, cherry-red Alexander McQueen gown of Fumi's, which fits me perfectly and might be the most gorgeous dress I've ever worn.

Sleeveless, floor-length, with a high neck in front and scooping all the way down to the small of my back, with a slit all the way up to my thigh. I've got on matching red, towering heels, and Fumi spent about forty-five minutes turning my straw-straight hair into a flowing, wavy master-piece that tumbles past my shoulders.

I've literally never once dressed like this in my life. And honestly, I *really* like it.

Fumi took so much time getting me ready that she herself is arriving a little later. So for now I'm flying solo as I float through the doors into the main event hall where the gala is being held.

"My my *my*!"

I blush, turning as Taylor waltzes over, looking absolutely stunning in a cream white gown that belongs on a red carpet somewhere, or in a royal palace.

"I *love* this color on you!"

I grin bashfully. "Thanks. It's actually Fumi's."

"Well, it's freaking stunning on you. You should wear red more often."

"Thanks," I beam. "And oh my God, you look incredible, too."

Taylor waves a hand. "Meh. I usually hate these things. So does Gabriel. These are more Alistair's bag. But, you gotta smile for the cameras and kiss some rings here and there, right?"

"*Do* you?"

She laughs. "Well, when you make equity partner next year, you'll find out just how un-fun it really is at the top."

I blink. Taylor stiffens, making a face before she smiles awkwardly at me.

"I did just say that out loud, didn't I."

"I...you can totally take it back."

She grins. "You should probably pretend you didn't hear that. But...spoiler alert, we're fast tracking you. You're *crushing* it, Elsa. And with the yearly partnership review coming up in five months, the brothers and I are in full agreement: you should be bumped up to equity."

My eyes threaten to fall out of their sockets.

"Oh my *God*, Taylor! Thank you!"

She grins, hugging me before pulling back. "It's not charity. You've worked your ass off, Elsa. For us, and to get here in the first place. You've earned this."

I swallow, shaking with the adrenaline rush of it all. Equity partner. Like, *fuck*.

"I—*wow*. Taylor, thank you so—"

"Just..." she grins. "Really. Keep that on the down-low for now, okay?"

"For sure."

She grins, turning to snag two flutes of champagne from a passing tray and then passing me one.

"Cheers. To you, and to your long and fruitful career at Crown and Black."

I END up having two more glasses of champagne with Taylor. Because how do you say no when it's your boss, and when she's just told you you're getting the promotion of a lifetime, which, by the way, comes with about a four-hundred-percent pay bump.

Literally.

So by the time she gives me one last hug before going to make the rounds, I'm feeling *great*.

Which is to say, *drunk*.

Drunk enough that I flat out ignore Leo when he strides in with Gavan Tsarenko and glares at me from across the ball-room. Drunk enough that when he *does* manage to corner me and try and grab me by the wrist, I simply shrug him off and disappear into the crowd.

No. I'm feeling too good right now to deal with his shit or his threats. They'll still be there tomorrow, anyway.

Tonight, nothing can bring me down.

I make the rounds myself, talking to a few of our VIP clients. Alistair introduces me to a handsome older Scottish guy named Cormac Heath, a client of Crown and Black that I've never met before.

I'm stunned when I'm introduced to his wife, and realize she's the super famous modern artist Ella Veers. I mean, I've seen her work hanging in the Tate Modern in London, for God's sake. So when she tells me she loves my dress, it's sort of a surreal moment.

I drink more champagne, and enjoy the conversation, and focus on all the amazingly good things in my life.

But then, laughing at something Cormac just said, I turn, and my eyes lock onto Hades, looking *sinfully* hot in a black tux.

…With a pretty brunette hanging off his arm in a dress that makes mine look like rags.

I shoot daggers at him, even if he can't see me through the crowd. I've never seen Hades dressed up. His go-to seems to be dark jeans and white t-shirts, or occasionally, business casual slacks with a button up shirt, no tie.

But in a tux?

Sweet Jesus.

It's positively criminal. He looks like a fucking movie star at the premiere of his superhero action film. It's the chiseled jaw combined with the slightly longer dark hair and the piercing blue eyes. The high cheekbones. The broad, muscled shoulders.

The general "fuck the world" devil-may-care cavalier, cocky attitude that swirls around him like smoke.

Or maybe it's just the fact that when I look at Hades, I see pure *sin*. I see a man who has pushed me past every boundary I have and left me gasping there, aching for more.

Right this second, though, I see a man who has recently managed to occupy roughly eighty-five percent of my thoughts walking into the gala with *someone else*.

And it makes me furious, even though I know that's not fair, and that I have no right to feel this way.

But fuck that. I do.

I grab a flute of champagne off another tray. I'm still glaring at Hades and the little princess hanging off his arm as I drink, before I realize the glass went down *way* too fast.

Good thing there's more champagne at this thing.

A lot more.

I only hope it's enough to turn off the part of me that can't stop thinking about him.

26

HADES

HOLY. *Fuck.*

I spot Elsa the second I walk into the ballroom of the Plaza. She looks *amazing.* So amazing that I don't realize I've just stepped on Vanya's foot in her open-toed shoes until she winces and grabs my arm.

"Ouch!"

"Sorry," I mutter, still not looking away from Elsa.

She's talking to some older dude in a tux, along with a younger woman who'd *damn well* better be his wife, seeing as how Elsa is cracking up at whatever dumb joke he's just made.

"I'm going to go make the rounds." Vanya pats my arm before disentangling herself. "If you're going to the bar, could you get me a red wine? Something expensive and old."

I chuckle. "Such a trust fund brat."

"Yup," she grins before disappearing into the crowd.

I make my way to the bar, ignoring the suits who try and stop me for a chat. I order a whiskey and a glass of something red without getting specific. Please, it's the Crown and Black gala at the Plaza. *All* the wine is old and expensive.

A dark figure leans against the bar next to me. I turn, and suddenly find myself eye-to-eye with Gavan Tsarenko.

"Of all the gin joints, hmm?" he muses, a tight smile on his chiseled face.

"Funny, I wouldn't have pegged you for a *Casablanca* fan."

"I think it's fairly safe to assume we don't know a thing about one another, Hades."

I give him a flat smile in return. "Well, maybe that's for the best. If you'll excuse me—"

"Interesting move, by the way."

I shouldn't be talking to this motherfucker, for about a million reasons. The Albanian Acquisition. The bullshit he pulled with buying Jayden Robinson's warehouse. The fact that Donnie Petrakis' and Jason Eliades' sons were both jumped recently, and that Theo Petrakis had *Russian* vodka fucking poured on him before he was lit on goddamn fire.

Clearly , the appropriate, diplomatic response to Gavan right now is to walk the fuck away before we get into a full-blown shoot-out in the middle of the fucking Plaza.

Unfortunately, diplomacy has always been just about my very weakest suit.

Smiling thinly, I turn back to him. "And what move is that?"

"Bringing Vanya Mirzoyan as your date tonight."

"I think the really interesting move, *Gavan*," I growl, "is lighting kids on fucking fire."

His brow darkens. "Theo Petrakis. Yes. I heard about that."

"Oh, I'm *sure* you fucking did."

His jaw tightens. "You don't honestly believe I'm capable of that, do you?"

"Honestly?" I shrug. "I do, actually."

He snorts, shaking his head as he sips the Belvedere on the rocks the bartender's just poured him.

"I'm insulted."

"Well, maybe you could go strong arm another old-timer into selling you a warehouse you don't need to make yourself feel better."

His lips curl at the corners. "Who says I have no need for Mr. Robinson's warehouse?"

"You're playing games with the wrong family," I mutter.

"I wasn't aware any of this was a game at all, Hades. But if you're just having *fun*," he snarls, "perhaps you could stop sniffing around Serj Mirzoyan and save us both a lot of headaches."

"Gavan, I wouldn't dodge a speeding train if it would save you a headache."

He smiles. "Perhaps you were right, before."

"About?"

"Excusing yourself before we even started this conversation. I'm not sure we have anything to talk about if this is how we're going to behave."

"Aww, I'm all broken up."

He shakes his head, lifting his glass in a toast.

"Enjoy your evening, Hades."

"Eat a bag of dicks, Gavan."

I glare at his back as he disappears into the crowd. I'm about to slam back my whiskey and order five more when Vanya shoves herself against the bar next to me.

"What's the holdup on that wine?"

"Russian embargo."

She arches a brow. "Huh. I did see Leo Stavrin prowling about. I figured the one holding his leash was probably around here as well."

"Your father is talking to them, too, isn't he?" I lock eyes with her. "The Reznikov Bratva, I mean."

She nods. "He is."

I turn, stabbing my gaze through the crowd, looking for Gavan.

When I find him, my jaw clenches tight.

What the fuck.

Standing right next to the Russian prick is a familiar dash of white-blonde in a stunning red dress.

Elsa.

I want to tell myself to leave it alone. Gavan is a client of Taylor Crown's, and it makes perfect sense for he and Elsa to be speaking in passing at a Crown and Black function.

Except I fucking *hate* it. I hate how close he's standing to her. And I see fucking red, as red as her gown, when he leans down and murmurs something into her fucking ear.

"Hades?"

My face is dark as I glance back at Vanya.

"Sorry. What would I have to do to throw a stick into the spokes of that situation?"

She smirks. "Of my father talking with Gavan Tsarenko?"

"Yes. And by stick, I mean lit fucking dynamite."

She nods slowly. "There is something, actually."

"I'm all ears."

"The whole thing is coming from Melik. He's been hanging around with some of the guys in Leo Stavrin's crew for years, trying to look tough."

I frown. "He can't hang around your own family's crews to look tough?"

"Not when they all hate him and think he's a joke."

I snicker.

"Melik's the one that brought Leo to my father, and then Leo brought in Gavan. My dad's willing to hear the Russians out, and I'll be honest, I'm sure he'd be perfectly fine with this thing turning into a bidding war between your family and Gavan. But the thing is, he *hates* the Russians."

"Because of the turf war between your family and them about a year ago?"

She nods.

"From what I hear, Gavan's still got an ax to grind about that," I continue. "Your father's men killed his top captain."

"Yeah," she mutters. "That was after the Reznikovs shot up a car they thought my father was in. He wasn't, as it turned out, but the woman he'd been dating for almost six years, after our mom died, was. He was planning on marrying her."

"Shit. I'm sorry."

She nods. "Thanks. Samantha. I really liked her, actually."

"And yet your dad is still entertaining Gavan's proposals on this deal?"

Her mouth twists. "Money talks, I guess. But he still fucking hates the Russians."

"So how's he feel about Melik hanging out with them?"

"He's forbidden it, literally threatening to write Melik out of his will if he keeps doing it."

My brow arches.

Interesting.

"*So*, if you can prove to my father that Melik is still chummy with Leo's crew, Dad'll lose his shit. I don't *know* if it'll torpedo the talks with Gavan. But it might."

I nod, grinning. "Thank you."

"You're most welcome."

I grin as I clink my glass to hers. "You know what, Vanya? We should have cleared this up between us years ago."

She laughs.

"*Cleared what up?*"

I blink, whirling to see Elsa glaring absolute *death* at Vanya, her hip cocked aggressively and her face very, very flushed. Judging from the lopsided way she's holding the almost-empty champagne flute in her hand, I'm guessing she's drunk.

And looking stabby as *fuck* right now.

Vanya smiles cordially, unfazed.

"Oh, a misunderstanding between from *years* ago. Hi, I'm—"

"Trying to suck his dick?"

Yikes.

Vanya looks more shocked than offended. But suddenly, I realize I was way off when I thought Elsa was just "drunk."

She's shit-faced.

"Um, *okay...*" Vanya glances at me sideways before smiling at Elsa. "I'm sorry, you might be confusing me with someone else. Hades and I are old friends—"

"No, you're absolutely right."

Except it comes out more like *"ur absholuely righ"* with the way Elsa is slurring.

I clear my throat. "Elsa..."

"Yes, I must be confusing you with the *thousands* of women orbiting him trying to get a little piece of him."

"Believe me." Vanya's smile is getting less polite. "That is *not* the case here."

"No? You're pawing all over him with your tits half out just because?"

Elsa jolts as I grab her upper arm and drop my mouth to her ear.

"*Stop it,*" I growl. "*You're way out of line and I don't think you realize it.*"

She shakes my hand off. "What? I'm fine."

"You're not—"

"Well..." Elsa drawls at Vanya. "At least I can tell by the way you're walking that he hasn't fucked you yet tonight, so there's that..."

Jesus fucking Christ.

Vanya's brow knits. "Oh my God, wait, are you two—"

"It's just screwing," Elsa says venomously. "That's it. Nothing more. No big fucking deal."

Vanya smiles not-at-all-cordially-by-now at Elsa as her eyes dart to mine.

"I'm sorry, I think I'm getting dragged into the middle of something—"

"You know what, I'd say maybe he hasn't screwed you yet because you're so fucking boring," Elsa slurs. "But, maybe that's actually his type. So, get on up there, sister. Ride that coc—*hey!*"

"*Excuse us,*" I hiss to Vanya, who gives me an arched brow and a nod as I grab Elsa and drag her away and out a side door.

"Get your fucking hands off—"

She gasps as I slam her against the wall of the quiet hallway.

"You are *way* out of fucking line," I growl.

"*Aww,* I'm sowwy," she coos sarcastically. "Did I offend your piece of ass for the night?"

"No, you insulted the daughter of a somewhat dangerous crime lord, but yeah, no problem."

She scowls. "It's fine."

"You're wasted."

"Hades… Why are you wasting your time with me?"

Her voice suddenly goes soft and quiet, with a broken edge to it. Her throat bobs as she drags her big, hazel eyes up to mine, her face falling.

"Why are you even bothering with a mere mortal like me?"

She's always so full of piss and vinegar, and so full of this all-business confidence, that seeing her so vulnerable like this is almost heartbreaking.

"You could have any woman in this city, Hades."

"Elsa—"

"So why are you wasting your time with me?"

I shrug my jacket off, draping it around her shoulders.

"Come on. I'm taking you home."

WE'RE BARELY a block from the Plaza when movement in the passenger seat next to me catches my eye. I turn, and my jaw clenches.

Shit.

"Guess I got your attention."

Elsa's still beyond drunk. But besides "angry" and "sad", drunk Elsa is also apparently *horny* Elsa. Because right now, she's turned herself sideways in the passenger seat with the slit of her dress open, giving me a really good view of her white lace panties.

"Elsa, you're drunk."

"So?"

Her hand slides up her soft, creamy thigh. My eyes return to the road, but then dart right back to her. I watch as her fingers tease over the waistband of her panties, and then suddenly slide right into them.

Fuck.

I'm not going to mess around with a wasted woman, especially when I'm stone cold sober myself. But, I'm only human. And watching Elsa's face melt, her eyes rolling back as her finger strokes her pussy under her panties has me hard in seconds.

Very, very hard.

"Does this make you want me?"

"You know it does," I growl. "Elsa, that would make a *dead man* want you."

She blushes.

"But you don't have to do a thing to make me want you." My eyes lock with hers. "I always fucking want you."

She shivers, chewing on her lip and then moaning softly as her fingers tease at her pussy.

"Do you want me right now?"

"Yes."

Of course I do. I *always* do. Day and night. No matter what the fuck else I have going on or should be thinking about or concentrating on.

I'm watching the road, because traffic is getting dicey, when I suddenly feel a hand sliding over my thigh.

"Elsa—"

I groan as her soft fingers wrap around my bulging cock under my tux pants.

"You're so hard…"

"Elsa, stop it."

"Whyyy?"

"Because you're drunk."

She giggles. "I know."

I hear the click of her seatbelt undoing. Frowning, I glance at her.

"What the hell are you—"

She spins, on her knees in the passenger seat now as she leans over and starts trying to open my pants.

"Elsa, *stop*," I growl, braking sharply and switching lanes.

"You just watch the road," she purrs.

My jaw clenches as she somehow manages to get my zipper down, snaking her small hand inside to wrap around my hard, throbbing dick.

"And just let me—"

"Elsa, that's *enough*."

She stops. Her hand suddenly slips back out of my pants, her eyes, big and wounded, looking up at me as I glance sidelong at her.

"Am I not as hot as your other girls?"

Fucking hell.

"Elsa—"

"Or is it the virgin thing? Am I not doing it right? Because I can do it however you—"

"Maybe it's because, despite your best fucking efforts, I kind of like you! A lot!," I snap. "And I don't want to fuck around with you when I'm sober and you're supremely wasted!"

The car goes silent, me staring at the road with a white-knuckle grip on the wheel, Elsa still on her knees leaning over the middle console.

"You..." she flashes me a sloppy, drunken smile. "You like me?"

I sigh, shaking my head. "Yeah, well, don't let it go to your—"

She pukes.

Directly onto my crotch.

"...Head."

27

ELSA

Like shit, that's how.

Like absolute. Fucking. Shit. At least I'm feeling relatively sober after throwing up all the champagne in my stomach, and I'm feeling a *lot* better after the shower I just took. But still...not great.

Wrapped in a robe, I step out of my bathroom into the bedroom. When he asks the question, I raise my eyes to Hades, who is currently in my room, sitting on my bed.

Why not sitting in, say, in the living room? Because he's not wearing *pants,* seeing as I threw up all over them an hour and a half ago. And Hades sans pants is *not* something I'm exposing the fifteen-year-old who also lives in this apartment to.

I mean, he's not naked. But he might as well be. Currently, he's wearing black boxer briefs and an old, super-oversized t-shirt of mine. On him, though, the fucking thing looks like it

331

was painted on. It would be comical if it wasn't so outrageously sexy.

"Like a steaming pile of hot garbage," I mumble. "But better."

And a lot more sober.

Which is unfortunate. Because if I was drunk right now it would be infinitely easier to face him, after throwing up in his lap. Not to mention the verbal diarrhea before that, not to mention whatever horrific things I blurted at that woman he was there with.

My brow furrows as I look at the floor.

"Hades, I—"

"Don't."

"Don't what?"

"You were about to apologize. Don't."

My throat bobs as my eyes lift to his. "It's pretty embarrassing."

"Don't sweat it. It could have been worse."

My mouth twists. "Exactly *how* could throwing up on you have been worse?"

He smirks. "You could have had my cock in your mouth when your fifteen thousand glasses of champagne came back up."

I blush fiercely. "I…yeah. Well, thank you for not letting me make a fool of myself while drunk."

"Oh, you did a solid enough job of that all by yourself."

I groan. "I mean the way I was acting in the car. Not all guys would have stopped me from...yeah."

"I'm not most guys."

"No shit."

I blush as the acknowledgement pops out of me, my face heating as I turn away.

"I have to apologize to that woman you were with for saying all of those horrible things to her."

He shrugs. "She'll get over it. We've all been there."

"Yeah, well, that was..." I shake my head. "Pretty bad. I was way, *way* out of line, and I don't know how—"

"If you seeing me with her made you feel even a *fraction* of how I'd feel seeing you with another man, you don't have to explain shit to me," he hisses quietly. "But to clarify, Vanya Mirzoyan and I are only friends. And barely that."

I shake my head. "That's none of my—"

"Yes, it is."

My eyes snap to his. "No, it's *not*. Who you choose to—"

"I'm not interested in screwing around with anyone else, Elsa."

My face heats, my teeth clamping down on my bottom lip.

"Oh." I clear my throat. "Have you...I mean, since we've been..." I whirl away to walk over to the window, unable to meet his eyes. "Wow, okay, please forget *any* of that just came out of my—"

"No."

I shiver at the low growl in his voice, turning to glance over my shoulder at him, sprawled against my headboard in boxers and a tight t-shirt, looking like original sin.

"No, I haven't. And for the sake of them continuing to breathe and remain alive, there had better not have been any other men."

There's a lethality to his tone that simultaneously scares me and turns me right the fuck on. I suck on my teeth as I turn to him.

"There haven't been," I say quietly. "Other guys, I mean. You're…" I press my lips together. "You're it."

Something savage, primal, and triumphant gleams in his eyes.

"Why hadn't you, before me?" he asks, turning and letting his gaze pierce into me.

"How did I get to twenty-six without screwing anyone?"

His jaw grinds. "Yeah. I mean, I'm not judging, but you're gorgeous, smart, successful…"

I shrug. "A boy I was sort of dating in high school was really aggressively pushy about us 'taking things to the next level'. And it just totally turned me off. Then as I got older, casual sex never really interested me, and I never had the time for relationships, not with my job and my life. That, and most men are awful, *especially* if you're—how did you put it?— 'gorgeous, smart, and successful'." My brow knits again. "And then you hit a certain age where you *still* haven't done anything, and by then it's become an issue. It's either a deal-breaker when you meet someone. Or it's the opposite. They fetishize it."

His jaw tightens, like merely mentioning a hypothetical scenario of me meeting and dating another man has his fury rising. I can see the violence he's feeling toward men who don't even exist written so clearly across his face that it has my pulse tingling like a flame under my skin.

"The last time I actually tried dating was almost four years ago. I went on a couple of dates—"

"Define *a couple of dates*," Hades rasps darkly, his blue eyes instantly turning stormy and vicious.

"Oh, strictly anal and gang bangs," I shrug with a grin, obviously joking.

...Or not so obviously, given the way Hades suddenly looks like he's planning summary executions in his head.

"I...that's a joke?"

"I think I was clear before how I felt when it comes to you joking about things like that."

I swallow, shivering with heat.

"Okay. For real. It was dinner out, three times. Except it turned out he was the kind of guy who fetishizes virginity. Like, *that's* what he was interested in. Not in me as a person, not in hearing about my career or other parts of my life in any capacity. Just in my worth as determined by whether or not I'd slept with anyone before. It was dehumanizing and gross. After a few dates, I told him it wasn't going to work out, and he proceeded to stalk me for three years—Nora, too —until I got a restraining order. Then I moved continents."

Pure, malevolent, *rage* explodes behind Hades' face.

"*Name*," he snarls darkly.

335

"What?"

"Give me his fucking *name*."

My face heats as I shake my head. "It doesn't matter. It's over and done with. I don't think a public execution is needed to protect my honor, Hades."

"It can't hurt."

I smile, shaking my head again. "I'd just like to forget about it, honestly."

I turn to take a seat. But the reading chair in the corner of my room is currently occupied by a massive stack of legal documents and some folded clothes. And my *bed* is currently occupied by a reclining, nearly-naked, Greek god.

And this is a tough choice because...?

Because I'm embarrassed about what happened tonight, obviously. But also, I'm scared what it says about me that all I want to do is slide onto that bed next to him.

Into his arms, preferably.

But this is only supposed to be fun. It's supposed to be wild, unhinged, no-holds-barred sex, nothing more. And snuggling in bed together after divulging a dark secret about myself seems like it crosses a line from "just sex" into something more than that.

"I'm not going to tackle you if you want to sit on the bed."

I blush vividly—both at his mind-reader ways, and the slight disappointment I feel when he says it. But just the same, I nod, smiling as I walk over to sit on the edge of the bed. It feels forced and awkward. So a second later, I move back to sit up against the headboard next to him.

I sigh, my mouth twisting. "I really am sorry I was such a bitch to that woman tonight. I just..." I shake my head, sighing. "It's just that this is all so new to me. Seeing you, I mean —" I blush. "I mean, not that we're *seeing* each other seeing each other. But...I mean, I...you—"

"Elsa."

I shiver when his hand drops to mine, taking it in his much bigger one and squeezing.

"This is new to me, too."

I scoff. "What, coming home with a girl and not getting laid?"

"Coming home with a girl when I've already come home with her before."

My brow knits. "Hmm?"

"I don't do repeats," he says quietly. "Ever. I've never once been with someone, or gone out with someone, and then done it again."

On the one hand, thinking about Hades going home with *anyone*, even once, makes me feel homicidal. And that alone is something I should probably unpack with the help of a professional. But also...hang on, *what*?

"And I *like* that I was your first..."

I tense.

He feels it.

"...*not* because of any fetish regarding your fucking virginity. But because it saves me from having to go find, castrate and murder anyone else who's ever touched you before."

I blush, grinning as I bite my lip.

"Why *did* you kiss me that night?" Hades suddenly growls.

My pulse quickens as he turns to me.

"I mean you just said you weren't interested in casual sex. But you picked *me* of all people, in a fucking sex club, to finally lose your virginity to, at twenty-six."

I nod. "And?"

"And I think I fucking deserve to know why."

He does. But I can't tell him. Part of me—actually quite a lot of me—*wants* to tell him about all of that. About Leo, and the pressure he was putting on me, and the threats. About how I went to that club that night with every intention of ripping the band-aid off and breaking my father's hold on me.

But I can't. Because I'm scared that if I do, he'll get up from this bed, walk out the door, and never come back.

"I..." A deep breath. "I guess I finally decided I wanted to. I was going to Venom with my boss for a client meeting anyway."

"With Dante?" he growls. "That's what you were talking about earlier that day at the meeting?"

I nod. "Except when we got there, I wasn't needed for it after all."

"And a sex club where everyone wears masks and doesn't use names is a pretty solid place to go if you're in the market to lose your virginity to a stranger but have a fear of that stranger bumping into you on the street afterward and forcing you to face your sins."

Mother. *Fucker*. He's good at this—reading my mind, peering inside my soul. Seeing my thoughts, however hidden I keep them.

"Yeah, basically."

He sighs. "And you picked me because of my…reputation."

My lips twist as I nod. "Yeah. Sorry. I figured if nothing else you'd know what you were doing."

He shrugs and sighs. Neither of us says anything for a minute as we sit there on the bed, holding hands. When I glance at him, I see that his jaw is clenched tight. Then he looks away.

"I don't do what I do because I'm this emotionally stunted sex addict that everyone seems to think I am, you know." His jaw ticks. "I was thirteen when I lost my virginity."

I wince. "Jesus, Hades…"

"My brother, Atlas, used to really beat on me, hard. I mean, he used to beat up on all of the brothers, but I was the only one stupid enough not to stay down, so he took a special interest in making my life hell. When I was thirteen, he decided the reason I was 'a pussy' and 'a threat to his author-ity' was that I hadn't been with a girl yet."

His face darkens, still turned away from me.

"He got me drunk, took me to a brothel, shoved me into a room with a woman twice my age, and said he wouldn't let either of us out until we were done. Until I was 'cured'."

My heart breaks for him. My very soul hurts at the idea of a young Hades—Jesus, younger even than Nora—being forced to do that.

"I'm so sorry," I say quietly. My hand squeezes his, twisting as our fingers entwine.

He just nods.

"That's why I don't like being fucked up or drunk when I'm being intimate. I mean, a drink or two is okay, but…"

We sit there for another minute in silence, just holding hands, allowing the openness of everything we've just shared with each other to settle as it will.

"For what it's worth," he finally says quietly, turning to me, "it wasn't easy."

"What wasn't?"

"Resisting you in the car tonight."

Heat blooms across my face and down my chest under the robe—which, I'm suddenly hyper aware, is the only thing I'm wearing.

In a bed.

With Hades.

I swallow as I turn to glance up at him. "Because I was drunk…?"

He nods, his jaw clenched tight and his eyes smoldering with ice-blue flame, as if he can barely restrain himself from touching me or doing so much more than that.

"I… I'm not drunk anymore—"

My words melt away to a whimper as he turns, grabs my face, and crushes his mouth to mine. His tongue pushes past my lips, tangling with mine as I moan into his lips and slide onto his lap.

The comically small t-shirt he's wearing is on my floor in a split second. And I'm shuddering and moaning as he pushes the robe off my shoulders. His fierce gaze slides over me slowly, drinking in every naked detail of me in the low light of the bedroom. I gasp as his mouth drops to my breasts, his teeth grazing over a nipple before he bites down.

Fuck.

I cry out, my back arching as he ruthlessly bites and sucks first one nipple and then the other, turning my core molten as I grind against the thick, hard bulge in his boxers. Hades growls, pushing me back as if to pin me to the bed. But suddenly, I'm shoving him back against the headboard, turning the tables on him as I shake my head.

"Uh-uh."

I kiss him deeply. Then, pulling away, I let my mouth trail first down his jaw, then his neck, relishing the way his muscles tense and coil under the touch of my lips. I move lower and lower, down over his abs, then even lower still.

"What exactly do you think you're doing, kitten?"

I blush as my eyes drag up to his, my fingers slipping into the waist of his boxers. "Finishing what I started earlier."

I peel the elastic down, and then whimper when his huge cock springs free, fully erect, slapping heavily against his abs.

Holy shit.

It takes my breath away every single time I see it. And just like every other time, the incredulity that this freaking thing actually *fits* inside me is both startling and outrageously sexy.

I keep my eyes on his as I reach for him, curling my fingers around his girth before lowering my mouth to the swollen head. I stroke him up and down, having to use both hands as I kneel between his legs.

My tongue drags over and around the crown, and the way Hades groans so deeply, the way his abs clench so tightly as his hips raise toward me, sends a pulse rippling through my core. I moan, licking him again, dragging my tongue down to his balls before lapping all the way back up to the top.

My lips part, and when I take him inside my mouth, Hades hisses in pleasure.

"*Just* like that," he growls. I shudder with electricity as his hand slides into my hair and holds it in his fist. "Such a good little kitten."

I moan, swallowing him deeper into the back of my throat. Hades groans in pleasure, fisting my hair as I bob my mouth up and down, tasting the salty sweetness of his precum on my tongue.

I go faster, and he groans deeply. Then I slow down, sensually making a big show of dragging my wet tongue around his head until it's slick and glistening with my spit. I suck the head between my lips, teasing the slit with the very tip of my tongue before I pull away and lock eyes with him.

"Show me how you like it," I purr softly.

Hades groans, his teeth flashing.

"I can get rough, kitten," he growls.

Heat explodes through me.

"*Good.*"

His fist tightens in my hair, pulling hard enough to make me flinch, but also hard enough for pure desire and heat to flood my core, turning my thighs slick with need.

"Are you going to be a good girl for me?"

I whimper and nod eagerly.

"Let's find out just how good you can be."

My eyes bulge as he suddenly rams his cock deep. I choke, but I force myself to open my throat wider, taking more of him. My eyes water, but the burning need and throbbing ache for him only grows hotter and fiercer as he gets rougher.

Hades hisses as his fist holding my hair guides my head up and down his throbbing, hard, glistening, wet cock. The lewd wet *gluck* sounds of his cock fucking my mouth has me more turned on and wetter than I've ever been, and I start to moan as I squeeze my legs together.

My mouth bobs faster as I swallow his cock deeper. Spit runs down his shaft as I stroke it, dripping onto his heavy balls as his thighs tighten and his abs ripple.

Our eyes lock as I swallow him deep, opening my throat all the way for his big dick as pure lust roars in his eyes, thrusting in and out.

"Come in my mouth, daddy."

I don't know why I say it. Perhaps a hidden kink I didn't know I had, or one he's brought out in me. Maybe from some porn I watched. Who the hell knows. But it just tumbles out, and when it does, suddenly *I'm* the one being teased and pushed to the edge. Saying it out loud has me so fucking wet, I could come right now just from touching my clit.

And Hades? For him, saying those words out loud is like pulling a trigger. His eyes flash, his jaw grinding viciously. He snarls as he grabs my hair in both his hands, his abs flexing as he thrusts hard up into my mouth, until he's fucking it as if it's my pussy riding his cock.

Our eyes lock. My world blurs.

"*Please come in my mouth, daddy,*" I blurt between thrusts.

And suddenly, with a groan, he's burying his cock deep in my mouth and exploding across my tongue.

I moan, greedily swallowing the thick salty-sweet ropes of his cum as he floods my mouth. But there's too much, and I can't do it fast enough. Whimpering, I pull back, stroking him fast as my tongue dances over his crown. I can feel his cum, hot and sticky as it spills out onto my mouth and my chin, dripping lewdly down my cheeks as I get it all over me.

When I'm done, I'm actually stunned at my own behavior.

What the *fuck* just came over me? It's like I couldn't get enough of his dick—like I was cock-drunk.

I blush fiercely as I look up at him, half expecting shock or a weird look in his eyes.

Instead, I just see pure. Fucking. Need.

All over his face. In his clenched jaw. In the way his cock is still rock hard in my hands.

In the way he looks at me like he wants to devour me.

And before I know what's happening, I'm gasping and my eyes are starting from my head as Hades throws me down on the bed, wrapping a hand around my throat and moving between my legs. I whimper as he lifts my ankles and throws them over his shoulders. He lines his throbbing cock up, easing it between my swollen lips as our eyes lock.

I blush, feeling his cum starting to dry on my skin. "Hang on, let me—"

I cry out, arching off the bed in pleasure when he thrusts every single inch deep into me.

"*Uh-uh*, kitten," he growls, his muscles rippling and his eyes blazing as he grabs my hips, my ankles still over his powerful shoulders as he starts to fuck me hard. "I want to watch you come on my dick with my cum all over your face like a good girl."

He slams into me, and my world explodes. The angle is so fucking perfect he's hitting places inside of me I didn't even know were there, and it feels like I'm drowning in him. I reach back, clawing at the headboard for dear life as Hades impales me on his cock over and over, letting me feel every thick, hard, swollen inch of him as he fucks me like he's trying to kill me.

He reaches out, wrapping a hand around my throat and squeezing just enough to send me into outer space as his cock rams into me over and over. The edges of my vision darken, and my sanity blurs. My eyes roll back, my face crumpling before I force my gaze to lock with his.

When I do, the dark, smoldering fire in his eyes utterly consumes me as he completely dominates my body. The pressure swells as my skin flickers with sensual fire. My core tightens and my legs start to shake, until suddenly, there's no stopping it.

"*Come on my fucking cock, kitten,*" Hades rasps, his eyes locked with mine. "*Come for daddy.*"

Holy. Fucking. *FUCK.*

When I come, it hits me like a bomb detonating, and everything goes white. I'm barely aware of his hand covering my mouth to muffle my cries of pleasure as I explode for him. The waves come faster and harder, growing more and more powerful as I come a second time, then a third as he keeps fucking me relentlessly.

Suddenly, he's leaning over me and slamming his mouth to mine, swallowing my screams of pleasure as he groans into my lips. His entire body tenses up as his cock swells even bigger inside of me, pulsing as his cum spills deep.

I'm fairly certain I'm dead. Or at least, not in reality anymore. I'm floating in the ether somewhere, barely aware of my own existence as I feel his body cocooning around me, his lips and teeth nibbling at my neck.

What. The. *Fuck.* Was. That.

That wasn't sex. That was a religious experience. That was nirvana. A brush with a higher power.

That was *insane.*

I'm flushed, slick with sweat, and still trembling when I can finally open my eyes. Hades is still poised right above me, his eyes locked on mine.

…and I'm fairly certain we've just left "causal sex" somewhere in the dust.

"What the *fuck* did you just do to me—"

I jolt, gasping and whipping my gaze to the bedroom door when I hear the pounding against it.

"Are you fucking *done* yet?! Or am I going to have to go for a walk!?"

Holy *shoot me now in the fucking head.*

It's my fucking *sister.*

I cringe as Hades grins devilishly at me.

"I'm so sorry, Nora!!" I blurt, my face filling with heat. "The TV was up too loud and—"

"Yeah, because I'm a fucking *idiot*, Elsa!" she yells through the door. "So? Am I going walking or not!?"

"You're not going for a walk at…" I glance at the clock and cringe. "One-thirty in the morning!"

"Then enough already!!"

When her bedroom door slams, I groan and bury my face in my hands. Hades chuckles, gently sliding from between my legs and moving off the bed. A second later, he's back, and I gasp as I feel something warm and wet between my legs.

A washcloth.

The lunatic, chaotic god of the underworld is *cleaning me* after sex.

What is even happening.

"Hades…"

"Shh," he commands with a finger to his lips. "We don't want to wake the sleeping dragon again."

I groan, blushing vividly. But I lie there, letting him clean between my legs, then wipe my face with a second cloth. When he's done, he clears his throat as he sits on the edge of the bed.

"I should go," he growls quietly.

"You don't have to." It just blurts out of me. "I mean, I know we're just—"

"I'd love to."

Heat tingles in my face.

"To?"

"Stay."

28

HADES

This is more.

More than I was looking for or expecting. More than I've ever felt I've deserved. More than I've ever wanted.

More...everything.

That, by the way, is a good thing.

In the darkness of the room, with just the lights of the city stealing in around the edges of the curtains, I watch Elsa as she sleeps next to me.

This is a first.

I've never slept—like actual *slept*-slept—with a woman before. I guess in the most technical sense, I still haven't, given that I'm awake and watching her. But I'm about to close my eyes and pass out, and when I do, it'll be the first time I spend the night with anyone.

I'm strangely okay with that. Actually, I'm a whole fucking lot more than okay with that. If I wasn't, I'd already be out the door and gone. But leaving her and her bed right now is the last thing I want to do.

Which is a goddamn *mind fuck*.

I've seen buttoned-up, stick-up-her-ass, tense, business Elsa. I've seen the other end of the spectrum, too, when she's shattering for me, clawing at my skin, and squeezing my cock tight with her sweet little cunt.

This is a new side I've never seen before: "at peace" Elsa. I drop my eyes to the woman lying asleep next to me, and my lips curl as I shake my head.

"What makes you so special?" I murmur, my eyes sliding over her bare shoulder as I tuck a strand of white-blonde hair behind her ear.

I already know what it is that makes her different. I've spent my entire adult life losing myself in strangers. Not to find anything out about myself, but to *hide* from myself. It was never because of a desire for pleasure and escape.

Rather, it was a need for the obliteration that meaningless sex with numberless strangers brought me. And that's the part that my family's always gotten so wrong with their jokes about my personal life.

I'm not a sex addict. I've just been trying for the last sixteen years to escape the memory of a room that smelled like chemicals, a woman who tasted like cigarettes and regret, and a brother who *did not care*. And the blank, black escape of giving small pieces of myself to people who didn't give a fuck about me as a human was always the easiest and fastest way for me to do that, even if it was only a temporary relief.

But I think I just found a better one. Except it's not an escape at all.

It's a cure.

She murmurs, stirring in her sleep only enough to curl her body back against mine as I slide in behind her.

My lips brush her shoulder. My arm encircles her.

Then sleep pulls me under.

When I wake to find an empty bed, instantly, my jaw tightens. The exhilaration of last night, while I watched her sleep and realized I didn't have to run from my demons anymore, breaks off like a choked breath.

Until I hear footsteps. Until her bedroom door swings open, and a panting, sweating Elsa wearing running clothes comes bouncing in.

She grins, pulling the headphones out of her ear as her eyes land on mine.

"You're awake."

I glance at the clock and groan. I am *not* a morning person.

"It's five-fucking-forty. Why are *you*? I thought you'd be hungover."

She giggles, shrugging. "I had Gatorade. I like to get a run in before I get ready for the day."

"Type A much?"

Elsa grins. "There's coffee in the kitchen if you want."

"Is there a kid sister in there, too? Because my pants are still in you dryer."

Elsa laughs. "She's on her way to dance class, actually. Help yourself. I'll be in the shower."

She steps into the bathroom, closing, but not latching, the door behind her. When I hear the water start to run, my cock thickens against my thigh.

I slide out of bed, but don't go to the kitchen. I walk into the bathroom, which is already filling with steam. Elsa's running clothes are discarded in a heap on the floor. Through the steam, I can see her naked body under the spray of the shower.

Coffee sounds good.

I can think of something that sounds much fucking better, though.

She gasps when I open the glass door and step in behind her. She whimpers when my lips crush to hers.

Then she moans when I pin her to shower wall and guide my cock between her legs.

I'm not a morning person.

But I'm pretty sure she could turn me into one.

THERE'S one thing bothering me about last night. I didn't bring it up with her at the time, because I was having *way* too good a time with her.

But now, I would very much like to know why Elsa looked so fucking cornered and scared while she was talking to Gavan Tsarenko.

And I'm about to find out.

A blonde woman glances up at me as I step into the lobby of the Russian bathhouse on 78th.

"dobryy den'. Imya uchetnoy zapisi?"

"Good afternoon," I answer, tapping into the extremely limited Russian I have. "No, I don't have an account."

She smiles. "You are here to see someone then, sir?" she replies in heavily accented English. "We are members only, I am afraid."

"Yes, I'm here as a guest of Pascha Andreev. I don't believe he's here yet, though."

Or will ever be again.

She taps something on her computer, and then smiles at me. "Ahh, of course, sir. If you'd like to wait for him in the lounge—"

"I'd love to unwind for a bit and just meet him in the steam room, if I could?"

This place is ground fucking zero for Russian Bratva business. It was a gamble whether or not Pascha had a membership here. But luckily, apparently he does. Or, did. Or…whatever.

The woman at the desk smiles. "Not a problem, sir. If you'd like to follow the hallway past these doors, your second right will be the locker room, which will lead to the rest of the facilities."

"Thank you."

"You've got bigger balls than I would have guessed, Drakos."

I take a seat on one of the tile benches in the giant steam room. Across from me, half-obscured by clouds of fog with a towel wrapped around his waist the same as me, a shirtless, tattooed Gavan gives me a pointed look.

I shrug. "If that's your way of asking me to take the towel off…"

He smirks, but his eyes stay lethally riveted on me.

"I wasn't aware you were a member."

"I've been thinking about joining, so I asked for a tour. So far I'm impressed."

He inhales deeply, rubbing his hand over his jaw.

"I own this place, in case you didn't know."

"Fantastic. Seems like that might take care of the sponsorship require—"

"What the fuck do you *want*," Gavan growls. "Because I come here not to be pestered by anyone, and for the silence." He glares at me. "I *do* love my silence, Hades."

I spread my arms. "Fine. Cards on the table. What do you want with Serj Mirzoyan?"

Gavan smirks. "I think it's obvious we want the same thing from Serj. But I also don't think we're *really* talking about the Albanians right now, are we?"

My mouth thins. "Who the fuck *is* she to you?"

He smirks. "Elsa?"

I want to knock his fucking teeth in for even saying her name. But I restrain myself.

"*Yes*," I hiss.

Gavan shakes his head. "As much as I'd enjoy fucking with you on this, she's no one to me. She's a lawyer who happens to work for the firm that I use for most of my legal needs."

"Then what the fuck do you want with her?"

"Me? I don't want a *thing* from Ms. Guin, actually."

"Bullshit. Your guy Leo—"

"*Perhaps*," Gavan hisses quietly, "you should find *Leo* when *he's* taking a fucking steam bath and ask him then. Or perhaps Pascha Andreev, who has so mysteriously vanished." His mouth twists into a thin smile. "Though I'm extremely curious to find out what it is that's stopping you from asking *her* directly."

"Careful," I growl.

Gavan pulls his towel away just enough to show me the knife in a sheath strapped to his bare, inked thigh.

"Believe me, I'm always careful, Hades." He flips the towel back down. "And I'm also out of fucking patience and answers."

I'm only half sure I believe what he just said regarding Elsa. I can also read him well enough to see I'm not going to get anything else from him. But that was only half the point.

The other half was to let him know in no uncertain terms that if he wants anything with Elsa, or even wants to speak to her again, it's going to be through *me*.

I start to walk out of the steam room.

"Hades."

I glance back to see Gavan watching me intently.

"This stunt you pulled today is amusing all of *once*. I can appreciate your balls. But don't mistake amusement for an invitation. We're not friends, Hades. Nor are we business partners. And we never will be."

"Does that make us enemies, then?"

He smirks. "If this happens again, I can promise you, you'll find out quickly enough."

"TOP OF THE MORNING, god of Hell."

Cillian nods, stepping aside and ushering me into his office. He's still working out of his late half-brother's office at the Kildare family brownstone on the Upper East Side, though his penthouse apartment is back in Brooklyn—not that far from my place, actually.

But no one meets him there. I got to check out the ridiculously cool penthouse built into the top of an old clocktower overlooking the Williamsburg and Manhattan bridges all of once, and that was before he met Una. Since then, to my knowledge, no one's been invited over.

I guess drinking each other's blood and fucking on pentagrams or whatever the hell those two get up to demands privacy.

So, yeah, today it's the brownstone where I'm meeting him. The psychotic, green-eyed Irishman looks me over curiously as we sit on two couches facing each other.

"To what do I owe the unexpected visit?"

I shrug. "Meh. I was in the neighborhood."

Cillian doesn't say anything. He just levels that typical slightly-unhinged look of his at me. Which, even if we're friends now, still has the ability to completely freak me the fuck out sometimes.

I exhale through closed lips.

"Actually, I need a guy."

"You'll need to be more specific."

"A guy who can look into people."

Cillian's brow arches. "All right. Friend or foe?"

"Friend. But it's complicated."

"And…blonde?"

I glare at him, my jaw tightening.

"Is there something you'd like to say to me, Cillian?"

He tilts his head thoughtfully, sinking back into the couch. "I'd like to remind you that I'm *very* good at reading people. But to answer your question, yes, I have someone. His name is Oren Frey, and he's good."

"How good."

"*Very.* He's arguably the best. If there's something to be found, he'll find it. The man's a bloodhound."

I nod. "And what does he need to start?"

"Money, and a name."

"Good. Can you send me his—"

"You're *sure* you want to go down this road, Hades?"

JAGGER COLE

Cillian's hand reaches automatically for his pocket before he stops himself, a gritted snarl on his lips. He's recently quit smoking. Which is great for his health, and pretty terrible for the health of just about everyone around him who isn't Una.

"I just want some...inconsistencies cleared up."

"Sometimes it's best not to go looking for monsters, or to ask questions you don't want the answers to. I need to ask you one last time: have you truly thought this through?"

Not really. But I need to know. I *have* to know what the connection is between Elsa and the Bratva. It might not actually involve Gavan at all. But it definitely involves Leo.

And I'm tired of wondering if I'm going crazy.

"Well?"

Cillian eyes me one last time before he shrugs. "If you insist."

He pulls out his phone, and a second later, mine dings with a shared contact.

"Thank—"

"People bury their ghosts and their skeletons for a *reason*, Hades," he growls. "And in my storied and fairly blood-soaked experience, I've found it's best to leave them where they are."

29

ELSA

HADES

you still haven't worn my presents. I'm
beginning to feel insulted

MY FACE BURNS HOTLY when I read his text.

ME

Who says I haven't worn them?

It's really quite disturbing how comfortable I've gotten playing with fire when it comes to Hades. How much I enjoy pushing his buttons, in ways I know he'll punish me for later.

…Maybe because I *enjoy it* when he does.

"Who are you texting?"

I jolt, slamming the phone to my chest as I whip my gaze to Nora.

"Nobody."

She smirks, arching a brow. "*Really.*"

"Just work stuff."

"It's amusing to me how you still think I'm six years old."

I roll my eyes. "Please. I don't think you're six."

"Oh, just not old enough to understand that you have a boyfriend? Or the concept of sexting?"

My mouth flies open. "What the hell do *you* know about the concept of sexting?!"

"I know it *exists*, El. I didn't say I *did* it. Jeez."

"Well—good. Keep it that way."

She snickers. "Your generation and older still doesn't seem to get that the internet is forever. My generation has zero interest in it. Like, sending people pics of your booty is insane."

"Correct. Completely insane. Which is why I am *not* sexting anyone."

"Just Hades."

My face burns hotly. "I am *not*. And he is *not* my boyfriend."

She frowns in an exaggeratedly thoughtful way, stroking her chin. "So…what you're telling me, as my sister, guardian, and role model, is that the man who you've screwed three different times in our apartment is just, like, some random guy? So I should just find 'some random guy' myself, and not worry about sex having meaning or an emotional component? Good to know, thank you."

I give her a look as she grins at me.

"You done yet?"

Her teasing grin widens. "For now."

Yes, Hades has been over twice more since the night of the gala a week and a half ago. Yes, he's slept over both times. And yes, we've done our best to be quiet in our...*activities*, including but not limited to, Hades muffling my moans with his hand, his mouth, my panties, and his cock.

But no, his visits have not gone unnoticed by my sister.

I sigh as the doors slide open and we get off the elevator onto our floor.

"What I as an adult choose to do consensually with another consenting adult is my own business, Nora."

"So, he's not your boyfriend."

I grit my teeth. "I don't know. No. Maybe." I glance at her. "It's complicated."

"Are you exclusive?"

"Yes."

Shit.

I answered that one *way* too quickly, and it hasn't gone unnoticed by the world's sharpest fifteen-year-old.

"Do you like him?"

I sigh. "Yes, Nora. I like him."

"So, let's review. You like him, you bang him—"

"Don't call it that—"

"He sleeps over, you get all mushy when he sexts—*sorry*, just regular texts—you, and you're exclusive. That about sum it up?"

I nod as we round the corner to our door. "Correct."

"I'm pretty sure that's called dating."

"It's not—*Nora!*"

My lungs go icy as I grab her hand back, just as it was extending to our door holding her keys.

…Because our door is already open, and ajar.

Nora's face goes white as she moves behind me.

Someone was in there.

My heart clenches.

Someone *might still be in there.*

"Elsa?" Nora whispers in a small, scared voice as she clutches my shirt. "I think you should call your not-boyfriend."

"ALL GOOD."

Hades is smiling as he steps back into the hallway, but there's a shadow of darkness flickering in his eyes when he glances at me.

"Probably just didn't click shut behind you when you left."

Nora exhales loudly. "Well, that was terrifying."

He chuckles. "I'll bet. It's all good if you want to go in."

When she's inside, he turns to me, his smile fading.

"The place is completely clean. But someone's definitely been through your things. *And* Nora's."

My stomach drops, my face turning white.

"*What?!*"

"They were good, but not that good." His jaw clenches. "I didn't want to scare her, but neither of you is staying here tonight. No fucking way."

I nod, my throat bobbing heavily. "Okay, I'll look at hotels—"

"I've got room."

I blink in surprise as I turn to him. "What?"

"I've got room at my place. Pack bags for the both of you. Don't freak Nora out. Tell her that you've found out that the door being left ajar was actually building maintenance, and they say they need to do some important upgrades to your electrical system tonight, maybe the next night too."

I stare at him. "Hades, we're not staying at your—"

"Yeah," he growls, making me gasp as his mouth lowers to my ear. "You are."

———

"Dude, this car is *sick*."

Hades glances up into the rearview mirror, grinning at Nora in the backseat. "Thanks. Do you drive yet?"

"*No*," she sulks. "The Queen forbids it."

I roll my eyes. "*I* don't forbid it, Nora," I sigh. "The *law* forbids it. You're fifteen."

"Well, she can practice."

I shoot Hades a withering look as he grins at me, clearly well aware of what he's doing.

363

"Yeah!" Nora chirps from the back seat. "I can practice!" She sighs, shaking her head at Hades in the mirror. "She thinks just because she doesn't drive, no one else should."

I blush as he swivels his gaze to me. "You don't know how to drive?"

"I've lived in completely un-drivable cities my entire life," I shrug defensively. "So no, I've never learned."

"Well, we should change that."

I glance at him, simmering when I see that cocky grin and those piercing eyes lancing into me. He clears his throat as he looks back at Nora again.

"Hey, by the way: any other guys at school bothering you these days?"

She shakes her head, her lips pursing.

"No. After what happened to Theo—"

"He's going to be fine, you know."

"He is?"

Hades nods. "I know his dad. Theo's got some physical therapy to do, and one more surgery on his shoulder. But he's a tough kid. He'll be okay. Nick's on the mend, too."

Nora smiles a little. "Well, I think the whole world had already heard the story of them getting kicked out of my apartment. So when they got jumped..." Her mouth twists. "Basically the whole school is now terrified of me. Or at least all the guys are."

I smile.

"Good," Hades grunts. "Keep it that way. Little shits should be scared of women with backbone."

Nora grins.

"Listen," he continues. "Do you carry a keyring?"

My sister nods.

"Here."

Hades reaches across me, opening the glove compartment and plucking out something small before closing it again. He twists his arm behind him, handing the fob with a button on it to Nora.

"Put this on your keyring."

"What is this," she frowns at it. "A tracker?"

"Emergency button. It pings if you push it twice."

"And then, what, you go full on Batman and come rescue me?" she says dryly.

Hades chuckles. "No, but your sister will. I'll hook it up to her phone when we get to my place."

"What, so she can spy on me?"

He grins, shaking his head. "Nah, it doesn't work like that. But if you're ever in trouble, or you feel unsafe..." His jaw tenses. "Push it. My younger sister is twenty, and I've got one on her keys, too."

Nora nods, eying the little fob a little less skeptically. "Cool. Thanks."

I glance at him, a smile curving my lips.

"*Thanks*," I mouth.

———

My jaw drops as the Camaro comes to a stop outside of a *stunning* brownstone on an idyllic street in Brooklyn Heights, across the East River from lower Manhattan.

"Wait—this is you?"

"Mm-hmm."

He pushes a button on the dash and then guides the car down a sloped driveway that leads under the brownstone to a garage with an automatic door. We park inside next to a couple of other gorgeous cars; some, old classics and others gleaming new performance roadsters. Nora whistles.

"Wow, are all the tenants of this building rich car nuts?"

"You could say that."

I stop him with a look. "*Are* there other tenants?"

Hades waggles his brows, saying nothing as he carries our bags to an elevator, which we all pile into.

"I still haven't redone the first three floors."

Nora sputters. "Wait, you own the *whole* building? And all those cars down there?"

When he nods, she turns and elbows me in the side. Hard.

"*Nice,*" she winks.

I roll my eyes.

The doors open on the fourth floor, and Nora and I just about trip over our tongues.

Holy. *Shit.*

The place is *stunning*, and honestly? It's not at all what I would have pictured the lair of the infamous Hades Drakos looking like. I imagined a BDSM dungeon, or some other kind of subterranean cave. Or maybe a frat-house type place outfitted in total bachelor-pad bullshit, like a tacky Sharper Image store.

Boy, was I wrong.

Almost the entire top floor of the brownstone has been converted into one big open loft space. Gorgeous exposed-brick walls, huge windows, and wooden beams and ceiling rafters have my jaw on the floor as I stare in awe.

The furniture is old, weathered farmhouse style wood and deeply tanned leather. And the walls...*holy shit.* The whole length of the place on one side is nothing but floor-to-ceiling wooden bookshelves. And they're *filled* with books—the same books I used to mock as some sort of "date bait" on his Instagram.

At the back of the loft space, an enormous kitchen area is framed by a back wall made entirely of black iron and glass, with matching doors that lead out to a lush, plant-filled patio.

"Dude, this place is *insaaaaane!*" Nora breathes, walking around with her eyes wide and her mouth hanging open.

"I...didn't imagine you having books."

"I *do* know how to read, as shocking as that may be."

I grin. So does he.

"Nora, this'll be you." He carries her bag to a large, gorgeous brick and wood-beam guest room.

"Yeah, I'm never leaving. Sorry, not sorry."

He chuckles. "And your sister will be in the room next door."

Nora arches a brow. "Oh, is that your room?"

"No. My room is upstairs."

"So, my sister *won't* be next door, then."

Hades cocks a brow, glancing at me. My face flushes twelve shades of red as I groan.

"Yeah, I'm *fifteen*, not an idiot," Nora snickers.

"Very good to know, thanks."

Hades ends up ordering food to be delivered, which arrives just as I begin to move from hungry to hangry. And sweet Jesus does it smell fucking amazing.

"Frankie's," he says, his face almost caving in ecstasy as he transfers all the delicious smelling gnocchi, cavatelli, and cacio e pepe from the to-go boxes onto plates for the three of us to share. "Fucking *amazing* Italian food. Possibly the best food in all of New York, actually." He turns and winks at me. "Just don't ever tell my grandmother that."

We eat on Hades' garden patio, laughing, listening to music, and drinking wine. Well, Hades and I drink wine. Nora has Perrier. When the music—a vinyl copy of Bob Dylan's "Oh Mercy" album we've been listening to via speakers out to the veranda—runs out, Hades glances at my sister and me.

"Who's picking next?"

Nora pops out of her chair instantly. "On it."

I grin as she darts inside to dive into Hades' huge record collection.

"That's all you, right?"

I smile as I turn to him. "What?"

"Raising her."

I nod. "Yeah, pretty much, I guess. Since I was seventeen and she was six."

"You did a pretty fucking amazing job," he murmurs. "She's a great kid."

A proud blush creeps over my face. "Thanks."

Then instantly, I cringe as the next song pipes out over the speakers.

Goddammit, Nora.

The devil herself comes skipping back out to the veranda, giggling as Steve Miller Band's "The Joker" hums out of the speakers.

Hades raises a brow at her grin and my embarrassed groan.

"Something I'm missing?"

Nora snickers. "It's Elsa's favorite song."

He laughs loudly, turning to eye me through my flushed face. "Seriously? Steve Miller Band?"

"Hey it's in *your* record collection, ass," I mutter as he grins at me. "And it was a *phase*, thank you very much."

"Yeah, right. She played it for like a year straight when I was maybe nine. 'Ah-whoo, whoo'!"

"A *long* phase," I sigh as the two of them crack up.

An hour later, Nora looks like she's ready to fall asleep at the table. She yawns, stretching her arms as she stands.

"All right, I'm going to bed. You guys can make out or whatever now."

I roll my eyes at her. "Love ya. 'Night."

She makes over-the-top kissy faces at the two of us before she heads back inside and disappears into the guest room.

And I'm suddenly very aware of two things: one, that I've been kind of craving Hades' touch all night, ever since he swooped in like a black knight to clear the apartment for us. And two, we're alone now.

"You know what I think?"

I flush, realizing I've been staring at Hades, lost in thought, while he's been looking right at me.

"Uh, what?"

His jaw tightens.

"I think you should come here."

Heat floods my core as I bite my lip. But slowly I stand, knocking back the rest of my wine before I saunter around the table.

"Where, specifically?"

He pats his lap. "Right here."

Blushing, I start to move to his lap. I shudder when he yanks me onto him faster, pulling me astride his legs, facing him. My breath catches as his big hands circle my waist, squeezing as they slide up my back into my hair. And before I know it, my mouth is dipping to his, and I'm kissing him deeply.

His tongue delves between my lips, teasing and tasting me as I writhe on his lap. It's like a Pavlovian response I get now just from being near him. My hips grind and roll, and my pulse thuds as I kiss him fiercely.

Tell him.

The thought is like a cold blade lancing into me. It's been burning a hole in the front of my brain for weeks: it has to come out, especially with what we are to each other now. Whatever this is, whatever label we want to give it.

Hades needs to know Leo Stavrin is my father, even if I want nothing to do with him. The longer I go on not telling him, the worse it will be when I finally do.

"I have to tell you something," I blurt quietly.

Hades lifts a brow, eyeing me.

"Do you now."

"I…"

My eyes lock with his fierce icy-blues, and suddenly, I'm lost, and my nerve vanishes in the face of the fierce god looking back at me.

I smile, shaking my head.

"It can wait."

It has to. I can't bring myself to ruin this perfect moment with something like this.

"You're sure?"

"Positive."

"Good," he growls. "Because I'm not sure *I* can."

I whimper when I feel his hand slide to my ass and grab a handful of my skirt, shoving it up to my waist. Desire pools between my thighs as his fingers stroke my bare skin and then slip under the back of my thong. When I feel one of them slip down lower and tease over my asshole, I gasp, and pull back from his kiss.

"*Hades...oh fuck...*"

His finger dips lower, finding my pussy already soaking wet for him. My back arches, pushing my ass out as his finger curls into me and starts to stroke against my g-spot. His lips sear to mine again, kissing me and swallowing my moans before he pulls back and slowly brings his other hand up between us.

My eyes widen, my face filling with heat as I realize what he's holding.

"Did you seriously buy *a second* one?"

Hades' eyes glint, his lips curling wickedly as he twists the golden butt plug in his hand.

"Not a second one, no."

I stare at him. "Did you... Is that from my apartment?"

"Sure is. Open your mouth."

I flush with heat, my pulse thudding hard just beneath my skin.

"*What?*"

"Open your mouth," he growls, lowering his lips to my ear and letting his teeth graze the soft lobe. "And *suck*."

Our eyes lock when he pulls back. My skin tingles, and something dirty and needy pulses in my core.

My lips part.

"Good girl."

Our eyes stay on each other as I wrap my lips around the shiny metal, swirling my tongue over it as lust explodes through my entire body. His other hand slips behind me, grabbing something I can't see. When he pulls my thong to the side again and slips a finger over my ass, it feels slick and warm.

I moan, sucking and tonguing the butt plug as Hades swirls his lubed finger around my asshole. He adds pressure, and I whimper before suddenly his finger slips into me.

I gasp, shuddering on his lap as he groans against my neck. The plug slips out of my mouth, and I'm shaking all over as he brings it behind me. The warm metallic tip of it centers on my hole, and I try not to tense up as I feel him start to gently push.

"*Open up for me, kitten*," he growls thickly into my ear. "Relax. Let me watch your tight little ass swallow it like a good girl."

The plug didn't look very big in my hands, nor did it feel very big in my mouth.

Against my ass, it feels *huge*.

But slowly, my breath catching, I can feel the tapered, bulbous head start to stretch me open. Hades' teeth drag down my neck, turning me to jelly before suddenly, the plug gets sucked in, as if my body's swallowed it up right past the thick part to clench around the narrow base.

"*Oooh fuuuckk*," I choke, gasping and shaking.

It's a weird sensation. I feel full in a way I've never felt before. But it also feels *incredible*. Like there's this background pressure there, throbbing in my core.

"*Such* a good kitten," Hades rasps darkly.

I whimper again. "It's…it's so big…"

I gasp as his teeth bite down on my earlobe again.

"*Not as big as me.*"

He kisses me hard, and I melt when I feel him slip my thong back into place, holding the plug inside me. Then we're standing, and my legs are so shaky it's a struggle not to wobble as he takes my hand and starts to lead me through the gorgeous loft space.

I can feel the damn plug filling me and rubbing against me with each step. And fuck, it feels *amazing*.

We get to the spiral metal staircase that leads up to Hades' room, which I haven't seen yet. Just as I'm about to take my first step up, he stops me. He cups my face and lowers his mouth to mine, and I'm so lost in the kiss that I barely even register him tugging the zipper of my skirt down, until the whole thing falls to my feet.

"Hades…"

My eyes dart to the guest room door, with Nora right on the other side.

"You'd better get walking, hadn't you?"

I flush deeply, eyeing him and then turning to walk up the stairs in just my blouse and a pair of thong panties.

And a butt plug up my ass.

I can feel it shift inside me with each step, just as I can feel his eyes leaving a scorching path across my ass as he follows me up.

The stairs wind up, and suddenly, at the top, my jaw drops.

Woah.

Hades' bedroom is all glass, like a huge greenhouse on the roof of his building with panoramic views of all of Brooklyn, the entire East River, and the whole of Lower Manhattan. A huge bed fills the middle of the room, and I shiver as I feel his hand take mine, leading me to it.

I pause at the foot of the bed, gnawing on my lip as I turn to him.

"So, do all your guests have to climb that treacherous spiral—"

"You don't honestly think I've ever brought anyone here before, do you?"

I blink, my heart swelling. "I—"

I whimper as he slams his mouth to mine and fists my hair. My blouse and bra are tossed aside. His shirt and jeans follow.

"The windows..."

"One-way glass," he growls, slamming his mouth to mine.

I'm moaning into his mouth and sliding my hands into his boxers to wrap my fingers around his massive cock when he tosses me back onto the bed and I gasp. He drops between my legs, peeling my soaked panties down and spreading my thighs.

His soft, wet tongue drags up my seam, making me cry out as a shiver of heat slices through my body. Hades teases my clit, sucking the aching nub between his lips and swirling his tongue around it as he sucks. His powerful fingers dig into my thighs, shoving them wide apart as he devours me like he's a starving man eating his first meal in a month.

I jolt when I feel his fingers on the plug. He grips the base, and my breath catches and my eyes roll back as he slowly twists it inside me, like he's screwing it into me.

Holy. *Fuck.*

The sensations are insane as the smooth, slick plug slowly rubs across a million nerve endings. He twists it one way, then the other, then back again as his mouth descends to my pussy. And the combination of the plug *and* his tongue has me seeing stars as my eyes go out of focus.

"*Hades...fuck, I—I'm—*"

He starts to twist the plug faster, gently tugging on it as if he's about to pull it out of me, only to push it back in just as it starts to stretch me open again. The feeling is unreal, and my world begins to melt as I drown in the pleasure of it all.

His tongue on my clit. His fingers sliding into my pussy and stroking my g-spot. The plug screwing in my ass. It all comes together like a symphony of sin, and suddenly it hits me like a bomb going off.

I cry out, slamming my hand over my mouth as my back arches off the bed. I shake and shudder, writhing and moaning under his tongue and fingers as the blast of the orgasm rips through me.

I haven't even caught my breath yet when he slides up between my legs, naked and hard and so ready. The swollen tip of his huge dick sinks into my lips as my eyes bulge.

I already feel so full with the plug in my ass. And he's *so* big...

"*Take my cock like a good girl, kitten.*"

He rolls his hips, pushing his cock into me as my mouth goes slack.

Oh holy *fuck*.

I moan, clinging to him desperately, eagerly slamming my mouth to his. His thick cock sinks deeper and deeper, and the combination of him and the plug has me seeing double as the room spins.

Our eyes lock as his hands tangle in my hair. I grip his muscled shoulders, my nails dragging down his tanned skin as he starts to slam into me. Our bodies grind, hips slapping together as the wet sounds of our fucking fill the room.

I pant into his skin, kissing and biting his shoulder as he pounds into me faster. One of his hands reaches down, and when he starts to twist and pull at the plug again, a cry of pure ecstasy rips from my mouth.

Hades rams into me even harder, our bodies grinding together as heat explodes across both of us. I cling to him, wrapping my legs around his muscled hips and never wanting to let go.

"Hades..."

"Give me that cum, kitten," he rasps against my lips. "Give me all the fucking cum from this pretty little fucking pussy right the fuck now."

The plug slips all the way out, then he instantly pushes it right back in at the same time that his cock sinks balls-deep inside of me. And suddenly, my world is blurring at the edges.

His mouth slams to mine, swallowing my cry of release as the orgasm explodes in me. My muscles quiver and shake.

My skin lights on fire. My nails rake down his back as my body clenches and spasms around the plug and his cock filling me up completely.

Hades groans, pushing even deeper into me as his cock throbs and pulses, and I moan again when I feel the hot, wet spurts of his cum spilling into me.

I'm still shaking when he slowly pulls out of me and moves up next to me. I'm barely able to breathe, let alone form words, as he circles his powerful arms around me and pulls my back tight against his chest.

His lips graze the back of my neck as I tremble from head to toe.

"What did you want to tell me before?"

No. Not now.

My throat bobs. My teeth rake over my lips.

"Nothing," I finally murmur, twisting in his arms to face him and those blazing blue eyes. My lips curl into a smile. "Just that I really like you."

"Yeah, I think I picked up on that. I really like you too," he murmurs, catching my hand and pulling it to his lips. "A lot."

I grin.

So does he.

My eyes grow heavy, and I'm not sure my cheek is even resting on his chest before I fall asleep in his arms.

30

HADES

Elsa shudders, biting down so hard on my shoulder that there's a good chance she's drawn blood. But I can barely feel it, because I'm *way* too focused on the pure heaven of her pussy strangling my cock as we explode together.

I groan, my hand in her hair pulling her mouth to mine so I can kiss her as my cum spills deep inside her cunt. Her thighs clamp around my hips, her ankles locked around my back with her panties still hanging off one heel.

Slowly, catching our breaths, I pull my head back. Elsa's face is flushed scarlet, and split by a huge grin. But her brow caves suddenly as she snaps her gaze past me to the door of her office.

"We weren't too loud, were we?"

I only keep myself from saying "who the fuck cares" because it'll throw her into a tailspin. We probably *were* too loud, almost certainly. But I truly do not give a fuck.

I'm completely off the deep end with her, and I have no intention of swimming back to the edge of the pool any time soon.

"Nah, we were fine."

I grind my hips into her one last time, bringing a whimper to her lips as she feels my cock pulse inside her.

We're not even hiding this anymore. For two weeks now, I've been visiting "my attorney" at her place of work just about every day, where we have a closed-door meeting for a minimum of one hour.

By which I mean, I fuck Elsa absolutely senseless on every available surface in her office until my cum is dripping down her thighs and she can't walk or see straight.

Since the night that someone—"someone" almost certainly being Leo or one of his goons—broke into her place, I've had Drakos men guarding her building: two outside the front door, two by the back door, one on the roof, and two more patrolling the halls on her floor.

But even with that, she's been at my place a lot. At first, Nora stayed over too, which I'm completely fine with because she's a really cool kid. But once Elsa accepted that her apartment was one of the safest places in the city with my people guarding it, she pulled a few solo nights over here, with Nora more than happily getting their apartment to herself.

I kiss her slowly before I grudgingly slide from the wet warmth of her sweet little pussy. Without batting an eye, I pull her panties back up her legs and fit them snugly against her cunt.

I want my cum staying right where it is. I want her to feel me slowly dripping out of her for the rest of the day.

I want her panties to be sticky with it when she leaves work later, to remind her of me.

Like I said: off the fucking *deep end*.

"What do you want to do tonight?"

That's code for "who's sleeping where?"

Elsa's mouth twists. "I'd love to come over. But I feel like I'm neglecting Nora. She's been up and out the door to school or practice without me like three days in a row now."

I nod. I totally get it.

"Stay at your place then," I growl, buttoning my shirt back up. "And we can talk—"

"Why don't you stay over at mine?"

I grin. So does she, her face tinging with pink.

"I mean, if you—"

"I do," I growl. "Want to. Thought I'm supposed to meet up with Sean later for a sparring round."

She shrugs as she finishes adjusting her blouse and fixing her hair. "Come over after, then?"

"I'll be all sweaty."

She grins as she leans up to kiss me.

"*Good*. And, ah—here."

My brows shoot up as Elsa presses a key into my palm.

A key *to her apartment*.

Well, this is an absolute first, by a mile.

She blushes. "Come over whenever. I'll be waiting for you."

I SPEND the rest of the day running errands and then helping Callie and Eilish cart a bunch of beer deliveries for The Banshee down to the basement walk-in fridge. Then I head to Sean's local gym in the Lower East Side for some long-overdue sparring practice.

My phone rings just as I pull up. Glancing down, I spot Ares' name on the screen before I answer.

"Yo, what's up? I'm about to head into—"

"We just got hit."

Everything goes still.

"*What.*"

"How fast can you get to my place?"

"Office or apartment?"

"Apartment. And Hades? Watch your back. Someone's trying to start a war."

"On my way."

HOLY SHIT.

My jaw grinds as I lean on the kitchen counter in Ares and Neve's all-glass penthouse overlooking the Hudson. But I'm not scoping the views right now. I'm scowling over at where Castle is patching up a gash across Mike Karagiannis' forehead.

...A gash he received about an hour ago, when a crew smashed their way into a warehouse of ours that he was guarding, cracked a bat over his head, and made off with about two million dollars' worth of black market high-end electronics.

They left the *other* two million dollars' worth of gear that was being stored there smashed into smithereens.

This was someone sending a pretty clear message.

"Mr. Drakos," Mike blurts, looking terrified as he stares wide-eyed at Ares. "I'm so sorry, sir—"

"It's not your fault, Mike," Ares growls quietly, walking over to put a comforting hand on the older man's shaking shoulder.

That's the difference between Ares and me, and it's what makes him such a great leader. If it were me, well, I doubt I'd be this calm. As it is, I'm barely keeping it together, standing over here across the room.

One sixty-year-old man isn't going to stop ten armed guys from doing shit. The concerning thing isn't just the theft or the vandalism, though. It's that someone even knew that the warehouse was worth hitting in the first place.

There are a couple of spots around this city where our family hides its more... *underground* activities and products. Sometimes cash, too. And when I say they're hidden, they're fucking *hidden*. That shit is locked down tight on a strictly need-to-know basis.

Except these assholes clearly knew.

"Tell us again what happened," Ares mutters. "Try and focus on any small details too, if you can."

Mike nods, wincing as Castle finishes stitching up the gash in his forehead.

"I'd just done a round of the perimeter and was headed back to the office. They came through the side door...used a plasma torch to cut the damn hinges right off and come storming through like a bunch of commandos."

"How many of them were there, again?"

Mike looks down. "Ten of 'em. I pulled my gun, Mr. Drakos, I swear—"

"No one's doubting that, Mike," my brother grunts. "We just want the details."

"They cracked me one good," Mike sighs. "I winged one with my piece. But they got me hard on the noggin. Then another one tied my arm to the radiator. It was lucky I could use my foot to get the phone off the desk to call you later. They went through the whole place like they knew exactly where everything was. Grabbed probably half the merch and then went to town on the rest with bats and tire-irons."

Ares glances at me, then Kratos, before his eyes slide back on Mike.

"Okay, I want you to try and remember this all on your own, without me prompting you. When you first called, you mentioned—"

"They were fuckin' Russians, Mr. Drakos," Mike growls. His eyes dart to Neve. "Begging your pardon for the language, ma'am."

"Fuck that," Neve mutters back. "You're *sure* they were Russian? Could've been some other Balkan—"

"My ex-wife's mother was Russian," Mike grunts. "Trust me, I hear that shit in my nightmares."

Ares' jaw clenches as his eyes lock with mine and Kratos'.

I clear my throat. "Family meeting." I growl. "Patio. *Now.*"

Castle, who was with Ares and Neve when Mike called, stays in the kitchen with the wounded guard. Ares, Neve, and Kratos follow me out onto the glass penthouse's sprawling patio.

"It's Gavan."

Ares looks grim. "We don't *know* that. It could be—"

"It was a clear shot across the bow, Ares," I mutter. "A warning shot."

"Yeah, but Gavan has no reason to—"

"He, uh…" I frown, clearing my throat. "He might."

My brother's eyes narrow. "*Hades…*"

"It wasn't a big deal. I went to see him the other day about something, and—"

"Something you *completely* neglected to inform me about?!" Ares snaps.

"It wasn't family business."

"*Bullshit*, Hades," he growls. "You went to see the head of the fucking Reznikov Bratva—who, by the way, we're still in a silent fucking bidding war with over the Albanians. I don't give a fuck if you were popping over to have a fucking book club meeting with Gavan. When you see the head of *that* organization, believe me, it's business. And that means *you tell me about it.*"

I grit my teeth. "It might *not* be him. I'm just saying, things got heated, and Gavan may have interpreted my visit as a threat."

"Oh, you fucking *think*, Hades?!"

The door to the penthouse slides open. Castle clears his throat as he sticks his head out.

"I just got a call from a buddy of mine from the VA. He works security over at Mt. Sinai, and wanted to let me know that a known member of the Reznikov organization just came in for stitches." His eyes darken. "Bullet graze, left shoulder, from a thirty-eight snub-nose. Same place Mike winged one of them. Same gun."

Ares nods stiffly before he turns to me.

"Apparently, someone *did* take your visit as a threat."

"So what are we going to do about it?" Kratos rumbles.

My lips curl as I glance first at him, then at Castle.

"I don't know about you guys, but I think it's getting chilly. I'd love to warm my feet by a campfire tonight."

Kratos nods his chin, folding his arms over his big chest. Castle grins.

Ares glances at me and nods curtly.

"Do it. Pick something of similar value, and no loss of life, Hades. We're not trying to start World War Three here. But if Gavan wants to start fucking around, it's time to send a message of our own back."

Two hours later, my feet are getting *plenty* toasty next to a fire that's soaring into the fucking heavens. Gavan's four men who were guarding this particular Reznikov warehouse are bound, gagged, and blindfolded, tied up on a pier that juts out over the East River.

I glance at Kratos and nod, clinking my beer to his before turning and doing the same to Castle's.

"You didn't have to involve yourself in this, you know," I grunt at him.

He shrugs, sipping his beer as he watches the flames.

"Yeah, well, I didn't have a new episode of *Succession* to watch tonight. What else was I going to do with myself."

The three of us stand there watching the fire curl and snarl up at the heavens before we hear the sounds of sirens approaching.

Time to go.

31

ELSA

I STIR SLIGHTLY awake when I feel his weight sinking onto the bed.

"Shh. Go back to sleep."

I grin, my eyes still closed as Hades slides in next to me and pulls me into his arms. Then my nose wrinkles a little.

I was expecting him to be coming fresh from boxing practice. And while he's clearly just showered, probably in *my* shower, it's not the sweat of a workout I can still smell lingering on him.

It's smoke.

Not tobacco smoke. Real, acrid, woodsy smoke.

I chew on my lip, thinking. Then I push it away.

I don't need to ask about this. If he wants to tell me, he will. Yes, there are things about him that might scare me. But he is who he is, and I like that.

I like that, and him, so much. In fact, there are other words I should probably be using instead of "like".

"What are you doing tomorrow?"

I turn in his arms to face him in the near-dark.

"Nothing, why?"

"I need you to come to the family and friends soft opening for The Banshee that Callie, Eilish, and Neve are throwing."

"Oh?" I frown. "I didn't know there was anything left to sign—"

"Elsa…" he chuckles, cupping my face.

"What?"

"Not as their fucking lawyer. As my date."

I go still, our eyes locking in the shadows.

"You…you're serious?"

"Very."

"Hades, your whole family will be—"

"Yeah. That's kinda the whole point."

My lip catches between my teeth. "You're really serious."

"I really am."

"And you're sure that's a good idea?"

He sighs, leaning close and kissing me softly. "I think I'm fucking sick of pretending you're not the first person I want to talk to in the morning and the last person I want to see before I go to sleep."

Well…*fuck*. Way to knock a girl's legs out…

I'm grinning like an idiot when he kisses me again.

"Come tomorrow. That's not a request, by the way."

I giggle. "Then how can I say no?"

"You can't. You're coming. And right now…"

I whimper as he sinks under the covers and spreads my legs.

"Right now, you're coming on my tongue."

32

HADES

"Hey!"

My face splits into a grin when I answer the phone, the sound of Elsa's voice making my very skin tingle like it always does these days.

What the hell has this girl done to me?

Thing is, I no longer scowl in confusion or turmoil when I consider that question.

I just fuckin' smile.

"Hey yourself," I grin into the phone.

"So, I'm afraid I'm running a *teensy* bit late in terms of the soft opening tonight," she sighs. "I'm just finishing up a deposition in Brooklyn. But quick question, is that blue dress of mine at your place?"

It's almost surreal. I'm actually having the "whose house is that piece of clothing at" conversation with a woman for the first time in my life. And I fucking *love* that I'm having it with her.

Yes, her dress is at my place—still there from the night last week where she rode my cock on the kitchen floor before I fucked her bent over the counter.

"It is, yeah."

"Oh, wait, yes, I think I wore it the night…" she trails off, and I can practically feel the heat of her blush through the phone.

"Go on."

She laughs quietly. "I think we both know which night that was," she murmurs.

"Oh, we totally do, I just want to hear you say it out loud."

"I'm standing in the hallway of the Brooklyn Court House."

"And your point is?"

She giggles. "I'll talk dirty to you *later*."

I grin. "I'll hold you to that, counselor."

"Deal. Do you think I could stop by your place and grab it before I head home to change? I think I'd like to wear it tonight."

"Here's a better idea: just get ready at my place and I'll come give you a ride to the soft opening after I finish helping the girls with the last of the setup here."

"Really?"

"You know the code for my front door, right?"

"Yeah."

"Then do it. Get ready at my place and I'll call you when I'm on the way. Deal?"

"Deal," she gushes. "Thank you, you're the best."

"No problem. See you soon."

"Yeah, see you soon. Lo—" she stops short, clearing her throat. "Right. See you soon."

She hangs up abruptly. I'm grinning ear-to-ear as I slip the phone into my pocket and turn to head back into The Banshee, where there *is* a fair amount of setup still to do.

Callie steps right in front of me, giving me one of her patented "I'm about to give you shit about something" looks of hers.

"Yes?"

"Who was that?"

I shrug. "Nobody."

She rolls her eyes. "Bullshit. You're grinning like a schoolgirl."

"Not at all. Just psyched about the free cocktails tonight."

She shakes her head, turning to walk away. "Whatever, fine. Keep your secrets."

Fuck it.

I clear my throat. "That was Elsa, actually."

Callie turns, looking extremely curious. So does Eilish, popping up from behind the bar.

"Wait, what?" Neve's blonde sister arches her brow.

"That was Elsa."

Callie frowns. "*Aaaand?*"

"And she's coming tonight." I glance at the two of them and clear my throat. "As my date."

Callie's eyebrows shoot so far up they almost disappear into her hairline. Eilish grins impishly.

"No *shit*," Callie blurts, staring at me. "Like, a date-date?"

"Don't make it weird."

"My nearly thirty-year-old terminally single brother is about to go on his first date. It's already fucking weird, dude."

I flip her off as she and Eilish snicker. "Well, just don't be a bag of dicks about it."

"What's she being a bag of dicks about?"

I turn, grinning when I see Sean lugging three huge cases of liquor bottles into the bar from a van outside.

"Nothing. Thanks for helping, man."

"Any time. Drinks are free tonight, yeah?"

I snort. "Most definitely."

"It's *not* nothing," Callie smirks. "Hades has a girlfriend."

Sean smirks. "I think Hades has *lots* of girlfriends."

"No, no," Eilish grins. "Like a real girlfriend-girlfriend."

Sean glances at me with an astonished grin on his lips. "No shit?"

"Why the fuck is everyone making this so *weird*," I grumble, turning to head out the door.

Sean follows me out, helping me lug a few more cases of stuff into the bar before I see a familiar black town car pull up in front of the building. I head to the curb, opening the passenger door and helping my grandmother out.

She beams at the newly remodeled front of the Irish pub that her granddaughter, Eilish, and Neve are about to open.

"Hard to believe she actually pulled it off, isn't it, Ya-ya?"

Dimitra chides me, playfully slapping my hand as I grin.

"Not hard to believe at all, Hades. She's a Drakos, after all. A Dragon. The blood of the Spartans—"

Not the Spartans again. "Hey, Ya-ya?" I clear my throat. "I, uh, wanted to tell you something."

"Oh?"

"I've…met someone. She's not Greek, but—"

"But she's very smart, *very* pretty, and quite intimidating," she finishes for me, grinning at my confused look. "And British."

I blink. Dimitra chuckles, reaching up to pat my cheek fondly.

"I'm old, Hades. Not blind, or stupid. And I think she'll be *very* good for you."

I grin. "I do, too. She's coming tonight."

"Good," she beams. "Good. She should be part of this. We can toast to your sister, and your sisters-in-law, and to falling in love, and having lots of babies."

I snicker, rolling my eyes. "Yeah, let me get a cocktail in me before we start talking babies, okay?"

She laughs, patting my hand as I walk her into the bar.

"*Gamóto*," she suddenly gasps, frowning as she turns. "I left my bag in the car."

I grin, leaning down to kiss her cheek. "I got it."

"Hades!" Callie stops me on my way out. "Where's this hot date of yours?"

I roll my eyes. "Let me get Ya-ya's bag, then I'm going to get her."

She grins. "Good. And hey…" She lifts a shoulder and smiles. "I'm really happy for you, you know."

I give her a hug, kissing the top of her head. "Thanks. And I'm really proud of *you*." I raise my eyes, looking around the brand-new pub. "This place is insane, Cals. And *you did this*."

She beams.

"Okay, let me get that bag, then, you and I are drinking."

"Before Ares shows up."

I laugh. "Definitely before Ares shows up."

I head out, clapping Sean on the back as slips past me into The Banshee carrying in the last box of liquor. I find Ya-ya's bag on the back seat of the town car, and I'm turning back to the pub with a grin on my face when the blast shatters the world.

The explosion punches out the windows and blows the door off The Banshee, slamming me back against the car so hard I see stars as I drop to my hands and knees.

No.

I stagger to my feet, my eyes wide in horror and a ringing sound echoing in my ears. It's all I can hear as I stumble like a drunk toward the gaping black maw that not four seconds ago was the front of my sister's beautiful new pub.

NO.

I start to run, heedless of the shards of glass and flaming bits of wood raining down around me. Heedless of the blood pouring down my face. Heedless of anything as I charge into the burning wreckage.

Where my family was just standing.

33

HADES

At first, all I know is pain.

The white noise of distant screaming and faint sirens. The frantic and yet numbing task of clawing through rubble and fire, heedless of the way it's burning the skin from my hands. The roaring sound that I finally realize is my own voice when the firefighters try and pull me out of the wreckage of the Banshee.

It's finally Castle that manages to do that, and he does it in his own way: by punching me in the face. It's probably the only way I'd have ever left that smoking black hole.

It dazes me and quiets the monster raging within me enough that he can drag me from the smoldering building and shove me against the side of a car. Then he physically yanks my head to the side to show me where they're loading my grandmother, my sister, and Eilish Kildare into the backs of three ambulances.

Callie climbs into hers herself.

Dimitra and Eilish do not.

That sets me off again, roaring and screaming pure, blind rage and hatred at the sky as Castle forcibly throws me into the back of his car as the scent of death curls into the air around us.

"I'M SO FUCKING SORRY, BROTHER."

Ares hugs me tightly, his jaw clenched as I cling to him.

Callie is already up and moving around. Eilish is going to be okay once she's out of surgery to remove the pieces of shrapnel in her shoulder and her leg. Our grandmother, miraculously, is okay, fuck knows how. They're keeping her for observation, despite her protests, because they want to watch for internal bleeding from the hit she took. But she's okay.

They're all alive.

My eyes squeeze shut.

Sean Farrell isn't.

The firefighters are saying it looks like he took the brunt of the blast when he used his body to shield my sister and my grandmother from the worst of it.

They're calling him a hero. And that's fucking great and all, but I don't want to eulogize a hero.

I want to thank my fucking friend for what he did and then go buy him a beer.

I grit my teeth against my brother's shoulder and take a deep breath before I pull away, my face grim.

"Fuck," Ares hisses, looking away.

Neve blinks back tears as she comes over to hug me, shaking as she clings to me. When she pulls back to sink into my brother's arms, I turn to survey the scene in the hospital waiting room around me.

The faces and clothes streaked with ash and grime. The wounds, like the gash on my head, that aren't big enough for anyone here to give a shit about right now. Not while Dimitra is being monitored for internal bleeding and Eilish is having pieces of her pub surgically removed from her body.

The tears. The pain. The shattered spirits.

And then there's the anger. And even though it's simmering below the surface, it's plain to see on everyone's faces: Ares, Neve, Kratos, Castle, Cillian and Una.

With me, the anger's not so much under the surface. It's about to explode outward with a force that'll make what just happened at The Banshee look like a cheap bottle rocket.

Not the bomb it was.

And it *was* a bomb. Castle's just gotten off the phone with the Fire Marshall, who confirmed it. Not a gas leak. Not an act of God.

A fucking *bomb*.

They're saying it was wired up under the downstairs lounge bar, purposefully put in that central location so as to do the maximum damage to both the downstairs lounge and the bar above it, where most of our family was.

They're saying it was a relatively complex IED, too. One that took time to set up.

They're *also* saying that while the security camera hard drives have obviously been reduced to molten slag, the off-site logs show that the back door to the place was opened using a security code late last night.

Someone tried to murder our family. And they damn well almost succeeded.

I turn away, yanking my phone out to try calling Elsa again. But same as before, it goes straight to voicemail.

I'm not worried. Well, not *that* worried. My building is far more secure than it looks, despite all that glass. Plus, I sent three of our men over to guard the place, without worrying Elsa, while I was on the way here to the hospital.

I text George, one of the men I sent over there, just to check in. His instant "all good over here" reply has me exhaling slowly.

Maybe she's in the shower, or taking a nap or something.

Ares glances at Kratos and me.

"There's no reason to keep quiet about it," Neve chokes tightly, shaking her head at my brother. "We're all thinking the same thing anyway."

Ares' expression goes grim. But he nods.

"Fine."

The waiting room is full of nothing but Kildare and Drakos people anyway, and this obviously concerns both families. Ares exhales slowly, his eyes dragging to Cillian.

"Does Dominic know yet?"

As in Dom Farrell, Sean's father.

Cillian nods stonily. "He does. He's on a plane right now from Chicago."

Ares shakes his head. "I'm so fucking sorry, Cil. Sean was a good man. And they're saying he saved Callie and Ya-ya's lives. I know Dom won't give a flying fuck about that right now, and that's fine. But I want him to know that. Eventually."

The Irishman nods quietly. "He'll know."

Ares grits his teeth as his eyes slowly sweep the room.

"There's no easy way to put this. But we're all thinking it anyway, so fuck it." He pauses. "Someone just declared war on us. It could very well be the Russians, but before *any* of us, or any of the vassal families, goes out there and starts waging World War Three in the streets of Manhattan, we're going to be goddamn sure it is. Can we please agree to that?"

Cillian's jaw grinds. But he nods.

"I can tell our people to stand down." His eyes harden. "*For now.* But my niece is in *surgery*, Ares. And there's a limit to my patience when it comes to holding off on retaliation."

"Fair enough. If anyone has favors owed them, call them the fuck in, now."

My phone buzzes. I yank it out quickly, expecting it to be Elsa. My brow furrows when I see the name on the screen.

Oren Frey: Cillian's "detective".

I move to the corner of the room and answer it.

"I just heard what happened, Hades. And I'm very sorry."

Oren and I have only spoken once before, a few weeks ago. I'd almost forgotten I'd called him and asked him to do what

I did. Now, amidst the chaos of all this, it seems so fucking petty and stupid.

"Thank you," I growl. "Now maybe isn't the best time—"

"Unfortunately," he growls. "It might be all *too* good a time."

My eyes darken. "What are you talking about?"

"I'm talking about what, or should I say who, you asked me to look into."

Elsa.

I asked him to look into Elsa, and I've spent the last three weeks regretting it every time she's smiled at me or kissed me.

"Oren, this *really* isn't the best—"

"I'm not some yellow pages private detective, Hades. Nor am I unaware of the intricate politics involved with people like yourself and families such as your own when I do work for them. I'm fully versed in the dynamics of your family, and Cillian's, as well as of those who you both might call enemies. Which is why I struggled with even calling you right now."

My pulse quickens, a whining sound ringing in my ears.

"What did you find."

He exhales slowly. "Her background is clean. Mom died when she was eighteen and her sister was seven. They were pretty poor, but she worked two jobs—interning at a law firm, running coffees, making copies, that sort of thing, and also running the back office for a local grocery store. She managed to get herself into no less than Cambridge, where she was top of her class, all while playing mother to her little sister, Nora."

I already know all of this. It still makes me grin with foolish pride, even if the world is burning around me. But I'm not sure where he's going with any of this, or how it's remotely relevant to any of what's going on.

"Oren—"

"The reason I'm calling right *now*, and the reason I truly wrestled with this, Hades," he growls, "isn't because of how smart she is, or how driven, or the blood and sweat it took for her to get to where she and her sister are right now. I'm calling you because of who her father is."

The ringing sound in my ears grows louder. My pulse thuds harder.

"And he is?"

Oren is silent.

"*Oren—*"

"Stavrin."

The floor drops away.

"Leo Stavrin. I'd tell you who he is, but I know you already know. And given this evening's events, that's why I wasn't so sure about calling."

"Thank you."

"Look, Hades—"

"That's all I need," I say in a voice that sounds like the edge of a knife. "Thank you, Oren."

I hang up. In a trance, my face a mask of pure, livid rage, I turn and start to walk for the door.

Ares spots me first, frowning as he moves to intercept me.

"Woah, who was that?"

"Out of my way."

His jaw clenches. "Hades—"

With a furious roar I explode, shoving him back as I yank the gun from the holster under my jacket.

"HADES!" Neve screams.

Ares holds up his hand to her, his eyes still locked on mine. His face darkens when I chamber a round, my face a cold mask of fury.

"*Tell me what the fuck is going on*, man," he growls. "I can't help you if you don't—"

"I am going to *deal* with something, Ares," I snarl. "That's all you need to know."

He shakes his head, Castle and Kratos moving behind him, eyeing me and the gun warily.

"You're not going after Gavan fucking Tsarenko by yourself, brother," Ares growls quietly. "Let us settle things here, and then you and I, and the rest of us, can all go knock down Gavan's—"

"I'm not going after Gavan."

He frowns. "Then who—"

"*GET. OUT. OF. MY. WAY.*"

The room is silent after my voice booms through it. Ares and I lock eyes. Then, slowly, he dips his chin in a slow nod. He steps away, letting me surge past him and out the door like an avenging angel of death.

No, I'm not going after Gavan.

I'm going after the little fucking spy who's been playing me like a goddamn idiot. The little blonde *traitor* who's had me wrapped around her fucking finger while she fed intel to the enemy.

And when I find her, I'm going to fucking bury her.

IT's a miracle I don't die in a fiery car crash as I scream across the bridge from Manhattan into Brooklyn. It's as if I've got blinders on—like I'm seeing in tunnel vision, completely unaware of anything and everything around me as I plow recklessly through traffic.

It all comes in flashes—horribly, blindingly obvious flashes, now that I think about it.

That first night, when I was so caught up in realizing that the girl from Club Venom was Elsa that I didn't focus on the part where she was *leaving Leo's place* at one in the morning.

Of course she was. Because she's his fucking *daughter*.

I think of all the times I was so stupidly cavalier with her. All the times I left my phone open around her, or chatted away to Ares with her in earshot.

Listening. Writing all that shit down.

Plotting to destroy me and mine, all while slowly breaking down every wall I have. And now someone is dead—a *friend* is dead—and my grandmother and basically my sister-in-law are still in the hospital because I got careless with my feelings.

She fucking played me.

I'm going to *destroy* her.

The car mounts the curb outside my building as I come to a screeching stop. My eyes dart to the van across the street with "Athenian Dry-Cleaning" stenciled on the side of it, which is my guy George and his crew.

I storm over there to tell them to scatter—to get the fuck out of here before I start shooting. When I get to the van, I frown.

It's empty.

What the fuck is going on?

Suddenly, something catches my eye: liquid, dripping from the side sliding door of the van.

My brow knits, and when I lean closer, my veins chill.

It's blood.

Pulse racing, I yank open the sliding door, and instantly grit my teeth.

Fuck me.

George and the two other guys I sent are dead in a heap on the floor of the van, all with their throats cut.

I don't think. I just whirl, bolting across the street, smashing in the keypad code to my building, then bolting up the stairs through the unfinished floors until I get to the top.

I can't tell if I want her to be there so that I can kill her with my bare hands, or if I'm hoping she's gone so I don't have to.

So I don't have to kill the woman I love for being instrumental in the death of my friend, and in almost killing my family.

But, luckily or unfortunately, she's not there.

I tear through the house, looking under every bed and in every closet. But the place is empty.

Her clothes are missing from my closet. The toothbrush she left here a few weeks ago is gone.

Elsa is gone. And I have no idea if the roaring sensation inside of me demanding I chase her is so that I can kiss her as if my life depended on it…

…or kill her.

34

HADES

Anger is a powerful thing.

Anger is a drug that'll restart your heart if it stops. It'll keep you going when you just want to fall down and die. It'll sustain you when you're too broken and fucked up to eat, drink, even sleep—at least, for a time.

Maybe forever. So far I'm on day five of running on pure anger, and I don't remember the last time I did any of those things, so who the fuck knows.

Since the blast ripped through The Banshee, my world has upended. On the plus side, Callie is healing and Ya-ya was cleared to leave the hospital. She's doing okay aside from a bunch of painful bruising she took in the explosion. Eilish is on bed rest at Mt. Sinai, but she's going to be back home at the Kildare brownstone in just a few days.

So, those are all good things.

Everything else is on fire.

It started the night of the bombing, when the Russians went on *full* lockdown. When we got reports the next day of more Reznikov muscle being flown in from Europe and Russia, the defcon meter moved a little higher.

Then, three days ago, a laundromat that's a front for an underground high-stakes casino run by one of our vassal families went up in flames. The *next* day, Kratos and I blew a hole in the keel of one of the mid-sized yachts Gavan owns and keeps moored at Chelsea Piers Marina, sending it to the bottom of the Hudson.

And this morning, the expected return shot came, in the form of one of Ezio Adamos' construction projects getting shut down by Homeland Security because of "personnel security concerns".

Guess which fucking Russian bathhouse the head of the New York division of Homeland Security has a membership to.

At this point we've moved past bullshit.

Now, we're gearing up for all-out *war* with Gavan Tsarenko.

The good thing is, though, when you're mainlining anger, you don't have time to be sad. To feel the way your heart is shattering inside of you.

Betrayal stings. Losing the woman you were ready to hand your whole goddamn soul to is a motherfucker.

But anger? Anger's got your back. Anger will smother the whole fucking thing, until all you can taste is bitter rage, and all you breathe is revenge.

Well, currently, it's actually more a mix of revenge, gun-oil, and the plasticky scent of body armor fresh out of its packaging.

We're in the basement of my family's Central Park South building, which is an all-in-one armory, garage, and fortress: Ares, Kratos, and I, plus Castle, because an attack on Eilish or Neve is an attack on his blood, and now he's gunning to bleed more of it into the streets.

There's also about twenty other Drakos men and another fifteen from the Kildare side, all of us strapping on body armor and loading up magazines. In about forty-five minutes, the hounds of war are about to get loosed from their chains.

"Hades."

I glance up to see Ares giving me a piercing look.

"Yeah?"

"You know you don't have to do this."

My jaw tightens.

"I mean…" he clears his throat. "If she's working with Leo, there's a chance she'll *be there* when we—"

"I don't give a fucking shit."

Without another word, I go back to coldly pushing rounds into the magazine in my hands.

"Guys?"

We all turn at the sound of Callie's voice to see a fierce, hard look in her eyes.

I sigh. "If you're here to talk us down from this, you're wasting your fucking—"

"Oh, you mean all of *this*?" She snaps, nodding her chin past me. "This insanity?"

Ares looks up, frowning. "*This* is the game, Callie. When someone comes for you or hurts you, you make *them* hurt. I don't *want* a fucking war with Gavan. But what I want or don't want doesn't matter when he's the one that just bombed Pearl Harbor. We're *in* this now."

He sighs heavily, shoving his fingers through his hair.

"Now, please. Go back upstairs until—"

"I need you to *for once* listen to me!!!" she snaps. Callie bristles, stepping closer to the four of us as her throat bobs. "I also need you to come upstairs."

"*Why*," I growl.

"Because Vanya Mirzoyan just showed up at our door, and you really need to fucking listen to her."

I'VE SPENT the last five days drenched in anger. Bathing in it. Feeding on it, and becoming its closest friend. So when I see that same vicious emotion carved into Vanya's face when we walk into one of Dimitra's sitting rooms, it gives me pause.

Ares grimaces. "I owe your father a phone call, I know, apologies. But there's a bigger issue at—"

"You're going to war with the Reznikovs," she says coldly. "Yes, I know."

I glance at my brothers and Castle, then shrug. "And?"

"And I think you might be going to war with the wrong people."

"Excuse me?"

"My father is a *liar*," she spits, her eyes darting from me, to Ares, to Kratos, to Castle, to Callie.

Ares frowns. "Kindly elaborate?"

"*With pleasure*," she hisses venomously. "My father decided to spend the last three months telling me he was dying of fucking cancer. That *that* is why he wanted to make this deal happen, so that my brother and I would have more money than we'd ever know what to do with once he was gone."

My jaw grinds. "What do you mean, he's been *telling you* he has cancer?"

"Oh, should I be clearer?" she snaps, shaking with anger. "I mean he's been *lying to me*. I just found out that he's not sick at all. The bastard's completely *fine*. He's just been using me as a fucking pawn to push that message."

My brow furrows. "Jesus. I'm sorry, Vanya."

"Yeah, well, I'm done. I'm done playing the ditzy mob princess daughter for him. I'm also done being his chess piece. And I'm *really* done pretending that all I want in the world is for some big macho he-man to come marry me and put me in a goddamn ivory tower somewhere. Because all of that is fucking *furthest* thing from what I actually want!"

She looks away, raking her fingers through her long hair. "I have an undergraduate degree and a master's degrees in business from goddamn *Harvard*, for fuck's sake!"

I glance at Ares and then turn back to her.

"What can we do for you, Vanya."

She smiles bitterly and shakes her head, looking away like she hasn't heard me.

"My father thinks I went to Harvard to have something pretty to put on my socialite resume, and to maybe meet a husband." She grimaces, rolling her eyes. "You know what I did instead?"

She glances back at me, smiling triumphantly.

"I minored in linguistics. He doesn't even know that I speak four languages."

I clear my throat. "Vanya, I hate to rush this, but—"

"Including...." Her smile widens, darkening. "*Russian*. Now, Hades, do you know when it's nice to be able to speak and understand Russian when no one around you realizes that you can?"

"No," Ares growls. "But I think I'd very much like to."

Her eyes narrow to murderous slits. "It comes in handy when your lying *asshole* of a father has been having regular meetings, both in person and over the phone, with Leo Stavrin. *In. Fucking. Russian.*"

I stiffen. Ares swears under his breath.

"I wasn't happy about it. But I was willing to keep his secrets and let him play his little games, because I was focused on my own exit. But that was before he lied to me about *dying*, and before people started to get hurt. Before..."

She shakes her head, brushing a tear away from her eyes. Callie moves towards Vanya as if to comfort her. But the Albanian woman shakes her head, holding a hand up.

"No, let me finish. Please." She swallows, sniffing back the tears. "I don't know what they're planning. I honestly *don't*. But Leo and my father are working together. *Not* Gavan as well," she quickly adds. "I mean just Leo, with just my father."

Her lips twist.

"Oh, and I'd bail on this deal you're so hellbent on working out with my dad."

Ares frowns. "Why would we do that?"

Vanya's lips twist. "There's a sub-basement under the main office of that parking garage you've got your eye on." She smiles wryly. "The one you think is going to get rezoned."

My brothers and I glance warily at each other.

"Or, should I say, *is* going to get rezoned," Vanya continues. "Believe me, he knows all about that."

I frown. "So why on earth would he be willing to sell it to us for the price on the table?"

"Because it's not the deal of the century you think it is." She swallows. "I don't know exactly what it is, but I've heard them discussing something that's in that basement that'll kill any development deal. He's selling you a lemon."

Vanya draws in a shaky breath, smiling sadly at me.

"My father is *not* a good man, Hades. And he has *not* forgotten the bad blood between your family and ours, or between Gavan's and ours."

Ares folds his arms over his chest. "I have to ask…"

"Why I'm helping you?"

"It's crossed my mind."

She sighs heavily. "Because I never asked to be born into this life, and I don't want it."

I frown. "Okay, but you telling us all of this is a bit more than giving the middle finger to your old man, Vanya. This could —and probably will—have consequences for you…"

"I was in love with someone."

Vanya looks away, tears brimming in her fierce eyes.

"Her name was Katja, and she was our household chef. Seven months ago, after hiding it my entire life, I came out to my father. *We* came out; Katja and I." Vanya turns to level a broken look at us. "Do you know how he reacted?"

My jaw ticks at the pain and rage in her face.

"He fired her, got her visa revoked, and had her deported back to Ukraine." Her face shatters. "She was killed by a Russian bomb outside Bakhmut last night. I just found out."

Jesus.

"Vanya," I growl quietly. "I'm so fucking sorry—"

"*He killed her.* So, Hades?" Her voice is like broken glass as she looks at me with tear-filled eyes. "There already have been 'consequences' for me. It's his fucking turn now."

She pulls her phone out, her face a mask of livid anger as she taps on it. Mine buzzes in my pocket.

"Watch that."

The video she's just sent me is blurry and shaky. But it's pretty obvious what it shows: Serj Mirzoyan and Leo fucking Stavrin, along with the late and unlamented Pascha Andreev, talking on what must be Serj's back garden patio.

"I don't actually speak Russian myself…"

"Then *allow me*," she hisses thinly. "They're talking about starting a war between the Reznikovs and the Drakos-Kildare alliance. Serj is giving them a list of potential targets, including a warehouse full of stolen high-end electronics that belongs to your family. Pascha is talking about plans to start using violence on the streets against the children of Kildare and Drakos vassal families, made out to look like Reznikov Bratva aggression."

Fuck. Me.

My mind flashes to poor Theo Petrakis getting lit on fire with Russian vodka, and Nick Eliades losing his prestigious spot on the Cornell hockey team after getting beaten to shit.

"They want to stoke the anger between you and the Russians, until you're all forced into open war. When it gets bad, my father's plan is to pretend to side with you, to get close, while Leo will cozy up to Gavan. At a certain point, they'll both make moves to kill their respective kings—Gavan by Leo's hand, and you, Ares—along with Cillian Kildare if possible—by my father's."

I glance at my older brother, whose face is a stony mask.

"Your father left a message for me this morning, actually," he hisses quietly. "Asking how he could help with the mounting hostilities between our family and the Reznikovs."

Fuck.

On the video, Leo and Serj grin and shake hands.

"That handshake is Leo and my father agreeing to split the spoils once both empires are up in flames." Vanya's face is lined as she looks up at me. "You *do not* want to go to war with the Russians, believe me. You're all being played."

An hour later, Ares, Kratos, Castle and I are using a crowbar to break down the door to the sub-basement under Serj's parking garage at nine-fifty-two Lincoln Place. Kratos hits the light switch on the wall, and a string of construction site bulbs illuminates an old staircase that leads down to what looks like an earthen floor basement.

"The fuck is this?" Ares mutters as we all carefully descend the stairs.

It's mostly full of nothing but old boxes. But at the far wall, there's a plastic curtain drawn across a black hole. I frown, yanking it back and peering into the darkness beyond.

Castle steps next to me. "What is it?"

I shake my head. Just then, Ares steps forward, turns on the flashlight on his phone, and shines it into the darkness.

Woah.

The first thing I see is the skeletons—*old* ones, too, from the looks of it, covered in dust and dirt. Past them, there are two honest-to-God *cannons*, and a giant pile of huge-ass cannonballs.

"What the fuck?" Castle mutters. "This shit looks like it's been here for a century."

"Two and a half centuries, actually."

We all turn to Kratos, who is staring at a big, yellow, official-looking notice tacked to the wall next to the plastic curtain, with "New York City Historical Preservation Society" emblazoned across the top of it.

My brother grimaces as he turns to us.

418

"This says all of this was discovered six months ago while they were trying to expand the sub-basement. It's an old storage house from the Revolutionary War."

"Mother. *Fucker*!" Ares groans, turning and kicking a piece of rock across the dirt floor. "It's a fucking historical preservation site. Rezoned or not, it *can't* be developed."

Serj, you sneaky. Mother. Fucker.

Ares scowls as he takes a breath.

"Vanya's right. We've all been fucking *played*—"

"Thank you."

The four of us whirl, yanking guns out at the sound of the voice behind us.

Gavan Tsarenko's voice.

And he's not alone. There's four of us, but Gavan's brought three times that, and every gun in every Russian hand is currently pointed straight at us.

Tsarenko smiles, cracking his neck as he too raises a gleaming gun in his tattooed hand.

"Thank you for saving me the trouble of digging you all a grave."

35

ELSA

ALL I KNOW IS DARKNESS.

All I feel is the ever-present fear, hovering over us both.

Lurking.

Shivering, I pull close to Nora, glancing down at her as she sleeps. In the near-total darkness of the place that has been our prison for the last five days, I can barely make her out against the blackness that envelops us like ink. But I can hear her breathing.

Hopefully dreaming of a place that isn't *this*.

I know it's night-time, because the train I occasionally hear rumble by not too far away hasn't been past in a while. During the day, it's more like every hour, which suggests it might be a commuter train of some kind.

It could be a train full of cops, for all it matters. I blew my voice out the first day we were here, screaming and screaming for help.

But nobody heard us.

Nobody came for us.

Not here.

My blood runs cold at the sudden metallic scraping sound of the door to the basement room opening. It wrenches inward on rusty hinges, and I wince at the blinding stab of light that hits me. It's just a single bulb on the other side, but after five days in the blackness, my eyes sting at the sudden glare.

"Are you ready to come out yet?"

I shiver violently and peer as hard as I can, but even so, when I look at the door, all I see is the darkness of his silhouette with the light stabbing past him like knives.

"I only come out if she comes out, too."

I hear the impatient cluck of his tongue against his teeth.

"But it's not her I want."

"If you want me, then you want her, too."

He's quiet for a second. Then he sighs.

"Perhaps tomorrow, then."

I swallow. "Both of us. I'll do whatever you want," I choke. "But *both of us* come out of this room."

I can just barely make out his foot tapping on the floor.

"Let me think on it."

He turns to go, but then stops, his silhouette twisting back to look at me again.

"Soon, we'll laugh about this, Elsa. Soon, this will all be an amusing story we tell at parties."

Venom, bile, and fear rise in my throat.

He chuckles fondly.

"I'm so glad I found you, my love."

The door shuts with another metallic clank, and the sob I've been desperately holding back in front of him bursts from my throat.

Nora stirs next to me, and I turn to pull her head into my lap as I drop mine against the stone wall behind me.

Please find me.

Wherever you are, Hades.

Please.

Find me.

36

HADES

"You don't want to do this."

Gavan smiles coolly. "*Want* has very little to do with it. You've chosen a path against me, Hades, simple as that. All of you have."

Ares licks his lips, trying to remain calm. "Gavan, you need to listen—"

"I outgun you three-to-one, and that's before the twenty other men I have upstairs. So, no, Ares," he rasps coldly, "I don't *need* to do a goddamn thing. Lower your guns. All of you."

I glance at my brothers and Castle. Ares gives a quick nod of his chin.

There's no reason to have a shootout right now and go down in a hail of Russian bullets.

The four of us lower our weapons to the floor.

Gavan smiles again. "Yes, I thank you for so conveniently leading me to you and walking into a hole in the earth without any other men with you. You've made erasing your empire from the face of the fucking planet *so* much easier for me."

His eyes narrow as he raises his gun.

"For that, I'll be quick with the rest of your family—"

"Stop! We're being fucking *played*, Gavan!" I snarl. "Look."

I gesture behind me, to the gaping hole in the wall. Gavan frowns, turning and nodding at one of his men. The guy steps forward, shining his phone flashlight into the darkness.

The Reznikov leader's brow furrows.

"The fuck is this?"

"A Revolutionary War era weapons cache, along with the remains of the men who were guarding it."

He stiffens.

"It means this whole fucking garage is a historical preservation site, and Serj is fully aware of that."

Tsarenko's lips curl dangerously.

"He's fucking playing all of us, Gavan. And the deal is just the beginning. Here."

I reach for my pocket.

Twelve Russian fingers suddenly get *real* tense.

"It's my *phone*," I growl, leveling my gaze at Gavan. "There's something you need to see."

He eyes me suspiciously. Then he nods.

"*Slowly.*"

I slip the phone out of my back pocket, unlock it, and hand it to him.

"It's the most recent video in my camera roll. Make sure the volume is up."

Gavan's face is impassive as he plucks the phone from my hand and clicks on my camera reel. Suddenly, the sound of Leo and Serj speaking in Russian fills the dirt room.

…And Gavan's whole expression turns *livid*.

I see the rage and the realization of the betrayal creep over him as he watches the video in its entirety, twice. Then a third time.

His eyes raise to mine as he hands me my phone back.

"Well?"

I watch the muscles of his neck ripple.

"Where did you get this."

"Does it really matter?"

His nostrils flare as he looks away.

"No," he growls. "It doesn't. Though it might explain my top *avtoritet* being missing for the last four or five days."

He swears viciously under his breath in Russian. Then he turns to level his gaze at the four of us.

"*opustite oruzhiye,*" he growls.

Around him, his men gradually lower and holster their guns. Gavan draws in a slow breath.

"You burned my warehouse," he hisses quietly.

"And you tried to blow up *my fucking family*!" Ares roars.

Gavan's face darkens. "I did not. I don't imagine it means much to you right now, but you have my word on that. I did *not* set that bomb. I don't believe in killing innocents and grandmothers, just as I don't condone setting children on fire," he rasps. "In case no one's translated the complete video for you, that little weasel Pascha Andreev is clearly outlining his plans to go after the children of your vassal families in order to get us at each other's throats. He very well may have been the one to set the bomb in your pub as well." His jaw grinds. "Frankly, his actions disgust me. When I find him—"

"You won't."

He glances at me sharply. I lift a non-committal shoulder.

"Consider that a peace offering. You *won't* find him."

Gavan raises a brow. "Duly noted. I will admit… I did torch your casino."

"Hope you had insurance on that boat," Kratos grins darkly.

"How's your collection of stolen televisions and Playstations doing these days?" Gavan tosses back.

"*Enough*." Ares shakes his head, holding his hands up. "We can play this game all day. Who shot first, who did more damage. *It doesn't matter*. This was all a setup, and we've all been playing right into Serj and Leo's fucking hands. They want us to burn each other's empires to the fucking ground, so they can paw through the ashes."

He glances at Kratos and I, and then levels a look at Gavan.

"I'm *choosing* to believe you about The Banshee bombing. I hope I never find out that I'm wrong."

Gavan nods as my brother continues.

"And being that all of this was set in motion by someone who is clearly a common enemy, I'm prepared to forget about the shot-for-shots regarding each other's property. No lives were lost on our end."

"On my end either," Gavan growls.

"So we don't have to go to war. We don't have to be best friends, either, but we don't need this to go nuclear."

Gavan smiles mirthlessly. "I have a difficult time seeing us as friends, Drakos," he growls. "But, that said, war is terrible for business." He takes a slow, deep breath, and then sticks out his hand. "Shall we agree to lower the temperature?"

Ares glances at Kratos and me. When we both nod, he turns back to the Russian and shakes his hand.

"Consider the temperature lowered. We have no open hostilities with you, starting now. I'll put the word out to my people immediately."

"Same."

"I'll talk to Cillian," Castle growls. "But consider the Kildares standing down as well."

Gavan allows himself a small smile before his face darkens.

"Now, are we going to flip a coin to see who gets to skin Serj Mirzoyan alive?"

———————

"M—Mr. Drakos?"

I pause in the hallway of the long-term recovering wing of Mt. Sinai hospital. Frowning at the sound of a voice I recognize, I turn to peer into the open doorway of the room beside me.

Theo Petrakis smiles nervously at me as I step into his room.

"I—I saw you walking by and just wanted to say hi."

I nod, smiling at him. "How's the recovery going, kid?"

He shrugs. "It's okay. The skin grafts itch like hell, but it's all healing pretty well. And, hey, my dad came by this morning and told me the good news. We're not going to war with the Bratva?"

I frown. "*We*? Theo, you're just a kid."

He blinks. "I'm eighteen, Mr. Drakos. My dad's already teaching me about running the business."

I smirk, nodding. "Fair enough. But no, there's no war. We've dialed it back. It's all settled."

"That's good to hear."

I nod.

In the last twelve hours, a *lot* of things have been settled. First and foremost, no, the Drakos-Kildare alliance will not be shooting it out in the streets with Gavan's people. All parties on both sides have been informed, and a total cease to any hostilities has been issued.

Gavan *did* end up flipping a coin in that sub-basement. He even won the toss, too. But he's not going to be skinning Serj alive.

No one's going to be doing *anything* to Serj alive.

Because he's fucking dead.

Apparently, he and Melik got into a heated argument about the pending sale of the empire. They were both drunk, and when Melik drew a piece *on his own father*, meant only to intimidate him, it discharged, blowing a hole in Serj's gut. At which point, Papa Mirzoyan pulled his *own* gun out, and shot his kid in the chest. Which sounds cold as *fuck*, unless you'd ever met Melik.

If you had? Yeah, you'd kinda get it.

Both Serj and Melik bled out before anyone found them, and now Vanya is the new head of the Albanian family. It's currently a big fat "to be determined" what she does with it.

"That's great to hear," I sigh. "Look, Theo, I didn't mean to come down so hard on you that time at Nora Guin's apartment. Your dad's an okay guy, and I know you're a good kid. I just want you to know that."

He smiles. "Nah, I get it. It must have looked super sketch. But honestly, Mr. Drakos, I wasn't, like, trying to *get* with Nora. Nick wasn't, either. We really were just wanting to chill and hang out. Seriously."

I nod, my brow furrowing. "Have you talked to her recently? Nora, I mean."

Elsa hasn't been seen since the night of the bombing. According to her building super, she hasn't been to her apartment, and when I dropped by Crown and Black, her friend Fumi told me she was on vacation, after giving me an earful about not hurting her friend.

She didn't mention not *killing her*, though.

It's a thought that keeps me up at night, twisting me back and forth: whether I *do* want to find Elsa, to wreak my vengeance on her, or if I never want to set eyes on her again, so I don't have to do that.

Because if I do find her, I will. There's no question about that. *Elsa's* the one who was feeding info to Leo. *Elsa* is the one who knew about our hidden warehouses, and the passcode for the back door of The Banshee.

Presumably, she's with her fucking father somewhere, given than no one can find either one of them. But something doesn't sit well with me about her having brought Nora along for the ride as well. Because I checked her school and her ballet class—she's been missing since that night, too.

"Nora?" Theo shrugs. "Probably having the time of her life on a beach in Thailand."

I stiffen. "What?"

"She's in Thailand. At least that's what her last TikTok said. She and her sister are there island-hopping for like a month-long vacation."

Jesus Christ. At Crown and Black, Fumi only mentioned that Elsa was on vacation. Even Alistair, when pressed, too, didn't seem to know where she'd gone. Only that she'd cashed in a bunch of vacation days that they were all too happy to give her, seeing as she's their new darling lawyer over there.

"Thailand."

He nods. "Guess so. I've never been, have you—"

"I have to get going. Get well soon, Theo."

Outside in the hallway, my eyes blaze with fury. Before I know what I'm doing, I duck into an empty waiting room and yank out my phone.

Technically, New York City Director of FBI Operations Shane Dorsey is Cillian's "guy", not mine. Cillian's done him some serious solids that basically made his career. In return, Shane makes sure the FBI turns a blind eye to any questionable Kildare—and now Drakos, too—activity in New York.

It's a mutually beneficial arrangement, and Cillian's made it clear not to rock that boat even in the slightest.

But I need to know this, and I need to know it now.

Dorsey answers on the third ring.

"Hades," he growls. "I'm sort of in the middle of—"

"I need the location of two passports."

He sighs. "It doesn't *stop* with you people, does it?"

"Hey, we scratch your back, you scratch—"

"*Cillian* scratches my back, Hades," he mutters quietly. "*That's* the deal. Look, I can help your family out when I can. But only when Cillian is looped—"

"Remember the time my brother took a fucking bullet, and we let *you* take the credit for killing the bad guy, which, if I recall correctly, gave you the promotion of a lifetime? Remember that?"

Shane sighs. "It rings a bell."

"Fucking *great*. Now can you or fucking can't you look up the locations of two passports."

"I'm the Director of New York City Operations for the fucking FBI, Hades," he mutters. "What the hell do *you* think?" He sighs again. "Okay. Names?"

"Elsa Guin and Nora Guin."

"Hang on."

The line goes silent but for the clicking of a keyboard. Then, he swears.

"What?"

"These are both UK nationals, Hades."

"And?"

"And the FBI is an *American* policing force."

"*And?*" I growl, growing impatient.

"*And* it creates serious fucking issues if we're spending our time spying on the whereabouts of citizens of one of our biggest allies, if not *the* biggest," he snaps.

I fight to keep my cool. "Shane, I've never asked you for shit. But I really *need* this."

"I *can't*, Hades. I can't fucking tell you where they are for about fifteen different legal and international treaty reasons." He sighs. "*But,* I can tell you where they are *not.*"

My brow arches. "That works. So, where aren't they?"

"Anywhere outside the continental United States."

"They're not in Thailand?"

"I can't tell you that."

"But they're *not* there."

Shane sighs. "I have to go, Hades. I can't touch this with a mile-long pole."

He hangs up. I stare at the floor, thinking.

Why is Nora Guin telling her friends she's in Thailand, when neither she nor Elsa has left the country?

EILISH, the actual reason I came to Mt. Sinai today, smiles as I step into her private room.

"How're you feeling, blondie?"

She makes a face, shrugging. "Meh, I'm fine."

"Brought you something to brighten the place up."

She grins at the bouquet of flowers in my hands. "Such a charmer."

I shrug, taking the lid off a pitcher of water on her bedside table and putting the flowers into it.

"Hades..."

I glance at Eilish. Her brow is furrowed, her mouth twisted with words she's not sure about saying out loud.

"Eilish, I don't want to talk about—"

"Hades, *c'mon*. She didn't do any of this. She can't have."

"She *did*," I growl. "And I know that's not a pleasant or convenient truth, and I know it fucking stings, *believe me*, I do," I snarl. "But it is what it fucking is. She betrayed us all."

Eilish shakes her head. "I refuse to believe that."

"Yeah, and I refused to believe that my older brother Atlas was telling the truth when he told me Santa wasn't real when I was six. But, ho-ho-fucking-ho."

She looks down.

"She's the reason you're *in* here, Eilish," I growl. "She's the fucking reason Sean is—"

I wince as her face contorts.

"I'm sorry," I say quietly.

Yes, Sean was a good friend of mine. But he was also like a cousin to Eilish and Neve.

Her mouth goes small. "It's okay," she murmurs. "I'm coming to the service next week."

"Want a ride?"

She smiles softly. "Yeah, that'd be nice."

I sigh, rubbing my jaw. "Anything I can get you right now?"

Eilish rolls her eyes. "Honestly? A decent cup of coffee. They've been limiting me to one cup in the morning, but that's like a quarter of my usual intake, and I'm losing it."

I grin. "One contraband coffee. I can do that. Back in a sec."

I get up to leave the room. As I brush past the door to Eilish's ensuite bathroom, the gym bag that was hanging on the doorknob falls off. When I turn to pick it up, I freeze.

"No, you're not crazy," Eilish says quietly. "It's Elsa's, I know." She shrugs. "She left it by accident when she came over a few days before"…her face darkens…"you know, *what happened*. I guess Neve thought it was mine and packed it with my stuff to bring here."

I swallow, unable to tear my eyes from the bag I've seen in Elsa's office over a dozen times. In her bedroom.

In mine.

"You know how I know she didn't do any of this?" Eilish says quietly.

I grit my teeth as my eyes raise to hers.

"Because she really liked you, Hades." Her mouth twists. "I mean, I think she loved you. Or...*loves*."

Pain slices into me.

And I love her.

I still fucking love her.

And that's why this hurts so much.

"I'll be back with that coffee," I growl quietly as I turn to leave.

A metallic beeping sound chirps through the room. When my brows knit as I glance at the gym bag on the ground, Eilish sighs.

"Yeah, it did that twice yesterday. Once this morning, too. It just beeps like that. But I'm pretty sure the bag's empty. Maybe it's like fob for the front door to her gym or something?"

My frown deepens as I lean down to pick up the bag. Eilish is right: it's totally empty. No smart watch, no gym fob, no anything like that that might be the source of the beeps. My eyes scan it inside and out, my hands running over the nylon material.

Suddenly, I go still.

There *is* something in the bag. It's just not *inside* the bag.

It's in the lining.

My pulse thuds as I grab my knife out of my back pocket and flick it open.

"Hades?" Eilish peers at me like I'm insane. "What the hell are you—"

I slice open the lining of the bag just as the beep goes off again. My fingers close around the little metallic disc as I pull it out and hold it up into the light.

A small round circuit board, with a tiny wire, like an antenna, sticking out of it. And a little black circle glued to the back.

No, not a circle.

A *microphone.*

Someone's had Elsa's gym bag bugged. And when my eyes land on the letters printed right above the small watch battery on the circuit board, my whole world goes numb.

It says "battery".

In Russian.

"What is that?"

I swallow as my eyes lift to Eilish's. "It's a short-range surveillance bug."

"*What?*"

I hand it to her. Eilish twists it in her hands, her brows furrowing as she peers at it. "The writing on this is Russian."

I nod.

"Okay, but if Elsa was working for the Russians—"

"Then why the fuck were they bugging her goddamn gym bag," I finish.

Elsa took this bag *everywhere*. My house. Her apartment. In locker rooms, and bathrooms. All places she'd never knowingly bring a hot microphone.

And suddenly, it starts to click.

Her drive. The way she's been married to her job her whole life. The carefully hammered armor around her emotions and her heart. The way it's always seemed, since the first day I met her, that Elsa was the type of person who was constantly moving forward, because there *was* no way backward.

But I'm suddenly realizing it wasn't because she was hungry for tomorrow.

…It's because she was being *chased*.

Holy fuck.

Maybe she is Leo's kid. But I've been blinded so completely by my rage that I've overlooked the obvious.

She raised Nora alone.

She goes by Guin, her mother's maiden name, not Stavrin.

She came to New York for a new job—a new *life*. And then Leo dropped in less than a month later.

She was so cagey about her motives that night at Club Venom—why she went there that night to, come hell or high water, lose her virginity.

Oh shit.

"And he's angry about a girl. There was a marriage proposal recently concerning the daughter of a would-be ally that is no longer favorable to a traditional man like my son."

Holy shit.

The would-be-ally was fucking *Leo*. And Elsa was the goddamn marriage trophy. Her fucking me and losing her virginity that night was to torpedo that arrangement.

She didn't go to Leo's place that night afterward to reveal information to him, or to report back on spying on me.

She went there to *tell him what she did*. And I don't think it was because she felt like sharing intimate details of her goddamned sex life with her father.

It was a fuck you. A middle finger.

It was finally severing a tie between them.

When it all hits at once, I literally choke from the weight of it slamming down on me.

Holy fuck.

"Hades?"

I raise my wild eyes to Eilish. She frowns.

"What—"

"I don't think Elsa and her sister ran away *with* their father," I murmur. "I think he fucking *took them*."

Her eyes fly wide as her hand claps over her mouth.

"Oh my God..."

I yank out my phone and start typing away frantically. I haven't done this before, because it would be ethically fucked for *me* to be tracking Elsa's fifteen-year-old sister. That's why I linked the keychain panic button I gave Nora and the app monitoring it to *Elsa's* phone, not mine.

But I still know the password.

My heart is racing as the app finishes downloading, and I log in with the account I set up for Elsa, hoping and praying Nora's as smart as I think she is. If I'm right about Leo taking them, I don't know if he did it separately, or together. But either way, if Nora kept her wits about her, I'm hoping to God she remembered to push—

The app pings with a map location.

The button.

Nora fucking pushed the button. And right now, it's giving me an exact location to where she is, accurate within a six-foot radius.

Now, I just have to hope that she and Elsa are together.

"Hades?"

"Call your uncle," I hiss, racing for the door and texting her a screenshot of the map. "Call my brothers. Call Castle. Call fucking *everybody*! And tell them to get their asses to that location, NOW."

I bolt out the door and sprint down the hospital hallway.

Praying that Elsa is with Nora.

But mostly….

Praying I'm not too late.

ELSA

"I've prepared your breakfast. Just the way you like it, my love."

To describe what I'm feeling as "creeped out" is like referring to a hundred-year-storm as "a spot of bad weather".

I'm not "creeped out" to be tied to a chair at the kitchen table of the dingy little house, across from my terrified sister, while Hugo Johansen sets two plates of poached eggs down in front of us.

I'm absolutely fucking *horrified*.

"Oh-oh-oh, mustn't forget!" he chuckles to himself, turning to grab two grimy glasses with orange juice in them, setting them down in front of Nora and I as well. "Fresh-squeezed, just the way you like it, sweetheart."

My stomach turns as I eye the man I once worked with. The man who hounded me for fucking *years* after our three whole dates, before I filed a restraining order against him.

The man I thought I'd left in my past forever once I moved us to New York.

So stupid.

None of my past has ever stayed there. None of it has remained in England. First it was Leo who followed me across the Atlantic. And now, it's Hugo who's back to shake my life apart.

As if it's not already shattered into enough charred, wrecked pieces.

When the bomb blew up The Banshee on the night of the soft opening, I was at Hades' place getting ready. My phone started going crazy with texts and social media notifications about it, and when I couldn't reach Hades, I bolted out the door in a blind panic.

...Right into Leo.

Leo, with a gun, a bloody knife, and the slain bodies of three men behind him in the open sliding door of a van with "Athenian Dry-Cleaning" stenciled on the side of it.

Leo, who demanded I get in his car.

Leo, who then crumpled to the ground as the brick broke in half over his head, revealing the other nightmare from my past standing behind him, smiling chillingly at me.

Hugo.

I shiver as my mind replays the manic hours that followed: the sight of Hugo dragging an unconscious Leo to his car. My freakout when I saw my sister bound and gagged in his back seat which was only silenced by Hugo digging the barrel of a gun into my side.

My sobbing pleas for him not to hurt her as I let him shove me into the passenger seat. Leo's horrible groans from the trunk as Hugo drove us north out of the city, following the Hudson up into the Catskills.

The groans finally going silent right before we pulled up to this little house, which has been our prison ever since.

I swallow, my gaze stabbing out the kitchen window to the brownish lawn outside with the fresh little mound of dirt in the far corner.

Leo's final, inglorious resting place.

I'm not sure if the irony that one of my demons was slain by the other has sunk all the way in yet.

Hugo turns away, and my eyes instantly snap to Nora's across the table.

"It's going to be okay," I mouth to her.

Her face is pale as a ghost's, and her eyes are wide and full of terror. But she nods back at me.

"Don't you want your breakfast, my love?" Hugo purrs in a voice that feels like cold slime being poured down my neck. He turns, smiling this creepy, way-too-focused smile on me. His pupils are dilated, and when my gaze slips past him, I see the answer to my unspoken question: a little hand mirror streaked with white powered lines and a rolled-up dollar bill sitting next to the stove.

"I—"

"I made it just for you. *Just* the way I know you love it."

I glance down at the egg in front of me. I've had poached eggs maybe twice in my entire life.

"Don't you remember?" He smiles a sloppy, cocaine-fueled grin at me. "It was our second date. We were at La Tua Pasta, that little Italian place next to Borough Market."

I have *zero* idea what he's talking about. But I can see the mania in his eyes, and it's not just from the coke.

There's a reason this man stalked me, and that reason isn't necessarily "me". He's insane. And between that and the drugs—not to mention the fact that he's just kept Nora and I locked in a goddamn windowless basement with a bucket for a toilet for five days—I am very, very afraid of him and what he's capable of doing right now.

Not for myself. But for Nora.

"Oh, of course!" I smile. "Yes, I remember now. Mmm, poached eggs, thank you!"

He grins widely. "You're so welcome, sweetheart." He lifts his brow. "Well? Why haven't you touched it?"

"My…" I swallow. "Hugo, my hands are tied."

He glances down to my wrists, which are in fact bound to the arms of the chair, just as Nora's are to hers.

"Silly me," he sighs, chuckling to himself. "I've been so worked up about making this utterly perfect for you, I wasn't even thinking. Forgive me?"

Not in a million fucking years you absolute dirtbag creep.

"Of course," I smile broadly at him.

Hugo walks closer, and I shiver as he uses a pocketknife to slice off the rope. But only on one of my wrists.

"Dig in, please," he beams.

443

Even after five days of nothing but water, and peanut butter and jelly sandwiches with a couple bananas here and there, I have zero appetite. But again, this man is insane. As would I be not to do what he says.

So I smile as I start in on the bland poached egg, making a big show of nodding and chewing eagerly.

"Good?"

"*So* good," I gush.

Hugo grins, turning and lowering his face to the lines of cocaine on the mirror.

"Hugo?" I venture.

He turns, renewed mania in his eyes as he sniffs loudly and wipes his nose.

"Yes, my love?"

I shudder again at the term of endearment.

"What is this? I mean…all of this? Us being here?"

His eyes lock with mine.

"Can't you guess? This is our fresh start, my love."

"*Don't.*"

It tumbles out of me, and I can't stop it. Every time he calls me "love" I want to throw up.

Because I don't know if the man I *do* love is alive or dead. I don't know if his family is, either. And I've spent five days in a black hole doing everything I can not to think about that, but every time Hugo says that word, I get closer to exploding.

444

"Don't what—"

"*Don't call me that*," I choke, cringing in my chair.

Hugo frowns. Fear stabs through me. Then he nods slowly.

"Yes, I know, Elsa," he sighs. "I know. I was *too* in love with you, and it frightened you away. And I'm still in love with you to this day, which is why it hurts so much that you cheated on me."

I go still, my face paling as my eyes snap to his.

"What?"

"You were *weak*, my love."

"Hugo, I don't know what you're—"

Nora and I both scream as he whirls violently and punches the flimsy wall next to the stove, sending his fist through it in a cloud of plaster dust.

"You were weak!" he snarls, turning back on me. "And you took another man."

I shake my head. "No, Hugo—"

"I found his *cum* on your panties when I broke into your apartment, *my love*."

I almost choke, my eyes flaring as the words hit me like a slap in the face.

When I broke into your apartment.

It wasn't Leo that broke in that time we went to stay with Hades. It was Hugo.

"Hugo—"

He spins again, dipping down to snort another line of coke. When he whips his gaze back to me, it's glassy. I flinch when he suddenly rushes to my side, a horrified expression on his face as he crouches down to my eye level.

"Dear God," he chokes. "Did he…" he swallows. "Did he *rape you*, my love?"

I want to vomit.

"It's all right, you can tell me, Elsa. Just tell me, and I will forgive you. I know it would be hard for any man to resist you."

My stomach turns.

I could say yes. I could just say it, and end this. Or at least temper his mania and his anger.

I can't.

"No," I choke out, shaking my head. "No, he didn't…"

The worry in his eyes dissipates.

"…because I love him, Hugo."

He stares at me, eyes unblinking and the color draining from his face.

"*No*," he whispers.

"Hugo… Sometimes you feel things for someone, and they don't feel the same way back—"

"*NO!*"

I gasp as he screams in my face, lurching to his feet and backing away.

"Elsa…"

"I love him," I choke. "Hugo, there's someone out there for you, I know there is! *Please*! Just... Just let us go."

Hugo starts to cry. My gaze slips from him to my sister.

I will *not* let her come to harm.

She will *not* die here.

"Please, *Hugo*—"

"NO!" he roars. "No, I can't! I won't! My love," he hisses, "I refuse to believe that you don't—"

"Okay!"

My gaze snaps back to Nora again, so pale, so terrified.

I'm getting you out of here.

"Okay!"

I swallow, turning back to Hugo.

And *smiling at him.*

"I, I... You got me."

It takes everything I have—all my energy, all of my theatrical skills honed in the courtroom—to force the huge sappy grin to my face. I almost can't do it.

So instead of Hugo, I imagine it's Hades who's standing in front of me. I don't even know if he's alive or dead, but *he* is who I pretend I'm looking at when I look up into Hugo's demented, frenzied eyes.

"I... I was wrong."

He frowns. "What?"

"I've been so scared of my own feelings. So afraid of what they meant, and that they were too strong."

His lips curl into a smile. "What are you saying?" he breathes.

"I'm saying… You're my person. I…."

I swallow back poison and bile.

Pretend it's Hades.

"I've always wanted you. Madly, to a truly crazy degree. I was just always so afraid of how big that felt inside."

Hugo looks like he's going to burst into tears again.

"*Elsa,*" he chokes. "That's…poetry. It's *exactly* how I feel, too!"

"It was meant to be," I whisper. "*We* were meant to be. It's why and how you found me again. To show me what true love is."

He grins widely. "Fate, my love."

I nod. "Yes, exactly. Fate."

My eyes slip to Nora. Then back to him.

"I want to…to be with you, Hugo."

He beams. "You do?"

I nod vigorously. "Yes. *Yes.*"

I swallow the bile down again, beckoning him closer. I shudder when his hands slide up my arms.

"What is it, my love?" he murmurs into my ear.

"I…I *want* you. I want a real man, like you."

He groans. "God, Elsa. I've waited so long to hear that from your lips."

But Hugo, I…." I lock eyes with him, then flick them to Nora and back again. "Not with my sister in the house, you know?"

He grins.

"Can we have some privacy? So that you can show me what real pleasure is?"

He stares at me, his eyes bulging, his breath coming faster.

The seconds tick by.

"Hugo?"

His smile suddenly drops. Hard.

Shit.

His brow furrows, and he slowly starts to shake his head.

"Hugo—"

"*No*," he snarls, turning to pace the small kitchen. "No, no, no, no, *NO*! I remember now why you were always such a good lawyer, Elsa!" he snaps.

"Wait, Hugo—"

"Because you're such. A. Good. Fucking. *LIAR*!"

Nora screams, and I cry out as his palm smacks me across the face, stunning me. But when he turns his attention to my sister, it's my own roar that explodes through the kitchen.

"You stay the FUCK away from her!!"

He ignores me, stalking closer to her, leering down into her face.

"Has your purity been sullied, my dear?"

Jesus fucking Christ.

Nora pales.

"STAY AWAY FROM HER!" I scream again.

Hugo snarls, spinning to glare at me before marching over to the kitchen cabinets. He yanks one open, and I blanch when he pulls out a snub-nosed revolver. He waves it at me, sneering before he moves back to Nora's side.

"Answer me, sweetness."

My sister's face goes white.

"W-what?"

"Has anyone taken your chastity yet?"

I gag.

"*GET AWAY FROM—*"

He whirls, levelling the gun at me before turning his monstrous gaze back to her.

"Answer me, Nora."

She starts to cry.

"*No,*" she sobs, shaking as tears trace down her cheeks.

"You're a virgin?"

Another sob rips from her throat as she nods miserably.

"*Good.*"

He turns back to me, smiling thoughtfully.

"She looks so much like you, Elsa."

I scream, trying to lurch from my chair even though one wrist is still tied to it. I fumble for my fork, then jolt as Hugo fires a shot into the ceiling.

"SIT. *DOWN.*"

He turns back to Nora, ignoring my screams and her shaky sobs as he cups her cheek.

"Don't cry, my little one. God has saved your innocence all for me. For today."

That's not going to happen.

His back is to me, I don't know for how much longer, but it's all I've got to work with. I grab the fork from the table, turning it and madly raking and scraping at the old, frayed rope tying my other wrist to the chair. My skin rips and bleeds, but the rope gives way.

Hugo starts to turn at the sound of my chair falling backward, but I'm already on him, stabbing down into his shoulder with the prongs of the fork.

"You *bitch!*"

I scream, stabbing over and over before suddenly he backhands me again hard.

But I'm not done, and I am *not* going down without a fight. I scream again, lunging at him and stabbing wildly with the fork. Over and over, I only manage to hit his free hand and the one holding his gun as he stumbles back trying to block my blows. Finally, I get one thrust past his hands, right into his face.

Hugo *roars* as the fork rakes over his eyes, bloodying one of them. He sobs, falling backwards and writhing on the floor as he clutches his face.

I don't have much time.

I use my fingers and the fork together to rip and shred the ropes from Nora's wrists before yanking her from the chair and out of the kitchen door. It's foggy and gray outside, and the ground is wet as it heads down a slope towards a set of train tracks. The opposite way, the slope leads up to a patch of woods.

Nora gasps as I grab her face, my eyes locked on hers.

"You need to *run!*" I blurt, turning and shoving her up the slope in the direction of the trees.

She twists, whipping around to shake her head at me.

"No! Elsa—!"

"*RUN!*"

I shove her and shove her again, looking deep into her eyes.

"PLEASE. RUN."

She looks at me once more, mute. Then she's off, zigzagging up the slope and disappearing into the woods.

Thank God—

I cry out when something slams against my head from behind, turning my vision blurry as I drop to my hands and knees. I groan, seeing stars, finally able to stand.

…Only to come face to face with Hugo and his gun. Vicious fury twists his face—one eye focused lethally on me, the other a horrific, bloody mess.

"You'll fucking pay for that."

I choke as he grabs my throat, hauling me up and slamming me hard against the outside wall of the tiny cottage.

"But first…"

Fear and adrenaline stab through me like twin knives as Hugo starts to undo his belt.

"*First,*" he snarls, "I'll take what I've dreamed of. Not quite *how* I dreamed it," he mutters as he paws at his zipper. "But I bet your cunt still tastes just as fucking sweet—"

My knee jerks up, hard, slamming into his balls.

I don't pause to see how much damage I've done. I just turn, and I fucking *run.*

Don't look back. Don't look back. Don't. Look. Back.

When I hear the roar of Hugo's wrath behind me, I can't help it. It's like an automatic response.

I look back.

Oh God.

He's running like a maniac after me, one eye gushing blood down his face. His good one is locked onto me.

But he's coming for *me.*

Not Nora.

Right now, he wants revenge, not her.

I bolt down the hill towards the commuter rail tracks. On the other side of them, there's an even steeper hill that plunges down toward a road that runs parallel with a river I'm just now realizing is the Hudson.

I'm almost at the rails. If I can just get to the road—

I scream when something slams into me from behind, shoving me down to my hands and knees, skinning both. Adrenaline explodes through my veins, and I try to stagger to my feet.

Hugo's fist crashes into my face. The taste of copper floods my mouth as I go toppling backwards, crying out as the back of my head slams against the ground. Lights and black spots swim through my stunned vision.

A dark shape looms over me.

Oh God...

I scream, choking as Hugo grabs me by the hair and yanks me up. He pulls me sobbing and screaming to the tracks, holding me down, my heels kicking against the rail closest to us.

It starts to vibrate.

"Fourteen past the hour, Elsa," Hugo growls, his good eye piercing right through me. "Like fucking clockwork."

The rattling sound of the rails grows louder, and the vibrations against my heels become harder. My eyes swivel to the side, and whatever color is left in my face drains right away.

Holy fucking shit.

Down the tracks, maybe a mile away, a commuter train is barreling straight at us.

"Hugo—"

"You could have had me," he hisses, his eye twitching. "I would have given you the world. We were soul mates, Elsa."

"Never," I spit.

He smiles cruelly. "Then your sister will become my new obsession."

The grin on his face curls demonically as he leans close.

"And I bet she tastes even. Fucking. *Sweeter.*"

My lips curl, and my teeth flash.

"You are *never* going to find out."

The thundering sound of the train roars closer. The pebbles over the rail struts begin to bounce and jump.

He's never putting his disgusting hands on my sister.

Not. Ever.

My eyes drop to Hugo's belt. It's buckled again from when he was trying to yank it off before, but it's loose.

I love you, Nora.

"And when you're dead," Hugo grins wolfishly, his arms tensing as if readying to throw me into the path of the train. "I will *feast* on your baby sister's screams. But you won't be able to hear them. Because you, my dear Elsa...well, you'll be dead."

My hand juts out, slipping through the loose belt around his waist until the crook of my elbow is tight against it. Hugo's eyes go wide.

"So will you."

I throw myself backward across the tracks, Hugo slamming down on top of me.

His eyes bulge as the deafening scream of a train whistle rips over us; once, twice, over and over, as the very metal of the rails underneath us begins to shake like the world itself is breaking apart.

Hugo's screaming and roaring, trying to break free. But I lock my legs around his waist, and my eyes stab into his.

"You will *never* touch my sister!"

"LET GO OF ME!"

The screech of the approaching metal wheels on metal rails is deafening.

"LET GO!"

I close my eyes.

I think of Nora.

Then I think of Hades.

I love you—

I jolt as the train slams into me.

Except, I'm not underneath it. I'm rolling sideways off the tracks, a firm body holding me, powerful arms gripping me tight as I roll to a stop.

…And look up into piercing, ice-blue eyes.

Hades.

The train whistle rips through the air. The sound of wrenching metal splits my ears. My head whips to the side just as Hugo lurches to his feet, feverish mania in his eyes.

"SHE'S MI—"

I scream, unable to look away as the Metro North commuter train turns Hugo into a crimson mist.

Hades covers my face with his arm, turning me aside and holding me tight as I cling to him.

"You're okay," he chokes into my ear, kissing my face as I sob against him. "You're okay."

"Nora—!"

"—is in my car. She's *safe*, Elsa."

We lock eyes as the train roars past us, speeding away down the tracks.

Silence descends over us.

"It's over," he murmurs quietly, both of us breathing heavily as our eyes lock. "It's over, and I love—"

I crush my lips to his, kissing him madly as the tears stream down my face.

"...*You.*"

EPILOGUE

One month later:

"CALL ME, OKAY?"

Nora rolls her eyes in the dramatic way only a teenager can pull off.

"Yes, *Mother.*"

I glare at her. "Don't do that. You know I hate when you call me that."

She grins. "I'll call, Elsa."

I stick my tongue out at her. "Have fun."

"We won't be out late, Ms. Guin."

I cringe. Theo calling me that sounds so...*mom-ish.*

"Good *night*, Theo," I sigh, giving a wave as the black Escalade pulls away from the curb and cruises away.

"Feeling old yet?"

I groan, turning to see Hades behind me, lounging on the front steps of his building.

"Slightly, yes."

He grins. "She'll be fine."

I turn back, watching Nora drive off with Theo, another boy and a girl I know from her grade, and another girl I don't know.

"Theo's not after your sister, don't worry. One, he knows I'll fucking castrate him if he even tries to touch her. And two, he's got a crush on Galina."

I frown. "Galina?"

"The other girl in the car." Hades smirks. "Russian. Her dad works for Gavan. So that could get real interesting real quick."

For now, when it comes to the Reznikov Bratva, there's still a ceasefire. Not a truce, a ceasefire. The Drakos and Kildare families are *not* now suddenly allies of the Russians. But no one has any plans to kill each other in the streets. At least, not today.

So that's a plus.

"Also, she's still got that panic button on her keys," Hades adds.

"Yeah? Good."

He wraps an arm around my shoulders, leaning down to kiss my cheek.

"C'mon upstairs. Let's have dinner."

A smell of pure deliciousness hits me the second we step off the elevator and onto the top floor. Dinner tonight is takeout from Shank that Hades went and picked up earlier, which I know was also an excuse to check in on Maya, Sean's girlfriend.

She's doing well, or at least the best that can be expected right now. Since Sean's memorial service, which was really lovely, his family has taken her in as one of their own. Last I heard, she's actually living with them.

My eyes slide to the piles of documents and contracts covering the dining room table.

"Hang on, sorry, I'll clear these."

Hades shrugs. "Leave 'em. We can eat outside."

I stack them up anyway, sifting through them as I go: insurance claims, structural assessments, building permits.

For the *new* Banshee.

I'm seriously in fucking *awe* of Callie and the Kildare sisters. Nothing stops them, not even a bomb that almost killed them.

Since the damage from the blast pretty much totaled the building, including the floors above it, the rest of the unit owners took their insurance money and ran, selling cheap to Neve, Eilish, and Callie. The plans for the new and even better Banshee include not just a pub and a downstairs lounge, but a *restaurant* taking up the top two floors.

They're in talks with Maya to see about luring her away from Shank. I hope she agrees to the plan.

On the plant-filled balcony, Hades is already setting out plates and opening a dusty and old looking bottle of barolo when I step outside.

"Hang on."

He stops me before I take a seat, walking me across the gorgeously lush patio to the edge of the roof overlooking lower Manhattan, across the river.

"I might need you for some work."

"Oh?"

"Yeah. Building permits."

"For?"

He grins. "I've been thinking about finally getting around to doing the rest of this building. You know, finishing up the lower floors."

My brows arch as I sink against his firm chest, relishing the feel of his strong arms around me.

"Oh, really?"

"Yeah."

"Any particular reason?"

"I could use the space."

I laugh. "Hades, you already have, what, three thousand square feet up here?"

"Thirty-three hundred, but who's counting."

I giggle as he shrugs, leaning in to kiss my neck, making me shiver like always.

"But I was thinking I might have two new roommates to think about, too."

I go still. My eyes blink rapidly.

"I'm sorry, what?"

"Sell your place," he growls. "The market is great right now. You'll clean up."

I stare at him.

"Are you asking me to move in with you?"

"Maybe. Or if you would prefer, I could tell you to."

I blush, my thighs clamping together. Goddammit, he knows "controlling" me—at least to a degree—is my weakness with him.

"And Nora?"

"She could have her own floor. Literally."

I slowly shake my head. "You want a *teenager* in your house?"

"I want *you* in my house," he growls. "So yeah, that's a sacrifice I'm willing to make. She's a good kid, anyway."

My brows knit. "You're actually serious, aren't you?"

"About as serious as I am about this."

When he drops to his knee, my heart almost flies out of my mouth.

"*Hades...*"

He holds up the box, opening it and letting the garden lights twinkle over the huge solitaire diamond ring inside.

"I want you to marry me, Elsa."

I can't say a word. Hades arches a brow.

"This is the part where you say yes, if that wasn't clear."

I bite my lip and look at him coquettishly.

"And what if I say no, Mr. God of the Underworld?"

A dark, lethal shadow crosses his face. "Then I tie you to my fucking bed like a proper Persephone and keep you forever anyway."

I grin.

"So," he shrugs. "Yes just seems like an easier—"

"*Yes*," I whisper. My cheeks bloom with heat. "I'd love to marry you."

"Yeah?"

"*Definitely.*"

Suddenly, our mouths are slamming together, and I'm kissing him hard and falling back into one of the lounge chairs.

He pins me down, stripping my jeans and panties off together, followed quickly by his shirt. I bite my lip, my eyes sliding over his muscled torso with all its ink, loving the way his body coils when he's about to devour me, like he's going to war.

"*Spread your fucking legs for me, kitten.*"

And *God* do I love when he calls me that.

I cry out as his head slips between my thighs, and when his tongue drags up my wet pussy lips, I melt. He's a mix of aggressive and soft, and being with him is always like dancing with a loaded gun. His tongue swirls around my clit,

463

driving me up the wall as his powerful hands shove my knees up and back.

He groans when his fingers slip lower, finding the gold plug already in my ass.

I *might* have gotten more than a little comfortable with wearing it these days.

All the time.

And by "comfortable" I mean "obsessed with."

I whimper when he tugs on the base of it, turning it in a slow circle inside my ass as his tongue does the same thing to my clit. The sensation is mind-blowing, and when my body starts to shake and writhe beneath him, he only drags it out even more.

"*Eager little kitten,*" he growls against my thigh before plunging his tongue into me.

I throw my head back, my cries filling the night air as Hades teases my body into a sweating, whimpering, shuddering mess.

His lips fasten around my clit, his tongue swirling around it as he sucks. And suddenly, my whole body convulses as the trigger inside me is pulled.

"*I'm fucking coming!*"

I scream and scream, my thighs clamping around his head and my back arching as the orgasm rips through me. I'm barely over the brink, and still clawing at the edges of my sanity when he moves up between my legs.

Oh God yes.

His swollen cock slams into me, forcing the air from my lungs as my eyes go wide. I moan, crushing my lips to his as my legs wrap tight around his muscled hips. One hand wraps around my throat, the other pinning my wrists above my head.

And I lose all control. Like I always do with this man who *destroys* my control. My inhibitions. My walls. As if that's exactly what he was born to do.

I moan into his lips as he kisses me, our bodies grinding together desperately as his hips roll. His gorgeous cock rams into me over and over, his pubic bone hitting my clit with each thrust as my nipples drag electrically against his chest.

Hades doesn't just fuck me.

He *consumes me*. He captures me and drags me off to his underworld lair, seemingly to keep me there forever, every single time we do this.

"Hades..."

"I want you to fucking come for me, kitten," he groans into my lips. "Let me feel that sweet, juicy little pussy come for my big fucking cock, like a good girl."

He sinks all the way into me, making me feel *so fucking full* between him and the plug. His hand squeezes around my throat just enough to send me reeling into the stratosphere.

And suddenly, I slam my lips to his, screaming my release into his mouth as I come like a thermonuclear explosion. Hades groans out his release, kissing me like I belong to him as he buries his throbbing cock deep. His cum spills into me as my legs lock around his hips and my lips sear to his.

And then, we do it all over again.

Three more times.

When we're done, we both look like we've competed against each other in gladiatorial combat. I'm covered in delicious bruises and marks from his mouth and hands, shaking and trembling on the couch back inside with one leg and one arm hanging off it. Hades is collapsed on the floor next to me, both of us gasping for air with a sheen of sweat across our spent bodies.

"You know, if Nora and I move in—"

"The fuck is with this *if* bullshit?"

I giggle. "Sorry. *When* Nora and I move in, I'm not so sure you and I will be able to do this."

"Sex?"

I blush. "On the dining room table, the living room floor, and against the refrigerator? Uh, *no*, not so much."

"And why is that, pray tell?"

I roll my eyes. "Because we'll have a third person living here."

"Exactly *why* do you think I'm going to be renovating a whole fucking floor for her?" he grins, groaning as he pushes off the floor and onto the couch, scooping me into his arms. "Not to mention making sure it's got extra sound proofing?"

"Um…"

"So that she *never* has to come up here, where we'll be spending our time fucking on every goddamn surface at every goddamn hour of every goddamn day."

I grin lazily, shaking my head.

"Which might, in fact, kill me."

"Hell of a way to go, though."

"You might *actually* be insane. You do know that, right?"

"What does that say about you?"

I shrug, blushing as his mouth lowers, hovering millimeters from mine.

"*Guilty as charged,*" I murmur.

"*I love you,*" he growls quietly.

"I love you, too."

"Will you love me less if I mention that my cock is *still* hungry for you?"

I groan, giggling as I twist in his arms. I shiver as my legs spread over either side of his grooved hips.

"*Nope.*"

"*Good kitten.*"

The Dark Hearts series will continue with Gavan's story in *Twisted Hearts*, coming August 3rd.

Haven't gotten enough of Hades and Elsa?
Get their extra scene here, or type this link into your browser: http://Bookhip.com/BMWLSBH

This isn't an epilogue or continuation to *Sinful Hearts.* But this extra hot "follow-up" story is guaranteed to keep the steam going.

ALSO BY JAGGER COLE

Dark Hearts:

Deviant Hearts

Vicious Hearts

Sinful Hearts

Twisted Hearts

Kings & Villains:

Dark Kingdom

Burned Cinder (Cinder Duet #1)

Empire of Ash (Cinder Duet #2)

The Hunter King (Hunted Duet # 1)

The Hunted Queen (Hunted Duet #2)

Prince of Hate

Savage Heirs:

Savage Heir

Dark Prince

Brutal King

Forbidden Crown

Broken God

Defiant Queen

Bratva's Claim:

Paying The Bratva's Debt

The Bratva's Stolen Bride

Hunted By The Bratva Beast

His Captive Bratva Princess

Owned By The Bratva King

The Bratva's Locked Up Love

The Scaliami Crime Family:

The Hitman's Obsession

The Boss's Temptation

The Bodyguard's Weakness

Power:

Tyrant

Outlaw

Warlord

Standalones:

Broken Lines

Bosshole

Grumpaholic

Stalker of Mine

ABOUT THE AUTHOR

Jagger Cole

A reader first and foremost, Jagger Cole cut his romance writing teeth penning various steamy fan-fiction stories years ago. After deciding to hang up his writing boots, Jagger worked in advertising pretending to be Don Draper. It worked enough to convince a woman way out of his league to marry him, though, which is a total win.

Now, Dad to two little princesses and King to a Queen, Jagger is thrilled to be back at the keyboard.

When not writing or reading romance books, he can be found woodworking, enjoying good whiskey, and grilling outside - rain or shine.

You can find all of his books at
www.jaggercolewrites.com

Made in the USA
Las Vegas, NV
26 September 2024